T0375696

Open Wide

Open Wide

Chas Coakley

authorHOUSE®

AuthorHouse™
1663 Liberty Drive
Bloomington, IN 47403
www.authorhouse.com
Phone: 1-800-839-8640

© 2011 by Chas Coakley. All rights reserved.

No part of this book may be reproduced, stored in a retrieval system, or transmitted by any means without the written permission of the author.

First published by AuthorHouse   07/30/2011

ISBN: 978-1-4567-8483-6 (sc)
ISBN: 978-1-4567-8484-3 (ebk)

Printed in the United States of America

Any people depicted in stock imagery provided by Thinkstock are models, and such images are being used for illustrative purposes only.

Certain stock imagery © Thinkstock.

This book is printed on acid-free paper.

Because of the dynamic nature of the Internet, any web addresses or links contained in this book may have changed since publication and may no longer be valid. The views expressed in this work are solely those of the author and do not necessarily reflect the views of the publisher, and the publisher hereby disclaims any responsibility for them.

SYNOPSIS

When you have read this story, think back to this beginning. Could this really happen. There are people sitting in meetings, now as you read, right now, that are wired to the outside world. With accomplices listening to every word, they recite back the very answers required to make their colleague the stand out person at that meeting.

Then think how technology has move on in the electronics and explosives industry and how the military and secret intelligent are at the forefront of that technology to protect and keep you safe now as you read.

Then go pc mad, it's just amazing how much information the internet is willing to reveal to a hungry vengeful young mind as in one of the main Characters Anthony. He hides a secret that burns inside him; many people will be subjected to his lust for revenge. Now think have you ever wanted to hurt someone be it a Human or Animal out of revenge, especially as you know they can't hurt you back. Now you're thinking like Steven Anthony's accomplice. Together in everyday life butter wouldn't melt, their outer coating normal, polite. Through the beatings they endure, the horror of watching their beloved mothers suffer, the damage is done. The scars of their torrid childhood run deep and both developed split personalities. Playing off each other their personality's turn like a switch and all hells let loose. Now follow them through childhood, through their teens to adult young men as they mix and match their hobbies resulting in a lethal concoction you wouldn't wish on your worst enemy.

CHAPTER 1

Bicknell Council Estate was a noisy place at the best of times but the ear splitting squeal of pure terror cut through the heavy air of the late summer evening like a knife. From inside his house a young boy muttered "yes!" under his breath, running outside to his makeshift trap. Steven Smith could hardly believe his luck, inside was a rat. It had been worth sacrificing that piece of his sandwich from his lunch box Steven thought as he looked into the glittering round eyes of the terrified animal. He could see glimpses of its teeth as it tried ineffectively to escape. This was the biggest animal he had caught, and Steven was eager to get started. As he held up the trap to examine the rat he thought it looked like the trap might have broken the rat's leg. He made for the battered shed at the end of the garden.

He had just shut and latched the rickety shed door when his mothers voice drifted down the garden

"STEVIE". "Oh damn, yes mum?". "Dinner". "Ok be there in a bit." "No come in now, I've dished it up "OK" "Damn and double damn" transferring the rat to another box, he reluctantly closed the lid and made his way indoors for dinner.

Steven was smaller than most kids his age; he was fourteen years old, fair-haired, blue eyed, and an only child. His father a dark big hairy man had regularly beaten Steven and his mother. Steven's childhood memories were mostly of the acrid smell of stale alcohol on his father's breath and the stinging of his belt on his legs or the dull thud that his fist made when he punched his mother in the face. Sometimes there was a cracking as well if a bone broke. He grew used to the look of terror in his mother's eyes, not unlike that on the face of the rat he had just caught. There had been times, many times, when fearing for their lives had given way to wishing their lives would just end, the nothingness of death seeming attractive compared to the daily hell they lived in at the hands of this sadistic man. But two years ago the heavy drinking had eventually claimed his father.

When they buried him, with only a couple of winos his only friends, one being Anthony's drunken father to mourn him, Steven had been surprised to see his mother cry. As far as he was concerned, there was no sadness only relief from a tortured existence, the absences from school while his injuries healed, the terrible sound of his father bellowing Mary! Mary! as he came in drunk from the pub.

"What have you been up to in that shed?" his mother asked as he sat down at the table.

"Oh I've caught a rat, I want to try and put it to sleep, and then when it wakes I'll let it go."

"What on earth for? Oh look, I don't want to know" she shuddered "but Steven, you be careful, rats are full of disease." She said.

Since his father had died his mother had been gentle and kind with him, maybe trying to make up for how things had been.

"I will mum don't worry". His mother was aware of his experiments, amidst much complaining she had seen him put mice to sleep, who once they came round he would let go. Although she moaned at him a bit, she obviously thought that it was better than worrying about him hanging round getting up to all sorts with the local lads, like that revolting creature Greg Barton who spent the summer evenings noisily kicking beer cans up and down the streets, smoking drugs, and generally causing trouble. Besides which, Steven had hinted to her that he would like to be a vet and she did not want to discourage his interest.

As she cleaned, Mary would look around Steven's bedroom, marvelling at the books he had collected containing all types of information on animal's anatomy, and the human body. Despite everything, and against all the odds, Mary dared to hope that her son might make something of his life. Other books in her son's room were on explosives, electronics, and science fiction, typical boys interests she thought, all in all Mary was, for the first time in years, feeling a cautious optimism for the future.

Mary Smith was tall, dark haired and blue eyed, with an attractiveness that came as much from her spirit as her striking looks. She was hard working, and had toughness about her, the result of or maybe the reason that she had survived years of hell from her husband. She had a natural elegance, chose her clothing carefully from charity shops and carried herself in a way that hid well the fact that she was penniless. She held firm to the belief that she deserved much better than life had thrown at her and as she sat in front of the television night after night, she dreamed of company and a little love in her life, a love that did not end the night by beating her to a pulp. For now though she was grateful that she and Steven had survived and now lived in relative peace. But someone to love and care for her would be nice.

After gobbling his dinner down, Steven said. "Can I go out to the shed Mum?" "Yes but not for long, I'm going out with some friends so I want the place locked up with you in it before I go"

"Ok, thanks", he replied sprinting down the garden.

When Steven opened the box he had placed the rat in though, he found himself looking at its lifeless body. "Damn bloody damn" he muttered. Picking the rodent up he inspected the leg he had suspected had been broken. The skin was torn and beneath it he could make out the bones. "Wow ", he said putting the rat down. Scanning the workbench he selected a couple of books, and opening them at the pages he needed, he compared pictures of rat anatomy and the real life rat that lay on the bench.

Steven fumbled around on the bench feeling for what he wanted, he couldn't take his eyes off the rat, and eventually his hand closed around the handle of his scalpel and with the skill of a surgeon he started to cut away the skin of the rat revealing more of its anatomy, his hand shook slightly as the more the scalpel exposed the more excited he became. Within no time he had completely dismembered the whole rat. He paid particular attention to the rat's skull and teeth. Ideas and theories crowded his head, could he somehow control the rat? Could he track the rat? Could he blow up the rat? "STEVEN" his mother yelled. "Coming just clearing up", he replied. "OK ten minutes no longer".

Steven scraped the remains of the dissected rat into a bucket, then wrapped the skull in a rag and slipped it into his pocket then went indoors. "Blimey mum you look nice". "Thanks son, I'm off out with some of the girls, I wont be late, don't answer the door."

"No mum, I'm not a baby! Have a nice time." "Yes. See you in a bit, couple of hours tops." This was the first time she had left Steven by himself, although in truth he had been alone most of his life in his own little world. Sometimes he had an overwhelming compulsion to punish anyone or anything for all the suffering he had been through.

Every time he was punished or beaten as a child he would punish his pets or even once or twice kill them to make him feel better. Then he would be punished again. It became a vicious circle.

As soon as the door shut behind his Mother he raced to his bedroom. Removing the skull from his pocket, he surrendered to the crazy thoughts that clamoured for attention in his head.

Looking along the rows of science fiction books, each one reminded him of stories that had captured his interest in the past. The idea of being able to track and find something appealed to him. Glancing at title after title his thoughts progressed from tracking something to tracking it and blowing it up.

Engrossed in his thoughts world time slipped by and a knock on the door made him jump out of his skin.

"What an earth is that Steven?" his mother pointed to the skull lying on the rag in the middle of Steven's bed.

"Oh it's a rat's skull," he said calmly. "Take it out at once, and don't ever bring anything like that into the house, never, do you hear me?

"Yes mum" he said bundling the skull up. As he passed he was half expecting a clip round the ear. Bracing himself for the familiar pain and deafness that resulted from a good slap, he ducked.

There was no need. His Mother was in a very good mood, and she very rarely clouted him, they had both suffered enough violence at the hands of his father.

Having hidden the rat's skull Steven returned to the kitchen where his mother was sitting at the kitchen table.

"Had a nice time mum? Tell me all about it." Smiling she opened an old photo album that she had on the table. "You won't remember these girls son, who do you think that is?" she said placing her finger under the grainy image of one of the girls, "Emm don't know",

"That's me silly, with two of my school friends. That's Emily and that's Sarah".

"Doesn't look like you Mum". "Yes I know, time changes us all son, anyway those are the two girls well, women now I suppose that I met tonight, we had such a good time that I'm going to meet them again next week". Steven was pleased to see the happiness on his mothers face. She had a lovely smile and warmth in her blue eyes that had so often been clouded by pain.

As she looked through the album Steven said he was going to bed.

"Yes I'm tired as well, see you in the morning and don't forget to wash your hands".

"And clean my teeth, yes mum". Steven chuckled to himself, how many times had his mother given the same instruction to her son at bed time, unnecessary now that he was a fourteen year old, but somehow comfortingly familiar.

With the urgency of a pee foremost on his mind by the time Steven got to the bathroom any recollection of his mothers instructions had vanished and hands and teeth unwashed and un-brushed he climbed into bed to live out his fantasies through his dreams.

"Steven quick I've overslept" his Mother said, her hair unbrushed and stood at his door, he could see the outline of her legs through her nighty.

"Come on you'll be late for school".

Dressing quickly, he rushed down for breakfast. "No time for breakfast, quick here's a banana, drink this milk" as he downed the contents of the glass, in big gulps, a fleeting image of his father glugging down his beer came uninvited into Mary's mind.

"Not so fast son". "Well you said hurry mum." "I know, I know, right off you go, see you this afternoon" she kissed her fingers and held them fleetingly to his cheek.

Steven dashed to the shed, slipping the rat's skull into his pocket he ran most of the way to school.

The school was a big Victorian building, lovely red brick with beautiful architecture, unfortunately hidden beneath the grime of ages that had built up on it's arches and gables, the large windows sent sheets of sunlight into the high ceilinged classrooms.

As the bell rang for class, Steven could not wait to show his prize to his best friend, Anthony. As they sat down, Steven elbowed his friend and whispered,

"Ant look at this" "Cool! Where did you get that?" "It's a rat I caught it, but it died." Said Steven "It's still got bits of meat on it. Gross!" Anthony said, but his eyes were bright with interest. "I thought we could experiment see if we can blow it up." "Yes that would be awesome man". said Anthony.

Anthony and Steven came from similar backgrounds but Anthony could not have been more different to look at than Steven. He was kind of geeky looking, with dark greasy hair tied in a ponytail, spotty skin, Joe Ninety glasses, and buckteeth that made him lisp.
Another only child from a broken home, Ant was pretty much left to his own devices, which allowed him to study his passion, explosives, which in turn had led him to Energetic Technology. He had scoured the Internet for information, till one day he had come across smart weapons, a device called a fuse, a detonator as small as one millimetre square. Anthony knew that if you added this to a small amount of explosive you got a mini bomb. After months of experimenting, Anthony finally made a small explosive device and was itching to find a use for it. Now with Steven's proposition, he'd found an answer.

"Pay attention Smith." "Sorry sir" Steven said, ducking as a small rubber hurtled his way, missing its target it came to rest behind him on the floor. Cathy Barrett picked it up and returned it to Mr Porter, brushing past Steven as she returned to her desk. "Crawler, teachers pet". Steven whispered

Cathy's hand shot up. "Sir, Steven just called me a crawler." "Smith see me after class." "Yes sir." Cathy smirked at him

"She'll get what's coming to her one day." promised Steven. "Yes the little prick teasing bitch" Anthony agreed.

Cathy Barrett was a stunner and well developed for a fourteen year old. She teased all the boys especially Steven. Although smaller than his classmates, he had inherited his mother's good looks.

Cathy would often lure Steven behind the sports pavilion, where with only a three-foot gap between pavilion and fence they were guaranteed privacy. Cathy would always lead the way placing Stevens hand on her breast; they would kiss for a while. Steven had begun to think these rendezvous were pointless, he was sick of feeling her breast through her jumper he wanted the real thing flesh on flesh.

The next meeting he had tried for a bit more. Holding his breath, while she was distracted with a kiss he slid his hand up inside her blouse, when she did not resists, and excited by the touch of her soft skin, Steven pushed gently at the edge of her bra with the tips of his fingers and moved first his fingers and then his whole hand inside the bra cup. "That's enough." She said "Aw just a little bit more" Steven said his voice hoarse "You'll like it, I know you will." "Ok just a bit longer then" Cathy said reaching around to unhook her bra. Free of restriction, Steven's hand explored every inch of her breast feeling its hard nipple pushing against his palm. He slid his hand across to the other breast, and in his excitement and in desperate need to be touched; he placed Cathy's hand on his crotch. "Wow that's big" she said, feeling the outline of his straining penis beneath the thin fabric of his school trousers.

Having touched and teased many boys, she had experience with adolescent cocks and this was the biggest she had encountered so far.

"Right that's enough" "Aw come on just touch it please", Steven begged. Breathing hard now he unzipped his flies, revealing his cock, distended and much bigger than anything Cathy had seen before although the truth was that while she had felt many cocks through trousers she had never seen one uncovered.

Steven placed her hand on it just under the head, with his hand over hers, moving up and down along the shaft of his straining cock. As he felt his knees go weak she continued for a few moments and just at the point that he thought he was going to explode, she stopped

"What's the point in this?" "Don't stop keep going you'll see." Steven gasped Shrugging; she replaced her fingers around his cock and began to go at him again. "Faster" he demanded. "Nearly there . . . . Yes!" he said as he climaxed.

Yuk what's that?" Cathy said snatching her hand away from his pumping cock. "No don't stop!" Steven grabbed his cock to finish himself off, "You have to keep going till it stops coming out". "Sorry I've never done it before"

Steven stared at her.

"You must have! What about all the other boys? "No"

Steven thought about the boys who had said they had done it with her. "Bloody liars" he muttered. What?" she said.

"Nothing" said Steven "No come on I want to know" she demanded. "Well some of the boys said you had done it with them" said Steven warily. "Done what?". "You know "*it*" he said. "No you're the first I've done it with" she insisted wiping her hands on her skirt.

Steven was pleased with his first sexual encounter, he could not believe how different it felt to have someone else wank him off. He looked forward to more sexual discovery with Cathy and they did meet again a few times, Steven wanted to get past the quick wank that was becoming almost perfunctory and although he tried to persuade Cathy to let him touch her below, for such a prick tease she was surprisingly shy and eventually he gave up.

But on that magical day when he had first come in the presence of a member of the opposite sex Steven was delighted with himself and even a little proud of the barely perceptible stain from his cum on the leg of his trousers.

Spurred on by her recent sexual conquest, perhaps even a little aroused, Cathy was up to her usual tricks in the afternoon maths class, teasing the boys and this time she went a stage further. As the teacher turned his back to write on the blackboard, she signalled with her eyes that the boys nearest her should look down, then opening her legs, gave them a brief glimpse under her skirt. It was so quick some were convinced that she was wearing no knickers and a debate raged for the rest of the week.

"One day she's going to go to far the silly bitch," Steven whispered to Anthony, a little bit hurt that she was showing off what he hoped to claim as his conquest, one day soon.

The class started to disperse as the bell announced home time and with Anthony waiting impatiently outside Steven could hardly sit still for the telling off from his teacher. Eventually a detention for Friday agreed Steven and Anthony set off for Anthony's house a few minutes away, where the boys were soon preoccupied in his bedroom. Anthony proudly showed off the mini bomb he had made "Shit, that's big" Steven said as he examined the gadget.

"It will have to go inside somehow" explained Anthony, "I can't get it any smaller, there's lots of information about these smart weapons on the net, but obviously they're not going to show you exactly how to make one are they what with terrorists and all that!".

"No I suppose not, we'll have to go to mine later to try this baby out". "Ask your mum if you can stay to dinner Anthony and I'll ask mine". A quick call and some wheedling got them the permission and invitation they needed and barely able to contain their excitement they hurried round to Steven's home. Opening the door Steven called to his mother. "How long is dinner mum?" "A couple of hours, I've got some ironing to do first." "We are going down the shed." "Okay". "We are best off in my shed 'cos mum never comes down here" said Steven. "Awesome" Anthony followed Steven inside and closed the door.

Anthony gave a low whistle as he looked at all the equipment stacked up in the shed. Lying on the benches were knives saws, electric cutters, drills, screwdrivers, vices, all his father's tools that Steven used in his experiments. Picking up one of the small saws he cut a square trap door in the skull, as he lifted the small bit of bone, the odour of the rotting brain hit them. "Bloody hell that stinks" Steven said holding his nose. "Aw man that's rank" Anthony agreed pulling the corner of his hoody over his nose and mouth.

Steven shook the tiny skull over a bucket and the brain dripped out like jelly, then packing it with kitchen roll placed Anthony's explosive device inside, he replaced the little square of bone and secured it with tape.

"Right Ant lets give it a whirl"

Steven placed the skull on an upturned bucket outside, so that they could see it through the small grimy window of the shed.

Steven passed Anthony some welding goggles, and they both put them on, feeling very much like scientists present at the dawn of a great new invention. Steven nodded and Anthony pressed the button on the remote control. The noise of the explosion was like a thunderclap rocking the shed and shattering the window, showering them in glass. "Bloody hell you alright Ant?". "Yes awesome man! Awesome!". Anthony was shaking, his eyes bright under the goggles! "Mum's going to go mad." Steven said

"Maybe she didn't hear, then you won't have to tell her, you can get glass down the high street shop."

"Yes I suppose, it can't be that hard to fit," Steven said his eyes fixed on the back door waiting for his mother to appear. After several minutes the door remained closed, and he relaxed, she had not heard, or at least had not thought the explosion was anything to do with him.

Inspection of their handy work revealed that the bottom of the bucket had been blow through, and the skull was in a million pieces,

"A tad to much explosive?" suggests Steven. "Yeah I've got to try and get it smaller" said Anthony disappointed.

But childhood was giving way to adulthood and for a while the boys found themselves preoccupied with study and growing up with no time to pursue experiments in Steven's shed. But the success of that day in the shed was never far from either boy's mind.

CHAPTER 2

O ver the next few years the two friends met less often while they worked separately on evolving their own techniques, and their schoolwork, until one day Steven took a call from Anthony who sounded breathless and excited.

"I've done it!"

"Done what?" Steven asked. "Come round and I'll show you" "Okay mate I'll be round in a bit" As Steven walked into the kitchen, his mother, her hand nervously fiddling with her necklace said.

"Hi son there's someone I want you to meet, Brian this is my son Steven" "Hello Steven" the man said holding out a hand. "Hello" Steven replied warily taking it and noticing the well-manicured nails.

"Your mum and I, well, we're planning to see quite a lot of each other, and as you're the man of the house I thought I'd run it past you, make sure you're OK with it?" Brian smiled at Steven and Steven wondered if Brian thought he was dealing with a much younger boy, so patronising was his tone. He half expected Brian to lean over and tousle his hair, he suppressed a smile, the guy had obviously been watching some half arsed TV show telling you how to behave with kids whose mother you were going to poke, but he held his tongue and said "As long as mum's happy, I'm happy." "Good," Brian smiled "just got in from school Steven?"

"No I'm just taking time out till I decide what I want to do". "One of those gap year holidays eh?" suggested Brian. "Something like that", Steven replied "What do you do Brian?". "Oh I'm a dentist; I have my own practise not far from here". "That's crazy I have a fascination for teeth, I have a big collection" Steven enthused.

"Sorry?" said Brian his smile faltering for a moment

Steven laughed

"Oh! Not human teeth, animals, I was thinking of becoming a vet"

"Oh I see, had me going a bit there", said Brian with a nervous laugh.

"Tell you what Steven, perhaps you might like dentistry, I could show you a bit of what we do, fancy it?"

"Yes, I'm up for it," said Steven. And at the same time thinking Perhaps this man could be quite useful. "Good I'll sort out a day, Saturday's are normally quieter, mostly emergencies or mop up from the week, if you'd like, you can have a good look around"

"Great see you Saturday then?". "Yes Saturday it is then". "I'm off to have a shower, see you in a bit"

"Okay love" replied his mum. She smiled at him, a smile that told him that she was relieved and pleased with him, she had obviously been worried about introducing Brian, but she didn't need to be, Steven genuinely wanted to see her happy, and if Brian did it for her, well, hey!When Steven was out of ear shot, Brian crossed the kitchen and took Mary in his arms

"Well that was pretty straightforward', wasn't it love?" said Brian "Yes it was, I must admit I was a bit nervous, but yes he seemed fine," she replied.

As he kissed her tenderly on the neck, Mary luxuriated in the feeling of his arms around her. She loved everything about him, not least the fact that his appearance gave an impression of wealth. Brian was tall and dark, with rugged features and excellent posture, Brian was kind, gentle, generous and loving, and a complete contrast to the man she had spent so many wasted years with. Since they had started seeing more of each other, she had often felt like pinching herself to see if it was all a dream, for the first time in years she felt that her life was complete.

"Right I've got to dash", said Brian kissing her on the lips, "this won't buy the baby a new bonnet". Mary laughed, she liked his little sayings.

"See you tonight?" she asked, "Oh I can't tonight, got to do evening surgery, see you tomorrow sevenish?"

"Okay" she smiled. Brain kissed her again and was gone.

"Hearing the door shut Steven came back down stairs. "Blimey Orielly he looks like he's got a few bob mum, where did you meet him?"

"Sarah introduced us" "Sarah?"

"Yes, you remember, one of my friends in the photo I showed you." "Oh yes, Sarah" he said.

"He split with his wife over a year ago, now the divorce is settled he's his own man."

"I'm really pleased for you mum." "Thanks son, come here and give your mum a kiss". Steven protested but gave his mum a quick peck on the cheek.

"Right I'm off to Anthony's." "What about dinner?" "I'll be back later, It'll be okay warmed up, see ya" he said, over his shoulder.

"Yes see you." Mary frowned "I don't know what that boy's up to, he's never here", she muttered.Steven flipped open his mobile and dialled his friend's number.

"Alright Ant, you in?"

"Yes where are you?" "Outside yours mate." "Right I'm coming down".

"Mum, Steven's here". "Okay "Oh that's nice we haven't seen you for a while, she said as Steven came in behind Anthony. Would you like to stay for dinner?" "No thanks Mrs Grace, my mum's keeping some for me." "Okay love", "Anthony make Steven a drink there's a good lad"

"What do you want mate? there's orange or there's orange." "I'll have orange then" said Steven. "Good choice" says Anthony smiling. "You go up I'll get the drinks".

Steven went up to Anthony's room, there was stuff everywhere, wires, gadgets, tubes of stuff, it looked like someone had thrown the lot in the air a left it where it landed.

"There you go mate, get that down your neck"

"Blimey it's a mess in here, how do you find anything?" "It's an organised mess, I know where everything is". Anthony paused "Now where is it?" he scoured the mess,

"Ahh here it is" he says picking up a tiny little gadget the size of a pea.

"What is it?" asks Steven. "A smart bomb, blow your head off", replied Anthony. "What, that little thing?" Steven stared at the tiny gadget. "Yes that little thing". "Have you tried it?"

"Yes put one inside a grape fruit, blew it to smithereens, it was awesome man; we got to try it out on one of your animals" suggested Anthony. "Yes, lets try it tonight, meet me round mine later, after dinner". As he left Steven called out

"See you Mrs Grace."

"Good heavens that was quick, bye love." "See you in about an hour Ant."
"Okay". "Have you two fallen out Anthony?" "No mum, I'm going round his in a bit." "Here give us a hand son"

Anthony's mum was wheelchair bound a legacy of his violent father, a former drinking buddy of Stevens father, who in a drunken rage had pushed her down the stairs. Frightened for her life, she had always said that she slipped and fell. Anthony was only five years of age, but the memory of that terrifying night had made an indelible mark on him. The loathing he felt for his father followed him like a hateful demon, and coloured everything he did. On the nights that he could not sleep for the bitter burn of hate in his throat he would comfort himself that one day he would find his father and kill himNow grossly overweight the once pretty delicate woman that had been his mother no longer laughed and smiled very much, and although she could do most things, she often played on her disability, but Anthony would do anything for her, and she knew it.

"Right dinner's nearly ready, set the table son" Anthony did and when dinner was over he loaded the dishwasher, a luxury, along with the chair lift on the stairs that his mum was entitled to because of her disability. Right I'm off mum, see you later" "Okay love, don't be late there's a pet."

A few short minutes later Anthony was at Stevens door. "Hi Mrs Smith, is Steven in?" "Yes he's down the shed, how's your mum Anthony?"

"Yeah, not bad, thanks" he said anxious to get to the shed. "I'll go round the back shall I?"

A nod from Steven's mum and he was off down the garden. Steven saw him coming and kicked the shed door open with his foot. "In here mate, you had dinner? ""Yes a lovely roast." "I haven't, I wanted to get on." "Blimey it's changed in here" said Anthony as he took in the caged creatures, staring back at him warily; rats, a mangy looking fox, pigeons, even a badger.

"Ahh let that one go mate I love them" Anthony indicated to a badger pacing up and down in its cage.

"Yes he's quite a character, I wasn't going to hurt him anyway let him go if you want"

Anthony picked up the cage opened the door and watched as the creature made for the undergrowth and disappeared. "What are you doing?" he asked Steven. "Look I've made an incision in the rats head, we can put the gadget inside sew it up, when it comes round we can release it somewhere and watch it blow up" "Awesome" said Anthony. With the operation complete they waited for the rat to wake. "Looks dead to me mate." "Give it time" said Steven. "There, it's moving, told you!""said a smug Steven. "Looks like someone's whacked it on the head, it's got a little bump" laughed Anthony.

"Yes does look funny don't it". "What now?" asked Anthony. "Let's just take it out, look around a bit see what opportunities present themselves" replied Steven.

They walk the streets the woozy rat wrapped tight in a rag under Steven's jacket.

"Look! There's Barton's car", pointed Steven.

Barton was the local bully, almost a stereotype, his slovenly overweight carcass topped with a small head and a face that only a mother could love, with sly rat like eyes that darted this way and that looking for new victims to torture.

As the boys looked at the car the image that both of them would never forget played out in each of their heads, and although they did not say a word, never had done and never would do, they both saw the image of themselves, their trousers pulled down, their naked genitals crushed together on view to the whole school on the playing field where Barton and some of his cronies had tied them to a goal post in their first year.

Above their heads Barton had tied a sign on which he had written.

"We are best friends, we are qweers we luv each other and do it up the bum!

"Let's blow it up?" Steven said a hard edge to his voice. "Yes awesome go on then, let it go" said Anthony. "But hang on how are we going to get it to go that way?"

"Hmm, don't know, lets just let it go see what happens" Steven released the rat from the rags he was carrying it in. It immediately scuttled in the wrong direction. A woman passing by on the other side of the road screamed scaring the rat and forcing it to change direction back towards the car. "Go on! Go on!" the pair urged in excited unison. Seeking the only available shelter the rat disappeared under the car. "Go on mate". Anthony pulls out what looked like a mobile phone, tapped in the number 999. A slight pause then

BOOM!

The car lifted slightly off the road.

"Awesome man that was brilliant." Anthony said his voice hoarse with excitement

Suddenly Steven spotted something. "Hey what's that?"

"What was what?"

A face had appeared in the rear window of the car. "Quick, get down, it's Barton!" Anthony hissed.

Before they could move, another face appeared. "Look,He's got his bird with him, lets leg it mate"

They ran as fast as their legs would take them, until they had gained a safe distance. As they slowed down Anthony began to laugh, bending over trying to catch his breath he said "He got a bigger bang than he bargained for eh mate?"

"And I bet it's the first time the earths moved for his girlfriend!" The pair collapsed in uncontrollable fits of laugher.Barton got out of the car. "What the fuck was that Sharon?" His florid face was even more blotchy his eyes wide with fright, "Uhh don't come out love there's blood everywhere". Barton was half expecting a body. There was blood, bits of flesh, and hair, but no body

"What the fuck is all this about?" His voice took on a babyish whine, and he realised he had wet himself.

The bomb had done its job, blowing the rat apart into a million pieces. The only regret the boys had was that they were unable to witness Barton and Sharon walking away from the scene, Barton walking with his legs apart as his urine stung the places on his legs where he had picked spots, Sharon, half undressed, looking every bit the desperate slag she was. Saturday came and Steven arrived at Brian's surgery nice and early. A Mercedes purred down the road, "lucky bastard" Steven thought before he realised it was Brian.

As the car pulled onto the hard court and the driver's door swung open Steven said

"Blimey I definitely want to be a dentist if I get to drive a car like that." "A lot of hard work!" said Brian, getting out of the car, smelling expensive "I like hard work" "Then you'll definitely have one".

"Right first things first, kettle on for a nice cuppa, do you take tea Steven?" Brian flipped on the lights and turned off the alarm.

"Not really." "Well I'm afraid that's all we have." "Tea it is then", Steven said.

"She really is a lovely woman your mum" Brian said, "I am so sorry about what you both went through in the past" before Steven could speak he continued "she's told me all about it." "Yes dad was a right arsehole, it was drink that made him that way, and I'm never going to drink".

"Good to hear it, learn by experience, I mean other peoples experiences. Still that's all going to change now; your mother and I get on so well," said Brian smiling at him. "That's good, mum deserves a bit of happiness".

Right let's show you round before the clients start arriving. The clinic door opened "Ahh this is Chris one of my partners. Chris this is Steven the lad I told you about." "Hello Steven." "Hi." "Just going to show him around before people start arriving, kettle's boiled" "Thanks." Chris barely acknowledged Steven apart from a rather arrogant look down his patrician nose, and Steven took an instant dislike to the man. Chris was tall, blonde highlights, full of himself and had a perfect set of pure white teeth, in the sort of smug face you'd like to punch.

"Right Steven this is where the action happens, this is my room, next door is Trudy's, she just takes care of hygiene, you know cleaning all the grunge off, gum treatment etc. That's Chris's door next, then the tea room you know, toilets, waiting room, x-rays, stores, offices".

"Where will I be?" "Probably in the toilets mostly, this isn't a job for the faint hearted" Brian laughed at his own joke.

"I'm not afraid of blood"

"Okay if you say so," Brian said with a smile that said we'll wait and see. "No really I'm not" "You can stay in with me today, see how it goes" said Brian. "Okay"

Steven looked around the surgery as a young girl dressed as a nurse came in.

"Hi ya, you must be Steven, I'm Lucy pleased to meet you," she said planting a peck on Steven's cheek. To his horror, Steven felt himself blush "Err yes pleased to meet you", he replied.

Steven watched, fascinated as Lucy prepared the instruments for the days work. I'm going to enjoy working with her, he thought.

Lucy was well endowed in all the right places with a smiley sweet face, and jet-black hair. "Ahh, I see you two have met, said Brian now dressed in blue with white clogs.

"I like the outfit" commented Steven. "Whose mine or Lucy's"?

"Both" Steven said casting a shy glance in Lucy's direction

"That's what I like, a happy ship, right first victim, I mean patient" said Brian with a smile.

Lucy disappeared to the waiting room. "Right, remember Steven these are high class clientele with big bucks to spend, best behaviour!"

"Sure no worries" Steven said.

"Ahh Mrs Spendlebase how are we today?" Brian asked solicitously as the first patient a matronly woman in very expensive clothes waddled to the chair.

"Not at all well" she said sulkily, glancing in Steven's direction. "Sit yourself down here; let's see if we can't put you right". Brian peered into her mouth the stench of drink nearly knocking him out. "I" think I'll just apply some pain killer." Brain reached his hand out towards Lucy who put a syringe in it. "Of course get on with it, can't you see I'm in pain". "Oh yes I see the problem, look Steven see that hole in the tooth there, he said gently jabbing a pointed tool into it, causing the woman to protest loudly. She batted his arm away. "You fool what are you trying to do kill me?" "Calm down Mrs Spendlebase we'll soon have you feeling a lot better". Brian said in a reassuring voice "Nurse can you mix some white filler?". He continued.

Steven watched as Brian injected all around the old cranks bad tooth. "Just give that a few minutes", she lay there with her eyes closed muttering to herself and Steven noticed her hairy chin. He shuddered.

"Open wide my dear", said Brian as he jabbed the pointed tool into the hole harder, this time with no reaction from the old woman.Brian raised the drill, looking at Steven

"Here we go just relax".

Steven imagined Brian with a set of devil's horns and wearing an evil grin. Grinding away and loving every minute of it. Eventually Brian stood up straight and said.

"Right that's you finished, you'll be fine now." "Thank you Brian" the old dear replied lisping through her paralysed lips. "Your most welcome" he said showing her gently out of the room.

"Managed to stay on your feet then?" he said to Steven. "Yes that was nothing, easy; and I could see that look in your eye when you were hurting her!".

"Perks of the job, the ruder they are to me, the more it's going to hurt," Brian said with a big grin. Right cup of tea then the next . . . ." "I know, victim!" said Steven laughing "Your turn, I made the last one" "I've never made tea"

"Well then, now's a good time to learn, come on!"

"How long is the training for dentistry Brian?" "Four years normally, you need qualifications in maths, biology, chemistry". "I got A grade at A level in them all, as well as physics" said Steven. "Perfect, so if dental college is for you, if you're serious, after you qualify you could practise here".

"Would you really take me on?" "Yes, and I have contacts, but give it a couple more Saturdays you may change your mind."

"Okay but I think I like it already". "We'll see, come on drink up, the next poor soul is about to feel pain." "Yes a pain like no other, I remember the dentist drilled my tooth once and hit a nerve, I nearly pissed myself, it's the worst pain I've ever had" ""Lovely" said Brian with a twinkle in his eye.

"Hello young lady" "Cathy!" said Steven surprised. "Steven what are you doing here?" "You two know each other"? Brian asked. "Yes we went to the same school. How you doing Cathy?" "I'm fine, do you work here then?". "Just on Saturdays, at the moment". "Cathy's been coming here since she was a little girl," Brain said smiling at her, "a fondness for sweeties eh Cathy?"

Chris popped his head in.

"Can I borrow Lucy for a bit?" "Yes just routine filling here, I'll be fine." "Thanks". "Right, in the chair my girl, lay back" said Brian.

From Steven's viewpoint he could see right up Cathy's dress. Following his gaze Cathy moved her legs slightly apart.

Still the same old prick tease, he thought, he wondered if she had done" it" yet. While Brian was engrossed at the head end, Steven ran his finger up one of Cathy's legs, which made her jump. "Oops sorry, did I hurt you?" "No" she looked at Steven wide-eyed. "Try and keep still there's a love, here Steven look

I've cleared all the rot" Steven moved forward trailing a hand up Cathy's leg to her panties. This time with no reaction from her, he slipped his fingers under the elastic of her panties, sliding his fingers into the moist warmth of her vagina.

"Oh yes that's a big hole" Steven said with a smile. "Steven quickly removed his hand as the door to the surgery opened and Lucy entered the room. "Ah Lucy, there you are, can you mix some filler please?" "Sure", she replied. "Are you okay, Lucy, you look a little flushed?" observed Brian. "Yes I'm fine just a little hot" she replied.Steven smiled, he thought he was going to like it here; he thought he was going to like it a lot!

CHAPTER 3

A few months later and Steven had seen just about every gory detail from fillings and tooth extraction, to deep root canal, and had heard a wide range of screams from little children to fully-grown men. He looked forward to his Saturday mornings and was seriously considering dentistry as a career. Brain was a good teacher and made his mother very happy and apart from the odd embarrassing noise from their bedroom on a Friday night when Brian stayed over, they were very careful not to gross him out too much. So every Saturday he and Brian drove to work in the Mercedes and every Saturday without fail Chris would pop his head in to borrow Lucy. One Saturday as Lucy left for Chris's room Steven followed, passing the door to Chris's surgery he pushed his ear to the shiny paintwork, unintelligible grunts followed by a sort of muffled screaming, then silence although Steven thought he could hear heavy breathing.

"Will that be all Chris?" he heard Lucy say "Yes thank you Lucy, and they'll be the usual little extra in your wage packet this week" Steven made a speedy run for the toilets slowing down just before he got there. Walking the last few steps he was stopped in his tracks. What was Cathy doing here again?

He was about to go into the waiting room when a voice behind him said "What you up to Steven?" It was Lucy.
"Oh Lucy, it's you, just seen one of my friends.

"Cool" she smiled, and he noticed that Lucy's face looked sort of shiny, her eyes bright and her lips puffy and bruised looking.Steven turned his attention back to Cathy

"What you doing here again?" "Filling came out" "What time is your appointment?" He asked. "Ten past" Steven looked at his watch. "That's ten minutes, quick, in here" Steven pulled her into the x-ray room. "Remember all those times behind the pavilion", he said, his cock stiffening. Unzipping his fly he said "remember this big boy?, well he's even bigger now".

"Wow that's huge" Cathy looked at his cock hungrily, she had often regretted not going further with him when they were younger, she had a bit more experience now. In fact Cathy had been through many boys in a short space of time, Without a word, she slipped her knickers down and positioned herself on the desk, her legs hanging down, the lips of her shaven pussy on display

"Come on then big boy lets see what you got"

For all his bravado and despite the tantalising, ball aching view of Cathy's shiny hairless pussy he felt suddenly unsure of himself.

"I've never done it before Cathy," he said quietly. Would she laugh at him? He held his breath. She looked surprised but, her breath coming quicker she said. "You'll soon get the hang of it" she said grabbing his manhood and guiding it towards her. As he pushed forward she let out a cry.

"What?" he said anxiously. "Nothing, it's just very big, try again" she said hoping the pain would ease and that she would be able to accommodate his huge prick. She couldn't

"No stop that's too painful, she pushed him away. "Now what?" Steven was in pain, his balls aching as his erection bobbed between them. "Wankey, Wankey" she laughed gripping his cock and working both her hands up and down his huge shaft,

Steven shot his load almost immediately. "Just like old times then" he said as the final spasm squeezed out the last of his cum. As he zipped himself up Cathy said. "Hey, not so fast, what about me then"?

"What do you mean?" "You've had your fun what about me?" "You said it hurt" "There are other ways" "Like what? show me." Cathy guided Steven's hand to her pussy, "Can you feel that hard little bit?" Steven nodded, "Rub it, no, not too hard, it's called a clit, and it feels sooooo good" she threw her head back as Steven worked his fingers in and out of her and over her clit, slick with her juices. He leaned over and parted her lips, curious to examine this previously unknown part of a woman anatomy.

"Actually what is really the best is if you use your tongue to lick my clit"

Steven sniffed cautiously between her splayed legs. He could detect a faint smell of talc and a musky smell that wasn't unpleasant. He could feel his cock stirring in his pants again and as Cathy bit on her sleeve to stop screaming out loud he began to lick her little clit "

"Yes that's it keep going like that, faster, yes that's it, yes, yes, yes", she screamed, the sound muffled in her sleeve. Steven was not quite sure what he had done, he assumed she had come, although he had never really thought much about women coming. She was straightening herself up now with the same glassy look in her eyes as he had seen in Lucy's just a little while earlier. He felt quite pleased with himself as she left the x-ray room winking at him as she went and planting a soft kiss on his lips. He could go again, but maybe there would be another day.

He had to wait for a moment to let his erection subside before he re-entered the surgery.

"Look who's here Steven" "I know we met in the waiting room" Cathy gave him the same sly wink and he had to suppress a smile.

"Where have you been?" asks Brian "I didn't feel that great, so I went for a bit of fresh air". "You okay now?" "Yep fine"

"Well take a look at this, Steven, all my work ruined by a toffee, now Miss Sweet Tooth you'll have to stop eating sweets or it'll be dentures for you." "Sorry I'll try and stop, I promise". Cathy said "Only teasing, seriously though you have to be careful, right that's you done." Said Brian

"Thanks Brian, see you then Steven" "Yes see you Cathy" Chris came into the surgery "Oops sorry" he said as he bumped into Cathy as she was leaving.

"Right I'm off, see you Monday have a good weekend, what's left of it",

"OK, bye Chris, come on then Steven, just one more and we're done, you ready Lucy?"

"No I'm scared" she wrinkled her nose. "Come on, you've seen it all" Brain smiled at her

"That's why I'm scared". She gave him a nervous smile "I'll leave you to it" Steven said. Once out of the surgery he headed straight for Chris's room. Looking around Steven wondered exactly what went on each Saturday when Lucy did her Saturday morning stint with Chris. Picking up one of the drills he pressed the trigger, enjoying the whining noise. With Brian still working the compressors were still on, and Steven quickly drilled a fine hole in the lower corner of the opaque glass window, then he stepped back to admire his handiwork.

"Nope can't notice that" he muttered, and going over to the window. He was surprised at how much he could see through the hole, carefully replacing the drill he went outside. The window of Chris's surgery was at the back of the practice and after negotiating an alley full of bins, old computers and other junk Steven identified the window and looked through the tiny hole he had drilled, He could see the patient's chair, perfect he thought. That should make things a lot clearer! He chuckled to himself. "All done Steven, you can shoot off if you like" said Brian emerging from his treatment room. "Okay see you next Saturday?" Steven said. "I'll probably see you during the week; me and your mum are out for a meal Tuesday". "Okay see you then". "Wait for me, I'll walk with you "Lucy said struggling into her jacket, "That last one was a doozy, horrible" she shuddered and Steven wished for a moment he had stopped to see it. "Nice girl that Lucy, you should invite her out" Brian said as Lucy went down the corridors putting off the lights.

"She wouldn't go for me" "Well, you won't know if you don't ask, go on go for it" "Maybe I will""

"That's the spirit" said Brian with a wink.

"Ready Steven?" "Yep, lets go."

They walked casually along the tree-lined avenue, Steven's trying to pluck up courage to ask Lucy out.

"Got a boyfriend Lucy?" he eventually blurted out. "No." "Want one?" "Why, are you asking?" said Lucy smiling at him. "Yep, I suppose I am" he smiled back "Okay" "Great" he said "Pictures Tuesday?".

"Oh yes I love the pictures!" she said excited. "That's settled then" Lucy suddenly stopped walking. "What's up?" he asked "This is my house!" she laughed

"Oh right".

She offered her cheek for a kiss and Steven bushed his lips on her smooth face. Steven went on his way like a dog with two dicks. Looking back at the end of the road he shouted

"See you Tuesday, Oh what time?"

"Meet you here at seven?"

"Okay see you then".
Tuesday found Steven and Lucy sitting in the more expensive seats in the back row of the cinema, In front of them there were a handful of people in the cheap seats. "We might get thrown out" Lucy said worried. "No we wont, even though I never buy the more expensive ticket, I always sit up here, and the place is empty anyway", he reassured her.

The lights dimmed and the film began, Steven put his arm around Lucy's shoulder, when she did not object, he began, millimetre-by-millimetre to slide his hand down towards her breast.

After a torturous ten minutes of this slow progress, Lucy lifted his hand and put it on her breast whispering.

"Its okay I don't mind". Having been given free reign Steven squeezed and caressed Lucy's soft flesh and explored her stiffening nipple. He tried to put his suspicions about what went on Saturday mornings in Chris's surgery out of his mind and wondered if she would do" it" with him although he doubted it on their first date.

He fidgeted in his seat trying to hide his obvious arousal. Lucy kissed him gently on the cheek and reached over to undo his jeans. She took out his cock and he heard her intake of breath as she saw how big he was. She began stroking and Steven found himself unable to stop his ejaculation.

"Now then, maybe we can sit and watch the film" she said with a smile. "Good idea" Steven smiled back, as he got his breath back

"That was a good film I really enjoyed it, thanks for asking me", said Lucy, as they walked home together.

"No thank YOU! Steven squeezed her hand, the film was a bit soppy for me, shall we walk across the park?".

"Yes okay", Lucy thought the park looked romantic in the half-light.

They sat on the swings chatting and laughing for a while.

Suddenly the wind got up and clouds covered the moon, and darkness fell. As they began to walk towards home a familiar voice stopped Steven in his tracks.

"Oi, Oi Savoloy", what we got here then".

"Barton",. Shouted Steven.

"It is I", Barton said with a mock bow, with him was another low life, Eddie Swan, a vile character, heavily tattooed, with a scared face, shaven head, and big black bovver boy boots.

"Bart, I can smell pussy", he said.

"Help yourself", without warning, Barton hit Steven, knocking him to the ground then jumped on him pinning him to the ground.

Swan had a tight grip on Lucy who was kicking and screaming. "Shut the fuck up bitch", he growled hitting her hard in the face with his grimy fist. Shoving her to the ground he straddled her and started ripping at her clothing.
"Look at them fuckers Barton". Swan pinched Lucy's nipples hard. "Yes nice I'll be having a closer look in a bit"

"Leave her alone you fucking scum" Shouted Steven

"Shut the fuck up", said Barton punching Steven again," just shut the fuck up and enjoy the show". "Go on Swannie give it to her" said an excited Barton holding Steven by the hair with his face towards the unfolding events. Lucy was wriggling kicking and screaming for all she was worth, Steven shouted again. "Leave her alone you scumbag!". Swan lost his patience.

"Shut him up Barty, and you shut the fuck up", he said to Lucy bringing out a knife and pushing it against her throat. Pressing down he brought a thin line of blood to the surface of Lucy's skin.

"Any more out of you bitch and you're history", said Swan, his foul breath thick with alcohol as he leaned over her.

Lucy lay paralysed with fear. He was going to rape her or kill her or both maybe. She struggled then spat in his face.

"You dirty bitch", he said slapping her again.

She was at his mercy. He used the knife to cut the crutch to her panties, fumbling with his flies, he shoved his cock into her, pumping furiously as fetid drool dripped on to her face from his slack mouth.

"Go on Suwannee!" Barton said egging him on. "Look at them, look at them", Barton squealed and Steven felt bile rise in his throat.
Swan howled like a wolf as he reached his climax.

Steven shut his eyes tight and croaked through broken teeth, "God no, leave her alone, please".

"Your turn Bart"

"Fuck off I'm not going there after you".

"You'll have to fuck her up the arse then". Said Swan laughing.

"Should be a nice tight one", Barton said, joining the laughter

Swan walked towards where Steven lay. Lining him up he takes a footballers kick to Stevens head, "Now shut the fuck up" he shouted stalking around Stevens still body like a predator circling its kill. Barton picked Lucy up and laid her over the small wall around the play area.

"Oh this is going to be nice and tight", he says pulling her skirt up to her waist

"Get it while you can, that's what I say Bart".

Swan had a particularly evil and repulsive smile. He had some teeth missing; the remainder were yellow with a tinge of brown, if truth were told even Barton was apprehensive of Swan and never trusted him, you could never tell what the mad fucker would do next.

Coming over to where Barton was about to enter Lucy he lifted her head.

"You're enjoying that bitch aren't you"

Sobbing, she spat in his face again.

"You dirty bitch I warned you"

Pulling out his knife, he ran it across her throat severing it in one deep cut.

Lucy's body slumped further over the wall, the blood was draining from her and she twitched as her life ebbed away.

"You Bastard, why did you do that?" Barton said looking down at his wilted erection

"I fucking warned her Bart" Swan replied looking at him with wild black emotionless eyes.

Barton's mind was racing, Swan was out of control,

Pulling a knife out of his belt, Barton lunged and planted the blade deep into Swan's neck, Swan fell to the ground, screaming, a grotesque, wet gurgling sound. "You fucking bastard I'll kill you" he shouted but his voice was getting weaker as blood poured out of his mouth. It took a long time for him to die, longer than it had taken Lucy. Once he was gone, an eerie silence engulfed the park. Barton glanced at Steven, Swan's last kick to the head had obviously killed him. Barton felt piss streaming down his leg. He vomited in the bushes and then disappeared into the blackness of the night.

CHAPTER 4

The next morning, Oscar and Jake raced ahead of their mother, Milly Downs to the play area in the park. As Milly stopped to pick up the dummy that her toddler had thrown out of her buggy, her children's screams reached her over the still morning air.

Running at full tilt towards them, the buggy and its occupant forgotten she shrieked in a voice that did not even sound like her own;

"My God boys, what's the matter?"

As she reached the scene, clouds of flies flew up from the gaping wound in Swan's neck. Her boys stood ashen faced, their innocence and childhood snatched away in the single moment that their young eyes had taken in the scene of horror. Their mother, could not speak or move, her eyes unable to tear themselves away from the sight of Lucy's bare buttocks, faeces streaked down her legs from the moment her bowels had relaxed in death. Her teeth chattering, Milly snatched her sons to her and stumbled back to the buggy. A dog walker and some joggers, hearing the commotion hurried over. Milly was trying to dial the police but her hands were shaking so much she repeatedly dropped her phone.

As the dog walker and jogger took in the scene, one of the dogs, a Labrador ambled over to Lucy's body lying half over the wall and sniffed at her soiled leg.

Milly and the dog owner screamed together before the older woman threw up where she stood. One of the joggers made the call to the police while the other led the two women, the children and dogs to a bench.

Sirens far away, then closer cut through the morning air, a morning that should have been full of summer scents and promise but that was now black with the stench of death.

The police swung into action like a well-oiled machine, with screens up around the bodies first.

"Clear the area Roberts".

"Yes Sir"

"Right, you lot get this area cleared" Andy Roberts assumed control of the new arrival of police officers.

"I'm afraid you'll have to move with your children Miss, and you Madam, and get those dogs on a lead! Hold on, were you two ladies first on the scene?" The women nodded.

"Oh right, then in that case, stay right there I'll get someone over to you."

The jogger who had made the call to the police made himself known and Roberts took him over to his superior.

'Sir, this is the gentleman that called us' 'Detective Sammy Matheson' the senior officer said, flashing his badge.

"The woman over there with the children was first on the scene, by the looks of it" Roberts said. pointing out Milly sitting hunched on the bench, her face almost grey with the full horror of the ordeal, her children's faces buried in her shoulders, as she tried to spare them any further horror. Their nightmares would be graphic enough.

"Roberts get one of the female PC's over to look after this woman and her children till the ambulance arrives"

"Right you are Sir"

"You, yes you, name?" demanded Roberts homing in on a nervous trio of young WPC's

"PC Jane Crouch sir"

"Right officer Crouch I'm leaving you with this woman and her children, go with them to hospital, and take down everything she says"

"Yes sir"

The Policewoman ran back to the squad car and returned with blankets for Milly and her children while they waited for the ambulance.

Detective Matheson walked over to where the murdered girl's body lay half over the wall, close to Swan's.

"Roberts, over here! There's another one, looks like there's been a bloody battle, take a look at this".

"What the fucks gone on here?", said Roberts kneeling down beside Steven. "Shit, this one's still alive!" he said holding his fingers to Steven's neck.

"Where's that bloody ambulance?", Matheson shouted.

"On its way" a PC shouted back.

"Call another one' demanded Matheson. "How bad is he Roberts?" he continued.

"Hard to say sir, looks like a head injury; he's been hit with something"

Ambulance crews were arriving now, the first, sirens blaring, took Roberts and Steven to hospital.

Forensic examination was beginning now with the familiar tents erected over the bodies.

After a couple of hours Matheson could no longer contain his impatience.

"What we got, anything"? He said, popping his head inside the tent.

"Yes a fair bit" was the reply

"You keeping it a secret then, Connor?" he said and Isabel Conner, head of the forensic team smiled a tight smile.

"The girl was most probably raped by the dead man, both show obvious traces of semen. We also found blood on a knife the deceased man had on him, and there is also signs of anal penetration, some tissue bruising and tearing, but that looks older, possibly not related to this incident.

Matheson put his hand up stopping Isabel in mid flow. "Hang on".

He called Roberts. "Roberts watch that lad like a hawk, he may have molested the victim as well"

"Yes Sir" Roberts replied, looking at Steven's lifeless body, this boy was going nowhere, he thought.

"Sorry, please continue", Matheson said closing his mobile

"We'll just take some more samples for DNA testing then we're done"

"Okay good job lads and lasses' Matheson squinted as the powerful flashes of the incident cameras went off around him.

A day later the lab results were on the Matheson's desk.

He ran through them expertly piecing together relevant strands of information.

Pubic hair taken from the clothing of the girl had turned up as a match to an old regular customer of Matheson's

"Greg Barton." Matheson muttered under his breath, this was pretty hard-core even for that animal "what a scum bag" he said out aloud.

"That's a name I recognise Sir". Said Roberts, back from the hopstial,he had come into the office with fresh coffee. "That fucking low life piece of shit, it was him that abused that girl." Matheson growled. "Roberts go and pick that turd up, and take some blue coats with you"

"Yes Sir". Matheson carried on with the report. A DNA test of the semen in the girl was a match to the dead man. DNA tests to the handle of the knife in the dead mans neck a match to . . . . Greg Barton!

Tests on the handle of the dead mans knife matched only his DNA. The blood to the blade was a match to the dead girl.

The Girls hand had traces of semen. "No match to either Barton or Swan".

Scratching his head, Matheson said aloud again. "The dead man fucks the girl. Barton kills the dead man, Barton's pubes are on her, and she's got spunk from another bloke on her hands'. "This is some fucking gang bang!".

Steven had cheated death by millimetres. In a medically induced coma, a blood clot had been removed from his brain; He had no ID on him so a press release and a spot on the national news was arranged. It was Brian that realised the boy in the report was Steven and raced round to Mary. As he arrived at the house he found her sitting on the settee her face drained of blood, shaking. She had seen the same broadcast. Taking her in his arms, Brian coaxed her out into his car.

"I thought he was having a lie in" she said over and over again on the way to the hospital. Brain said nothing but kept her hand in his all the way.

As Mary stared around the Accident and Emergency department where Brian was trying hard to get information, she thought that it really looked no different than it had when she had been a frequent visitor before her husband died. She felt sick and helpless, much the same as she had then. Eventually a harassed young doctor who looked like she had not slept in a month came to see them.

"I'm sorry but you can't see Steven just now, he's just come from surgery, he's critical but stable. Tonight will be cruciall; I am afraid it is very much a wait and see approach at the moment. But if he can make it through tonight, then we will be more optimistic"

"Where is he?" Mary said, her voice didn't sound like her own.

"On the 3rd floor, but" the doctor looked uncomfortable "he, um, he's got police guarding him"

Mary sighed and nodded. She knew what that was like. "Can we sit near his room.?"

"Of course," the young doctor jumped up eager to end the interview.

On the third floor, they were shown to small room a few doors away from where Steven lay fighting for his life, two police officers at his door.

A couple of hours later detectives arrived, but Brian refused to let them speak to Mary, she was still deeply shocked and barely talking. They slept the night in the little room, Mary eventually falling asleep on Brian's shoulder. In the morning, Mary awoke and her first word was, "Steven?"

Brian, his arm numb from Mary's weight on it all night called a nurse. She gave them a small smile, "He's holding his own!"

Brain and Mary returned to Mary's to wash and change. They had agreed to meet detectives there, Brain thought it might be better in Mary's familiar territory. As the detective filled them in on the horrific details of the attack, they sat holding each other's hands tight, almost unable to take it in.

Daily visits to the hospital became routine and Mary spent almost all the day with her son. He began to make real progress, and the doctors were pleased with each hurdle he passed. Two weeks later Steven was off the critical list and in a single room guarded by a policeman.

Having been given the news that Steven was doing so well, it was not long before Sammy Matheson arrived on the ward.

"Inspector Sammy Matheson, and this is Detective Constable Roberts", the detective said showing his ID to Steven's doctor.

"Dr. Black?"
"Yes inspector what can I do for you today?" "Would it be okay to ask Steven Smith a few questions?"

"Ten minutes, no more" the doctor said, he still tires easily."

"Okay Doctor Black, thank you"

"Ten minutes" he emphasised showing Matheson and Roberts to Stevens room. "Okay, thanks doc." "Ten lousy minutes Roberts"

"We'll have to slip in the old watch trick" offered Roberts

"Yes" Matheson smiled briefly

"At ease officer", Matheson says flashing his ID and looking at his watch—ten to three, "We arrived at five to three, right officer"

"Loud and clear sir"

In the room Steven was sitting up in his bed, looking surprisingly well.

"How you feeling son? I'm detective Matheson and this is my colleague Detective Roberts, you're looking well".

"Yes I feel fine; don't know why I'm still in here"

"Can you remember the events of Tuesday the 11th?

"Yes I went to the pictures with my girlfriend". said Steven.

"Would that be a Lucy Crowstone?"

"Yes is she Okay? Where is she, no one here seems to know? Steven said.

"I'm afraid it's bad news son, she was murdered" said Matheson gently "That fucking Barton, that bastard I'll kill him" Steven said sobbing. Matheson felt sorry that he had suspected Steven of attacking the girl, but it was only a fleeting feeling.

"Yes we know he was involved we're searching for him now, did you know the other man?"

"Swan, yes, oppo of Barton's, he's evil", said Steven his throat aching with his attempt to control his tears.

"Times up", said the nurse.

"Hang on we've only had five minutes right officer"

"Yes nurse they arrived at five to three"

"Sorry we got lost", said Roberts.

"God call yourselves Detectives? she said shaking her head, right I'll be back at five past" she said looking at Steven with concern. "What are you doing to this patient?"

"I'm sorry we had to break bad news "Roberts said.

"I'll be okay nurse, really", Steven reassured her. He wanted to help the police find the animals who had killed Lucy. His sorrow for the lovely girl had turned to black hatred of her killers.

"Okay see you in five".

The nurse disappeared.

"Right Steven, can you remember anything that happened." "Yes that evil bastard raped Lucy, then he said to Barton it's your turn, and to do it up her arse, the dirty fucking bastard." He choked the words out. "Calm down now Steven we don't have much time, the more we know now the quicker we can catch the scumbag". "Yes Sorry". Said Steven, taking a deep breath. 'I don't remember much more just getting kicked in the head and blacking out'.

"Who by, Barton?" Roberts asked

"No, Swan", replied Steven.

"Well Swan is dead, looks like he was killed by Barton". Said Matheson "I hope he suffered a long and agonising death" said Steven hoping for confirmation from the officers. Matheson did not respond but said.

"Yes, the unhappy part is Barton's still on the loose somewhere". "Any idea where he could be?" asked Roberts "He's quite well know locally isn't he?" "He is but I don't have a clue, kinda made it a habit to avoid the scumbag. Steven said

"Time gentlemen"

"Yes nurse we have just finished, right Steven that'll do for now, we will get the full interview done later but if you think of anything else however small, make a note of it and do get in touch, here's my card" Said Matheson handing the card to Steven

"Okay I will" Steven assured him.

"Right officers you're dismissed get back to the station" said Matheson

"Yes sir"

As the detectives walked along the corridor Steven's Mum and Brian were just arriving.

"Ma'am" said the Detectives.

As they walked out of the hospital Roberts said. "What about the semen on the girl's hand, you didn't ask him?"

"Roberts, Roberts, how long you been a detective, two young lovers at the pictures?". Matheson stood there looking at Roberts, "Penny dropped now?" he said as Roberts smiled.

"Yes Sir"

"What did they want Steven, what's a matter? You've been crying?"

"Yes, they told me about Lucy" His mother took his hand.

"Oh my poor boy, I know, it's horrible, I wanted to tell you before but the doctor said you weren't well enough, I'm sorry you had to find out like this."

Steven dried his eyes.

"What else did they want?" Brain asked.

"Oh just a few questions, don't worry Mum." Steven squeezed his mother's hand.

"Nurse said you could come home in a couple of days isn't that good news son?"

"Yes the grub in here not a patch on yours Mum"

"Ahh that's nice, I'll do your favourite, stir fry"

"What every night for a week?"

"We'll see" Mary said smiling.

"Be good to see you back at the surgery Steven, poor Lucy she didn't deserve that" said Brian.

"Yes the evil bastard, the one that did it, he's dead, the detectives told me".

"Small consolation," Brian said "but at least he can't hurt anyone else".

"There's bad news though, Barton's on the loose" said Steven grimly.

"Barton, I know that name, he's been to the surgery, his girlfriend too, her name's Bright, Sharon Bright" said Brian.

"Yes that's the scum bag; perhaps you could slip with the drill and bore into his brain?" "Steven!" Mary scolded him.

"Sorry mum, Sorry Brian".

"It's to be expected after what you've been through, if they turn up at the surgery of course I'll let the Police know don't you worry, but I doubt that dental treatment is uppermost in his mind at the moment", said Brian.

His mother smiled at him. "We'll just give you some good news before we go son, Brian and I are getting engaged".

"That's great news Mum I'm pleased for you both, Mrs Ginger got a good ring to it eh mum?"

"Were not that far ahead son, but yes in the future"

The door opened as another visitor was ushered in by the nurse.

"Oh hi Ant" said Steven beaming at his best mate. In fact Anthony was his only mate.

'Sorry didn't know anyone was here' said Anthony looking awkward and embarrassed.

"That's fine Anthony we were just leaving. Hope you didn't mind Steven?, I rang Anthony told him where you were, come on Brian"
"That's fine Mum".

After a peck from his Mum and a handshake from Brian the two friends were left alone.

"How you doing mate?" Anthony asked.

"Don't know why I'm still here" said Steven getting up and walking around, "I feel fine honestly mate" "Must say apart from the missing hair you look good"

"What happened mate?" Anthony said cautiously.

Steven went through the events that he could remember. Anthony sat still as he listened a frown creasing his forehead

"Should have blown that wanker up when we had the chance" said Anthony.

"Yes, I know, with all this time on my hands, I've come up with a plan, think I'll use it on him or her. He took my girlfriend I'll take his, eye for an eye".

Steven ran through a rough outline of the plan with Anthony.

"That's awesome man, I love it, you need to come round I've got something to show you, just the right thing for your plan".

Anthony gave Steven a brief rundown of what he had to show him.

That's brilliant mate'.

"I thought you would like it". 'And we have the right equipment now right Ant?'.

"Yes right, its taken months but it's perfect now. 'How's College, or rather how was it before . . . . ?' asks Anthony

"Yes great just three years to go and that's it I'm qualified. Couldn't of got in without Brian, he is letting me do quite a few things at the surgery now as well"

"Really?" Anthony looked surprised.

"Yes even got my own room all kitted out, well it's not mine, but I am allowed to use it Saturdays to practice on Mavis. It was the old store room". Think it's going to be mine eventually though.

"That's awesome Steve, who's Mavis?

A dummy's head, with real teeth."

"Oh right"

"You haven't heard the latest mate. Mum's going to marry Brian, so he'll be my dad, I reckon he has to give the surgery to me!"

"Talking of Mums I'll have to get going Steve, cant leave mum too long these days" Anthony was his mum's full time carer now that she was almost bed bound.

"When they finally let me out of here, I'll have to pop round"

"Yes, that'll cheer her up" A week later and Steven was at last at home convalescing. He spent a few days watching telly, playing on the play station, and reading. Restless he eventually said to his Mum.

"I think I'm going round to Anthony's Mum"

"Are you sure you're okay?" she said

"Yes I'll be fine"

"Okay love". After a pause, she said; "Do you want a lift Son?' Brian had bought Steven's mother a little run around, she had passed her test years back but couldn't afford a car at that time.

"Oh, yes please"

"Right give me ten minutes, just got to finish preparing dinner".

"Okay Mum no rush really", he said picking up another magazine from the coffee table

Steven's mum dropped him off at Anthony's. "Give me a ring if you want picking up"

"Sure Mum, will do".

Steven knocked loudly on Anthony's front door.

'Come in mate! Great to see you up and about!'

"Hello Mrs Grace, blimey you look cosy in there". Said Steven following Anthony into the lounge.

Anthony had done his mother proud; everything she needed was within reach. "You're looking well Mrs Grace" Steven said giving her a peck on the cheek where she sat in the middle of the room in a large armchair. "I feel fine, just lost a bit of strength, old age you know" she said smiling, a tired smile that looked like it took a lot of effort. Mrs Grace was in her fifty's not old at all, but Steven humoured her as he thought with gratitude of his own Mother. "You're not old Mrs Grace!"

"You know what I mean Steven, I feel old"

"Yes my mum says that sometimes"

"Anthony?"

"Yes Mum"

"Make Steven a drink there's a pet, I'm tired, and I think I'll have a nap"

"Okay Mum", Anthony walked over and planted a little kiss on his Mums cheek tucking a blanket around her.

"Thanks love" she said snuggling up and closing her eyes

"Keep well Mrs Grace, see you soon"

"Okay love" she said with a smile. "Good lads" she whispered to herself.

"You all right mate you look a bit tearful?' said Steven concerned. "Yes I'll be fine, it's Mum she's a bit down, and depressed I reckon"

"Seemed fine to me"

"That's just a front, all she wants to do is sleep all day that's not right, whenever I say something she just says I'm fine there's nothing wrong"

"Sounds like depression to me. You know Pete?"

"Pete who?"

"You know little Pete, Pete Harris"

Anthony frowned then said "Ah Yes I know who you mean"

"Well he locks himself away for a couple of weeks, won't answer the door, the phone, nothing, that's depression, week, may-be two and he's fine, fucking weird eh?"

"Yes it is" agreed Anthony thoughtfully.

"Do you reckon I should get the Doctor then?"

"Yes mate soon as, where's that tea? I'm parched"

"Give us a chance. Go up to my room, I'll bring it up" Steven climbed the stairs to Anthony room.

"What the fuck" he said out loud as he entered Anthony's room. It was spotless. The pair hadn't seen each other for a good few months, with Steven at College and working week ends. They had mostly kept in touch on the phone.

"There you go mate"

"Cheers, what the fuck's gone on here then mate?" Steven said, taking the cup of tea.

"Oh I'm all domesticated now, what with looking after Mum and the housework, it just overflowed into my room, I quite enjoy it really, keeps me busy"

"What's all this lot?".

"They're remotes, here have a look at these babies!" In Anthony's hand was what looked like a collection of tiny ball bearings in two different colours, gold and silver.

"What the fuck are they then mate?" Steven took one the small gold balls.

"Bombs, same as before but smaller, blow your head clean off into a million pieces".

"Woaw!" Steven replaced the ball bearing hastily in his friend's hand.

"For real?"

Anthony nodded proudly.

"I can think of a use for these, mate" Steven said his face momentarily clouded with pain.

"That's what I thought when I found out what had happened to you, I thought I'd keep these babies as a surprise"

"Why are they different colours?" Enquired Steven.

"The silver ones are the transmitters so you can talk. Here take one and go out to the landing Steve. Steven took the ball cautiously and cupped it in his hand and walked the few steps to the landing. "Put it to you ear mate"

Steven obeyed, feeling the cold of the metal on his warm skin.

"Little willy" came a voice from the ball. Steven jumped as the voice from the little ball crackled in his ear.

"Oi, I heard that"

"Awesome isn't it mate?"

"Fucking brilliant", Steven said staring at the tiny ball, "What's it range?"

"Fifty yards at least"

"I'm trying to fit the two together that's the next step" Anthony said

Steven gave a low whistle," Now that would be something special" he said.

"You could put one in a sandwich, no fucker would know!" said Anthony.
The pair bounced ideas off each other for the next couple of hours. Many were so outrageous that they fell about laughing. Steven thought how good it felt to laugh again

As he wiped tears of laughter from his eyes, Stevens's mobile started to ring.

"Yes mum I'm fine, no mum think I'll take a slow stroll home, yes Mum bye".

"Mums!" Steven smiled at Anthony, "she's worried about me, better make tracks" "Okay mate take a few of these with you just in case I can't get away because of mum, give me a few minutes just got to set the frequency on them"

Steven watched as Anthony set up his equipment.

"There mate", said Anthony placing three little brown envelopes into Steven's hand. Be careful with them mate they can take a bit of a knock, but just be careful"

"I will mate" replied Steven warily placing them separately in different pockets.

"I've written the detonation numbers on the envelopes, don't mix 'em up!"

"I won't". Said Steven

"Right see you when I can Steve, keep in touch".

"Will do mate, I'll ring you"

Steven descended down the stairs. "See you Mrs Grace keep well!" no answer. "She's probably asleep mate I'll tell her you said good bye"

"Cheers Ant, see you soon mate". "Let's not leave it so long this time eh?

Steven had not been home long before dinner was ready

"Brian should be here in a bit Steven"

"I bet he'd like a glass of wine Mum, I'll pour him one, got to be room temperature you know".

"Ooo a wine connoisseur now are we?" she said

"Nah just read it in one of those magazines this morning" replied Steven

"Yes go on then love". Steven poured a glass out for Brian

Taking his coat off, Brain came into the lounge, giving Mary a kiss on the cheek as he passed her laying the table.

"What's all this then? Is it a special occasion?".

"No love, well yes I suppose having Steven home is special, he thought you might like one"

"Come here you" said Brian grabbing Steven's mother for a hug.

Steven smiled as he saw how happy his Mother was with Brian.

"Alright Steven, d'you think you're ready for work yet?" asked Brian

"God yes, I'm going mad sitting around all day"

"You don't think it's a bit soon Brian?" said Steven's mother looking concerned "After all with the memories of Lucy . . ." she tailed off

Brain's jaw tightened. "Yes that has been tough for all of us, Chris has taken it really hard, but it is something we all have to come to terms with."

"It will be alright Mum, I'm fine"

"Oh well if you're sure?" she said

"That's settled then.", Brian took a sip from the wine glass.

"Yes Pinot Noir at room temperature sir!" said Steven smugly.

'Thank you my good man' replied Brian with a mock bow.

They all laughed

"Would it be Okay to work on a real patient soon Brian?". "Don't see why not, you've already started at college haven't you? But it would be just fillings mind, you seem to have got them off to a fine art on old Mavis!"
"I could do them in my sleep" said Steven. "Get back in the swing of things for a week or so, then we'll see what you can do", Brian said encouragingly.

"Great, can't wait!"

"He'll make a good Dentist, Mary, mark my words"

"I've always hoped, right from when he was a little boy that he would do something like this Brian" Mary smiled proudly at Steven.

Two weeks later Steven was back at the surgery. It was painful not to see Lucy there but he knew he had to keep himself busy and taking a key he locked himself into the small file storeroom.

Looking along the boxes of files he came to 'B' in the alphabetical filing system and checking each file he came to what he was looking for, "Sharon Bright" he murmured and writing her address down he locked the room and slipped the key back in the key box.

"Fancy having a go at some fillings today Steven?."

"Do I!", said Steven, then 'Are you being serious?"

"Sure, you said you could do them in your sleep"

"I can, but I'll keep my eyes open, right?" he said with a chuckle.

"Yes that would be good, I'll inject, and you do the rest. I'll be by your side just do as you have done in practise and it will be fine" Brian reassured him.

Steven's skill and craftsmanship improved week by week with the combined experience he got at college and with Brian Saturday after Saturday.

And all the time Steven was working a plan was formulating in his head, he needed to be on his own, but Brian was still watching him like a hawk. The frustration was killing him. t was nearly a year later before Steven finally got his chance. Brian appointed him a nurse and pointed him to his own room for Saturday surgery.

Full of anticipation he wrote to Sharon Bright on surgery stationery asking her to attend Saturday surgery for a check up. The following Saturday he had her in the chair.

He was surprised, close up she was a lovely looking girl, what she saw in that ugly pig Barton he could not imagine. She was not as lovely as Lucy and the thought of poor Lucy brought him back to his plan. An eye for an eye he had decided a year back, nothing was going to stop him now, revenge was all he could think of.

"Right Miss Bright open wide, a little wider if you can, that's better". Steven went through the list of teeth and the nurse noted them down.

"Right then Miss Bright you're going to need a couple of small fillings, we can do those now if you would like?"

"Yes please, I've only just plucked up the courage today, I don't know if I could again!" said Sharon, her eyes wide with fear.

"Okay just a couple of injections; you may feel a little stinging sensation"

Sharon winced as Steven injected her. After a few moments, Steven asked

"OK Miss Bright, nice and numb are we?"

"Feels like it" she replied

Steven got the drill and asked her, "Can you feel that?" as the drill began to grind into her tooth".

"No that's fine" She replied.

Lovely he thought, drilling away till there were two nice cavities in her mouth. "Nurse, Can you mix me up some filler please". With the nurse distracted he slipped the silver and gold tiny balls into the cavities. They popped in easily. "Perfect" he said. "Is that it?" she said

"Oh no that's just the packers, I've got to fill them yet, won't be long, soon be done"

Steven placed some spongy packer to protect the balls from any undue pressure, which could set them off.

"Thanks nurse", he said as she handed him the filler.

With the teeth filled and smoothed off he said, "I'm just going to call my colleague to have a look and see what a great job I've done!"

"Nurse could you call Chris?" he continued.

"That's a lovely job Steven. You're so lucky to be the first patient of Steven's Miss Bright"

"Oh right, well thanks"

"You're most welcome. Now you have a great weekend" said Steven. "Yes thanks bye". She said gathering up her handbag.

"Nice work"

"Thanks Chris" said Steven as they watched Sharon Bright walk out of the surgery.

"Miss!" shouted the receptionist.

"Yes?" answered Sharon.

"Sorry would you like to pay"

"Oh yes silly me!"

With the surgery cleaned ready for Monday, Steven was left to savour his first taste of the real thing. He sat in the chair then lay back and let his thoughts wander through his mind. Most were disturbing evil thoughts, almost as if he was trying to exact revenge for all the punishment he had received as a child, someone had to pay and he was going to make sure they did.

CHAPTER 5

"Right I'm off," said Chris popping his head round the door, Steven almost jumped out of his skin "Oh and great work today, you can lock up, see you"

Chris called over his shoulder.

"Yeah, thanks', Steven said, muttering under his breath, "Cheeky bastard—I can lock up? That's taking the piss"?

Sitting down at the deserted reception desk, he gave Anthony a call.

"Hi mate how trick's?"

"Fine mate, I've had the doctor round, like you said, and Mum's a bit better"

"Did he think she was depressed"?

"Think so, I told him I thought she was so she's on some tonic and some pills, seems to be working, she's even been in her wheelchair",

"That's great mate must pop round and see her again".

"Yes that'd be good she always like seeing your ugly mug, God knows why!" Anthony chuckled.

"Tosser! Anyway Anthony my son we're in business, I've planted one of your babies"

"Really? No way! What already?"

"Yep Barton's bird is pregnant". Steven said

"Sorry mate you've lost me". Anthony said, confused.

"Pregnant, thought that made a good code word for when someone's carrying the bomb, you know, your babies as you call them".

"With you now, yes that's actually bloody cool mate, nice one" Anthony was relieved, for a moment he had thought . . . well it didn't matter now.

"Thanks", now we've just got to wait till she meets Barton".

"Do you think she'll still be with him?" asked Anthony "Don't know. Don't even know if he is in this country, the police haven't caught him yet, but they must be tailing her surely? Anyway he's excrement and needs flushing away. I'll find him somehow, even if they can't. You going to be able to get out of the house do a bit of reccy work?"

"Yes give it a few days to see how Mum is, if she improves at the rate she's going, I should be able to get my own life on track".

"Great, ring you in a couple of days then" said Steven.

While he was speaking to Anthony, Chris's patient list caught Steven's eye, he had developed a penchant for reading other peoples notes and letters, in fact anything at all and he had become an expert at reading upside down. Curiosity got the better of him. Glancing down the list he noticed that what each of Chris's patients did for a living was written in a small space at the bottom of the page. He put down the phone and picked up the list. Unusual, he thought, why would he list their occupations? Judge, builder, doctor, accountant, secretary. Interesting he thought putting them back as he had found them. "Fuck look at the time" he said, he was cutting it fine for a very important appointment.

"This could be third time lucky, don't want to be late" he mumbled to himself running for the bus. Steven had failed his driving test twice before; his nerves had simply got the better of him. Today he concentrated on the thought of revenge and of how much more easily he could achieve it if he could drive, and it spurred him on.

"Right Steven, pull away and take the first left", said the driving instructor, "good, next right, pull over, three point turn please, good."

Steven was managing to hold it together.

"Right Steven I'm happy to say you have passed your driving test"

"Brilliant", he said shaking the instructor's hand.

At home his mother was waiting in the kitchen, her expression enquiring." Hi Mum" said Steven setting his features to a sad expression.

"Don't worry son, next time" his mother put her arm around him.

"There won't be a next time! I passed!" he said.

"You little so and so!" she said hugging him.

"Can I borrow the car Mum?" Mary laughed,

"Okay but be careful, Brian bought that for me"

"Thanks, I love you, keys please," he said with a cheeky smile.

"On the hook, and put them back". She said smiling proudly at him. He had grown into a handsome young man.

"Will do!".

At first, Steven practised around the streets where he lived, places he knew. After a week, his confidence buoyed, he wanted to venture further afield—to one place in particular.

He drove to Sharon Bright's address, as he parked opposite he saw another car with a man and a woman sitting in it, four cars down.

"Cops" he muttered to himself. Within the hour Sharon came out and got on a bus. Steven and the detectives followed. The bus pulled up at the stop in the High Street, Sharon got off and started walking. Probably going to work, he knew that she worked in Boots just before Byfleet Broadway. Steven parked up and decided to follow on foot. There was no sign of the cops, it was starting to rain, and they probably didn't want to get wet!

The Streets got darker and darker and it soon dawned on Steven that they were heading past Boots towards Byfleet Broadway itself. The name gave false promise of the place, in fact the road was wide and litter strewn with many disused buildings, and drab grey corrugated steel panels lined the entire Street on both sides, the odd one missing here and there, some bent up at the corner, enough for a druggy or wino to squeeze through. Behind the panels was wasteland and more derelict buildings, a real rat hole. Steven felt a thrill of fear.

Peering round the corner he jumped and said "Barton!" out loud. Realising, too late, his mistake, Barton's head swivelled towards him and Steven ran as fast as he could not even daring to look back. Once he was back on the High street he ran into a rank smelling shop doorway trying to get his breath back.

"Oi this is my spot fuck off", said a disgruntled tramp whose foul breath stank of liquor

"Fuck, you scared the shit out of me!" said Steven, "here take this" rummaging through his pocket he offered a few coins, "get a cup of tea or something"

"Cheer's Fella, you hiding from someone then?"

"Something like that"
"Old Bill?" asked the tramp "No, just keep quiet for a minute, thanks"

Steven thought if Barton had followed him, even that lard arse would have caught up by now, besides which he was wanted for murder, he was not going to expose himself in broad daylight.

His legs shaking, Steven left the darkened doorway, the tramp talking to himself still in his ears as he paced the street.

As soon as he got home he was on the phone to Anthony. "I've found him mate".

"Found who?"

"Barton, he's holed out in Byfleet Broadway' said Steven

"Awesome, that means one of my babies is going to be aborted!"

"That's funny man", said Steven with a chuckle, "how's your Mum today?"

"Yes slight improvement, I think the gears working, whatever it is".

"Good that means you can get away then?" Steven said

"I reckon.".

"Right it's time for Barton to lose his head!"

"Awesome man can't wait to see him blown to bits!"

"Yep that's going to be one hell of a show" Steven said grimly

"When we going to do it then Steven?"

"Don't know yet, I'll have to follow her for a few days see if they meet in the same place as last time".

"Give us a bell then."

"Will do" Steven hung up.

Over the following few days Steven kept tabs on Sharon. He was worried that Barton might have seen him and moved on somewhere. But it seemed as though he hadn't. Sharon met up with Barton every day at Byfleet Broadway usually going to work first so that the cops would be put off the scent.

They would talk for a while, then kiss and cuddle, Barton often tried to get more intimate, but Sharon is having none of it, even she had some standards, and was not about to drop her knickers on the street, it seemed. Not on the street where tramps and winos lurked in the shadows and would have a good old wank-fest at her expense.

Steven watched amused as Barton became more and more frustrated, desperate to shag Sharon. Eventually Barton could take no more and to Stevens's amazement, broke cover to steal a car.

The next day, Steven and Anthony waited for Sharon to leave Boots, as she always did out of the back entrance. She made her way to Byfleet Broadway and jumped into the car that Barton had stolen.

Steven put his foot down and raced after the vehicle.

It soon dawned on Steven that they were heading for a disused collection of industrial buildings on the edge of the Broadway.

As Barton and Sharon disappeared into the Industrial estate Steven and Anthony followed on foot. They found Barton's car parked hard up against the corrugation offering some protection from prying eyes. But there was no protection from the eyes of his eager assassins. They had positioned themselves commando style on the ground by one of the panels, its corner bent up, giving them a clear view of the car.

"Looks like Barton's is getting stuck in mate, said Anthony as he watched Barton's head rocking back and forth.

"Yes mate, his last fuck!" he said laughing, a hard-edged sound. Anthony held the remote in readiness.

"Go on you piece of shit, kiss her, go on" Steven hissed and as if by telepathy Barton began to slobber over Sharon, his huge tongue probing her mouth and her newly filled teeth.

"Having a nice snog Barton?. Hit the button Ant!". Steven said, his voice hard his expression grim.

A horrible squealing noise, like someone trying to tune a radio filled Barton's senses for a moment before an explosion shut his brain down instantly as it spattered in a thousand pieces along with the glass from the windows of the car. As the vehicle settled back on its axis pools of blood formed on the roads surface.

"Fuck me man that was AWESOME, wasn't it mate?" said Anthony his voice shaking.

"Fucking right it was!", said Steven his breath coming quickly" That piece of shit got it big time.". Looking into the car they could see two body shapes and could just about make out the shoulders.

"Perfect mate, heads gone, worked a treat" said Steven.

As they watched, several rats appeared and started lapping up the blood from the roads surface; others were homing in on the car, the smell of fresh meat in their nostrils. Soon the rats were crawling all over the corpses.

"Fuck me you couldn't make it up could you Ant?, just desserts for a rat, eaten by rats"

They watched for as long as they could before the noise of sirens echoed towards them. Emergency vehicles started arriving as the two boys slipped away.

Looks like the bomb squad mate," said Steven, "we better leg it!".

"Wait for me Steve I can't run that fast"

"Come on mate round here" Steven had remembered the route out from following Sharon. Just then he had a thought, "Quick mate in there", he said pointing to the shop entrance. "Oi fuck off I was here first" Shouted the tramp "What the fuck?", Anthony almost fell over backwards.

Steven fell about laughing.

"What?. Aw you fucking knew didn't you?, that wasn't funny Steve!"

"Sorry mate couldn't resist, come on let's get out of here".

As the Emergency vehicles pulled up beside the damaged car, rats scampered everywhere to escape the light cast from the vehicles.

"Roberts keep away; let the bomb squad in first". Matheson said.

"Right you are Sir"

Detective Matheson walked a few steps then stopped. Lifting one of his shoes he noticed bits of glass and other matter caught in the tread. Picking a bit off he realised it was a bit of skin.

"Stay where you are Roberts we're walking all over the evidence"

Roberts stopped.

"What is it Sir"

"Skin, bits of skin, human skin I think", said Matheson looking at the ground. The bits of glass reflected the light making them shine like diamonds. Matheson crouched down to pan the area around him.

"Fuck me Robert's there's bits everywhere, what the fuck have we got here?" he asked.

"All clear Matheson", said the chief of the bomb squad "you got two bodies, well nearly two, both have their heads missing, you might want to prepare yourself, it's not pretty"

"Okay good work we'll take it from here" said Matheson.

Most of the vehicles left the scene leaving forensics, some bobby's and the detectives to continue their work.

Matheson looked into the car, the interior was splattered, every inch of the upholstery covered in blood. In all his years in the force he had seen nothing like this before. Turning his attention to the bodies he wondered if the heads had been cut off.

"Excuse us Detective" said two forensic men, who proceeded to tent the entire area. Others were painstakingly collecting the debris from the road ready to be bagged.

"Oh, Detectives we will need to clean our shoes' "Yes, Roberts, shoes"

"Sir?"

"Give them your shoe's"

"Oh, right, I see". Perkins nervously removed his shoes

"Yuk" he said looking at all the bits attached to his under soles.

Matheson picked up a battered handbag that had somehow survived the blast and been flung clear of the car. As he opened it he caught his breath. The face smiling back at him from the Boots staff badge was well known to him. In fact he had tried his luck with her once; she had a cracking figure and dimples in her cheeks when she smiled. He could never understand what she was doing with Barton. But she, predictably, had wanted nothing to do with him. Now he stood sadly looking at the badge and the happy girl of a few years ago that smiled back up at him. Her life could have been so different. Sensing that Roberts was watching him he shoved the badge back into the handbag

"Find anything sir"

"Yes She was Sharon Bright, according to her credit card in her purse, Barton's bit of stuff, she didn't deserve this, poor girl, such a shame. Matheson's said. "I wonder if the man here is Barton?"

"Any clues as to what might have happened sir?" Roberts said.

"Yes they were blown up by some sort of explosive; trouble is any evidence was blown up with them. There was no sign of anyone else being involved. It just doesn't make sense. And I want to know what those useless wankers who were supposed to be following Sharon were doing when all this was going off?" Matheson said, his voice tight with anger.

"Maybe it was some sort of love pact", suggested Roberts, "If there was no one else involved they must have done it themselves" he continued

"A double suicide? Possible, but a bit unlikely, not the usual modus operandi for a suicide, anyway I doubt Barton, if it is him, would have the brains to come up with anything so sophisticated."

"Well, he certainly hasn't got the brains now" Roberts said suppressing a smile

"What did they use? There's fuck all left, nothing!" Matheson said.

In the following weeks the police identified Barton's body but Steven thought that their investigation into who had blown him and Sharon up lost a bit of impetus after that. To be truthful Steven did feel some regret about Sharon but he saw himself and Anthony as nothing short of heroes for ridding their streets of Barton's particular brand of menace. As each news bulletin came out, he had held his breath to see if the detailed forensic examination had shown up what had caused the explosion. They did, of course narrow it down to something in the mouth of one or other of them, probably Sharon but that was as far as they got. Given that the two heads had splattered and scattered in a million fragments, Steven felt pretty confident that they never would discover what had happened to the pair. As the weeks turned into months he felt a deep sense of satisfaction for a job well done. He and Anthony would meet up now and again. Anthony's Mum was up and about now. She was even venturing out on her little disability car to the shops. Mary Smith and Brian were making plans for a big wedding. Steven started taking evening surgeries as well as Saturdays, which allowed him to buy his own car.

One particular evening the lads were in Anthony's room.

"Mate I've done it!" said Anthony

"Done what?" Asked Steven.

"Put the two devices together, better still let me show you".

"Here take this" Anthony placed a little square shaped metal object in Steven's hand, slightly larger than the balls, but still small enough to place neatly into a cavity in a tooth.

"Right go out to the street put it to your ear Steven".

Once outside Steven placed the little object to his ear. Nothing happened for a moment then Anthony's voice sounding tinny emanated from the little object.

"Are you there yet?" he said sniggering.

"Yes" Steven shouted as loud as he could to try to make his voice reach Anthony in his room.

"Fuck! You don't have to shout mate, just talk normally!" said Anthony holding his hand over his painful ear. "You nearly burst me eardrum"

"You haven't?" said Steven.

"I fucking have mate!"

"You're a fucking genius!"

"I know" said Anthony delighted that they could now communicate with each other through the device.

Steven came back up to Anthony's room; they went over different scenarios of uses for the device. Anthony gave two of the devices to Steven, "There you go mate, check these little babies out". Steven looked down at what Anthony was showing him. Two little golden balls like the others he had given Steven lay in the palm of Anthony's hand.

"These are for us mate, transmitters so we can talk to each other wherever we are, Awesome aren't they?"

Steven gave a low whistle "Fucking brilliant, pop to the surgery tomorrow night we'll put them in".

As he drove home Steven's mind was alive with ideas. After nearly hitting a parked car he decided to pull over and explore his thoughts. The possibilities were immense!

During evening surgery the next day Steven went to the waiting room to call his next patient and caught sight of two drop-dead gorgeous women.

By the time one and then the other had lain fragranced and lovely in his chair Steven had fallen in love with them both!

His mind was working over time again, imagining the power he could have over them. The thought of being able to get just what he wanted, to have such an advantage, almost blew his mind. He just couldn't resist it, he planted Anthony's tiny devices in the teeth of both of them.

By the time that Anthony arrived at the surgery, Steven had already implanted himself. With his friend in the chair he set to work. While he was working he said to Anthony.

"Ant, you ever fucked a women"?

"No, why have you?"

"Sort of, I had me knob in Cathy Barrett once".

"No way?", said Anthony surprised

"Yes straight up, it was in the x-ray room here in the surgery. I was just getting started and she pushed me off the bitch said I was too big" Steven remembered.

"Yeah right mate, in your dreams, that one's always been a fucking tease, wants teaching a lesson" said Anthony.

"What if I said you could fuck the woman of your dreams?, what would you say to that Ant?"

"I'd say bring it on baby" Anthony's words came out garbled as he tried to speak with Steven's hand in his mouth, packing in the cement on top of the filling.

"Right that's you done".

"Let's give it a try, Oh hang on though you need to say a code word to turn them on" Anthony said.
"Bet you thought of a good one Ant!"

"Yes—Babies" "that's clever mate! Babies.'

There was an almost inaudible bleep.

"Don't say it again mate, the code word also turns it off, say it once on, again off." yours is on, mines off—Babies" said

Anthony and again there was a little bleep, "there you go mate"

"Hey I can hear you" said Steven, "put it there mate" he said, putting out a hand and shaking Anthony's. "Right lets celebrate, bring on the pussy" said Anthony.

They drove to the place where the girls who had visited the surgery earlier in the day lived. It was a nice cottage style building recently renovated and on the end of a row of dilapidated farm buildings that were in various stages of renovation. Anthony got out the two remotes and turned them on.

"Hi girls, up for a bit of fun?"

"What? Did you hear that Trace?" One of the girls shouted to her friend in the bathroom.

"Yes what the fuck was it Terry?" she answered

"Someone's in the house Trace", Terry said rushing for the phone.
"There's no one in the house, we're outside, don't do anything stupid like phoning the police or you'll die" Steven said laughing.

Confused Terry stood with the phone in her hand.

"What the fuck's happening?" she whimpered.

"'Terry, the voices sound like they're in my head!' Tracey stood beside her friend, eyes wide with fear.

"They *are* in your head, we put them there!" Anthony laughed. "This is fucking brilliant mate!" he said turning to Steven

'What's going on' Terry was crying softly now, "who the fuck is this?"

'Did you by any chance visit the dentist today?' asked Steven.

"Yes why? "The girls voice was shaking with fear, "How do you know this, how do you know us? What do you want?" Terry was crying openly now.

'Well ladies it's like this. You both have bombs planted in your teeth; listen to this' said Steven.

Anthony adjusted the frequency so that it screeched inside the women's heads causing them to scream.

"Stop it, stop it, what do you want?" Tracey sobbed

"Well I want a fuck love, that's what I want", Anthony said

"Me too" said Steven.

"No, please, leave us alone!" said Tracy'

"Yes please just leave us alone, don't hurt us!" said Terry.

"Now, now girls, don't be playing hard to get, it's not worth dying for, surely!

Give them another blast mate!' said Steven

Anthony subjected the women another blast of brain numbing noise.

"Okay, Okay!" sobbed Tracy. "Please stop!"

Anthony turned the remote down.

'They're not touching me Trace, I'm telling you', Terry's voice was shrill with fear. Anthony turned up Terry's frequency.

She screamed holding her head, shouting through her pain "Never!"

"Leave her alone you fucking bastards", Shouted Tracey. Anthony turned her remote up—

"Alright! 'I'll do it! I'll do it!" Tracey screamed through the pain in her head.

Anthony turned off the remotes.

"That stubborn one, she isn't going to budge mate, what we going to do?" said Anthony

"I want a fuck" said Steven.

"So do I. I should be first, after all it's my device and you've already done it" Anthony said.

"Well I don't fancy going after you" said Steven.

"Yuk, same as, mate" replied Anthony.

"We'll toss for it", suggested Steven.

"Okay I'm up for that"

"Heads or tails?"

"Tails never fails," said Anthony.

Steven flipped the coin. It landed heads.

"Best of three" Anthony said.

"Okay", another flip. Tails.

"Go on" said Anthony.

The last flip caught one of Steven's fingers as it fell rolling under one of the seats.

"Bollocks! turn on the light" Steven said. The pathetic little light slowly illuminated the car, revealing the coin, 'it's a head', said Steven triumphantly

"Bollocks! You jammy fucker", said Anthony.

"Well, you never know, the other one might come round" said Steven.

"Yes she might" Anthony sounded unconvinced "go on then you jammy bastard go fill your boots!"

"Turn the remotes on mate" Steven said.

"Name?" Steven said into one of the remotes.

'Tracey'. Said one of the girls.

"Ah the blonde one, that'll do for me, tell your mate to make herself scarce, and you come to the door'.

Terry went upstairs and Tracy opened the front door.

Steven approached, "We meet again."

"Oh its you!" she said her eyes wide her face deathly white. "No funny stuff or my friend will blow your fucking head off; 'babies' a tiny bleep "Give her a blast mate".

Tracey held her head. "Okay, okay turn it off "she said backing into the cottage. "Turn it off mate" Steven said, not wanting Anthony to hear what he was up to.

Steven followed Tracey and shut the door behind him. He turned to Tracey "Strip" he ordered. He had watched many porno films and now he wanted a show all of his own. He had often fanaticised about this very day, and someone who would do it just for him.

'Yes, yes that's it', he said getting hot and excited as Tracey peeled off the layers of clothing down to her knickers and bra. 'And the rest' he demanded sternly.

Reluctantly she obeyed his command and peeled the rest away to reveal full breasts the nipples taught with their exposure to the cold air her bush full and a slightly darker shade of blonde than the hair on her head.

"Spread your legs" Steven felt drunk with power and desire. His cock was hard in his trousers and he undid his fly. His cock emerged, huge red and so swollen it almost hurt. He saw her terrified eyes flick down to his massive organ her eyes widening slightly and her terror deepening.

He scanned the room, hmm sofa nah, floor nah, dining table yes.

'Right over there, on the table'. he said his breath coming faster now.

Tracey sat on the table and laid back shutting her eyes tight, this was going to hurt, she knew it but she did not want to die, maybe if she let him, they would leave . . . .

Steven walked up to her and holding his distended cock to the opening of her vagina, he forced his way into her. Tracey turned her face away from him tears of pain, humiliation and fear squeezed out from behind her closed eyelids. As Steven pumped, he was in ecstasy, and his ejaculation was very close now.

Suddenly he felt a pain and he started to slip into unconsciousness.

"Leave her alone you fucking bastard" Terry shrieked still holding the baseball bat she had hit him over the head with. She had not hit him full on; just the right side of his head but it was enough to knock him out.

"You okay Trace?"

"Yes I'm okay, is he dead?" Tracey sobbed

"I don't know" Terry said

"What about the other one?" asked Tracey.

Just then Steven started to move regaining consciousness.

Tracey screamed.

Summoning all her strength Terry aimed another blow at Steven's head. He deflected part of it by putting his arms in front of his face, but the bat caught him again on the right temple, and he lay still.

"What we going to do Terry?" Tracey was crying, sobbing, her face white, with blood tricking down her leg from the force of Steven's rough entry.

"Get dressed I'll phone the police"

"What about the other one, he might come, we should just leave now" said Tracey struggling into her clothes. "Yes, Terry agreed, "we'll phone the police on the way, we'll go out the back"

Neither girl had noticed that Steven had come around again. He lay still his eyes closed until his chance came.

"Right Tracey ready?" Terry asked her voice tight with fear.

"Yes" she replied then looking at Steven's body lying on the floor his genitals exposed.

"One thing before we go" she said grimly "give us that bat Terry. Let's see if he still feel so randy with his balls smashed in! Right you dirty bastard" Tracey raised the baseball bat.

Steven leapt from the floor and tackled her to the ground knocking Terry off her feet as they fell. As they grappled and wrestled furiously on the floor, still woozy from the blows to his head and desperate to protect his exposed genitals, the girls began to get the better of Steven.

"'Babies"—a small bleep—"fucking abort" he shouted as the girls gained the upper hand.

"What the fuck is he on about?" Terry gasped "Who cares" said Terry as she grabbed for the baseball bat.

"Abort now, both?" Anthony's voice spoke in Steven's head.

'YES NOW' Steven screamed, with a huge effort, he freed himself and rolled into the corner of the room, curling up into a ball, his arms over his battered head.

BOOOOMMMM.

His ears ringing, Steven curled himself tighter to protect himself from the shower of flesh raining down on him. The headless bodies of the two women fell to the floor almost on top of him. Blood spouted like fountains from severed arteries like a flood of red around him.

He raised himself from the floor the blood weighing down his clothing. On his feet he nearly slipped twice in the enormous pool of blood.

He met Anthony at the door.

"Steven you okay mate?" With his heart pounding and his head feeling as though it had been split open Steven said. "Yes I'm okay"

"Fuck me, the state of you" said Anthony looking at his friend who was covered from head to foot in blood.

"That's not all mine you should see the state of the place in there, look out its slippery mate"

Anthony looked into the room his eyes resting on the two women for a moment, and then he panned around the room. Blood was everywhere; the ceiling was spattered in a spectacular pattern almost as if a can of red paint had been thrown onto it.

"Fuck what a mess mate" said Anthony awed by the scene in front of him.

"What a fucking waste, eh mate?" said Steven looking down at the headless bodies.

"Yes come on we got to get out of here and get you cleaned up mate" said Anthony. "We'll got to the surgery, there are showers there

"We'll have to mate, you can't go home looking like that can you?"

They listened but could hear no sirens. Amazing, thought Steven, because normally it seemed that no matter how far you seemed to be from civilisation there was always someone to call the old Bill.

At the surgery Steven cleaned himself as best he could putting all his clothes in a clinical waste bag along with the blanket he had sat on in the car. As he showered fragments of skin and bone and other stuff he did not like to think of gathered in the plug guard. When he had finished he scooped it up and threw it in on top of the blood soaked clothes. He nearly gagged.

Anthony slipped home for a change of clothes for his friend, choosing the most generic tee shirt and jeans he could so that neither mother would notice. Looking into the mirror of the small bathroom Steven studied his reflection, his face was OK, he had taken quite a bit of the force of the blows to his hands as he held them up to defend himself, the rest of his injuries were to his head.

There were some deep splits in his scalp, lesions that he thought he could repair himself.

"Right we got to get out of here, take everything with us, look around mate check we've cleaned everything we touched" Said Anthony.

The two friends retraced their steps and cleaned. "You were lucky mate", said Anthony.

"I know just seconds away from having me bollocks smashed in, and all for a fuck eh?"

The next morning the builders doing the renovations arrived on site. All three called at the cottage for the cup of tea the girls usually provided them with.

They knocked, nothing.

'That's strange, they can't be out, they're usually still in their nighties at this time!" "Maybe if we get here a bit earlier we'll catch them out of their nighties!" a muscle bound Geordie said placing a huge fist in the crook of his elbow and jerking his forearm up towards him.

"Jesus Joe, don't you ever think of anything else?" the lanky foreman said peering in the window.

"Oh fuck!" he said as the contents of his stomach rose to the back of his throat.

The Geordie looked over his foreman's shoulder, swore and flipped open his mobile.

"Emergency, which service to do require?"

"Police, there's been a murder at the cottages on Porter street".

CHAPTER 6

Matheson and Roberts were at the scene within 10 minutes.

"Right you lot don't move a muscle" Matheson ordered the shell-shocked builders.

'What the fuck? It looks like it's the same scenario Roberts," said Matheson his face grim, what the fuck's going on?"

"I don't get it sir."

"Me neither, where are forensics Roberts? This is beyond us."

"Yes sir."

"And get someone to take statements off this lot". Matheson, nodded in the direction of the hapless builders.

"Will do sir."

An hour later the cottage was crawling with professionals trying to piece together what had happened. Matheson watched intently, paying special attention to Isabel Connor.

"Like what you see Sammy?" she said, feeling his eyes on her shapely rear as she leaned over to take blood samples from the carpet. There was a definite connection between them; she knew it and she felt he did too.

"Who wouldn't, I'm a man, aren't I? Reluctantly however, although I'd like to talk about your rear end all day, I think we better get down to business, are you getting same MO?" he asked.

"Identical I'd say", she said flashing her big brown eyes in his direction. There was something about the gruff policeman that always gave her a thrill. Pity she only ever seemed to meet him among the debris of someone's exploded brain these days; it was hardly a turn-on, but then again . . . !

A few days later her report arrived, and was as baffling as the previous cases had been.

"Again, no sign of any break-in Roberts, are these people blowing themselves up? What the fuck is going on?"

"Don't know sir, perhaps its aliens?"

"Fuck off Roberts now you're being stupid"

"Sorry sir, well it might as well be, you know firing lasers or something like that".

"You've been watching too many star wars movies Roberts"

"Yes sir" Roberts said.

Matheson started pinning the gruesome pictures up like some sort of horrific picture gallery.

"That's lunch fucked, I couldn't eat a thing now, come on Roberts, lunch in a glass, I think—pub, I'm buying".

"*YES sir*" Roberts followed Matheson out of the station. "Makes a fucking change", he muttered under his breath.

"Morning Steven"

"Morning mum, got any head ache pills? I've got a splitting head ache" Steven called from his bedroom, he dare not let his mother see his battered head and he was ready to pull the covers up if she came into his room. But she didn't.

"Yes son in the bathroom cabinet" she called from the bottom of the stairs.

"Right, thanks, I'm going stay in bed for a bit, see if I can get rid of this stinker"

"OK, son, I'm going out now; remember to lock up if you go out"

"Will do Mum."

Upstairs Steven was about to get back into bed when he noticed blood on his pillow.

"Fuck, got to wash that off" he mumbled to himself. He waited till he heard his mother drive off, and then set about cleaning the pillowcase.
As he soaked and scrubbed at the pillowslip, finally wringing it out and laying it over the boiler to dry, he had a thought. His headache had almost gone now thanks to Anadin extra and thoughts were now crowding his mind.

He picked up his phone to call Anthony. Twenty minutes later, a beanie hat pulled down over his bruised head he arrived at Anthony's house.

With a cup of tea Anthony had made him held gingerly in the hand that had fended off the blows from the baseball bat, he let his friend know what he had been thinking.

"Hmm our own surgery? That would be Awesome Steve, but how we going to do it?"

"Money mate, there's enough rich people come in the surgery, plant a bomb in a few, job done".

"Where would the surgery be?' asked Anthony.

'Don't know we'll have to look around see what takes our fancy."

"Okay mate whatever you say, I'm up for it!"

Over the next few weeks Steven kept himself busy planting as many of the little bombs as Anthony could produce. His hand healed fast and the bruises he could mostly cover with his hair. The wall of Anthony's bedroom began to look like the cockpit of an aeroplane. Row upon row of remotes, all with their own little flashing lights. The light they emitted was so bright that it illuminated the room, and Anthony had to cover them up so he could get some sleep.

It was soon obvious that the project was out-growing Anthony's room, and he desperately needed more space. There were files on all the 'babies' and their surrogate parents containing information, which with the chronic lack of space were in danger of getting mixed up. "Something needs sorting" Anthony rang Steven.

"Mate we got to sort a place we can't carry on like this." he said.

"I know, let's just stop production for now and look for something," suggested Steven

"Okay good." said Anthony.

That evening, as they sat watching telly, Steven broached the subject with his Mum.

"Mum I'm thinking of getting my own surgery with Anthony, I know I am only newly qualified and normally I would joining a practice to gain experience, but with the Saturday work, I feel I'm ahead of the game, I really feel I'm ready for it, but what do you think Brian will say?"

'Blimey that's out of the blue, how long have you been thinking about that son, and what will Anthony do? He's not in dentistry is he?"

Steven thought quickly

"No but he is very interested in the prosthetic side of things, you know making false teeth, plates, bridges that sort of thing, he's starting a course soon."

"Oh really, I didn't know that, how nice the two of you working together! How long have you been thinking about it?"

'Ages, do you think Brian might help, you know set me up?"

"I really don't know Steven, you'll just have to ask him at dinner."

"Okay I will Mum"

"Oh and Steven I am glad you've stopped wearing that silly little hat, it really didn't suit you."

"No mum." Steven smiled to himself.

Over dinner Steven brought up the subject of going it alone. Brian was clearly disappointed that Steven did not want to join the practice with him and Chris but he understood Steven was young and ambitious; there would be no holding this one back. So Brian agreed to help Steven set up a practice on the other side of town, far away enough not to affect his own practise.

A few weeks later Brian found the ideal place, an old surgery. Although it was in a bit of a rundown part of town it was apparently what Estate Agents called an up-and-coming area. The original owner had died and the surgery was to be sold with all the equipment in it.

Steven drove Anthony to the place. They pulled up outside and sat for a while to admire the building. It was a two story building, a large house that had been converted with the entrance to one side. Once through the door they climbed the stairs to the small reception area. To the left was the waiting room, further along another two rooms, two surgeries fully kitted out. Towards the back of the house were a kitchen and some rooms used for storage. At the back was a door; the lads opened it to find stairs leading downward. They followed the stairs down along a small corridor eventually arriving at a door above their heads

Steven and Anthony were bemused by the strange position of the door. Steven opened it and they found themselves in the back garden.

"It's some kind of coal bunker door" Suggested Steven

"That's fucking Awesome Steve, what the fuck's that all about?" "The mind boggles mate, haven't got a clue", he replied shutting the door and locking it.

"Come on let's explore." Steven said. They went through the rooms again and decided that Anthony could work in the back of the house.

It was not long until the surgery was ready for it's first patient. Taking his first tentative steps into the world of fulltime dentistry Steven was grateful for the help that Brain gave, and the odd patient he sent his way. Eventually he had a respectable client list and at last he could stand on his own two feet. Brian was curious about Anthony.

"How is he doing with his training Steven?" he asked.

"Oh he's doing Ok he finds the denture technician training really interesting"

"Well that's certainly very useful, if he's any good, I might send some of my patients over for moulding."

"Sure!" Steven said. He was very pleased with his masterstroke with Anthony studying to be a denture technician, it gave them the perfect cover for his laboratory in the back of the practice.

It was Saturday morning. With no college or work Anthony was busy doing the chores.

"Anthony love I'm going out for a while".

"Where are you going Mum?"

"Oh just a bit of shopping", she dropped her voice "and getting my hair done"

"I heard that!" Anthony teased "next you'll be telling me you're going on a date!" "No son, just the hair for now" his mother smiled up at him.

"Okay see you later."

Anthony's mum was improving almost daily now, and Anthony was pleased that he was able to build his newfound career without worrying about her. As he heard the front door slam behind her, he decided he was going to spring clean her bedroom. He moved everything out of the room into the lounge, this was going to be the mother of all spring-cleans. There were old magazines and letters under them, stuff that needed sorting. Black bags at the ready he sifted through, stopping at a letter that caught his eye. He decided to open it. The letter was stained brown on the edges and brittle to the touch, and had never been opened. Carefully he opened it and started to read.

"Fuck! It's from Dad!", he said aloud. The writing was just about decipherable.

> Dear Rose, how can you ever forgive me? I can never forgive myself. It was the drink not me, you know that. You haven t told anyone have you Rose? Remember what I said, I meant it, don t forget that Rose. Anyway Rose look after the lad.

"Fuck me, is that it?" Anthony looked at the back of the letter, nothing. Looking through the mountains of paper he couldn't find any more letters from his father. Studying the letter again he noticed a phone number scrawled at the bottom. "I wonder if he's still around." Anthony said out loud.

He decided to finish the room first, and pluck up his courage. Two hours later he eventually rang the number.

"Hello?" it was a male voice.

Anthony wasn't sure if it was him.

Warily he said" Hello, Dad? It's Anthony your son".

"Anthony!" Then Silence.

"Hello dad, are you still there?"

"Yes, yes sorry I was just shocked to hear your voice, where are you?"

"Still at the same address, living with mum".

"How is she son?"

"Yes she's fine." No thanks to you, Anthony thought bitterly

There was a long pause, then

"You know it was an accident don't you son?".

"Yes, mums told me all about it, but why did you leave?"

"Me and your mum fell out and I couldn't stay son".

"Why didn't you stay in touch then?"

"Your mother wouldn't let me, she stopped me seeing you."

What a fucking liar Anthony thought to himself.

"I'd like to see you dad, if that's okay?"

"Bit tricky at the moment, but yes we should see each other, and soon."

"Is it all right if I ring you then?"
"Yes son that would be nice".

"Okay I'll ring then. When?" asked Anthony.

"Give it a week or so, I've got a bit of business to sort."

"Okay I'll ring next week." Anthony put down the phone.

He phoned Steven

"Steven! I'm . . . com . . . ."

"You all right mate? you sound out of breath" Steven interrupted.

"Yes I'm coming over, got some great news"

"What is it?"

"Tell you when I get there"

Leaving a note for his mum Anthony set off for Steven's.

Up in Steven's bedroom, Anthony's said

"You'll never guess what mate?!"

"Don't tell me you've had sex!" said Steven laughing.

"No, I've found my Dad"

"That's great mate, but I didn't know you were looking for him."
"I wasn't but now that I've found him, I can't wait to kill the fucker!"

"Eh? Sorry you've lost me" said Steven

Anthony told Steven the story, a story remarkably similar to Steven's own story, culminating with the dreadful night that Anthony's mother had been thrown down the stairs, while her terrified son stood in the shadows helpless to do anything to help his mother. Well not any more, it had been a long time coming but he was finally in a position to make his father pay for what he had done to them both.

"Jesus mate, why didn't you tell me all this? You knew what I went through with my own dad, why didn't you tell me?" Steven could not help feeling hurt that his friend had not trusted him with his story.

"Mum told me not to, I sort of promised. But anyway Steven it's his fault that my mother is like she is, that bastard pushed her down the stairs making her a cripple for life. He ruined her life and pretty much put the mockers on mine too, I've been waiting all my life to get that fucker, since I was five years old. Now he's going to get his, I'm going to arrange a meeting."

"Fuck I'm shocked, you kept that a secret all these years"

"Yes it's been on my back like a boil, now I'm ready to burst it" said Anthony, with real hatred in his voice.

"Fuck mate, I've never seen you like this, you must really hate him."

"I do mate, I do". said Anthony with passion.

"What you going to do?" asked Steven.

"Don't know yet, you'll help me I hope?"

"Yes mate, of course" Steven replied.

"When you going to meet him?"

"Next week I hope"

"What's he like?"

"A fucking piss-head"

"That's right!" Steven said remembering the day they had buried his father. "He was at my dad's funeral, only bugger there apart from me and mum, one piss head mourning another piss head. I'm never drinking".

"Me neither" said Anthony

On Monday morning, Steven and Anthony arrived at the surgery bright and early.

"Steve I'm not too happy about the set up, someone might come in here and I need to have my gear out of sight, just leave the denture stuff on display, in this half of the room. I need a partition with a door really."

Steven nodded

"We need some money first mate".

"We'll have to liven up a few of our adoptive parents, get some dosh, . . . I know! That rich lawyer, what's his name?' Said Anthony.

"You mean Richard Bellman?"

"Yes money dripping from him, you can tell can't you mate?"

"Yes, get his remote".

Looking along the rows of remotes, Anthony said "bingo here he is" and handed the remote to Steven.

"Mr Bellman!"

Across town a short balding man rose from his plush leather buttoned chair in his equally lavish office. It was called the green room, with Victorian windows looking over the city of London. Although there was plenty of light the room it still felt dark and oppressive. Low beams and green-flocked wallpaper supported a cream ceiling stained with nicotine. The walls were adorned with many souvenirs acquired from distant countries he had visited. Alongside them were artefacts from his other passion, with crossed swords, shields and statues dressed with armour. All testament to Richard Bellman's fascination for history and war memorabilia.

"Mr Bellman" Steven said into the remote.

The man stopped in his tracks as though he had been struck.

"Who's there?" his voice was tinged with panic as he poked a finger into his ear and wriggled it, he called again, "Who's there?"

"It's your friendly dentist, Steven, Mr Bellman."

"Where are you?" said Bellman striding to the door of his office and flinging it open expecting to find Steven on the other side of it.

"We're at the surgery Mr Bellman, of course!"

"What? How are you doing this? How is this possible"? The man voice took on a slight whine, he was frightened but so arrogant that he still thought he would get the better of the situation.

"You have been impregnated with a highly sophisticated state of the art device; we can hear your every move, your every word and we can track you wherever you go. You also have an explosive device in one of your teeth so don't do anything stupid, One press of a button and boom, you're a million pieces". Anthony said.

Bellman rushed to the toilet adjoining his office and with his mouth open wide, inspected his teeth. He saw the two new fillings and realised with a growing horror that threatened to open his bowels where he stood that the truth of what Anthony was telling him was indeed staring him in the face.

"What do you want?" Bellman said his voice choked with fear.

"We want money, and lots of it" Steven said.

"How much money?" Bellman asked

"How much d'you think?" Steven asked Anthony.

'Fuck knows mate, whatever, a million pounds?" suggested Anthony laughing.

"A million pounds" Steven says his voice flat. He nodded to Anthony who turned the knob on the remote. The excruciating noise that seemed to explode in his brain sent Bellman crashing to the floor clutching his head.

"Okay! Okay, a million!"

"Fuck did you hear that Ant? Seems we have a deal!" Steven said.

'Yes, fuck! I can't believe it, a million pounds we're rich mate!" Anthony clapped Steven on the back "We're rich, we're fucking rich!"

"Are you there?" Bellman asked his voice strained, he was obviously in pain.

"Yes we're here, when can you get the money?" Steven said.

"In a few days" replied Bellman.

"Right, no funny stuff, remember we can track you 24/7 any move towards the police or another dentist and you're history!" Steven said with authority in his voice, he had stretched the truth a bit, but hey, Bellman wouldn't know that.

"Give him a blast Ant"

Anthony turned up the tuner blasting the excruciating noise through Bellman's head and knocking him to floor again. Clutching his head, he screamed,

"Make it stop! Please! You'll get the money!"

"Good that's settled then, we will be in touch", said Steven.

A week later Anthony was on the phone to his Father.

"Hello is that you Dad? it's Anthony".

"Yes son it's me".

"Can we meet?" said Anthony

"Yes son, business is sorted, got a few days off, where do you want to meet?"

"I can come round yours or we can go to the pub?"

"Pub would be better; my place is a shit hole".

"Okay pub it is then. The Red Lion, you know where that is?" Anthony said.

"Yes the local watering hole, don't suppose anyone will recognise me now?".

"No chance, it's been under new management three times over the years. How about tomorrow night? Say about seven?"

"See you at seven Son."

"Okay great" Anthony said, flipping his mobile shut.

The next morning Anthony brought Steven up to speed. Steven agreed to position himself in the pub, keeping an eye out, and to give Anthony moral support.

That evening as they arrived Anthony entered the pub first looking around, the place was busy but no one looked familiar.

Perhaps he isn't here yet, he thought, ordering a pint. Steven came in and looked in Anthony's direction. Anthony shrugged.

Just then, a man looking, for all the world, like Fagin from Oliver came over to Steven, "Anthony is that you son?"

"No I'm Steven, that's Anthony over there", Steven said pointing in Anthony's direction.

"Anthony son, by God you've grown, give your old man a hug!" He said grabbing Anthony. Unable to avoid the hug the smell of body odour immediately hit Anthony making him catch his breath. The smell of BO and the stale smell of alcohol on his father's breath made his eyes water.

If his father noticed, he gave no sign of it and Anthony said "Let's sit down Dad" Sitting opposite each other now Anthony thought, what a fucking mess.

His father had long grey greasy hair, he had thin, gaunt, almost skeletal features and a stubbly chin, cold black eyes, and rotten teeth. His clothes were stained, old and threadbare.

"Well son look at you, fine strapping man, are you working?"

"Yes I am, what do you want to drink?" Anthony said.

"Oh a drop of the old whisky son, with just a smidge of water."

Anthony went to order the drink; Steven was propping up the bar.

"How's it going?"

"Okay so far", Anthony said. Paying for the drink he returned to his Father.

"There you go!"

"Thanks son." He said taking a sip. Why don't you ask your friend to join us?

Steven came over and sat down next to Anthony.

"Look at you, Anthony all fine and fancy bet you got a good job, what line of work you in?"

"We're both in the dentistry business." answered Anthony.

"Ah, a dentist, I could do with one of those." he said showing his rotten teeth to Anthony.

"Yes I can see, you must be in agony?" said Anthony. His father's teeth were in various stages of decay, some were black and flat to the gum, others brown stumps.

"We might be able to help, what do you think Steven?"

"I should think so Mr. Grace."

"Call me John, and I couldn't afford it son, you boys charge a fortune".

"Let me worry about that, call by the surgery tomorrow, don't you think your long lost son could help his old dad out?" Anthony said with what he hoped looked like a genuine smile.

"Thanks son I will, it would be nice not to have any pain for once!"

"Got him!" thought Anthony. For the rest of the night he plied his Father with drink and when he was no longer able to stand the two friends escorted him home. 'Home' was along a balconied walkway of a two-story block of flats. As they progressed slowly along the walkway, various smells assaulted their senses.

"Mmm, curry" Said Anthony

"Yes, smells nice", agreed Steven, "wouldn't want to live with it every day though",

"I bet this is his flat, it smells like him—rotten drains," Steven stopped outside a battered front door that had obviously been kicked in a few times. "Where's your key dad?" Anthony shook his father slightly to rouse him from his drunken stupor.

"Whaa?" he slurred, belching loudly and enveloping the two lads in a foul cloud of alcohol fumes and stale tobacco smoke.

"Jesus Christ!" Steven said

Fishing in his pockets, Anthony's dad eventually pulled out a long bit of string that was tied round his neck, on the end was a key.

"Move him nearer mate it won't reach" Anthony shuffled him nearer. Steven slid the key into the lock, with a turn and a push the door opened.

Once inside Steven turned on the light.

"He was spot on describing the place, your dad, it is a fucking shit hole".

"Yes, what a fucking mess!"

Clothes, black bags,newspapers and books were piled high, rubbish was every-where, empty cans, bottles and what looked suspiciously like rat droppings. The sink was full of dishes and pots and pans that were encrusted with mould. A trail had been forged out over the filthy threadbare carpet between the piles of rubbish that led from an ancient television to an equally ancient stained and filthy chair. The pair guessed this was where he slept and eager to get rid of their malodorous burden, dumped him, unceremoniously onto the disgusting chair cushion. An indignant rat, the size of a small cat, jumped out from under Anthony's father's bony backside as it hit the chair and ran off into the kitchen.

"Jesus H Christ!" Steven said, again, he was beginning to feel sick. "Let's get out of here Ant!"

Anthony pinned a piece of paper to his father's coat giving the location of the surgery and they left.

"How the fuck do people live like that?" asked Anthony gulping in lung-fulls of the cool night air outside the fetid squalor of the flat.

"I can remember a certain person's bedroom not so long ago!", said Steven with a smile

"Come on mate there's no comparison" said Anthony, slightly annoyed

'I suppose, it was clean mess, but hey, you've seen the light now eh Ant?" They both laughed giving each other a high five.

As they arrived the next morning Steven and Anthony were surprised to find Anthony's dad waiting on the steps outside the surgery a battered looking roll up dangling from his stained fingers. As he saw them approach he got up, cleared his throat and spat out a long string of browny-black filth.

"I didn't expect you here so early" Anthony said dodging the foul smelling remnant of something he would rather not even guess at on the pavement.

"Always up bright and early me". He hawked again.

"Why is that?" asked Anthony dodging a gust of foul breath as he let his father into the surgery.

"'Cos I might get a job come through" he replied, stubbing out his rollie as he went through the door.

"What type of job?"

"Oh I collect and deliver parcels, ask no questions, nudge, nudge, wink, wink, know what I mean?"

"Yes I think I get your drift", Steven led Anthony's dad up the stairs and into the surgery.

"Right rinse your mouth with some of this" Steven said handing him a cup full of the pink fluid and reaching for a mask.

Once in the chair Steven set to work. There were two decent teeth that would be suitable recipients for the devices, the rest he scraped and bodged over, after all he wasn't going to need them for long!

"Right that should do you." He said finally.

"That's lovely, and no pain Steven, you're a talented man!"

"Thanks, but I'd wait for the anaesthetic to wear off before you count your chickens, but it shouldn't be too bad." Steven reassured him

"I can't pay much".

"That's okay, I've had a thought, I might want you to pick up a parcel for us." Steven said. "If you can do that we'll call it quits."

"Yes I can do that; here take my number" John Grace said, bringing out a state of the art phone.

"Wow some phone!" said Steven.

Bloody piss taker how comes he can afford that? He thought

"Oh it's not mine" John Grace said, his voice lispy from the anaesthetic, "it belongs to the bloke I do work for, he just lets me have it to keep in touch".

"'I see', said Steven taking down the number. "Right, we'll be in touch".

"Anytime, just ring! See you son" he called to Anthony

Anthony poked his head through the curtain,

"Yes, see you, Dad"

"See you in hell!" he muttered under his breath

"Sometime soon I hope son?"

"Definitely, Yes! . . . . Sooner than he thinks", Anthony chuckled to himself.

"How did it go?" Anthony joined Steven where he was clearing up in the surgery.

"Yes sorted mate, I had a brain wave, your dad delivers parcels, we can get him to pick up the money from Bellman".

"Fucking good idea mate, we can meet him at his shit hole, get the money then . . . boom! Fucking good riddance to bad blood, eh mate?".

"God Anthony you really want to see the back of him that bad?"

"Yes Steve, if I had known where he was before, I'd have killed him already. All those years of watching my mum suffer because of him. We got him now, as you say we'll use him for what we want, then I want rid, you'd be the same if it was your dad wouldn't you?"

"Yes, I suppose I would, scumbag, still he did us all a favour and drunk himself to death!".

A week later they were back in touch with Bellman again.

Anthony spoke into the remote.

"Bellman you got the money?"

"Yes, one question, if you get the money will you take this out of my mouth?"

"Can't, I'm afraid, that would be too dangerous, it might blow up"

'WHAT? I'm stuck with it forever?" Bellman shouted

"Afraid so me old mate, best I can do for you is that once we get the money I'll destroy the remote, that way it cannot be detonated, and then I'm afraid it's fingers crossed you don't need a dentist" Anthony said.

"That's intolerable, outrageous!" Bellman blustered.

Steven gave an exaggerated sigh, "It is really, I suppose, but that's what we're stuck with and if you want me to destroy the detonator you will put the money in a box, then wrap it in brown paper, someone will collect it, you can't miss him he looks like a tramp"

"How do I know that you will destroy the detonator if I give the money?" Bellman's voice sounded as though he was on the verge of tears.

"Again, you don't really, you'll just have to trust us. Life can be so unfair, don't you think?" Steven laughed and Anthony laughed with him.

Anthony arranged for his Dad to pick up the parcel, and then to wait for him and Steven at his flat on Friday night.

"What's in there then lads?" John Grace said handing the parcel over.

"A million pounds' said Anthony.
'Fuck off! A million pounds, you're joking right?"

"Nope" said Steven opening the parcel.

Inside were neatly stacked piles of money.

"Fucking looks real doesn't it Ant?"

"Yes mate let's have a feel" he said holding out his hands.

"And to think I could have fucked off with that lot!" John Grace said his rat like eyes bright with greed.

Anthony looked at his father sharply.

"Not that I would have of course, steal from my own boy? Never!" he said unconvincingly.

Yeah, right. Anthony thought.

"Here take this" Steven handed Anthony's dad a wedge of money.

The older man sat on his chair flicking the money like a pack of cards over and over. He'd never seen so much money and he couldn't stop playing with it. "Right let's shoot mate" said Steven.

"Yes, we got to go now Dad, don't drink it . . . I mean spend it all at once!"

"Yes see you son!" John Grace replied not taking his eyes off the money.
He counted the money. "A thousand pounds" he said out loud.

He held up the money again, flicking through it and causing a slight breeze to fan his face. He was just holding the crisp notes to his nose to take in the smell of new money when . . . . BOOM.

As tiny fragments of bank notes fluttered down to the street outside, Anthony said.

"That's the end of that fucker. At last I'm free, what a feeling!"

"What we going to do with Bellman?" asked Steven

"Fuck we got more money than we could ever dream of, get rid shall we?"

"Yes, let's see what he's up to" Steven said

"Bellman?"—silence. "Oh Bellman?"

"What? You've got your money, now leave me alone!"

"Aw come on Bellman don't be like that there's a good boy, what are you doing now?"

"None of your damn business!"

"Now, now, that's not very nice, give him a blast Ant"

Bellman shrieked and held his head to try and contain the pain.
`"What do you want?" he whimpered

"Nothing" said Anthony

"Except to say, bye-bye Bellman" . . . . BOOM!

"Fuck that was funny mate!" said Steven

So now, what say we get back to the surgery and discuss the plans we have for this little lot?" Steven patted the parcel on his lap.

"What about a nice bottle of champagne to help us decide?
"Anthony said

"Oh I reckon we could just about run to that!" Steven
laughed.

CHAPTER 7

Matheson rushed into the noisy general office where, hearing his name, Roberts looked up from his desk.

"Get your coat we've got two separate explosions, looks like the same MO as the others"

Roberts was on his feet and out the door before Matheson could finish the sentence.

Sirens blazing they raced first to Bellman's house, that could more accurately be described as a small mansion. The only person who had been in the house at the time of the explosion was a cleaner, a woman in her fifties, with her teeth chattering, she was wandering around explaining in hysterical tones to anyone who would listen that she had heard the explosion and had come upstairs to investigate. Each time that she reached the point of describing what she saw, she would drop her head into her hands and sob, and then start from the beginning of the story again.

An ambulance and it's crew, with Bellman way beyond any help they could give, took the jibbering cleaner away describing her as being in 'an advanced state of shock' to the hospital.

At the crime scene Matheson's stood his face grim. "What the fuck is all this Roberts? I just can't believe what I'm seeing; this is getting beyond a joke!" Bellman's naked headless body sat in a chair his right hand still cupping his blood-spattered penis. Opposite him the TV was playing pornographic films now partly concealed by blood and bits of bone brain and skin, dripping in trails down the screen.

The whole room was splattered with the contents of Bellman's head.

"Anything to go on?" Matheson said to Isabel Conner as she examined the area closest to Bellman.

"No nothing," she replied, "no break in, no struggle—nothing, same as the others. One thing I do know is we are getting a bit sick of this, it's becoming a bit of regular occurrence, can't you boys get your fingers out and sort it?" Isabel flashed her brown eyes at him. They held a challenge and, Matheson realised, it was a challenge to more than his crime solving skills.

For a moment, he didn't reply, God she had the most beautiful eyes.

Then, ignoring her jibe he said. "Okay let me know if you find anything. Come on Roberts" As he left the room he could feel Isabel's eyes following him.

"'I reckon you're in there" Roberts said. Matheson ignored him

"Where to now sir?"

"Back into town that's where the other case is"

"I thought we might have gone there first sir, it being so close and all?"

"Should have, I just had to come here Roberts, its way out of the area of the other cases, and I thought it might be something different, but it appears it isn't!"

"Exactly the same sir."

"Yes Roberts, only this time he seemed to be preoccupied with playing with himself, just doesn't make fucking sense. Why would he do that? Who would want to off themselves with their greasy mitt round their old fella, for everyone to see?"

"Perhaps he was ashamed of what he was doing"

"So why make sure that every other bugger knew what he was doing, after he was dead? No it doesn't make any sense at all."

"Yes sir"

"Right, this is it, we're here."

Matheson pulled up on double yellow lines. On the balcony outside John Graces' flat a crowd of curious onlookers had gathered.

"Where's plod? You can fuck that lot off straight away Roberts; have we got to do everything round here?" he said

"Looks like it sir"

"Put a report in, procedures are lax, they need tightening Roberts"

"Yes sir"

"Come on, then let the dog see the rabbit." The two men ran up the filthy stair well.

"Right, everybody back." Roberts shouted, "That's it, right back, go home there's nothing to see here."

Despite the fact that there was obviously quite a lot to see, the crowd grudgingly dispersed leaving the detectives to their work.

Matheson gagged as the smell of the flat hit him.

"God alive! Hanky Roberts!"

"Sir"

Matheson put the hanky to his face and proceeded along the corridor, he had become hardened to this type of case now, and was expecting a similar scenario.

In the lounge he tightened his jaw, it never ceased to amaze him what absolutely filthy conditions a human could endure. The spattered colour from the brains of John Grace had almost improved the place. 'Fucking degusting' he said out aloud, 'there's only just about room for one person in here Roberts'

Looking over Matheson shoulder Robert's said, "Can't imagine anyone else would be that interested in being in here anyway."

'It's not as though he was skint either; there's money everywhere, Said Matheson as he neared the corpse. "Strange choice of pet, too" he said noting a rat lying dead across John Grace's legs.

"Same as, blown to fuck, brains everywhere, forensics have got another delight here Roberts."

"They certainly have, sir."

"Come on, leave it to them, we'll have to look at the reports, but I can't see them throwing up anything new. I'm starting to believe in your theory Robert's, suppose someone was firing a high voltage laser at them? Find out all you can about lasers Roberts."

"Yes sir"

Two days later the reports were on Matheson's desk.

"What the fuck is going on Roberts? This just doesn't make any sense!"

"What do you mean sir?"

"I mean rich man, poor man, beautiful women, scum bag. Where's the connection other than them missing their heads?" Matheson said, "The Super is doing his bollocks, we haven't got zilch, and our necks are on the block Roberts."
"Yes sir"

"You got anything on the laser idea, Roberts?"

"I have. You could take someone out at distance with a laser, they would be burnt or vaporised, in each case there would be some scorching, burn marks, but not an explosion like this."

"That's fucked that idea then, no burn marks clean as a whistle, apart from the missing heads" Matheson said. He was disappointed; he really had no idea what it was they were dealing with.

"Got to be suicide sir, they must be doing it themselves"

"Don't be so dense Roberts, the victims are so diverse so different, what do you think the chances are of all of them thinking that blowing their heads off would be a good way to off themselves, let alone all of them happening on the same really bizarre way of doing it? Besides which none of them have any obvious reason for wanting to kill themselves. Even the tramp was fucking rolling in money, seemingly. Bellman was rich, the girls had everything to live for, no problems at all according to their family and friends, none of it makes any sense, but one thing is sure it was not suicide. We are going to have to go back, fine tooth comb everything Roberts."

"Yes sir" As Matheson and Roberts dealt with the aftermath of their handiwork Steven and Anthony enjoyed their bottle of champagne. "What are we going to do with all this money mate?"

Anthony said running his hand over the neat piles of bank notes.

"Well first things first, I'm going to get me the best whore money can buy" replied Steven

"I'll have some of that," said Anthony, feeling his cock twitch.

"Where can we get them?"

"Look on the computer there are loads of sites, just pick one out, money no object!"

Steven laughed.

"Right come on then let's have a look," said Anthony "What shall I type in Steve?"

"God Ant, you really are a clueless fuck aren't you? Type in high-class call girls".

"You've done this before haven't you Steve?"

"No I haven't I'm just using this!" Steven pointed to his head. "I believe you thousands wouldn't!" laughed Anthony.

"Here we go!" Anthony pushed his glasses up on his nose as a dozen pictures of gorgeous women in various states of undress appeared on the screen, every imaginable nationality, body type and hair colour.

"I like the look of her!" said Steven pointing to a stunning blond. "She's well fuckable!"
"Me too, that was my choice!" said Anthony.

"Okay I'll have her," said Steven, pointing to another stunner.

'Give the number a ring then mate' said Steven.

Anthony rang the number.

"Hello?" A low sexy voice answered

"Err yes hello, is this Classy Call Girls?"

"Yes, what can I do for you lover boy?" the voice purred

"Err how much is it?" said Anthony

"One thousand a night."

Anthony covered the mouthpiece of the phone with his hand, his eyes wide.

"Fuck Steve she wants a thousand just for one night!"

"Ask her what you get for that, mate."

Anthony cleared his throat "What do you get for that?"

"Everything you've ever wanted," the voice oozed "straight sex, blow job, anal, smacking, whipping. What do you want big boy?" she asked softly

"I just want a fuck love, so does my mate Steve, we've never done it before, well Steve sort of has, but I haven't."
'Two grand and I'll bring a friend to your place" she said

"Oh, we haven't got a place, just loads of money!" Anthony said breathing fast.

"Fuck don't tell her that you numpty!" Steve punched his arm.

"Sorry mate!" said Anthony flustered, completely missing the woman's reply.

"Err sorry, what was that?" he said into the phone.

"Another five hundred and I can arrange a lovely hotel for the night," she said in honeyed tones.

"What do you reckon mate?" Anthony relayed the offer to Steven.

"We want blonds!" Steven shouted into the phone.

"Okay two blonds, nice hotel, pay up front," the voice said, becoming slightly more business like now.

"Done" Anthony said. His hands shaking he took down all the particulars and put the phone down.

"Tomorrow night, it is then mate, I'm nervous already Steve!"

"You don't say!" Steven teased, mimicking Anthony's shaking hands, although if truth were told he was just as nervous.

"Right where we going to stash the cash, we got to be careful can't go splashing it about, we don't want to draw too much attention."

Anthony nodded "Yes I agree might raise suspicions, we can get the door fitted here though can't we?"

"Yes mate and what about a wall across here separate this lot off? Then another door?"

"Yes a secret door that no fucker knows about". Said Anthony pleased with his brainwave.

"Hmm yes I know just the man, Bob the builder!" Steven said.

"Yeah, yeah, Come on mate I was being serious!" said Anthony.

"So was I, Chris has a builder on his books called, wait for it, Bob! I've already planted him. Oh I'm so good"

Steven laughed. "Fucking Brilliant, Bob the fucking builder!" Anthony fell about laughing.

Anthony looked around, "What about stashing the cash up there for now?" he said pointing to a loft hatch in the ceiling.

"We haven't got a ladder," said Steven.

"Even better, with no ladder on hand no one would be tempted to use it to have a look up there and we can use a table and chair for now."

'Yes you're right', said Steven pulling the table from the waiting room. With a chair on top Steven was able to reach the hatch. Pushing the box to one side he let the hatch down.

"There that should do it, God knows what else is up there, we'll have to have a proper look later, it might have possibilities for all sorts of things!"

"Like what?" Anthony asked.

"Man oh man you're a bit lacking in imagination aren't you old chum?"

"I manage!" Anthony said, it was true he was not a leader like Steven, he was a follower, he knew it, but it was like they said, it's often the quiet ones you have to watch! Every dog has his day!"

With the surgery locked, they said goodbye and agreed to meet the next day at the Station. Steven could have driven into

London for the night but the parking was so expensive, they decided it would be better to go by train.

At home Anthony found his mother polishing some brass. He said nothing but he was secretly delighted. It was months, no years since she had taken any interest in the brass pieces she had inherited from her mother that were displayed over the mantelpiece. Anthony, although he had dusted them, had no idea that they needed to be polished with Brasso and was amazed to see how bright and shiny they were.

"Hey they look good mum!"

"Yes, they do don't they?" She held up an old brass bowl admiring it.

"Mum, I won't be home tomorrow night, will you be alright?"

"Yes pet you don't have to worry about me, I'll be fine!

"But I do worry" But a lot less now that I have disposed of the mysterious exploding father Anthony thought to himself.

"Yes I know that son, I've had a lot of time to think, and I realise what a burden I've been, I've virtually taken your childhood away from you, and made quite a pain of myself in your adulthood so far as well, and I regret it son."

"Don't be daft mum, it wasn't your fault, it was dads, I was there, I saw it all, I never told you because you seemed to want me to believe that you fell, but I saw him push you, I was hiding behind the door in my room."

"My God Anthony, I never realised!" She said, "Why didn't you say anything before?"

Anthony shrugged "Its' a long time ago now, I'm over it, onwards and upwards. That's the new motto in this house. I don't want to go into the ins and outs, the why and why nots, Let's just forget it forever, it's taken enough of our lives already, lets not let it take any more. We will never, and I mean never mention it again, promise?"

"But son . . . ." Anthony's face stopped his mother in mid sentence, she could see there was no point in arguing with her son, however much she wanted to talk it through with him, however much she felt she should somehow try to find out how much he had suffered in silence all these years. She sighed deeply, a sad sound that seemed to come from her very soul. "Ok, Anthony, I promise."

"Good, now, are you sure you're going to be alright? I'll will be back Sunday, probably about midday."

"Of course, I'm sure" His mother smiled although Anthony thought he could see tears in her eyes

"What are you planning? Something with Steven? He's such a nice young man, and it's great that the two of you are going to work together, you were always good with your hands, making things and whatnot, this job could have been made for you!"

"Yes, we're going up into London, just for a night out, you know the sort of thing!"

"Maybe you'll meet a nice girl up there?" his mother said hopefully

"Maybe" Anthony answered, He was definitely going to meet a girl but just how nice she would be by his mother's standards was debatable!

"You go and enjoy yourself!'

"Thanks mum, I will!" Anthony planted a kiss on her cheek.

The following day dragged for both Steven and Anthony and Anthony had had to take emergency action four times when unwanted erections interrupted his day as he thought about the night to come. Finally, as the evening crowds of Saturday shoppers returning from London were starting to disperse, their train drew out of the station.

Steven said, "Let's call into a pub on the way mate get some Dutch courage eh?"

Anthony nodded, "I'm going to need a lot of it, I'm nervous as hell!"

"You'll be alright Ant, once you're on you'll know how to ride her." Steven sounded a lot more confident than he felt.

"Hope so!" Anthony said.

After a couple of quick drinks in the pub the pair found themselves waiting nervously at the reception of the Plaza Hotel.

"The man behind the reception desk seems a tad preoccupied or is he just ignoring us Steve?" whispered Anthony.

"Excuse me" Steven said loudly.

"Yes?" the man said not looking up from the register he was studying on the desk.

"Sorry are we invisible?" Steven felt anger bubble up inside him, he was looking forward to this night and this prick was not going to spoil it for him. "We have a reservation for Smith and Grace."

"Smith and Grace" the man said in a bored voice then suddenly, "Oh I'm very sorry gentlemen" the clerk looked up hastily as he located their names in the register.

His expression was both fearful and deferential and Steven liked it.

"That's okay don't let it happen again, my business colleague and I are trying out various hotels for regular business meetings, don't make us write yours off before we start."

Steven said and Anthony had to turn away to hide his smile. Steven really did have balls!

"Yes of course sir, I mean no, I mean … You're in the penthouse suite, top floor, have you any luggage?"

"No none" said Steven, just our brief cases. He held up the briefcase he had brought the money in. Anthony had an old laptop bag.

"Of course sir, very well, Now if you'd be so kind as to sign the register?"

Steven obliged writing in a fictitious address

"Thank you." The receptionist said smiling the sort of cheesy smile that made Steven want to punch him, not so bloody dismissive now that he could see they were in the most expensive suite in the hotel eh mate?

Steven thought. He was pleased to see that the receptionist seemed to be breaking into a sweat as his broadest smile failed to illicit anything other than a withering look from Steven and he nervously clapped his hands for a liveried porter who scurried over from the concierge desk.

"Porter take these gentlemen to the Penthouse lift."

"This way gentlemen."

Once inside the lift Anthony counted thirty floors before the lift finally whispered to a halt at the Penthouse

"Blimey that's a long way up Steve!" said Anthony, farting loudly.

"'You smelly bastard!" "Sorry mate I'm nervous!"

The porter stood expressionless, he had seen it all before, no doubt.

"God, Ant, I can taste that, thank God we're here!" The lift doors opened and the lads were met with a plush grey wall papered hallway with big golden doors at the end.

"How do we get in?" Steven asked the porter.

"No need for a key sir, this lift is for the exclusive use of the penthouse, it does not stop at any other floor, you may just go ahead and turn the handle."

Steven did as the porter said and the door opened to reveal a fantasy world that neither he nor Anthony could have imagined even in their wildest dreams.

As Steven and Anthony stood speechless taking in the opulent interior of the Penthouse suite, Steven realised that the porter was hovering, even though they had no luggage he was obviously expecting a tip.

Steven slipped him a twenty.

'Wow' said Steven as they entered. The room had subtle muted grey walls with gold cornicing, a dazzling chandelier hanging from the ceiling and cream carpets with plush deep pile that felt almost like sheepskin. Steven sunk his hand into the lush pile.

"Quality, mate quality" he said delighted. Fine art adorned the walls with the odd mirror. Anthony and Steve walked from room to room looking at the artwork.

"I'm surprised that no one has them away!" said Anthony.

"My dear fellow" Steven put on a posh accent "One would not accept the kind of clinetelle who would 'ave them away' in one's penthouse suite!"

"Pratt!" Anthony laughed,

"Mind you, that one's shit," said Steven pointing to the reflection of Anthony in one of the mirrors.

"Oh, ha fucking ha, speak for yourself you're no Rembrandt" said Anthony.

Anthony dived on to one of the Sofa's, they were like big beds and gave a low whistle as he saw one of the biggest Plasma screen he had ever seen.
"Stick the telly on mate, I'm going to see what's in here, he said walking over and trying one of the three doors.

"Wow can this get any better? Look at this mate!"

Anthony joined Steven to scan the bedroom that was predominately cream with gold accessories a King size four poster, and dark antique furniture.

'That's the bollocks mate, Said Anthony trying another door which was also a bedroom. It was the same in style but was decorated in gold and ice blue.

"Lovely." Steven said looking over Anthony's shoulder.

"This has to be the bathroom then mate!"

"I think you might be right Steve or at least one of them, I saw an en suite in the bedroom."

"God look at that, you could fit a football team in there!" Anthony said staring at the enormous Jacuzzi set in the centre of the mirrored bathroom.

"Fuck this is weird mate, look I'm everywhere!" said Steven looking at his reflection on the walls and ceiling.

"Hmm kinky!" agreed Anthony.

Just then there was a knock at the door. Steven walked over and opened it. Outside a giant of a man almost blocked the whole doorway. Dressed in a navy blue crombi, shaven head, dark glasses wrapped around his eyes.
With a lisp and in the most unlikely squeaky gay voice he asked

"Anthony?"

"No I'm Steven." Steven was in danger of laughing.

"Have you got the money Theven?" The huge man lisped

"Yes" he said, going to his briefcase and trying not to smile. He noticed Anthony sitting on the couch one of the cushions pressed to his face, his shoulders shaking with laughter.

"You're not helping mate," Steven hissed returning to the door.

"There you go"

'Thankth' said the giant and as he moved to one side. Behind him were two beautiful blonds.

"Steven?" One of the girls said. "I'm Kelly and this is my friend Sam."

Both girls were wearing fur coats.

"Can I take your coats girls?" Steven said.

The girls removed their coats to reveal that they were only dressed in the flimsiest of knickers and bras.

"You like?" said Kelly giving them a twirl

"Yes I like very much!" said Steven his cock beginning to stiffen.

Kelly and Sam disappeared into the bathroom to turn on the Jacuzzi.

Steven looked at Anthony "What do you think mate?"

"I'm fucking scared Steve" Anthony looked pale, but Steven noticed a bulge in the front of his jeans.

"Come on mate, stiff upper lip, or something a bit lower! We've paid now, just go for it, come on!" Steven said

"Oh boys . . . we're lonely" called Kelly from the bathroom.

"Coming!" said Steven stripping his clothes off and throwing them on a chair.

"Oh that's fucking great, typical!" Anthony said.

"What's wrong now?"

"The size of your fucking todger that's what!"

"You stay here then, I'll fuck them both!" Steven offered.

"Not bloody likely, mate, ask Sam if we can go in the bedroom"

"Oh you're having Sam are you? I see, and when was that decided?"

"Alright ask Kelly if she can come to the bedroom, I don't give a fuck, or rather I do!" Anthony said.

"Only joking mate you can have Sam, I'll send her out!"

Steven walked into the bathroom his cock almost fully erect.

"Well, hello big boy!" said Kelly

"Sam, Anthony's shy, he wants to do it in the bedroom"

'Does he now' she said reaching out to touch Steven's cock. Easing him towards her she slipped her lips over the tip, while Kelly took his balls in her hand rolling them around like two marbles, then raising herself up she sucked them into her mouth licking them gently with her tongue.

"Fuck, I'm coming!" Steven gasped.

"Not so fast!" said Sam removing her mouth and flicked the tip of Steven's cock with a long crimson painted fingernail, making him wince with pain.

"Fuck that hurt!" "Oh so sorry, let me kiss it better" said Kelly in a baby voice stroking his semi erect cock.

"Ahh that's better" she said as Steven's cock stiffened again.

She climbed out of the Jacuzzi and spread her legs as she balanced on the side of it. Kelly came up behind her and Sam layback with her head on her friends shoulder. Steven groaned, as Kelly began to play with Sam's broad brown nipples that were fully erect. Gently she leaned forward and parted Sam's thick bush of neatly trimmed blond hair, with the bubbles from the Jacuzzi making it look like her pussy was adorned with diamonds. Pulling Steven towards her by his cock Sam held him to her swollen pussy lips for a moment before letting go and throwing back her head on Kelly's shoulder, as he pushed his cock into her.

'Oh yes that's it, come on big boy. She may have been a prostitute but Steven was pretty confident that she was enjoying this as much as he was. As Kelly gently pinched her nipples Sam groaned at the twin pleasure of the huge cock inside her and the delicate touch of her friend on her over stimulated nipples. Steven pumped in and out, revelling in the luxury of the tight hot pussy, all the time with the sense he was being watched by his own image that was reflected in the mirrors that covered every surface of the bathroom and he started admiring himself and the girls from all angles. This titillation spurred him on and he felt his ejaculation nearing. This time he was saying nothing, and with a groan he pumped his cum into her.

"Fuck!" he said as he collapsed into the water.

Meanwhile

Anthony is sitting on the huge bed in the bedroom stark bullock naked and was feeling decidedly neglected. He could hear the sounds of passion coming from the bathroom and had resigned himself to the fact that the girls had obviously decided that Steven would be the better ride. He was about to get dressed when the girls walked in. Both were as naked as he was.

"Ahh is Anthony a shy boy?" said Kelly in her baby voice.

"Does Anthony want the light off?" Sam switched the light off, and then on again. "Only joking, you wouldn't want to miss seeing this would you?" She parted her pussy lips and stuck a finger inside herself"

Anthony's cock sprang to attention, not as big as Steven it was still a good size and the girls lay down on either side of him, running soft fingers all over his body, but not touching his cock. If it was his first time he was likely to go off like a rocket, they wanted to give him some build up before hand!

First Sam then Kelly offered him their full breasts and distended nipples. His balls were aching now; they felt three times their normal size. Soon Anthony had forgotten his fear overcome as he now was with an urgent need to shoot his load. But these girls knew what they were doing and caressed him to the brink and then left him alone while they played with each other, being sure not to let him touch his cock. Looking down at his aching cock Anthony could have sworn that it was almost the same size, as Stevens' now, and he had to come, he was in physical pain. At last, pushing him onto his back Kelly got on top of him, lowering herself gently onto his cock.

"Who's a big boy then, you can come now, Anthony, fill me up, we can go again later," she whispered. Anthony had only ever climaxed from wanking before so he was not prepared for the intensity of his orgasm that was long and deep and sent his whole body into spasm. Kissing him gently on the lips, Sam returned to Steven in the bathroom leaving Kelly curled up next to Anthony, already getting a response to her gentle mouth on his cock, still wet from her pussy and his own cum. In the bathroom Steven had been enjoying the warm massage of the soapy bubbles of the Jacuzzi. Leaning over him Sam stuck her tongue deep into his mouth. As she whispered filthy suggestions in his ear, Steven's cock did an impressive impression of the Loch Ness Monster emerging from the watery depths of the Jacuzzi. Sam sat astride him and rode the sea monster. He groaned with pleasure as the warm water caressed their writhing bodies, his urgency having been spent with his first orgasm he could enjoy the ride more now and his next orgasm was simultaneous with Sam's. Kelly taught Anthony all she knew over the next few hours until he was almost too weak to walk. By the time morning came the girls had slipped away.

"There is someone at the door" Anthony called and Steven went to answer it.

"Breakfast sir."

"Oh yes thank you" Steven picked up a twenty from the table beside the door and gave it to the porter. Steven saw the man's eyes flick down his naked body to his huge cock, and he looked up at Steven deliberately licking his lips. Steven suddenly felt self-conscious.

He kicked the door shut. It was too early to be grossed out!

"Come on mate grubs up" Steven shouted wheeling the big trolley towards one of the giant sofas and pulling on one of the complimentary dressing gowns.

Bleary-eyed Anthony appeared from his bedroom, a towel tucked around his waist.
"Fuck what a night eh Steve? That Kelly sucked my cock, licked my arse, and sat on my face, I fucked her till I thought I was going to die."

"Welcome to sex my friend!" said Steven laughing.

"Yeah like you were the big expert to start with!" Anthony said.

"I've had my moments, which is more than you can say!" Steven said, and it was true he had had a few partners at college, mostly one-night stands, but he supposed it all counted!

"Any worries I had, she soon sorted them mate!" Anthony said

"Told you, didn't I?"

"Yes, you did Steve, thanks!"

"No worries mate, eat up we got to be out of here by eleven."

The two lads were starving and ate their breakfast with the same enthusiasm with which they had approached the night before's activities. At reception they were waved off with earnest entreaties from the reception staff that they come back again very soon. The bill had been taken care of, as the girls had promised. On the train ride home they talked over the night before, and came to the conclusion that they would probably be making a booking at the Plaza on a regular basis.

"Had a good time?" said Anthony's Mum.

"God yes I need to sleep it off, I'm going to bed, give us a shout later Mum will you?"

"Okay son" Sarah Grace smiled. She was glad that her son was at last getting a life of his own; he had been deprived for too long. She had heard from the police that his father had died in an explosion. She was eternally grateful that Anthony had been in London when they called round to see if she knew anything. They had asked a few questions but seemed convinced by her insistence that she had not seen John Grace for years. After they left Sarah had sat for some time in silence. She was not sure what she felt about John's death. She should hate him, she knew that, but somehow she didn't. They had been so in love when they met, before the drinking had got hold of him. But it was his fault that she was in a wheel chair that Anthony had missed out on so much and for that she could never forgive him. None the less, a single tear ran down her cheek for the man that she had once known and loved.

CHAPTER 8

Steven spent the rest of Sunday at the surgery drawing up some rough plans for the alterations. A few days later they had a quote from Bob the builder and decided to give him the job. Steven had also tried to secure the services of an old adversary Cathy Barrett to be their receptionist. She would be on extraordinary amounts of money, he said to her and the only other proviso was sex for both him and Anthony whenever they wanted. It was a once only offer, 'take it or leave it'. Steven said to her convinced she would jump at the chance. As he thought about the last time he had seen her, his cock twitched, he was owed a visit to that tight little pussy and he could not wait to take it.

Cathy laughed in his face. "You deluded weirdo, Don't you watch the TV Steven, haven't you seen me doing the weather after the local news?"

Steven hadn't. Not for the first time he felt completely frustrated by Cathy. He knew that she was becoming a bit of a fixation with him, the need to conquer her, something that had been denied him for so long now, since those days behind the bike shed. This was a disappointment, but there would be other chances to teach that particular bitch a lesson, he smiled as he wondered if she might be interested in some free dental work?
Over the course of the next couple of months they visited the Plaza on Saturday nights. They tried different girls, but the lads decided Kelly and Sam were their favourites. And the girls agreed that Anthony was a fast learner. Steve was more

a wham bam thank you ma'am type but Anthony showed a real tenderness, a desire to make sure that his partner got as much pleasure as he did, and the girls loved him for that. His technique improved all the time and he asked questions, "How does that feel? Is that too sensitive to touch? How much pressure should I put here?" The girls loved teaching the young man and were proud of the lover he had become. They also worked miracles with his appearance, and even met him on their day off to go shopping for the clothes they thought would suit him. They took him to one of their clients, a top class hairdresser for a make over, another who was a leading dermatologist to treat his skin, an optometrist for contact lenses. Steven was amused by Anthony's attempts to morph from a very ugly duckling to a swan and even fitted braces to Anthony's teeth but as the months went by and the braces came off he was more than a little rattled by his friends new look. Anthony was a lot taller than Steven but that had never been much of an advantage while he looked like he did all goofy teeth, unruly hair and spotty skin. The young man that the prostitutes had fashioned in smart clothes and looking hot was a different prospect and Steven felt uneasy about it. He tried to tell himself that it didn't make any difference, he would always be the cooler, the more sophisticated, but still, it bothered him. He had thought that the girls would introduce him to their contacts, the barber in particular, he would have liked a cool hair cut, but for some reason they were always all over Anthony and apart from doing what they were paid for with Steven, they really did not seem to want much to do with him.

Meanwhile back at the surgery, Bob had certainly done miracles and had totally transformed the place. There were secret camera's everywhere, Steven had even had a camera installed in the frame of his glasses, he didn't need glasses, they were just a good cover. Every detail of their work was relayed back to monitors overseen by Anthony in his secret hideout at the back of the building. And now with the addition of another dentist, a former student who had trained with Steven the money was rolling in. Jim, the new dentist was a bit of a brainwave of Stevens. Jim had been at college with Steven and had been deaf since birth. The young dentist worried that his deafness would prevent him being considered for a job, but for Steven he was just perfect. He lip read perfectly, but you had to be in the same room as him for him to do that, so Anthony and Steven could talk freely anywhere other than in front of him. Bob was no mug either and had quickly grasped the potential for a bigger profit by expanding the work that they required him to do. He missed no opportunity to expand his brief.

This did not go unnoticed and it was beginning to get to Steven. With the surgery almost as they wanted it, Bob's eternal 'final touches' were becoming an expense too far. He had not missed the chance for free dental treatment either and Steven had taken particular pleasure in implanting a 'baby' in him.

"We don't need Bob anymore do we Ant?"

"No, I suppose not, he's done a bang up job though!"

"Well the surgery's nearly done, and he's getting on my nerves, asking question's, coming up with yet another money making alteration, charging what he likes he's getting dangerous, snooping around, he knows too much about this place" explained Steven.

"Fuck! The wanker, I didn't realise that mate!"

"Well you're out the back mate, you wouldn't see as much as I do."

"So what, we lay him off?"

"Like I said, he knows too much about this place, always sticking his beak in, we'llhave to blow the fucker up."

"Awesome. It's been a long time mate!"

"Sure has, I think we'll invite him out, you know for a meal or something like that." Steven said

"You mean like a Topping out ceremony, job well done and all that malarkey?"

"Exactly mate, exactly" Steven smiled

"Even a topping off ceremony, get it?" "Yeah mate, but don't lose your head over it!" Anthony quipped back

"That's good, for you!" said Steven, and they laughed together a sound that had no real mirth in it, more a hard determined resolve.

They begin to plot Bob the builder's demise.

"It should be something spectacular, I reckon "Steven said.

"Yes like in a crowded restaurant? That would be awesome man!" Anthony looked excited at the prospect.

"It sure would mate, I know just the place, one of them big Chinese restaurants!" Steven arranged to meet with Bob at five, the builder seemed surprised but very pleased by the invite.

Sitting right in the middle of the crowded restaurant Anthony suggested they take a photo for the wall in the Surgery that had all their photos on. "After all you've been as much a part of getting this place up and running as we have!" Steven said and Bob beamed, delighted with the accolade. "That would be great, thanks fellas, I'm touched, really!"

"I'm just going for a slash, take a good one of Bob, Anthony." said Steven.

"Yes okay mate! I'll try to get the fish tank in the shot as well."

Steven retreated to a safe distance. He watched amused as Anthony stood back from the table and held the remote in his hand, turned sideways it looked for all the world like a camera.

"I'll just have to move back Bob, to get the tank in. Anthony took several steps back "Right nice big smile!" he said
Bob gave a big cheesy grin holding his beer glass. Anthony pressed the button. BOOM.

Bob's head exploded in a million pieces showering the restaurant. For a moment there was complete silence then a crack in the fish tank ruptured and a flood of water splashed onto the floor fish flapping helplessly in pools of bloody water. The diners started to scream and a couple women fainted as others dived for cover. Women's best evening dresses, men's shirts and tablecloths were all splattered with the contents of Bob's cranium. Waiters ran to the kitchen for cover. Bits of brain hair and skin and bone garnished the dishes of those tables closest to where Bob had sat only moments earlier, his pint in his hand. In the pandemonium Anthony and Steven slipped away, into the gathering gloom of night.

"That was the bollocks mate!" said Steven exhilarated, his eyes bright.

"Got to agree it was exceptional! I fucking loved it!" said Anthony "We got to do it again; it's the only thing that gives me a buzz!"

It's like nothing else mate" Steven said as they walked swiftly away from the restaurant,. Suddenly Anthony stopped dead and shouted "FUCK!"

"WHAT?" Steven said startled.

"I must have dropped the remote!"

"We'll have to go back and get it' Steven said starting off at a run back along the pavement Anthony close behind him.

Across town Roberts and Matheson had just put on their coats and were preparing to leave the office. Hesitating as the phone rang on his desk Roberts picked it up. For a moment he listened in silence then slammed the phone back on its cradle.

"Sir! Sir!" Robert's shouted across the office

"What is it Roberts? No forget it whatever it is, I'm out of here, I don't want to know." Matheson shouted back.

"We've got another one sir!"

"Another one?" Matheson asked, although he knew the answer.

"Another body with it's head blown off." Roberts said flatly

Matheson and the whole front office fell silent for a moment, the previous cases were no further forward and with five-weeks having elapsed since the last incident, Matheson had dared to hope that they had heard the last of this type of case.

"Fuck it," Matheson, said "Laura is going to go mad. It was our anniversary today and my nippers birthday at the weekend. Ok Roberts, where is it?"

"The Chinese in Purling!"

"WHAT? Jesus, I was going there tonight!" "Give me a minute Roberts" Matheson rang his wife.

"Yes dear, sorry dear, I've got to, don't be like that love, I didn't plan it did I? Anyway the Chinese has been blown up. I'll make it up to you, yes I promise, yes, yes, got to go bye!"

"Right lets go Roberts. And you lot can fuck off!' he said to two sniggering officers who had overheard his call to his wife.

Anthony reached the restaurant to a scene of mayhem, people confused, crying, not sure whether the blood on them was their own or the man's whose body still sat upright, an untouched chop suey in front of him. Quickly smearing his hands with some blood from the floor and daubing some on his face, Anthony milled around with the diners unnoticed, scanning the area where he had been standing. "Fuck, fuck!"

Real panic taking hold of him, Anthony left the restaurant as the first police car arrived. With no sign of the remote he plunged his hands into his pockets in attempt to wipe off some of the blood. His left hand found a gap in the corner of the pocket. Flapping the coat he realised that the remote had fallen through the hole and deep into the lining.

"Did you get it mate?" Steven said as they slipped down an alley at the side of the restaurant.

"Yes it was in my coat all the time, fell down the lining!"

"Thank fuck for that!" said Steven as more police cars and two ambulances arrived, sirens blazing.

Matheson walked into the carnage.

"Same MO?" he said to Isabel Conner. He felt a little stab of irritation, how the hell was it that she always got to the scene before anyone else. The chain of command should have her being called out after the initial attendance of the plod and themselves, but no she was always here first, God she must prowl the streets waiting for something to happen, he thought.

"Yes exactly the same pattern Matheson." "Call me Sammy.". He said. "And tell me how is it you always seem to get here before anyone else, in fact how is it you seem to get everywhere before anyone else?"

Isabel shrugged. "Okay, Sammy" she said his name in a tone laced with promise, looking at him from under long lashes, "You want to know how I always get everywhere before you and the boys in blue? Dunno, luck? Devotion to duty?" she smiled.

She went back to her examination of the meal in front of Bob favouring Matheson with another flash of her brown eyes.

Matheson caught her enticing glare, but stayed on the case.

"Anything different"

"No nothing different, except" she continued teasingly, Matheson took a step closer to Isabel.

"Except?" he said, staring deep into her beautiful brown eye's.

"There were two other men with the deceased". she said lowering her long sooty lashes slowly over her eyes for a moment.

"Where are they?" he said looking around.

"Gone, they disappeared" replied Isabel, fluttering her eyelids again.

"Bollocks! Oh sorry excuse the French!" he said, "did anyone see them?"

'Most people saw them, but it happened so quick they said that one minute the two men were here, the next they had gone", explained Isabel. She looked longingly at him; he had such a commanding presence, and if it was one thing that turned Isabel on it was power.

Although he was working, Matheson had not missed the signals she had been sending him, and he had filed them away for later. Throwing her a smile, he turned back to Roberts.

"Right Roberts get everyone together whoever saw them, take down everything; I mean everything, even if it takes the rest of the night!"

"Yes sir" Roberts answered wearily.

Isabel hung around for a while carrying out tests, all the while watching Matheson at work. A man of power really excited her, and the thought of getting her claws into him began to make her feel horny.
"Right I'll be off Sammy" Matheson thought she looked a bit flushed, "I'll have my report in a couple of days"

"Oh right, look forward to it Isabel".

"I might even deliver it personally", she said looking at him with those big brown eyes. 'Yes do that' he said admiring her profile as she turned to leave. Now that she had her overalls off he could see she was wearing a tight pink cashmere sweater her nipples erect and poking out at him through the thin wool. Unusually for him his mind was drifting off the case in hand. His thought's tumbled around for a while but he could not shake the picture that his mind had conjured up of Isabel her naked body under his, those eyes looking up at him in ecstasy.

"God" he thought as the warmth began to flood his groin "what I'd give for a piece of that!"

"Sorry sir, did you say something?"

"No Roberts just thinking out aloud, right lets get on shall we?"

They spent the rest of the night interviewing customers and staff. As dawn broke they returned to the office to sift through the information they had. It was the only lead that they had in all the cases, and Matheson was determined to make it work for them. But all they had amounted to the vaguest of descriptions of a short blonde man, and a tall dark haired man, both in their mid-twenty's.

"Fuck that could be just about anyone Roberts!" "Yes sir not much to go on, you'd have thought that with all those people, someone would have noticed a bit more." he agreed

"You would" Matheson said.

The next day they confirmed the identity of the dead man. "What the fuck? It doesn't make any sense! I mean what have we got, low life scum bag, the girls, rich man, poor man, builder man, what next Robert's, beggar man, thief? What's the fucking connection? Other than having their heads blown off."

"Don't know sir, it might be random, no link at all, in the wrong place at the wrong time may-be." suggest Roberts.

"Maybe" said Matheson looking at the many notes and the trail of gruesome pictures that now formed a macabre gallery stuck on the display board behind his desk.

"I was sort of hoping it had gone away" Roberts said stifling a yawn. "Me too" said Matheson as he looked at all the pictures of the dead people's faces. His gaze intense, he tried desperately to extract something from the pictures, looking intently into each of their eye's willing them to tell him their story.

"Fucking zilch, that's what I'm getting Roberts, zilch!" The phone rang and Matheson snatched it up "Matheson!" he barked into the receiver. "Who's stolen your teddy?"

"Sorry who is this?" asked Matheson impatiently. "Isabel Conner"

"Oh, sorry, yes Isabel what do you need, I mean what do you want?" The double entendre in his voice was plain.

"Now, what do I need?" she said seeming to mull over her own question.

"You still there?" he asked listening to silence.

"Yes I've got something for you." She said in a soft voice that immediately flashed up a picture of her nipples straining at her pink sweater in Matheson's mind. "Nice" he said, without realising he was speaking aloud.

"Sorry what was that?"

"What was what?"

"You said—nice."

"Ah yes, nice, I meant, what you got for me then, something nice?"

"Yes a couple of things." He could hear the smile in her voice.

This time the nipples appeared without their sweater and he sighed.

"Lovely!" he said.

"Well I don't know about lovely, but I have information when can we meet?"

"where do you want to meet" he said playing a reversal role.

"Meet me at mine, I live in River View Tower, number 71; I think you'll be interested in what I have to show you.""Okay give me an hour to clear my desk and I'll be round." He said putting down the phone.

While Matheson was finishing up in his office, Anthony was waiting outside the TV studios. Steven had told him about the offer he had made to Cathy and that she was not interested. Anthony had not said anything to Steven but he was very unhappy that he had told the girl that sex with both of them was a stipulation of the job offer. For one thing it was freaky and would raise suspicion and for a second thing it was crass, childish and he did not want her to see him like that. He had always had a soft spot for the feisty girl who had livened up many a boring afternoon in Maths but he had always known she was out of his league. Until now. Thanks to Kelly and Sam he really thought he had something to offer now. They had told him often enough about how selfish men usually were and how special he was and now he wanted to try out his newfound technique on a girl of his own.

For weeks he hung around outside the TV studios and eventually his patience was rewarded when one evening, Cathy, flanked by two men came out of the studio. "Damn" Anthony said, he certainly was not going to approach her with them in attendance. The trio stood for a while laughing and talking and then the two men waved goodbye, going off in different directions. Cathy stayed where she was, waiting for a lift? A taxi?

"It's now or never" Anthony muttered to himself crossing the road.

"Hi Cathy!" Cathy had not seen him coming and turned her face, an expectant smile on her lips that faded as soon as she saw who it was.

"Oh it's you, I hardly recognised you, it is Anthony isn't it? "she said warily. Her expression was quizzical and not completely hostile Anthony was glad to see and he was even more glad to see that she had obviously noticed the difference in him, despite her guarded expression he could see her taking in his hair cut, his cool clothes, the fact that his face no longer looked like a pizza!

"Yes, look Cathy, I'm sorry about what Steve said, he was just joking you know!"

"He didn't sound like he was joking!" she said.

"Well he was, I mean to say, as if he or I or anyone for that matter would think that a classy girl like you would, well, you know."

Cathy looked at him uncertainly, mollified, it seemed by his heart felt speech.

"Well it was a pretty stupid thing to say."

"It was, but you know Steven he can be a bit hot headed!" She smiled up at him and Anthony thought that she really was quite beautiful and she certainly looked good on the small screen!

"I suppose," she said, relaxing, what are you doing these days Ant?"

"I'm just finishing training to make dentures, plates and that sort of thing, that's how Steven and I come to be working together.

"Oh right." Cathy looked at her watch.

"Bloody taxi, it is always late or doesn't come at all, I've got to tell them to change the company, a girl could freeze to death out here!" Cathy said

"Take my jacket" Anthony said, whipping it off and putting it around her shoulders.

"Thanks Ant!" she said sniffing the lapel "Nice aftershave, what is it?"

"Boss, I've always liked it" Ant said, more pleased than he would admit that she had noticed. She was a petite girl apart from her big bust and looking down he noticed that she had gold flecks in her rich auburn hair.

"If the taxi doesn't arrive we could walk into town go for a drink if you like?" Anthony held his breath for her reply.

"Yes, why not? Bugger the taxi, it's already 10 minutes late, lets go!" Anthony was delighted and fell into step beside her. As they reached the end of the road a taxi sped around it obviously heading for the studio at the end of the cul-de-sac. Anthony looked at Cathy. Would she flag it down? She made no move to and then looking up at his enquiring gaze said.

"Too late!"

Town was quiet and the bar that they sat in was half deserted. A group of girls on a night out sat in a corner and Cathy was gratified to see that they all looked at Anthony appreciatively. She was wracking her brains to try and remember what he had looked like at school. Definitely nothing like he did now. His hair cut looked expensive, and more than a little like David Beckham's latest cut, and his clothes were top of the range but understated, trendy. His teeth she especially noticed, they were white and even, she was pretty sure they had been very far from that at school. It was warm inside and the music that was being played was soft and soothing.

"Do you want something to eat?" Anthony asked.

"That would be nice." Cathy said picking up a menu

Once they had ordered and the waiter had brought them drinks and cutlery they began to talk, to reminisce about school and to talk about what each of them had been doing since. Anthony had to be a little economical with the truth of his activities in recent months but the dental technician smoke screen worked well and Cathy was really more interested in telling her own rags to riches story, how she had won a competition to read the local news and while she had been less than a perfect fit for that, the evening news producer had thought that she might be a great weather girl and so it had proved.

"He's a bit handsy" she said wrinkling her perfect nose, "You know, thinks I owe him something, but he's OK really, besides, I'm really good at reading the weather don't you think Ant?"

Anthony found himself struggling with the twin emotions of jealousy and tenderness for this lovely girl. Suddenly he could not bear the thought of anyone touching her.

"Of course you are, the best I've ever seen anyway!" he said and she rewarded him with a kiss on his cheek.

After the meal they walked to Cathy's flat. As they arrived at her front door on the second floor she handed Anthony's jacket back to him.

"Thanks Anthony, I had a really nice evening."

"So did I!" Ant said, "We must do it again!"

"Yes, how about Friday night?" Cathy said, Anthony's heart leapt with delight.

"Definitely!" he said. "Shall I pick you up here at about 7.30?"

"Yes that would be nice." Standing on tip toes, Cathy held her soft lips to his for a moment and then darted her little tongue out to give him the smallest, briefest of licks to the inside of his upper lip. Anthony felt as though he had been electrocuted. He wanted more than anything to take her in his arms, to pick her up and take her inside, and explore every inch of her lovely body, but he knew that would be a mistake, he had to take things slowly. So he smiled down at her and said.

"Goodnight Cathy, see you Friday?"

"Thanks again Ant!"

Matheson pushed the button to take the lift to the seventh floor. He waited a while then pushed it again.! "Come on' he jabbed repeatedly at the lift 'UP' button.

"It's out of order mate" said a chap in overalls, walking to his ground floor flat and smirking as he opened the door, "hope you're feeling fit!" Matheson sighed and started up the stairs. A young man almost knocked him off his feet as he came down stairs struggling into a jacket. From the floor above someone called "Night Ant!" and the young man called "night!" back.

The pungent smell of disinfectant filled Matheson's nostrils and he noticed the freshly cleaned floor. "Lazy bastards'" he thought as he noticed the black 'tide line' of dirt left in the corners where the mop had missed. On the seventh floor, an array of greenery greeted him. Pots containing cactus and climbing ivy's framed a doorway. In amongst the ivy, a plaque contained what he was looking for, number 71, Isabel's flat. He tapped on the door tentatively with the knocker. A few moments later Isabel appeared at the door smiling.

"Hi Sammy come on in, dump your coat in there." she said pointing to one of the two bedrooms. Matheson entered the small bedroom looking for somewhere to hang his coat; eventually he just threw it on the bed.

"Would you like a drink? Tea, coffee, something stronger?"

"Something stronger, thanks."

"Scotch, Brandy, beer?"

"Brandy please."

Isabel walked over to the drinks cabinet and bent down to retrieve a bottle from the glass shelf. Matheson took in the perfect outline of her buttocks beneath her thin skirt. "Straight up, Ice?"

"As it comes, Isabel, thanks."

"There you go," she said, handing him the biggest brandy glass he had ever seen. "Are you trying to get me drunk Isabel?"

"Who me?, as if, she said smiling and flashing her eyes under half closed lids. "Right what you got?," he said.

"Well you'll probably go bananas but, do you remember the cottage? The two girls?"

"Yes go on."

"Well we have a different blood type."

"What do you mean?"

"Different to the girls." she said watching his reaction.

"When did this happen?' he said confused "and why now, five weeks later?"

Isabel shrugged "Different technology, everything was all mixed up."

"Oh I see." he said. "Mixed up how?"

"I don't know, some problem at the lab, heads are rolling, don't worry!" "I should bloody hope so, the time we've lost on this!" Matheson's jaw was set. "What blood type?'

"O"

"Great". Pause. "You don't know how much this case has tortured me Isabel. It's all but knackered my marriage, but hey things can change, two leads in two days, God I could kiss you!"

"Well, why don't you?" She said leaning towards him.

Matheson found himself mesmerised by her as her lips met his. He felt himself drowning in the depths of her eyes as her tongue entered his mouth probing gently, meeting his tongue, igniting a spark in his brain and he surrendered to her charms, her taste, and her smell.

"You sure?" he said softly.

"Never been more sure." she said, as Matheson's hands explored her body lingering on every curve. As their passion increased they started pulling at each other's clothing. Soon Matheson was kissing and sucking her breasts, delighting in the taste of the large full dark nipples. She took his erect cock in her hand exploring its length with her fingers then pushing him back gently on the couch, she replaced her hand with her mouth. Matheson groaned and slid his fingers between the wet lips of her pussy. The sensation hardened his cock until it ached and he was desperate to plunge his whole length into her. They rolled off the sofa onto the floor. Straddling his face she lowered herself onto him taking his cock into her mouth again. With her wetness over his face, he had an urge to taste her very being, her inner self, and his taste buds tingled as his tongue explored her sweetness. She moved her clitoris onto his tongue, the hard swollen bud a contrast to the soft folds of her vulva, she groaned, urging him on, and he circled her clitoris with his tongue, teasing it till she exploded raising her head from his cock and pressing her pussy down on him riding out her orgasm. Feeling her spasm as her orgasm ripped through her almost tipped him to the edge. Pulling her over he entered her from behind clasping her full hips, admiring her soft rounded buttocks. He moved slowly savouring every stroke, his hands moved from her hips to her straining breasts, the firmness the roundness, the hard nipples that he rolled between his fingers, his ejaculation was close. His breath ragged, he slid his hands around her waist gently stroking her skin then holding her hips firmly he pumped, each stroke of his cock bringing him closer to ecstasy. And then with a loud groan he exploded into her. As his climax ripped through him he felt her beginning to come again and as her vagina spasmed with another powerful orgasm, he carried on pumping, desperate to feel every exquisite moment of the best orgasm he had ever had.

Breathing hard, they lay beside each other, their legs entwined.

"What you thinking Sammy" she asked.

"Oh nothing", actually he was thinking of his wife and how he had just betrayed her.

"You're not regretting what just happened?" she asked

"Never!" He said reaching over to give her a kiss.

She threw her arms around him. "Now you're mine for ever Sammy!" she said holding him in a strong embrace. Matheson felt uneasy, her embrace was somehow too needy, too desperate. Ten minutes passed then half an hour and he was still in her embrace.

"Isabel?"

"Yes Sammy?"

"I've got to go" he said softly.

"Oh must you?"

"Yes I must, I haven't been home much over the last two days, I have a wife and family"

"Oh poo!" Isabel stuck her bottom lip out. "When will I see you again Sammy?"

"Soon! I promise!" He said struggling out of her grip.

As he dressed, she lay there like a naked goddess, and he could feel himself getting aroused again. He clenched his jaw and gave her a final kiss. He was about to leave the flat when she said

"Sammy wait"

Rising from the floor she walked naked towards the kitchen. Matheson watched every move of her swaying hips. She returned with something in her hand, but Matheson could barely tear his eyes away from her flawless body to look at what she was offering him.

"Here is my report" smiling, she was very pleased with the effect that her nakedness was having on her lover.

"'Oh yes the report. Thanks Isabel!"

"Just one more kiss Sammy?" she asked flashing her big brown eyes, which Matheson noticed were exactly the same colour as her wide nipples.

"Okay one more'!" He said as his resolve weakened. Her lips touched his and he could feel his blood pressure rising, he was lost and at her mercy. Raw passion took over his senses as she fished in his trousers and once again held his cock in her hand. Sliding down to her knees she took him into her mouth, moving up and down the length of his straining cock. He began to tremble and held on tight to her shoulders as molten semen exploded into her mouth. He almost collapsed as his legs gave way beneath him.

"Wow that was some last kiss!" he said

"That is the sort of kiss you can expect from now on!" she said digging her claws ever deeper into him. He was well and truly hooked, helpless to resist her charms. Grinning from ear to ear he made his way home.

Over the years Matheson had become an expert in slipping into bed without disturbing his wife, Laura.

In the morning she greeted him with

"Oh you're here then, what unearthly time did you get in last night?"
Matheson knew full well his wife was a creature of habit. She ran her life and the house almost like a military camp. She was a big woman, athletic, hard like a shot putter, dark hair, a bit of a Catherine Zeta Jones look alike. She was up at seven thirty, breakfast, only three cups of tea a day, eight thirty, eleven o'clock, eight thirty in the evening, all on the dot, then bed at ten thirty.

"Not that late love, somewhere around one, you were sound, anyway must dash got a lot on!" he said planting a kiss on her cheek.

At the station he found Roberts already at his desk.

"Morning Roberts."

"Morning sir you sound a bit chirpy today, got your leg over?"

"Maybe, or maybe I got another lead yesterday!"

"What's the lead sir?" Roberts looked up eagerly

"Remember the cottage murders?"

"Sure do, nasty!" said Roberts recalling the horror he had witnessed.

"Well forensics have found another person's blood, so there was someone else at the scene after all!".

"That's a turn up, who gave you the lead?"

"Oh forensics came up with it, new technology, some cock up, whatever, they gave it to me!Get up to the hospital Roberts, get the names of anyone treated that night". "Right you are sir!"

A few hours later Robert's arrived back at the office clutching a fist full of paperwork.

"There you go sir!"

"Blimey they were busy at casualty that night!"

"Yes Sir, one of their busiest they said.".

"Right let's lay them out, right, she's out, he's out, they're out" Matheson sifted expertly through the records.

"Why's that Sir?"

"They're all kids stupid'!"

Robert blushes, "So they are!"

Matheson continued sifting, "too old, too young, too ill, right that leaves ten possible, four men, six women, cutting out the women for now, we'll concentrate on the men." He paused a while staring at the four names.

'Right they're yours Robert's', he said handing him two of the records.

The phone rang.

"Matheson?"

"Sammy I need to see you." Isabel said in a silly baby voice.

"I can't just now, I'm following up that lead you gave me".

"I want to see you, please!" she said in a louder more insistent voice.

Matheson felt a twinge of alarm, he did not like the way things were going with Isabel, he hoped she was not going to be trouble. "I cant, I'll see you tomorrow evening."

The phone went dead.

CHAPTER 9

Matheson had a sense of foreboding as he replaced the phone on its cradle. "Fuck did she just hang up? She must have!" He frowned, started to ring back then stopped. "I don't need this shit"; he mumbled getting up and walking out of the office. On the way he rang his wife from his mobile.

'Hi love, yes sorry, I 'm running late again, just got a big lead on the case, hopefully I'll home for dinner, bye, love you!" Matheson drove away in his car heading for an address scrawled on his note pad. He walked up the path of the nondescript house and knocked on the door. The door opened and a man in his thirties with dark receding hair answered it. He looked bookish, pale and weedy, Matheson knew without asking a single question that he was not the man they were looking for. "Detective Matheson" Matheson flashed his badge, I just need to ask you a few questions" he decided to carry on, even although he knew it was pointless.

"Come in detective." the man looked puzzled. "What's this about detective?"

"Just routine investigations, sir," said Matheson. After ten minutes, satisfied that the man had been at the hospital after a fall on the stairs that required stitches, Matheson left. His keen eye had spotted get well soon cards on the mantel piece and, while the man was out of the room getting the sick note that the hospital had written for him, he looked them over. One of them had a hand drawn stair case with a stick man falling down them and the words *"What are you like, you clutz?!*

Matheson gave the sick note a cursory glance. "Sorry to have troubled you sir" he said.Once back at the car and being totally pissed off that he had wasted precious time he shouted. "Bollocks!" as he sat in his car he flicked open his mobile and rang Roberts.

"Any luck?"

"No sir, I've just been to one, the bloke passed away, died in a motorbike accident a couple of weeks back"

"Fucking bikes I hate them, I hope my son doesn't want one" Matheson said

"You know what they call bikers down at the hospital don't you sir?" Roberts said

"Yeah yeah, organ donors, very funny."

"D'you think we can call it a wrap for today sir?" Roberts asked tentatively, it was nearly 7 pm.

'Yeah, I did no better, Oh well two to go, fingers crossed, see you tomorrow Roberts.' "Yes, thanks sir, goodnight!"

But instead of going home, Matheson drove towards the other side of town. He was on the hunt. Picking up the piece of paper his eyes focused on the next address scrawled down, 41 Crowstone Road. On the drive to the address Matheson got a sort of butterfly feeling in his gut, the feeling he always got before something big happened. "I can feel it in me water!" he muttered to himself. Pulling up outside the address, he sat there rounding his shoulders as if warming up for a fight, for some reason he felt nervous. Right let's go he thought, and as he walked up the street he clocked the numbers of the houses counting them down to 41. He was about to ring the door bell when suddenly it flew open.

"Yes what do you want?" said a swarthy man abruptly he had a thick foreign accent and was holding car keys in his hand, Mathseson got the impression he was going out to his car to collect something. He did not have a coat on so Matheson guessed he was planning to go straight back indoors. He relaxed; this looked like a typical domestic scene. He took his badge out of his inside pocket and said

"Detective Sammy Math—"

The man's fist flew out and hit Matheson on the bridge of his nose. The punch knocked Matheson out cold and he fell to the ground. The man then returned inside the house for a few minutes, struggling into a denim jacket he jumped over Matheson's inert body, and then ran off down the street.

Minutes later Matheson regained consciousness, raising himself to his feet he stumbled, leaning on the wall to the front of the house he steadied himself. He shook his head to clear the fuzziness blurring his vision and drops of blood from his nose sprayed over the white paint of the half open front door. With his senses returning he gently pushed at the front door, wiping his nose on his sleeve he reached into his inside pocket to his 9mm Glock police firearm. Pushing the door open fully with one hand he carefully entered the house. He glanced at the stairs leading upwards from the left, he then moved commando style forward—room to the right, kitchen, nothing, inching forward, dining room, nothing, lounge nothing. Starting quietly up the stairs his back pressed to the wall, he reached the top where a small landing had three doors leading off it.

As he glanced into the open door nearest him, his eyes took in a grotesque scene. Two bedrooms led off the landing, and in the door nearest him and the other, there was a naked woman, their legs strapped and spread-eagled to the bedsteads. Not knowing whether his assailant was still in the house, Matheson pressed himself to the wall, and sliding along peered into the first room. The woman on the bed lay still, was blind folded and gagged, but had no obvious injuries, her nipples stood out like organ stops probably with fear and the cold and her legs were spread so wide that despite the fact that she had a thick dark mass of pubic hair the crimson entrance to her vagina was clearly visible. Judging by her body the woman was in her 40's at least, but not in bad shape, Matheson could not help noticing. He moved on. Checking the second bedroom the woman in there was much younger, but lay in an identical position her pussy shaved and affording Matheson a detailed view of her clitoris and the folds of her vulva. Her nipples, he noticed interestedly were the exact same shade as the other woman's maybe they were mother and daughter? Apart from being completely naked and vulnerable she also appeared unhurt.

Adrenalin pumped through Matheson veins as he looked at the last door on the landing, which was closed. "Come out you mother-fucker!" he shouted. A muffled noise from behind made him spin round. It was the younger of the two women struggling against her bonds. With as much reassurance as he could muster through the dull ache of what he was sure was a broken nose, he said

"It's OK, I'm a detective you're going to be alright!" His voice sounded nasal and the metallic taste of blood was bitter in his mouth.

Matheson moved towards the closed bathroom door and said "Police, open the door!"

Nothing. Matheson summoned his strength and kicked it in only to be met by a toolbox and tools set out on the floor.

"What the fuck?"

Returning to the two women he released them, and they both wrapped themselves in the bedding.

"Are you Okay, what did he do to you?" Matheson asked.

"Nothing," The younger woman replied, you were just in time!" They were both sobbing and shaking.

"OK get dressed and I'll get a female officer here and an ambulance.

"Matheson put a call in to the station and it was not long before blues and two were arriving at the house.

"Good God sir what happened to you?" the first officer to arrive took in the sight of Matheson his dried blood dark on his shirt.

"Never mind" Matheson said, his head was throbbing now.

Sipping tea that the female officer had made for them the two women began to tell their story.

They were, as Matheson had suspected, mother and daughter, Louise and Sarah Johnson, the daughter, Sarah was just visiting giving moral support to her mother while some plumbing work was being done in the bathroom; Sarah had taken the plumber a cup of tea, then turned to go back downstairs. He had grabbed her from behind and covered her mouth with a cloth." She sobbed into her mother's shoulder "It must have contained some sort of drug" she said, "because I can't remember anything else till I woke up lying on the bed. The thought of what he might have done . . . ." she shuddered, "I felt sick. Then I thought of mum, what had he done to her? I couldn't move, I couldn't speak, I felt so helpless." Her mother comforted her.

'I'm fine he didn't touch me, I came up to see where you were, and when I saw you tied up there . . . . ." The girl's mother shook her head. "He surprised me and grabbed me from behind". Louise Johnson turned to Matheson "Like Sarah I remember nothing till I woke up on the bed."

"I got a glimpse of him", said Matheson, 'Can you remember anything that might help us get him? Who recommended him for the work?" he asked.

"Oh he called one day saying he was doing odd jobs in the area, he gave his card, so I called him to fix the leak, silly really I should have known better."

"Have you got the card?"

"Yes it's on the little table in the hall." she said, going to get it.

"It's gone'" she said returning empty handed.

"Are you sure it was there Mum?" Sarah asked her.

"Yes love, quite sure."

"He must have taken it" Matheson said. "I think that's enough for now, you should both go in the Ambulance and get checked over" The two women nodded. While Matheson was outside calling in the ambulance crew, mother and daughter sat talking, and when he came back with the ambulance men, Sarah said

"I've remembered something!".

Matheson raised his eyebrows.

"He had a tattoo on his arm, a Chinese man with a knife through his head. I remember thinking how gruesome it was."

"Good, which arm left or right, high up, low on the fore arm?" Matheson asked, he had found that giving a multiple choice sometimes helped to get the right answer.

"Right, on the forearm." said Sarah

"Thanks ladies, Oh and I nearly forgot, the reason I came here tonight, I have a record of a Mr. James Johnson of this address having attended the A&E department of the local hospital on the 21st of last month. Do you know anything about that?

For the first time that evening, the women smiled and looked at each other. "Yes, that's my brother, Jamie, he's a bit clumsy. He originally tried to fix the leak in the bathroom, ended up slipping over and hitting his shoulder on the side of the bath, cut himself really badly!" Sarah said. "He's away on a field trip at the moment, he teaches history at the University."

As the women left with the ambulance crew, Matheson had an eerie feeling that someone was behind him, and spun round.

"Hi Sammy."

"Isabel." he replied.

"I need to see you" she said kissing him, some of his dried blood smearing onto her lips. She did not seem to care and her hand snaked down rubbing his crotch area.

"Pack it in, someone might see!"

"Who cares?" her eyes looked wild, challenging.

"Okay, Okay Look, I'll see you tomorrow night, I need to get home and get cleaned up now." he said pushing her away. For a moment he saw something dangerous flash in her eyes, and then she sidled up to him again and said
"Aw poor baby, you're going to have two lovely shiners!" she kissed his eyelids.

"See you tomorrow big boy" she said making her way to where her team were dusting for fingerprints. Matheson thought how that sounded more like a threat than a promise and he felt the feeling of foreboding again, a feeling that was becoming the most consistent feeling associated with any thought of Isabel, somehow he knew it wasn't going to end well. As she walked away from him, she slowly and deliberately wiped the blood off her face with a tissue, poking the end of a very pink tongue out at Matheson as she climbed the staircase.

Matheson shut the door of the lounge; his thought's disturbed by Isabel's demands and the thinly veiled threats that lay behind them. She did not seem to care who found out about them whereas he most certainly did.

Going outside to his car, he rang Roberts.

"Hi Sir, I just heard, do you want me to come down?"

"No Roberts, it's all over, I'm going home to clean up, maybe do a little detour to the hospital, I think my nose is broken, still I was no oil painting to begin with eh?" "Are you alright sir?"

"Yes." Matheson said but he was very far from it, he now had a very bad feeling about Isabel and the evening's events had done nothing to calm him.

He called at the hospital and was grateful for the attention of a young nurse who cleaned him up so that he would not look so frightening when he got home. A doctor confirmed that his nose was broken and packed it with gauze, Matheson knew the routine he had it broken a few times in the past, playing rugby.

There was nothing they could do about his shirt but his face looked better although his eyes were beginning to blacken now and he wanted to get home to Laura before he looked too much like the stuff of nightmares.

As she always did Laura vacillated between concern and anger when he got injured on the job. He knew that she worried and was always jumpy when he was working on violent cases, he tried to keep as much of the detail from her as he could but she always got to know, the police wives jungle drums were pretty powerful. But Laura loved him and he knew that however much she railed at the police force and the job she was only worried about him. He let her fuss over him and apply cold compresses to his eyes and the bridge of his nose, and felt even more guilty about what had happened between him and Isabel.

The next day was taken up by paperwork from the night before and a visit to an enormously overweight man in his mid twenties who wheezed loudly as he shuffled around his unkempt flat that smelt faintly of urine. He had, told them, he visited A&E after slipping on the floor and banged his head on the kitchen sink."

"Figures, slob" Matheson said under his breath to Roberts as the man showed them into a filthy kitchen its cheap aluminium sink bearing the indent of his large sweaty head.

"Another dead end." Roberts said as they stepped gratefully outside into the fresh air.
"I just know that I had one of the killers in front of me Roberts; he fit the description of one of the men in the Chinese perfectly, dark hair, tall, mid twenties."

"What happened, sir?" Roberts asked tentatively

"He gave me the slip, knocked me out cold, should have seen it coming, hell I'm always telling the men to be careful, I was sloppy." said Matheson

"At least you know what he looks like sir."

"Yes and that's not all', Matheson described the tattoo that Sarah had seen to Roberts.

"Can't be many with a tattoo like that, can there?"

"Right a drink I think." Matheson broke another couple of caplets out of a blister pack and swallowed them without water.

At the pub, the smell of a real log fire greeted them, its warmth enveloping them. "What will it be then Roberts?"

"Are we off duty sir?"

"Yes, come on what's your tipple?"

"Oh mines a Guinness and you can call me Jim!"

"Okay Guinness it is and you can call me Sammy."

"Cheers Sammy!" said Jim lifting the glass to his lips, hmmm, black gold you can't beat it!"

"Little bit bitter for me, I'm a cider man!"

'Yes I like a cider in the summer, very refreshing" said Jim

"Lovely pub this Jim" said Matheson getting up to go to the toilets. As he stood in the washroom he looked at his black eyes and swollen nose. The last thing he felt like doing was visiting Isabel but somehow he knew that he would suffer if he didn't. Maybe the drink would give him some enthusiasm.

As he walked back he glanced into the snooker room of the pub that had it's own little bar.

Hurrying back to the table Roberts looked up at him, reading his expression.

"What's up?"

"We're back on duty, he's in the other bar!"

"Who?"

"The killer, the one I saw yesterday, right, ready?" Matheson put his hand on his gun inside his jacket. Roberts followed suit.

"Police! Nobody move, stay where you are!" he shouted as they ran through to the snooker bar.

Two women screamed.
Matheson focused on his target, he then said,

"Stay where you are." He drew his gun, pointing it straight at the man. A stark reminder of the pain he had felt the day before made him want to shoot the fucker there and then.

"Cuff him Roberts" said Matheson.

"Yes sir!" said Roberts, expertly clipping the handcuffs around the man's wrists.

"Landlord!" Matheson called.

A flustered man stepped forward, his face red.

"Take down the names and addresses of everyone here" Said Matheson scanning the room making a mental note of the five people present.

"Everybody?"

"Yes everybody, you as well" he continued flicking open his phone and calling for back up.

"My officers will be here in a moment, make sure you get those names right, they'll be checking!"

The Landlord set about the task earnestly.

"Right you, out!" said Matheson as they manhandled their prisoner to Matheson's car.

"Please mind your head" said Matheson as he deliberately smacked the prisoners head against the metalwork of the car.

'Fuck. You bastards!" he said grimacing, his foreign accent making the work fuck sound more like fook.

"Shut the fuck up, you scum." Said Matheson, pushing him in further.

"In you get Roberts; we'll come back for your car later!"

Robert's aimed his gun at the prisoner.

"Sit still and not a word!" he demanded.

Back at the station the prisoner was booked in, and then thrown in a cell.

Matheson sat quietly in his office making notes, questions, likely answers that might come back at him, counter questions.

"Matheson!" came a familiar voice

Matheson looks to the doorway,

"Guv. What you doing here?" he said surprised. Andy Sims was his direct superior, although the two men had very little time for each other. They had trained together and matched each other rung for rung on the promotion ladder until Matheson had missed out on the board that had given Sims his latest promotion. Matheson was convinced that there had been some sort of sharp practice by Sims, he had always been a slimy bastard. But so far he had no proof and tried to keep out of the man's way.

"Hey up Sammy, I believe you got my prisoner in the cell?"

"What do you mean your prisoner?" Matheson said.

"The Romanian rapist, we've been after him for months!" explained Sims

"Get lost Andy, a rapist he maybe and I think he did make his intentions pretty clear at Crowstone Avenue, but he is also one of the ones that's been blowing all those people up!" Matheson countered.

"Yeah I heard about that, spread-eagled and naked the women weren't they? D'you get any photos?"

"Fuck off you perv, no I didn't get photos but trust me, he's not your man, we've got a description, he fits the bill perfectly.

"Watch it Sammy with the lip, I am your superior and I was asking about the photos because they could be material evidence."

"Yes, of course you were." Matheson was not reckless enough to think that he could be as rude as he wanted without repercussions.

"Sorry guv, uncalled for." He muttered.

"Sammy, Sammy, mate I'd love for him to be the one, but he's only been in the country a short while. There's no way he could have killed those other people, I know you have been struggling, I've been thinking about giving you a hand, it's obviously getting on top of you and now that I have finished with this case, maybe I will."

"But . . ." Matheson clenched his teeth to stop himself saying what he wanted to.

"Sorry Sammy!" Andy Sims said, looking anything but, "don't feel too bad mate, after all you are furthering the cause! We had him in on another case; he had an alibi so we had to let him go. I have his passport here in my hand, look" Sims handed him the passport.

Matheson's face dropped as he looked at the travel document and the realisation that this was not the man they had been looking for began to hit home.

"Bollocks, so basically you fucked up and let the low life go then I saved your bacon?" He said, throwing the passport on the desk. "Fucking typical, well you can have all this crap!" he moaned, shoving all the evidence they had collected and the statements from the women across the desk at his superior.

"Thanks Sammy, I won't forget I!" said Sims laughing, giving Matheson a pat on his tense shoulder. "Oh and if you find yourself out of your depth with the explosives case, just give me a shout!"

Matheson felt his head ache returning and took the blister pack of Anadin extra out of his pocket. There were none left. He threw them across the desk and they skidded off onto the floor.
Roberts picked the empty pack up as he entered the room
"Who died sir?"

"We did, well we might as well have", said Matheson, "fucking lost our suspect. Turns out he's some bloody Romanian rapist."

"I wondered what the Guv wanted; he had that smirk on his face, you know the one" said Roberts.

Matheson did know the one.

"No fucking wonder, we just sorted his case for him, bet we get no credit either." Matheson growled.

"Yep they'll take all the glory, bound to, the fuckers!" agreed Roberts

"Fuck it!" said Matheson suddenly.

"What?"

"I forgot to ring the wife," he said dialling his home number.

"Yes pet I'll be home for dinner, yes won't be long". He said "See you tomorrow Roberts"

"See you tomorrow sir."

Steam filled the air as Matheson showered away the day's grime. He dressed casually, T-shirt, track suit bottoms, slippers, no socks, and no pants. A habit formed over many years, he wanted to be ready for action just in case he sensed his luck may be in with Laura. When they had first been married, before the birth of their son Tom, they had often ended up naked in front of the fire on the sheepskin rug. Those days were pretty much gone now, but he still like the feeling of the brushed insides of the track suit bottoms against his skin. He came up behind Laura in the kitchen and lifting her dark hair from her neck he kissed her gently, she smelt familiar and her perfume made him remember the nights they had spent in his car when they were courting when the smell of her would fill his mini.

"Dinner won't be long, pour a glass of wine, I'll have one as well" she said.

Just then his mobile rang.

"Isabel!" he had completely forgotten that he had agreed to meet her. He pressed the red button cutting her off.

"'Who's that love, not more work?" Laura never normally asked who was calling him, he was always on the damn mobile for one thing or another, but she always got a bit clingy and jumpy when he got a whack.

"Roberts, I rung off, he can handle things by himself for once!" he said turning his phone to silent.

Across town standing in front of her 7th floor window looking down over the river that formed a dark ribbon through the town lit up on either bank Isabel stared at her mobile. She felt rage building inside her, he had a lot to learn that Sammy Matheson, no-one but no-one hung up on her! She dialled again.

'Detective Roberts." the young detective answered on the third ring.

"Oh hi, it's Isabel Conner."

"Isabel. What can I do for you?" said Roberts trying to impress

"Have you got Sammy's home number, I wouldn't ask only it's some information he asked for, he did give his number to me but I think I left it in the office. I've just had an email, something he wanted to know about. I should really let him know."

"Sure" Roberts said and reeled off the number. "Anything else I can do for you?" Like most of the men in the station Roberts was not immune to the promise and overt sexuality of Isabel Conner, and in that moment he had a vague hope that she might have phoned on a pretext of getting Matheson's number, and that them both being single, she might just be interested in him. He waited for her reply, but she had already hung up.

"Up yours, stuck up bitch!" he muttered to himself.

At Matheson's the phone rang.

"Get that love, will you, I'm just dishing up" said his wife.

"Christ, can't a man get a minute's peace for God's sake?" he grumbled aloud, taking the cordless out of its stand by the television.

"Hello?" he said abruptly.

"Sammy is that you?"

"Isabel!" he whispered, "What the fuck are you doing ringing me here, and where did you get my number?" he was past angry now.

"Oh that imbecile Robert's gave it to me, what a geek!" She laughed.

"Roberts! What do you want?" he said louder his voice low and menacing.

"You said you were coming round."

"I will, later, I promise!" he would have said anything to get her off the phone.

"You better or else!"

"Or else?" He paused, fear making the hairs on the back of his neck stand up. "What do you mean, or else?"

The phone went dead.

"Fuck, fuck!"

"What's up love?" Laura walked past him carrying his dinner to the dining room table.

"'Oh it's Roberts, just wanted a couple of pointers on this case we're involved with."

"My God Sammy, what's the matter with that place, does everything fall apart just because your not there?" she asked placing his dinner on the table.

"Something like that love, I may have to go in later, just for a bit."

He said waiting for her reaction

Sitting down at the table, Laura said "This is lovely having dinner together, it seems like ages!" Matheson knew this tactic, pretend it's not happening and it will go away.

"Yes, it is" he said placing his hand on hers giving it a gentle squeeze. "Where's Tom?"

"Round his mates, we have the place to ourselves" she said.

Matheson sensed a twinkle in her eye, one he had seen many times over the years. He thought of his betrayal again and his face clouded.

"Are you okay; you look miles away, what's up?" Laura said.

"Just thinking about the case it's getting to me, one step forward ten back!"

"Can't you just forget about it tonight? Please, just for me?" Laura said softly.

"I'll try love, I'll try."

They finished their meal and then moved into the lounge where they curled up on the settee in front of the fire, talking about this and that. After the 24 hours he had had it was lovely to sit and talk about whether or not they should cancel the milk delivery and get it from the supermarket with the rest of the groceries, and whether the gutters needed doing, or the windows cleaning, ordinary stuff, the stuff that marriages and life are made of.

The fire crackled in the grate and Laura's soft lips found his. He knew this kiss, it was the kind of kiss that she gave to show that she loved him, it wouldn't go any further, not because she didn't want it to, but because she knew he was too tired, and he was, the thought of his wife's familiar body was tempting but every fibre of his body was aching for sleep and soon his eyelids became heavy and started drooping. Laura's head was on his shoulder and her hand in his. He loved her and he knew that she worried about him. She really did not deserve him cheating on her, he didn't really know why he had done it, but one thing was sure, he was going to have to put Isabel straight, especially if she was going to be difficult. Maybe he would make love to Laura on the sheepskin rug after a little doze, the wine and the thought of that helped him drift off with a smile on his face.

Laura left him asleep and went to watch a movie in the dining room. She knew that he would not need much of a nap to revive him and then she hoped that they would make love, it seemed a long time since they had, and despite the fact that he looked so battered and bruised she wanted to feel him inside her again, she needed to feel that connection to him to know that they were alright.

From his deep sleep, Matheson could hear his name being called, 'Sammy, SAMMY'

"What?" he muttered as he forced his eyes open.

Laura was standing over him.

"What's up love? You scared the shit out of me" he said.

"Someone called Isabel's been on the phone, they need you at the office, something's come up!"

"Isabel? What did she say, I mean what did she want?" he was wide-awake now.

"She didn't say anything, just that you were needed, she wasn't going to discuss the case with me was she?"

"Fuck, what's the time love?"

"Ten o'clock", she replied.

"Oh I better go, you going to be alright?"

"Case of having to be." she said with a sigh.

"Sorry love I'll make it up to you", he promised. "Yes and how many times I have heard that?" she replied sternly
As he made his way across town to Isabel's flat Matheson was in turmoil, the woman had shown him clearly how easy it would be to get at Laura and he began to feel real fear. There was no doubt that Isabel was a lovely woman and sex with her had blown his mind, but did he want to sacrifice his marriage over her? The hell he did! And yet here he was, she only had to say jump and he said how high? He felt annoyed with himself but at the same time, thinking about the amazing night he had spent with Isabel had his cock twitching perilously in his pants. He was weak and pathetic and he did not deserve Laura, but he would do all he could to make sure that Isabel did not wreck his marriage, the thought of losing Laura made him feel physically sick.

He sat for a moment in his car at the foot of Isabel's block of flats. Most of the flats had light on over the 10 floors. As he tried to gather his thoughts into some semblance of order a young man, his arm around a much shorter woman came up to the front of the flats. As he watched the girl turned her face up and the young man took it in both hands, kissing her gently on the lips. The man, illuminated in the light of the street lamp looked familiar to Matheson, and then he remembered he had passed him on the stairs the last time he was here. The woman had nice hair, gold highlights picked out in the yellowish glare.

Sighing deeply, Matheson got out of his car and made his way to the lifts. They were working today. Although, he thought, his anger and adrenalin would have carried him up the 7 flights quite easily.

CHAPTER 10

He made a bee line straight for Isabel's, and rattled the knocker hard, the sound echoed through the corridors.

A door opened next to Isabel's flat and a man popped his head out.

"Where's the fucking fire mate?" he shouted at Matheson.

"Police, shut the fuck up!" he said flashing his badge.

"Oh" the man said shutting the door of his flat hastily.

Matheson was about to knock again when Isabel answered the door. 'There you are Sammy!' she said in a tone that suggested he was a bit late back from fetching a newspaper. Before he could answer, she put her mouth over his. He could smell and taste drink. She guided him, lips glued to his, along the hallway and into the bedroom.

Breaking away he said. "What's your game Isabel? I'm not your plaything to fuck about with!"

"Shhh Sammy no talking" she said kissing him harder, expertly hooking her leg behind his and toppling him onto the bed.

Despite himself Matheson felt his anger dissipating, He groaned as his cock stiffened, he seemed powerless to resist the passion and beauty of this woman and as her soft lips found the tip of his throbbing penis, her tongue pushing into the tiny opening he surrendered himself to her with a groan. Any thoughts he had had about telling her to lay off were forgotten now as his body responded to her teasing and he exploded in one incredible orgasm.

They made love for most of the night, until he fell into an exhausted dreamless sleep. She slept beside him her lithe body finally satisfied. She had made love like a wild thing, clung to him like a limpet, and her passion had overwhelmed him. He was immensely turned on but he was also un-nerved, with a deep sense of impending doom.

At some time just before it was light he felt her on him again her mouth around his penis. He kept his eyes closed and let her do what she wanted. She mounted him lowering herself onto his battered cock. She rode him with a hunger, a desperation that had him at the brink in minutes watching her from half closed lids as she played with herself as she worked up and down on his cock. She came noisily and collapsed beside him again and they slept. It was light when he woke again and he was alone. Padding through the flat he called her name, but there was no reply. Strange, he thought searching the flat, until in the kitchen he found a note. Let yourself out; see you when I see you, Isabel, X.

"She was a strange one, and no mistake, but a great fuck" he touched himself gingerly, his cock was throbbing pleasantly from over use and his balls felt sticky and smelly.

He showered, noting that she had a lady shaver and a tube of hair remover on the windowsill of the small bathroom, and he wondered which one she used on her pussy. He thought it must be the cream, his tongue had encountered no stubble in its frequent forays south over the night, he loved the smoothness of a hairless pussy, you could get to everything a lot easier, he didn't mind going down on his lovers, but he really did not like getting pubic hair caught in his teeth. He thought about Laura, how long was it since they had had oral sex? So long he could not remember, but still there was something comforting and familiar about their lovemaking and he felt a pang of guilt, he just didn't seem to be able to help himself.

After he had dressed and with his detective's head on he couldn't resist a quick nose around the flat. All the normal stuff that you would expect, nothing unusual, apart from the fact that everything was almost pathologically tidy. He left and as he did so he noticed the young man he had seen the evening before coming out of a flat on the 2nd floor.

They smiled at each other briefly, a man thing, they had got lucky and they both knew it.

Across Town Laura Matheson was worried, it was not like Sammy not to call. She remembered the call that he had had the night before, and dialled 1471 getting a mobile number as the last number called. She pressed 3 as instructed, to return the call. After a few seconds the call was answered.

"Hi, is this Isabel?"

"Yes who's speaking?"

"Sammy Matheson's wife, you rang last night, do you remember?"

Isabel paused to gather her thoughts; it was not hard to imagine what the woman wanted.

"Hello, are you still there?" Matheson's wife said into the silence.

"Sorry, yes" replied Isabel. "How can I help?"

"Sammy left his mobile last night, when he rushed out, I've called the office but he wasn't there. Do you know where he is?"

"Sorry no I don't" said Isabel thinking that the last time she had seen him; he had been lying on top of her duvet, his cock still wet from her.

"He was supposed to be meeting you at the office last night, that's what you said, you don't know where he went after that?"

"He never arrived", Isabel said, immediately wishing she hadn't.

Laura was becoming confused and was starting to get annoyed, surely after ringing up so late on urgent business, if that someone didn't turn up you would be concerned enough to ring to see where they were?" But this woman seemed to know nothing. Alarm bells were ringing in Laura's mind but she was not sure what it was she was suspicious of at the moment. First and foremost though, she needed to know where Sammy was.
"Okay, thanks" she said to Isabel putting the phone down.

Isabel stared at the little phone. What was she to make of that? Did the woman suspect anything? Isabel didn't think so, she sounded more worried about Matheson than suspicious of him, but she had dropped him in it, why the hell had she said that he had never shown up?"

In the kitchen Laura paced up and down the floor. Her mind considered all manner of possibilities. Was he hurt; was he dead, was he seeing someone else?

The thought that had been bothering her made her pick up the phone and ring Isabel back.

"Hello Isabel Conner?" Laura tried to imagine what the woman looked like. She couldn't.

'Hi it's Laura, Sammy's wife again. Sorry I'm a bit confused, I can't help wondering why you didn't ring when Sammy never showed last night, surely you must have been worried or put out or unable to complete the job, whatever it was?"

"We never worry about Sammy, he says one thing the does the exact opposite, I assumed someone else had called him to something else."

"But how could anyone call if he left his mobile here?"

"Maybe he had another work one in his car?"
"Maybe, well thanks." Laura hung up.

Looking up at the kitchen clock she noticed it had gone nine so she rang the office again.

"Hello detective Matheson please.'

"Who's speaking?" enquired the receptionist

"His wife."

"Hold the line I'll just put you through."

"Thanks" Two rings and then Sammy's voice "Matheson"

"Sammy! What's happened? What's wrong? Where the hell have you been? I've been so worried, you left your mobile here and I had no way of contacting you."

"Yes sorry love it was a busy night." He said, shifting in his chair, his balls still felt tender.

"Where were you?" she demanded "I rang the office last night, you never turned up." She said flatly, the accusation in her voice obvious.

'Why did you ring the office?' he asked, his heart began to beat faster.

"I was worried." Laura replied "Then this morning I rang Isabel who said you never arrived at the office."

"You did what?"
"I phoned Isabel!"

Laura heard him swear under his breath and alarm bells sounded again in her brain.

"Look Laura, I'm sorry I'm up to my neck in it, we'll have to talk later." he said hanging up, truth was he was desperate to give himself some time to get his jangled thoughts together.

For a moment he sat, stunned. Why the fuck did Isabel say I didn't get there? He picked up the phone.

"Isabel Conner."

"Isabel? Sammy, what the fucks going on? You've put me deep in the brown stuff saying I wasn't at the office last night. Why did you say that, and to my wife as well, what were you thinking?"

"I wasn't thinking Sammy, she put me on the spot, it just came out, I'm so sorry."

"You're sorry? Fuck knows how I'm going to dig myself out of this!"

"Perhaps you don't have to." she said

"What are you on about?" he demanded.

"You can always come and stay with me Sammy." he could hear the laughter in her voice, she was enjoying this!

'WHAT? Are you fucking mad? He fumed.

"Hang on a minute, did you fucking plan this?" He said reaching boiling point.

"You fucking did didn't you?"

"No I didn't honestly, come and stay with me Sammy, I want you, I love you, we're good together, you know we are!"

"What? Did you really think . . . . ? You *are* mad; I was never going to leave my wife. I love her!"

"Funny way of showing it Sammy!" she hissed, her voice brittle.

"You don't love her, you can't love her, you were with me!" her voice escalated. "No, no, you're mine now Sammy, you said!" her tone was wheedling now.

"I never said any such thing, you mad bitch!" he shouted to the mouthpiece.

"Don't you remember Sammy? We made love, then after I asked if you regretted it, you said no, and I said "now your mine forever?" The wheedling tone again.

"*You* said that, I didn't I would never leave Laura!" said Matheson. "Christ it was just a bit of fun, it's not like you haven't been panting for it for months!"

"And you haven't?" her voice was hard again now

"Whatever, it's obvious you've read much more into this than there is!"
"What you trying to say then Sammy?"

"Listen to me, and listen good, I love my wife; I'll never leave her for you! Got it?"

"We'll fucking see about that" she said slamming the phone down. Isabel was furious, how dare he? Well she would show him, she had no intention of letting Sammy go, let's just see how understanding his little Laura was when she heard all the details of the steamy sex scenes she had had with her husband.

'FUCK, FUCK' Matheson said even louder. Heads turned in the adjoining office. One of the plain clothes officers popped his head around Matheson's door.

"Everything OK sir?" he asked.

"Fuck off!" Matheson snapped.

"OK, OK, he said holding his hands up as if a gun was pointing at him. Doing a u-turn he went out pulling Matheson's office door closed behind him.

Matheson picked up the phone to call home. "Fuck, engaged!" he growled putting his head in his hands and rubbing furiously at his temples trying to ease the building pressure.

Meanwhile, wiping her hands from washing up a cake tin, Laura picked up the cordless that she had brought in and put on the kitchen table, hoping although not expecting her husband to call back. Laura answered the phone with a tentative
"Hello?"

"It's Isabel!" Laura thought the woman sounded as though she was on the verge of tears.

"Nasty news I'm afraid, are you sitting comfortably?" Laura said nothing.

On the other end of the line Laura heard Isabel draw in a lung full of air ready to make some sort of an announcement.

"Sammy was with me last night, at my flat, in my bed, we made love all night!" she continued a note of triumph in her voice.

"No you're lying!" Laura's mouth had gone dry and although the protest had escaped her lips she knew in her heart it was true.

"It's the truth, I'm afraid love!" insisted Isabel. Any hint of tears was gone now and Isabel's hard edged callous voice continued "Oh and where do you think he was the night before?"

Silence

"Oops, with me again I'm afraid, making love, going at it like rabbits! God don't you ever give him any? He was like a starving man at a feast! And that tongue of his, ooh he is so good at that isn't he?" Isabel heard a sharp intake of breath, she had hit a nerve. She had guessed that oral sex was not on the Matheson's love making agenda, it was always the first thing to go once the wedding rings went on and she could tell from Sammy's initial tentative approach that he was not practised at the art.
"Oh dear, hasn't he been doing that with you? Oh sorry, how embarrassing, but if he's prepared to do that with me, well it's obvious, he loves me not you, just give it up love, you're obviously yesterdays news now, make room for the new woman on the block!" and with a manic cackle, Isabel hung up.

Laura Matheson's sat looking at the phone for a full minute. She felt sick, she could not believe what she had heard, just yesterday evening, they were going to make love, she knew it, the signs were all there, if he hadn't been called out . . . . But then if that horrible mad woman was right, he was called out to her flat! It would make sense, and Sammy had obviously made his choice, he had chosen Isabel.

Eventually she started to cry, softly at first and then louder. As she sat at the table memories of other occasions when he had been called out came back to her, times when he had been secretive, elusive, absent. Hell she was describing their whole marriage!

She thought back over the years that they had been married. All those promises he had made to both her and their son. All the nights they had spent alone without him, how many of those times was he with someone else, how many times was he with that bitch Isabel? How long had this been going on? The questions crowded her brain, bitterness, anger, and hatred had taken over now. Suddenly she heard the familiar sound of a key in the front door.

Drying her eyes in case it was Tom, she called out

"Who's that?"
"Laura?" From the front door Matheson saw her sitting at the kitchen table, she didn't meet his eyes.

"Laura, love can we talk?" he could see she had been crying.

"Tell me you didn't do it Sammy? Come on lie to me, after all you're a fucking expert, you been doing it all our marriage, haven't you Sammy? Haven't you?" her voice shook with emotion.

Matheson slumped down on one of the chairs opposite Laura and put his head in his hands.

"It didn't mean anything, really it didn't"

"Well at least you're not bothering to deny it, not much point really with your girlfriend having given me all the gory details, she reckons I can't have been giving you enough, how was it she described you? Oh yes, like a starving man at a feast, she even praised your oral sex skills, how long since we've had any of that Sammy, I suppose I'm not sexy enough for you now, is that it? Too old, put on a few pounds, too boring, which is it, or maybe it's all of them?" Laura felt sick as she spat the words out at him. Looking at him she felt a white-hot rage, a hatred building inside her,

"You fucking bastard!" she said her tone was low but her voice was shaking. Matheson winced he was not used to hearing such foul language form her, he had really pushed her over the edge and he could say nothing in his defence.

"It was nothing like us, she's nothing, trash; I love you, not her!" He said

"Too late!" said Laura. She looked at the man she had loved for as long as she could remember and felt nothing but a deep contempt, a hatred that she could almost taste. How dare he humiliate her? How dare he stick his tongue into another woman? And how many women were they talking about? She must be the laughing stock of the town. The thought of people laughing behind her back pushed her over the edge and grabbing the big kitchen knife from the draining board she lunged at him with it. Matheson grabbed her arm but rage had made her so strong that she knocked his chair backwards and they tumbled together to the kitchen floor. Matheson felt a strange sensation, a physical draining away of his strength, his breathing becoming rasping, At first he thought he had knocked his head as he fell backwards but as he looked up at Laura he saw that she didn't have the knife in her hand anymore and the realisation hit him, he was hurt, badly. Looking down he could see the blade protruding from his chest. His dimming brain wondered vaguely why there was no pain. He could feel something but it was no worse than a splinter in his finger. He watched his brilliant white shirt turn to blood red, as his eyes closed gently and blood bubbled up in his throat, making him cough, streams of bright red blood pouring from between his lips. Almost calmly he realised he was dying. He closed his eye. Somewhere in the background he could hear Laura screaming his name "Oh my God what have I done?" She fell to her knees pulling at him.

"Sammy wake up!"

She shook him again, "Sammy wake up speak to me" she was sobbing now, her body shaking so much she could barely move.

Matheson opened his eyes and mouthed in a whisper.

"I love you Laura" with his last breath.

"Oh my God, he's dead" she whispered.

In the silence of the kitchen Laura stayed kneeling in her husbands blood at his side for what seemed like hours. As she studied his face a strange feeling came over her, this was not Sammy any more it was a dead body; she felt repulsed, she couldn't touch or even look at Matheson. She backed away from him, watching his blood drip off the end of her skirt onto the kitchen floor.

Just then she heard the noise of another key in the front door,

"Tom" she thought, home for lunch. For a moment she froze, then just in time, rushed to the kitchen door and shut it.

"Mum you in there?"

"Yes son, I'm just cleaning the floor, don't come in while it's wet, there's no school for you this afternoon we're off to Auntie Fiona's. Go up to your room and pack a few things!"

"Why are we going over there?" Tom said.

"Tom, just do as I say, please!" Tom shrugged, taking the stairs two at a time delighted with the thought of time off school. Up in his bedroom he tipped the contents of his rucksack onto the floor. In their place he threw in his I pod, the game boy, games all his favourite bits and bobs. On top of that he threw in some socks, pants, and t-shirts so it looked like a bag of clothes. He had heard his mother come upstairs, he glanced up as she ran past his door, it looked like she was in her underwear! Grown ups, who knew how their minds worked he thought to himself.

By the time that he got downstairs again she had gathered a few things and was waiting for him.

'Ready?' she said

'Yes mum, are you going to leave the washing machine going?"

"Yes, yes I'll pop back later and deal with it" Laura thought about her clothes covered in blood sloshing bright red water against the washing machines window, next to her husband's dead body and almost gagged.

Tom looked at his mother. She looked pale and worried, but that was nothing new, his fathers' job was always a worry for her.

"Right go and wait in the car, I just need to ring Auntie Fiona."

"Why? Doesn't she know we're coming, and how come Dad hasn't got his Range Rover?" Tom was beginning to worry now, something in the way his mother looked, the fact that he was being let off school and now it seemed they were making some mad dash to Auntie Fiona's in his dad's car, mad Auntie Fiona it seemed didn't even know they were coming? He shook his head getting out an old battered Game boy that he kept in the pocket of the back seat and started to play, he knew that if he asked he would only be told that it was nothing to do with him, so he wouldn't even bother.

Her hands shaking Laura dialled Fiona's number, they we're old school pals and had kept in touch throughout the years.

"Fiona? It's Laura"

"Laura what's up?" Fiona barely recognised her friends shaking voice.

"Big problem's, I need a big favour" Laura said through chattering teeth.

"Anything just name it, what on earth is wrong?"

"I'm setting off for yours now; I'll explain when I get there."

"Okay' replied Fiona hanging up the phone."

Laura jumped into the car, it still smelled of Sammy's aftershave, he always kept some in the glove compartment, he had told her it was to freshen up if he had a long day or a smelly assignment, but now she knew what it was really for, it was to cover the smell of another woman on him. She felt sick as she thought of him with another woman, his eyes enjoying bodies that were more voluptuous, less stretch marked than hers, she could see in her minds eye his face as it always was above hers when they made love. Did he bite his lip when he was about to come with other women or was it only with her? Well she would never know now. She felt a wave of panic wash over her and she drove the twenty odd miles to Fiona's in a daze, her head was full of the horrific scene she had left behind at her house and she could still smell the sickly smell of Sammy's blood. She looked at her hands on the steering wheel, there were dark half moons between each of her nails and the nail beds, dried blood, Sammy's blood. She shuddered, glancing in the rear view mirror. Thank God Tom seemed engrossed in some game, she did not know if she could trust herself to speak.

She wondered how Tom would react to his dad's death, she thought about the last chat they had had about him, it had worried her sometimes that they did not seem to be close but after one telling off Tom had seemed even angrier than ever.

"I hate him, I never see him, and when I do all he does is tell me off'!" he had said angrily.

She had thought about that at the time, it was true she thought, and it was her fault, every time Sammy came home, she would complain that Tom had done this or that. He was my way of controlling Tom she thought, "Wait till your Dad gets home!" had been her continual threat. Perhaps that was all Sammy was meant to be in his life, a chastiser an arbitrator.

In her jumbled thoughts she stopped herself going down the train of thought that would lead her to pity and regret for Sammy, he was the one that had strayed, God knows how many times, he was the one who had put a bomb under their marriage, not her! She had been a virtual prisoner in her own home, waiting night after night, promise after promise. He never played with Tom. We never went out as a family like normal people did.

Ahead of her was the turning that led to Fiona's farm house, the thought of the calm pastoral scene almost made Laura cry out loud, she needed this so badly, needed to see normal things, peaceful things, things not covered in blood and she needed to hear words not screamed in hate.

Inside Tom gave Fiona a peck on the cheek, and ran to the top of the stairs and into his very own bedroom. Fiona had no family, or a man for that matter, so they were welcome whenever they wanted. Tom had spent many happy school holidays here helping Fiona with the chickens and ducks she kept.

Guiding her friend to the big settee in front of the blazing log fire in her lounge Fiona said nothing. Laura was obviously deep in shock and took the tumbler of brandy that her friend offered with shaking hands.

The friends sat in silence for 10 minutes, Laura was not ready and Fiona did not rush her. Eventually her shoulders dropped a little and the shaking subsided and Laura began to tell her friend what had happened. She went through the whole sordid story speaking in a low calm voice, shutting her eyes tight as she described the moment that she had realised that her husband was dead. For the first time tears spilled down her cheeks and she sobbed onto her friends shoulder.

Fiona was stunned, couldn't say anything at first, but that was OK because all her friend needed was for someone to hold her, to let her cry her heart out to wash out her soul. "What are you going to do now?" Fiona asked gently

"I don't know, I just want it to be over." Laura buried her head in her hands. She wiped her eyes. "I have thought, maybe set fire to the place?"

"Oh now Laura, let's think about this." Fiona was alarmed at the way her friends mind was working, she had thought that when she was strong enough, Laura would call the police explain what had happened. This was dangerous territory.

"I mean with forensics and all that even if you did, when they found his body they would know how he died?" Fiona said.

"I've thought about that. He's a policeman and he has been involved with a lot of serious low life. They would assume one of them had done it."

Fiona thought about it.

"I suppose so, but Laura, surely if you explained . . ."

"No! I can't risk being sent to prison, Tom will find out soon that he has lost his father; he can't lose me as well.

For a moment Fiona sat quietly then she nodded.

"Right, if that's what you want, you know I'm with you all the way." The hugged.

"What about Tom?" asked Fiona.

"He will be on that play station for hours, and I told him that I would be going home again later to empty the washing machine, the clothes from . . . ." she tailed off.
"Right, you go then and I'll see you back here later."

"Fiona, you would look after Tom, you know if anything happened to me?"

"Nothing is going to happen, just be careful!" Fiona said hugging her again

Laura nodded her pale face disappearing into the darkness.

Laura returned to their cottage on the edge of town. It was nestled in a copse giving plenty of seclusion, which was the reason they bought the place originally. On the return trip she felt stronger and her thoughts became more focused on avenging the hurt she had suffered. Half way home she called into a petrol station and filled two petrol cans she had purchased. As she drove home from the petrol station she thought about Isabel and how much the bitch had cost her. A husband, even if he was part time, her home, which was heavily mortgaged, possibly even her freedom,

"The bitch has destroyed my life!" she kept repeating. Back at the cottage hands shaking she lifted the phone and called Isabel's number.

"It's Laura Matheson, you can have him, I don't want Sammy anymore we're finished!" She shouted down the phone.

"Where is he?" Asked Isabel.

"He's here at home with me, packing, you'll have to come and get him if you want him, I'm taking the car and going away for a while.
"Yes, yes of course, Isabel hesitated "Did he say he wanted to come to me?"

"Not exactly but he's weak and he obviously finds you irresistible, and I'm out of here, so he's all yours, you miserable bitch!" Laura flung the phone down.

Laura started to prepare the trap; she chose the dining room, small in area, just right for the job. She wet two towels placing one at the bottom of the door on the outside and one on the inside. Her hands shaking she sloshed petrol over furniture watching it bubble on the paint of the dining room table that Sammy's parents had given them as a wedding present. Quickly exiting the room she leaned down to pack the towel well into the gap at the bottom of the door to contain the fumes which were intense now, she sprayed copious amounts of air freshener then she stood back.

"That will do!" 'she said sniffing the air. Laura went up to wash and change, coming down the stairs a noise set her adrenalin rushing again, it was Isabel at the door. Laura opened the door, the atmosphere could be cut with a knife, and the pair eyed each other up. Laura held it together.

"Sammy's in the shower, you can wait for him in here" said Laura guiding Isabel to the dining room door. Isabel kicked gingerly at the towel on the floor then opened the door. The fumes immediately struck her and before she could react Laura had shoved her in and locked the door.

The petrol fumes burned Isabel's lungs as she pounded on the door. Her eyes smarted and tears streamed down her face. She ran to the window but Laura had made sure the steel security shutter was down.

Shouting through the door she said

"You fucked my life, now I'm going to fuck yours!"

Striking one of her kitchen matches Laura held it up for a moment then dropped it in the puddle of petrol that had pooled out under the door. The flames licked hungrily up the door blistering the paint as they went, forcing Laura back.

On the other side of the door Isabel was engulfed in an inferno of flames her blood curdling screams made Laura cover her ears until they gradually diminished into silence.

Now the noise of the flames was the only sound from the dining room and Laura felt a calmness come over her, her mind was now at rest, and the score was settled.

She walked calmly into the kitchen noting that the washing machine had erased any hint of blood of her clothing. She took the clothes out and carefully arranged them over the drier by the Aga. Better make it look as normal as possible she thought. Sammy's body stared sightlessly up at her and she felt bile rise in her throat. His blood had dried now and looked dark, almost black. A fly crawled out of his open mouth, and Laura thought she could see the white of its eggs on his tongue. She held her hand to her mouth to stop herself being sick. She tore her eyes away and splashed the other can of petrol around the kitchen.

She struck another match; the roar of the fire in the dining room was joined by a loud whoosh as the kitchen exploded like a bomb knocking Laura off her feet. The fire that lapped hungrily at the puddles of petrol on the floor enveloped her clothing and she patted at them desperately, trying to put the flames out. Gradually the pain of the flames melting her skin registered and as she breathed in flame filled air, her lungs filled with hot vapour and collapsed. As she lay on the floor beside her husband's dead body, suffocating flames licked at her and with her last ounce of strength she clawed at her throat, desperate for air. As the life finally left her, her arm fell away and her open hand landed on Sammy's, and as the flames shrunk their skin and burned the flesh from their bones, their hands remained together until bone lay on bone.

CHAPTER 11

So wooded and secluded was Sammy's house that it was a full thirty minutes later that a rickety old gentleman walking an equally rickety dog raised the alarm. By this time the house was well ablaze, ferocious heat and voracious flames licking at the walls and escaping through the windows. The metal shutters over the dining room windows that Laura had closed to stop Isabel escaping were melting in the heat and dripping like molten lava onto the path below.

Emergency services started to arrive at the scene in a blur of sirens and screeching tyres, in the police, those who knew Sammy Matheson and where he lived held their breath as they grew close to his house, surely it couldn't be . . . .but it was!

Struggling to raise anyone from his own department to investigate Bill Nyland the Super had a nagging gut feeling that something was very wrong. His years of hunches were about to come to roost as the news came through of a possible tragedy involving a member of the force. Suddenly his demeanour changed as he caught site of someone disappearing into his office.

"Andy?" Andy Sims turned round "Yes Super?" he replied, and then noticing his bosses ashen face. "What's up?"

"God where do I begin" the senior officer sank onto one of the chairs.

"Sammy's place has been destroyed by a fire and I can't get in touch with him." He paused. "Fire say that there are three bodies in there," he continued grimly.

Andy felt shell-shocked. "What the fuck? Who we got at the scene?"

"Roberts and McCracken, couldn't get hold of Isabel, but something's not right" Nyland said a tad weary, his voice thick with something that sounded suspiciously like tears. Andy pulled on his jacket. "I'd better get over there."

"Yes I'd be a lot happier if you were there Andy".

"You going to be okay?" the Super didn't look right, he was pale and sweaty and for a big tough man he looked somehow fragile, breakable.

Yes, yes I'll be okay, he replied attempting a reassuring half smile.

Andy Sims walked quickly through the corridors to the front office where he spotted Maria, a junior officer and asked her to check on the Super. Maria nodded and hurried down to the office where she found Nyland on the floor of the office, clutching his chest.

'Help', she screamed.

Officers ran from various sections of the floor one grabbing the phone to call an ambulance.

"Who's first aid?" Maria asked sitting cradling her boss's head in her lap.

"I am" said a tall lanky officer stepping forward his Adams apple bobbing nervously in his thin neck.

"Do something quick" said Maria. Around them a gaggle of officers stood motionless in shock, while the young officer tended to the Super till the ambulance arrived to take him to the hospital.

Meanwhile Andy had arrived at the cottage; He sat in the car for a while to gather his thoughts, preparing himself for what he had to face. He and Sammy went way back, they used to be partners in the old days. True they had had their ups and down, but it was more like banter than anything serious. He knew that Sammy had resented his last promotion but he had always respected Sammy, and he hoped that the feeling had been mutual.

Steeling himself he got out of the car.

"What we got?" he asked entering the charred building.

'Three bodies' said McCracken.

'Three?' Andy repeated.

'Yes, looks like a male and female in what could be the kitchen and another female in there' he said pointing to the dining room. Andy looked over towards the kitchen. McCracken intercepted him.

'Sorry sir the fire chief hasn't cleared us for in there yet, but they have over there', he said directing Andy to the other room. Andy disappeared into the dining room, his senses registering the acrid smell created by the fire. The ceiling of the floor above had collapsed in the middle but had missed the body crouched beside the door. Andy felt a strange sensation come over him, it was bizarre looking up into a clear blue sky with green leaves waving in the breeze, and a perfect 'V' of ducks, their quacking audible, flying overhead, all alive and all vital while around him all was black and burnt and dead. His eyes were drawn to the charred corpse, his facial expression turned to horror as a shiny familiar object caught his eye.

"Oh no" he muttered.

"What is it sir?" the bobby he had spoken to said, from behind him.

"I know her, that's Isabel Connor".

"How do you know it's her?"

"That ring on her middle finger, I bought that for her", Andy said shortly, not trusting his voice to say anymore and then seeing the look on the young officer s face he said "A special birthday, you know the type of thing." The young officer looked as though he did know the type of thing, trying, and not succeeding, to hide a smirk.

"God that's tough, sir, I can't imagine, how awful", the young officer struggled to find the right words.

"Please can you leave me to it for a bit? Andy said gruffly

"Sure I'll be just outside if you need me sir."

Andy knelt down beside the corpse, unrecognisable now as Isabel, almost brunt to the bone, the jaw gaping open in an agonised death throe. "What the fuck were you doing here Isabel?" he whispered. "What games were you playing this time?"

He thought about the many encounters he had with Isabel, she was a wild one and no mistake, always sailed close to the wind. "Bit too close this time eh girl?" he said touching the ring on the charred finger in a gesture that communicated his good bye to a woman he had known well.

Standing upright he set his jaw and struggled to regain his composure. As he passed the area that had been the kitchen he spotted Roberts now allowed in by the fire investigator.

"Hang in there mate" Andy said kindly guessing from Roberts hunched shoulders and the white drawn expression on his face, that the younger officer had identified Sammy and his wife in the kitchen. He looked at the younger man for confirmation.

"Sammy and Laura?"

Roberts nodded shortly; he could not trust himself to speak.

The obvious always bites you last. But knowing Isabel as well as he did, Andy had solved the case already. As he stood in what had been the hallway he looked around at the officers present, most in various states of shock and wondered if he should voice his opinion. He hesitated for a moment, hell they were police officers not girl guides they would have to know the truth sooner or later. He sighed deeply.

"I don't see any foul play here lads, I reckon that Sammy Matheson and Isabel were having an affair; Laura Matheson found out and killed them both, then killed herself." He said flatly.

'That's it then, case solved' said McCracken." making an attempt at levity but the expression on his face and that of many of the others present, registered renewed shock.

"You know better than that McCracken, for now that is just my opinion" Andy said.

"Yes Guv."

Pathology reports backed up Andy's theories and no one else was sought in connection to the fire. They traced the purchase of the petrol back to Laura and Roberts was able to provide vital evidence about what had happened in the last days of Sammy's life, the phone call from Isabel. Subsequent embarrassing DNA samples from the bedding of her flat confirmed what Andy had suspected.

Laura had obviously feared that the whole thing might go wrong and had left detailed instructions for her and Sammy's son to be cared for by Fiona. Andy had visited the boy at the farm and come away feeling rattled his nerves jangled by the raw grief of his colleagues son and the woman who had been his mother's best friend.

A week later Andy was deep in paperwork when a familiar voice reached him from the open door of his office.

"You're on the Kenly exploding bonces case, aren't you Sims? Well I need you to get some fucking answers before I really do have a heart attack!"

"Fuck! You're back on form Super, I heard that it was nothing too serious, you seem back to fighting fit now anyway!" he said looking up.

"No just a chest infection coupled with, well you know what, it was a bad day for us all." Nyland said

"Yes sad, sad, I don't think any of us are over it yet." Andy said softly and they were silent for a moment, lost in their own thoughts.

"Right, Andy." The Super shook himself out of it first, "it's you, Perkins and I'm sending a newbie over. I want no excuses, just results on this it's becoming an embarrassment. There was a big piece in the News of the World this weekend."

"I saw it."

"Who's the newbie?" Andy asked.

"Don't worry you'll like her, got a good brain. You've got a week to go over the case, and Andy, for fucks sake please find something!"

"I'll give it my best shot Super!"

"Good, Oh by the way, just had a call from HR, Roberts is on sick leave, he took Matheson's death very badly, so don't be bothering him."

"Sure thing," Andy replied, he had heard that Roberts was not well, he had taken a hell of a hit over Sammy's death, probably took it harder than any of them.

Andy took the lift down to Sammy's office.

"Fucking mess" he mumbled looking around the office.

Andy decided to set up base there for a couple of days, get the paper work and evidence in the case together and look at things as Sammy had left them. As he unravelled the chaos he would transfer the case to his own more spacious office where he could start again and do things his way.

Four days in and nothing, Perkins had been out to look at the murder scenes and, not surprisingly this long after the event, had found nothing.

Andy kept finding memories of Isabel crowding his mind and in the quietness he often drifted into the past. Like Sammy Andy had admired Isabel's professionalism at work and her subtle teasing ways aimed at him when they worked together at crime scenes. He recalled being on the trail of a particularly nasty rapist, there seemed to be no pattern, and it appeared he was picking his victims at random.

The chemistry between himself and Isabel was there from their very first meeting and unlike Sammy, Andy had honed in on the fact immediately. Single he could play the field at any time, and responded to her, tease for tease.

On their third meet the chemistry combusted.

Andy had been called out to a crime, a lady in her early sixties had been brutally raped and killed. Arriving after Isabel, she had already gone over the victim with a fine toothcomb.

"Isabel, where is everyone?" he asked as he walked in.

"Gone, you've missed the party, I'm afraid, where have you been?"

"Oh I got held up on another case, what we got?" he asked

"Female, probably sixty, raped, strangled, and.. bitten".

"Bitten?"

"Yes bitten, look here on her neck," said Isabel pointing to the bite mark. "He drew blood as well", she continued, "and look here" she said beckoning Andy closer.

"What am I looking at?"

"Look at the shape of the bite, no front teeth" she said he eyes bright with discovery and revelation.

"Well, well, that's hard to spot." Andy said peering at the mark on the woman's neck. "I would have defiantly missed that, thank God for forensics, thank God for you. This puts a whole different picture of the suspect out there, well done Isabel" he said and she had smiled at him a mixture of surprise and amusement as though she needed no praise for anything so obvious.

"Thanks" she said simply, and Andy remembered her big beautiful brown eyes smiling up at him.

"This deserves a celebration, drinks are on me!" he said.

Isabel nodded. "When would suit you?"

Strike while the iron's hot he thought. "Tonight?"

"Yours or mine?" She asked.

He was actually thinking more like a pub, but thought now about the state of his flat last time he had been home.

"Got to be honest mines a shit hole got to be yours Isabel!" He said.

"Seven?"

"Seven's fine" he had left her to finish.

He smiled to himself as he thought about that night, it seemed like a hundred years ago now./ He had no sooner got in Isabel's doorway when she was on him like a hungry dog on a bone.

They ended up making love there in the hallway; he couldn't control himself it was an urgent hot, desperate coupling and over in the blink of an eye. Later she prepared a meal, they ate and drank, and made love again, this time less hurried, deeper more satisfying. Then it was time to go and Andy had disappeared into the night.

There had been a few more encounters but then they stopped—perhaps she found someone else. "Perhaps she found Sammy," he said aloud. That's why she stopped answering his calls, Sammy, he repeated in his mind. Just then a voice interrupted his thoughts.

"All right Guv?"

"Yes thank you, and you are?".

"I'm Detective Denise Lawson, I've been assigned to assist you on the case."

"Great, a tea maker, pick a desk and sort yourself out." Andy looked at her to see how she would respond to his teasing. She looked annoyed.

Fucking cheeky bastard, she thought as she picked the desk as far away from him as possible.

"Hey I won't fucking bite, have the desk opposite. I shout enough as it is"

"Fair enough." she moved grudgingly to the desk opposite Andy's and he said.

"Come on cheer up, at least your opposite a bald, handsome specimen of a man".
Denise looked across at him, realised he was joking and smiled grudgingly.

Actually he was not bad, bald suited him, he must polish it, that was one shiny head, nice smile, appealing likable face, and the size of him, six foot odd, firm and fit looking. Yep, eminently shaggable she concluded.

Suddenly her thoughts were interrupted.

"Hey wakey wakey, Hope I haven't got a daydreamer on board".

"Sorry Guv, just thinking about the case, it's a strange one, you really have got no ideas or leads at all?".

"Nope not a Billy Boo, whoever or whatever is doing this is destroying the evidence. You would have to be an expert in micro jigsaws to sort this lot out."

"I'm good at jigsaws, but not that good", said Denise and despite himself Andy smiled. He gave her the once over.

Hmm, a bit short, and a bit tubby, big tits I'd like to get them babies out and have look. Not bad looking, rounded face, Blue eyes framed with glasses, brown hair tied back in a ponytail.

"Guv?"

"What?"
"Hope I haven't teamed up with a day dreamer", She chuckled.

"Okay, okay, let's get down to business, here's some case files see if anything grabs you, a fresh pair of eyes might spot something".

Denise spent a good part of the morning with her head stuck in the files, she was desperate to find something to impress.

"Right" Andy said. Completely out of the blue

"What?" Denise looked up, startled.

"Liquid lunch. That's what, let's go", He said. As Andy strode down the street outside the station, Denise found herself having to run to keep up with him.

"Hang on Guv, I've only got little legs".

"Oh yeah sorry, see anything in those files?" He asked her.

"No nothing." She replied

"Thought so, I've been looking at them for days, I'm sick of it, tell you what after lunch lets go to some of the crime scenes and have a gander. I've already seen them and Perkins has just finished another reccy, but again a fresh pair of eyes. Something might *pop up*".

Andy glanced at Denise for a reaction but the innuendo went straight over her head.

"Okay it's worth a try," she agreed eagerly

They arrived at the local, which was literally across the street. An old time bar, with upholstered bench seats everywhere. Heavily patterned wallpaper on the walls, very atmospheric.

"All right Guv?" shouted Perkins from a bench near the bar.

"Yes mate, where you been?"

"Doing a chore for the Super." Explained Perkins "he clobbered me when I got back from visiting the crime scenes"

"Anything?" Andy asked.

"Nope"

"This is Denise, she'll be working with us on the Kenly case"

"Hello luv," said Perkins

"Hi." Denise answered, "Why is it called Kenly Guv?"

"I don't believe you just said that, where the fuck are we?"

"In the pub Guv?" she replied

"No what town?" said the Guv impatiently

"Er Kenly, Oh I see" she said as the penny dropped

"Get her a coke Perky, don't want that brain getting fuzzed do we?"

"No Guv"

"Sorry lads, it was too obvious, and I'm not even blonde!" said Denise, red with embarrassment

"Were going over some of the crime scenes this afternoon, and you can mind the shop Perky.

Denise was watching Perkins while he and the Governor were in conservation. She had seen him around the station. He had a dark James bond hairstyle, didn't quite match his looks, not a lady-killer but reasonably handsome, tall, slim, pointy features. Always dressed in a suit and tie

"Drink up Denise lets go".

"Where we going Guv?' she said reluctantly tearing her gaze away from Perkins.

"To the first case, two victims, Greg Barton and Sharon Bright"

"Were they an item?" she enquired

"Yes, he was an out and out brute, a violent bully; we felt his collar many times". Andy said, frowning

"And the girl?" she said with genuine interest.

"Ah the girl. The Guv's expression softened, she was an angel, bit rough and ready, a real beauty though, don't know what she saw in him. I have a hunch he bullied her as well".

"Got his just desserts then wouldn't you say Guv?"

"Yes he did, shame that she went with him, she didn't deserve that. How's your driving Denise?"

"Not bad"

"Ok you drive then, show me what you got!"

Perkins looked disappointed. Andy smiled at him. "Pull your lip in Slick, there's a nice pile of paper work waiting for you back at the station!"

Perkins sighed and casting a resentful glance at Denise turned to walk back to the station.

"Where we going, Guv?" Denise asked slipping behind the wheel.

"Byfleet Broadway" he said

"I know it, rough area," said Denise

"Good place to get a blow job", Andy said with a smirk, looking for a reaction.

"Good place to get raped, stabbed, buy drugs, a right shit hole, why anyone would want a blow job there is a mystery to me, you would probably get rabies" she said

"You're right it is a shit hole, but you have to remember that Barton was on the run, after the murder in the park that he was implicated in, even though he did us a favour by offing an even bigger low life than he was."

"Drugs involved?" Denise asked

"We didn't find any."

Denise pulled the car up at the spot Andy indicated. They walked through the area. The low life were there, melting into the dark places of the streets as Andy and Denise approached. Only a trained eye would spot them, and Andy and Denise did, but they were not what the pair had in their sights today.

"Perhaps they were passing through wanted to stop for a cuddle, if he was of no fixed abode and on the run they might have found it a bit difficult to summon up a romantic atmosphere here?" Denise smiled, as she kicked a dead rat out of her way "perhaps they were after a little bit of slap and tickle, we know that he stole the car, it is amazing what men will do when the sap is rising isn't it sir?" Denise cast a sideways glance at her boss.

Andy smiled, he thought he was going to like Denise, she was feisty "Yes it would have to be something like that, the car started so they couldn't have broken down, or run out of petrol".

"Bet you a pound to a dollar they were at it!" She said

"Yep well we'll never know about that, right next stop 41 Porter Street"

"I've never heard of that one Guv."
"Oh it's right on the other side of town, head for the cinema it's nearby"

"Okay. You married Guv?"

"No never had time for a serious relationship, work always gets in the way. What about yourself Denise?'

"Not now, I was married once."

"What happened?"

"We just drifted apart; nothing in common really we had different interests. I guess it was lust rather than love, once it wore off that was it. Anyway you know what it's like, I can't remember the number of marriages that go to the wall amongst police officers but it's high."

Andy nodded. "Any kids?" he said.

"None thank God, we might have stayed together for kids. I'm sure a lot of relationships are that way."

"Of course they are, I know loads that would have broken up if they had no kids.

Pull over Denise, there by that sandwich bar."

Once inside the pair looked along the line of trays containing a mouth-watering array of sandwich fillings.

"What takes your fancy then Denise? I'm paying."

"Mmm chicken tikka, thanks Guv."

"I'll have the coronation chicken please luv." Andy said. "Will that be all sir?"

"Yes, oh and two cokes please, thanks."

"Five pounds fifty please." Said the girl holding out her hand

"There you go," he said giving the girl a hand full of loose change. "That should be right, check it', he continued.

"That's fine, thank you and have a nice day" she said with a smile that would melt butter.

"Aw I feel rotten now."

"Why's that Guv?"

"I just unloaded all my shrapnel on her, she was really sweet."

"Yes, but they are often glad of the change," Denise smiled at him and he thought, not for the first time, how she had the knack of making you feel better about things.

Once back in the car Andy tucked into his sandwich with gusto.

"You not eating yours?" he asked Denise

"I will, in a bit Guv."

"Denise drove away from the sandwich bar spotting the Cinema on the right.

"Where to now Guv?"
"Take a left at the bottom here, then second right" Andy mumbled through a mouth full.

"Right" she said

"That's what I said, right"

"I meant okay, Guv'

"Oh right, he replied, smiling. FUCK!"

"What?"

"There was something hard in there", he said pointing to the sandwich. Exploring the chewed pulped mess in his mouth he extracted a bone. "Think I've chipped a tooth".

"Let's have a look," said Denise pulling the car over.

"Hang on let me finish this mouthful first", he says swilling down the contents with a slug of coke.

"Have a look at that one near the back there", he said pointing with his finger.

"Ooo yes there's a big piece missing, that's going to hurt" she said pulling a face.

"It hurts already" he said wincing as an intake of cold air rushed across the damaged tooth.

"Dentist for you my boy!" Denise said firmly.

"There's one in the high street, leave me there, you go to Porter Street here's the keys, mind all the steps in there, it's all different levels"

Denise dropped him off. Up at the small reception area he put on an act. "God the pain luv, I think the nerve must be hanging out".

"Are you registered with us Sir?" asked the prim woman at the desk, whose name badge pinned onto a non existent bosom proclaimed her to be 'Pauline'

"No I'm detective Sims" he said flicking out his I.D, "I'm on a case and this is an emergency".

"Well" the woman's face showed that she was entirely unimpressed by Andy's attempt to impress her with the urgency of the situation "we have no appointments, fill in this form; you will have to sit in the waiting room, I'll speak to our dentist and we will try our best to fit you in".

"God you're a life saver, I could kiss you, Pauline" he said softly, giving her as much of a smile as he could manage.

The woman blushed; defrosting slightly "that won't be necessary" she said pointing him in the direction of the waiting room

Andy sat alone in the waiting room. Filling the form in took his mind off the pain for a few moments but once he had done it, another wave of pain washed over him. Placing his tongue in the hole and biting down the warmth and the barrier to the air created by his tongue gave him some respite. Just then a little old lady who had followed him in from the street to the reception desk came in to the little waiting room supported by the receptionist, "Detective Sims this is Mildred one of our regulars. Mildred this man's a detective-".

"Ooo a Detective, how exciting, has someone been murdered?"

"Err yes you could say that" Andy said removing his tongue from the hole in his tooth and bracing himself for the pain that he knew would accompany his inhaled breath.

"About time something exciting happened around here, been quiet for years." said Mildred

"Anyway" Pauline interrupted. "Mildred said it would be okay to take her appointment".

"Yes love you go ahead I can come here anytime, I'm a pensioner you know"

"Never. You look far too young, and thanks a lot, you've helped the police today, I'm on a very important case."

"Ooo I suppose you can't say anything about it can you?" the old lady said in a conspiratorial tone. Andy took her hand and shook his head gravely and she said again "isn't he a sweetie?" and Pauline smiled.
"Yes he is, now come on Mildred let's make you another appointment."

"Thanks again Mildred, you're a life saver." Andy winked at the old lady.
"Ooo did you hear that? I saved his life!"

"Yes come on Mildred let's get that appointment booked."

Detective Sims?" called the nurse.

"This way sir"

In the surgery, Steven smiled to himself as he asked Andy to sit in the chair.

"Hi my name is Steven, what can I do for you today?".

"Yes thanks for seeing me at such short notice, I'm on a case and really need this tooth sorting, I broke it on a bit of bone in a sandwich!"

"Let's have a look, lean back please"

Steven surveyed the detectives mouth, "Coronation chicken?" he said. Andy shut his mouth, embarrassed, "Yes sorry doc, didn't have time to clean my teeth.

"That's OK, I've seen worse" Steven said, "Mmm, not been to the dentists in a while then?"

"No I always think about going and then something else crops up" Andy said weakly. "I expect that you hear that all the time?"

"I do if people have enough teeth to talk!" Steven said smiling. The dentist's own teeth were perfect, Andy noted.

Andy smiled and winced as air hit the exposed nerve again. "Point taken doc, I'll mend my ways, promise!"

In reality, Andy was terrified, unreasonably so, he knew, but he had always hated needles, the last time he was injected he had had terrible palpitations and had thought he was going to die, before he eventually passed out. As he lay in the chair breathing in the antiseptic air of the surgery he wondered if he should tell the dentist, let him know that he might just peg out in the chair. He thought he probably should but he couldn't bring himself to. Not very macho was it, to admit that you were likely to keel over at the site of needle like a little girl?

"I'm going to have to give you an injection," said Steven. Andy felt the sweating begin in his palms and his heart pick up its beat. Steven glanced at him.

"Don't worry I've done this a thousand times" he said.

"I am a bit worried, last time I was in the chair I had palpitations and passed out, thought I was a goner." Andy said with a weak attempt at a laugh

"Ahh that's probably because you were injected into a main vein, rest assured you'll be fine with me" and as the young dentist began to inject all around the tooth Andy did begin to feel that he might be able to cope. From under the goggles that he had on he could see the dental nurse at the dentist's elbow ready with the equipment he would need. A pretty little thing, brown curly hair, round face, slightly olive skin, that looked lovely in her pristine white tunic. Andy tried to concentrate on his mental cataloguing of her assets to take his mind off the work being done in his mouth and found himself inching slightly back from the cliff edge, his heart rate slowing from a gallop to a canter and then the dentist was operating the chair and he was upright again.

"If you would like to wait in the waiting room I'll call you back in a few minutes", he said and Andy stood up on slightly wobbly legs.

In the waiting Andy sat near the window that overlooked the High Street. He loved people watching, a trait inherited from his mother. When he retired he could see himself in one of those little cottages by the seaside, sitting on his little bench watching the world go by. He tried to keep his mind off the horror that was to come, the noise of that drill that went right through you. At the battered bus stop opposite a couple of lads were trying their best to pull the roof off, dangling from it, their jeans that were already low slung almost falling off their skinny behinds as they swung like monkeys from the roof, which due to the council's anti vandalism reinforcement of structures campaign, they had as much chance of dislodging as they did Big Ben.

Andy felt his shoulders relaxing a bit as the pain began to fade and his lip began to go numb. Happy that the numbness was creeping steadily over the left side of his face, he began to breathe a bit easier, and the canter of his heart slowed to a brisk trot.

Meanwhile Steven had moved to a room to the back of the surgery, a secret room nobody knew about except for one other. Along the hallway towards the back of the building stood a big metal cabinet, to anyone glancing inside they would see many shelves containing pills, drugs, the usual paraphernalia that you would expect to see in a dentists surgery. But a quick flick of a button and the whole interior of the cabinet became a door, which could be pulled forward to reveal another door to the secret room, where Anthony worked, his array of ever more complex explosive and transmitting devices neatly placed on his work bench. A complicated chart that detailed who and where the devices had been implanted occupied the whole of one of the walls.

The coal hatch type door that Steven and Anthony had discovered the first day that they had looked over the rooms could be accessed down some stairs and the door leading out to the gardens was almost invisible from the outside with shrubs grown up all around it.

"Anthony?"

"Yes mate?"

"Guess who I've got in the waiting room, only a detective!"

"No?" said Anthony turning on the monitors to take a look.

"Yes mate straight up, I think he could come in handy if things get a bit hot."
"Awesome man, yes let's plant him, Oh and put the explosive in before the radio transmitter". Anthony told Steven.

"Why's that? We always do it the other way round".

"I think they'll be able to hear us much better."

"Okay" said Steven walking back through the surgery to the waiting room. As he passed the open door the detective looked up at him.

"Don't worry" Steven said, "We'll have you fixed up in no time!" Smiling to himself he went into the surgery and closed the door softly behind him.

CHAPTER 12

"**D**etective this way please". Steven showed Andy back into the surgery "On to the chair, please, there's a good chap, all nice and numb now?"

"Yes" Andy said the effect of the anaesthetic making him lisp.

"Right let's get started".

Half an hour later it was all over.

"Won't be a sec" Steven slipped out to the secret room,

"Give it a couple of minutes then run a test Anthony," he said hurrying back to his patient.

"Okay mate." Anthony busied himself setting up the remote, his practiced fingers making the task look easy.

Back in the surgery Steven asked Andy how he was feeling.

"Fine, much better thanks, is that it now?" "Yes that's you all done." Steven said raising the chair to a sitting position.

"Wow, what was that?"

"Sorry, what was what?" said Steven feigning surprise and concern.

"I just got, well it was a sound like a radio being tuned."

"Oh that sometimes happens with the new metallic elements we use to seal fillings, it's rare and usually clears" Steven reassured Andy.

Andy looked doubtful but the dentist seemed to be aware of the anomaly and did not seem concerned by it so he stood up and asked, "Pay at reception?"

'Yes please' replied Steven.

After paying Pauline Andy put a call out for Denise to come pick him up. Back in the waiting room he continued his observations of the street below. The lads who had been trying and failing to dismantle the bus shelter had now resigned themselves to daubing obscenities on it with spray cans of paint. He recognised one of them as Barton's younger brother. It wouldn't be long before he took up his rightful place as his brother's heir to crime in the area no doubt. Some part of him felt sorry for the boy. What chance did he and other lads have? Andy was very familiar with the sink estates that had spawned Barton and dozens more like him, filthy hovels of homes, rough worn out foul mouthed women with fags hanging out of toothless mouths, clipping the ears of filthy children hardened by years of depravation and rough treatment. Men who, if they did stick around in the homes in which they had spawned young, were even rougher, brutal and brutalised. Andy sighed; at least for the most part they all stayed together so it was easy to find them in their rat-infested enclaves. But this bloody case, the Kenly case, there was something different about this, something intelligent, sophisticated.

Steven went to back of the house to see Anthony.

"Nice job! Yes mate all went well, the test freaked him out"

"I saw. Laughed my bollocks off," said Anthony with a chuckle.

Looking over Anthony's shoulder Steven asked which amongst the rows of remotes was the detectives. Underneath each carefully itemised remote was a detonation number, enter this and—BOOM. Anthony's technological advancements meant they could now talk to recipients and receive replies even clearer than before.

"This one's his mate." Anthony pointed to it on the end of the last row.

Steven laughed, "007 that's funny mate!".

As Denise driving the police car, turned the corner, the boys in the bus stop scattered and Andy smiled.

"Blimey you look rough," said Denise as he got into the car.

"I feel rough, drop me back at mine, I'll take the afternoon off".

Denise dropped him off. Once inside he went straight to his pit and slept soundly for two hours. When he awoke he was greeted with a dull ache. The anaesthetic had worn off and the aching was much worse. He rang the surgery but got the answer phone. The pre-recorded voice told him to ring back during surgery hours. Nine till four. Looking at his watch he said, "Five! Shit!" in a loud voice.

Andy decided drowning his sorrows might alleviate the pain and went out to the pub opposite the station.

On arrival he spotted Perkins "Alright Guv?".

"No I'm fucking not alright". Perkins leant back a tad waiting for a rollicking. But it was not Perkins in Andy's sights this time and he sighed with relief as Andy told him of the unbearable pain he was in.

"Get us a double in Perky, I might be calling in a favour later when I'm pissed".

"What's that then sir?"

"You have permission to smack me in the mouth as long as you knock this tooth out" he said showing Perky the painful molar.

"Err I don't know about that Guv".

"I'll be pissed I won't remember, don't make me make it an order!" Perkins looked at him, alarmed, was he joking? He would love nothing better than to give his boss a good smack in the gob, but alas he had a better idea.

"I know an easier way," he said.

"What's that?"

"My mate Palmer is a dentist, he works out of his house, one of his bedrooms is a surgery, and I'll give him a ring shall I?"

"Yes mate soon as" Andy said through clenched teeth.

Starting on his third double he could hear Perkins in deep conservation with Palmer, laughing and joking, he listened till his impatience got the better of him.

"Could you have your little chat later, d'you think Perkins? Can he fit me in or not?" he shouted

"Yes Guv" Perkins replied, "We can go now."

Andy threw down the rest of his third double as Perkins terminated his call to Palmer.

All the drink had done was to make him unsteady Andy observed ruefully. The pain was still as intense as before. At

Palmers, Andy ignored the dentist's attempt at polite chitchat saying shortly.

"Where's the chair? I want this fucker out!"

"I'll just have to give you an injection."

"Fuck that. Just pull it out!" "Shame, I could have done something with that, it's a good strong tooth." Palmer said tugging away at the tooth. Andy yelled in agony.

"Injection?" offered Palmer.
"No just get it out!"

Once out Palmer threw the tooth in the yellow bin on the floor.

"Hey Doc, can I have the tooth I'd like to keep it if that's okay?"

"Sure" said Palmer rummaging through the bin, planting the tooth its long roots still bloody, in Andy's' hand. "Thanks" said the Guv with a weak smile.

"How much do I owe you?"

"Call it fifty."

"Worth every penny, thanks." Andy said through the wad of cotton wool in his mouth.

"How's the pain?" enquired Perkins.

"Much better" Andy said.

"Back down the pub then?".

"Na drop me off".

They bid farewell to Palmer, and Perkins dropped his boss off before heading back to his customary position at the bar of the pub.

Andy walked across his grubby little flat and put the tooth pride of place on the mantelpiece. "So much pain from such a small thing", he thought to himself staring at it, admiring its simplicity, its strength, its colour. Hmm. food, his stomach was grumbling and he hoped his tooth cavity had stopped bleeding. He knew he should not eat after an extraction but he was starving and he made his way to the fridge. Inside there was a bit of cheese wrapped in Clingfilm, not tight enough to stop it drying out, a couple of slices of ham, two tins of Strongbow cider, and some tomatoes. "Fuck it, I must do some shopping", he mumbled to himself slamming the fridge door shut. Reaching into the high cupboards he removed a tin of big soup, did he have any bread he wondered, he flipped open the bread bin, apart from an elderly and very mouldy scone, nothing. Fuck. Oh well, soup on its own then. After warming it on the cooker he turned on the T.V and settled down for what was left of the evening. Struggling to spoon the soup into one side of his mouth, as the third spoon-full splashed down his front, he gave up in frustration.

Just then the phone rang. It was Denise. "How's tricks Guv tooth ache gone?"

"Yep the little bastard's on the mantelpiece"

"How come?"

"Long story tell you tomorrow, find anything at Porters Street?"

"Not a dicky bird", she replied.

"Oh well it was worth a try, see you in the morning"

Andy spent a restless night and woke to a pillow soaked in blood.

In the office next day the phone rang and Perkins reached to pick it up.

"I think you'll find that's for me," Andy said, beating him to the call

"Oh yes good morning Super, no nothing yet, yes everything, yes sir, of course, yes sir, will do".

"Who was that?" Perkins asked

"Fuck off you piss taker, he's right though we've come up with sweet fanny Adams. All we got is a load of headless bodies, it's as if someone's placed a hand grenade in their mouths and blew them up".

"We've been over that Guv, says Perkins, there's no struggle, they haven't been drugged, there were no other injuries to their bodies, it's as if they wanted to do it, like a suicide bomber".

"Perhaps they were suicide bombers," suggests Denise.

Andy gave her a look that said you know better than that and said. "There's a link, and I'd bet my life it's not suicide the cases are too diverse, too random.

And a suicide bomber is supposed to kill other people, Denise".

"Yes Guv"
"Make yourself useful take Perky with you, go see some of the relative's, see if anyone had a death wish, see who they were in contact with, any recent acquaintance with suspect groups, cults, that sort of thing. Waste of time if you ask me, but hey we got fuck all else."

"Sure thing, come on Perky." Denise said with enthusiasm.

"Try and hold me back", he said, sardonically, following her to the door.

"And don't come back till you've got something!" Andy shouted after them.

"What fucking now?" he thought looking round at the empty office, "Fuck it, pub!"

The pub was noisy, too noisy for him to think so he stepped outside with his pint, and settling at one of the many wooden tables in the rear garden of the pub, he became engrossed in watching the people around him. Many were refugees from the station, he thought that the chain that had opened the pub here in what had been the old magistrate court, knew what they were doing. The force had a reputation for being hard drinkers and with the food that they served, tasty, not too expensive and a generous plate full, they were always assured of a good clientele.

At one side of the wooden tables he saw Sammy Matheson's old oppo, Roberts. The man looked pale and gaunt, he had obviously lost a lot of weight, normally Andy would have disapproved of someone appearing in a pub who was supposed to be off sick but in this case he could not bring himself to. Roberts looked haunted, and Andy knew he was single. He also knew what it was like to be alone and suffering the nightmares that Roberts would be suffering. He went over to talk to him.

"Hello Roberts." Roberts looked at him doubtfully obviously wondering if Andy would have something to say about his being off work and in the pub.

"Glad to see that you are keeping up with the crowd, it can get lonely on your own, being off." Andy said.

Roberts relaxed. "Yes sir, any luck with the case?"

"Not really, got Perky and Lawson working on it, but whichever way we go is a dead end it seems."

Roberts looked down at his pint and nodded.

"I wish I could, you know . . ."

"Yes I know you do, but it is more important that you get back up to strength first." Andy put his hand on the younger mans shoulder. Roberts looked as though he might burst into tears.

"A break down is as valid an illness as anything else, Roberts, take it easy and don't beat yourself up OK?"

Roberts looked up at the senior officer gratefully. "Thanks sir."

Andy drifted back inside to one of the booths and settled down for some people watching, often he would play games trying to guess what various drinkers did for a living, who was married to who? Who was cheating on their other halves? Most of the drinkers were members of the force tonight, but some nights there were rich pickings and he had got pretty good at picking up the signs; a white mark where a wedding ring had recently been removed, a nervousness with eyes frequently darting to the door or clocking anyone who came in, in case they were seen. It was a pub that was well known as a police hangout and as such put certain people off. Andy often wondered if the couples he saw having illicit assignations chose the pub because of that?. Was he ever right about what he guessed about the people he watched? He never knew, it was just an amusing past time, a break from the real world, which was, he found also full of wrong assumptions and disappointments. But tonight he could not concentrate. If only we could get a break on this case, something to get the Super off his back, he mused. He flicked mobile open.

"Hi, Denise it's me"

"Me who?"

"O Meowww, anything?"

"Not a sausage Guv"

"Where are you?"

"At Barton's place, the old man's as happy as Larry, glad to be rid of his low life son, his words not mine"

"His own flesh and blood, how sad, I'm going to do some food shopping, keep me posted"
"Sure thing", she replied and hung up.
Loaded down with shopping bags Andy unlocked the flat door and shoved it open with his foot. With the shopping unpacked he contemplated returning to work. "Quick cuppa first I'm thinking" he mumbled. With the television on he sat in his favourite chair. The mid day news has just started. Settling back to watch, the screen flickered then returned back to normal. Unusual, he thought. Then it happened again, "What the fuck?" he said as the picture settled once more. Then again. "What the fucks going on?" He said in frustration. Then having come to the conclusion that the network might be having trouble, he shut the set off and went back to work.

The afternoon was uneventful, and the several calls he made to his team failed to raise his spirits, they were consistently drawing blanks. None of the victim's had been suicidal, quite the opposite in fact, most had everything to live for. "It just does not make sense." He said aloud to his empty office.

A few jars at the pub and he was soon back at his tiny flat, surprisingly and unusually tidy, but dark and in need of decorating he concluded. With a freshly cooked meal on his lap he stabbed at the remote and the TV flickered into life. "Aww fuck no," he said looking at the screen, which was all wavy lines. A familiar faint noise registered in his brain. As he was racking his brains to make a connection with the sound, the screen returned to normal. Andy raised his fork to his mouth, and was just about to take a bite of his chicken tikka when the noise came again, followed by more wavy lines on the screen of his new plasma. Placing his meal on the coffee table he went to the TV, the noise quietened but the lines remained. Turning the volume down allowed him to hear the familiar sound more clearly. He scoured the flat for the source, and then, abruptly, it stopped. "Fuck it" he shouted. He stood still and waited for the sound to come again. He was about to give up when the high whine started again, and his eyes and ears were drawn slowly but surely to the fireplace, then straight to the tooth that had so recently been in his head. Cautiously he cocked an ear towards the tooth. That was it, it was the same sound as he had heard in the surgery the sound that the dentist said was common enough and would settle. He picked up the tooth frowning.

Looks normal, he thought. But putting it to his ear he could hear the noise, faintly but still unmistakable.

Something's not right, he told himself, and putting the tooth in his pocket he decided to take it to work." Get the lab boys to take a look". He mumbled.

"Bob, you been drinking?" Andy asked as Bob's uninspiring drone of a voice greeted him with "Kenly Police Lab?" only it came out sounding like Kellypleeselad

"Nope" said the Nerdy character on the other end of the line.

"Good, can I pop in and see you in the lab?"

"What now?"

"Yes now" demanded the Guv

Half an hour later Andy handed the tooth to Bob.

"Is that it, you interrupted me for that?" said Bob.

"Just listen to it before you go off on one." Andy said
Bob put the tooth to his ear,

"You're winding me up, this is some kind of joke right, who
put you up . . . .?"

Just then an unmistakable whine filled the air. "Hang on yes;
yes I can hear something, sounds like a wireless being tuned."

"Yes that's it, weird noise, had that before, just after the dentist
did the filling at the Dentist's,he said it was common it would
wear off, but what the hell is causing it?" Andy said

Bob placed the tooth in a small vice and carefully started to
drill away at the filling.

"Here there is something in here, have a look" he said bending
down to get a better look

"What is it?" said Andy impatient to take a closer look

"Don't know." said Bob delving and prodding deeper.

BOOOMMMMM.

With the sound waves from the explosion ringing in his ears,
Andy picked himself up, dusting himself down, his hands
brushed away a sticky mess, looking down he could see his
outstretched hands were covered in blood.

"Bob, Bob you okay?" he said gently lifting his friend from
the lab bench. "Oh God", he said as he caught a glimpse of
Bob's mutilated face, most of the front of his head had gone.
He was dead. Leaning over the tooth on the bench he had
taken the full blast. Another 3 seconds and I would have been

a gonner too, Andy thought, an icy fear gripped him and laying Bob back down he sat down on a lab stool, fighting a panic attack.

The puzzle that had tortured him for the last few weeks was, in that awful moment, as he sat next to the body of his dead colleague and heard footsteps running to help them, finally solved.

"It was Steven the dentist, he killed all those people." he murmured. What he wasn't clear about was motive.

"Why implant me?" Andy murmured then answered his own question, "obviously he knew we would find him one day, we were the enemy, I was a gift to him with my chipped filling.

"Has he done all his patients?" He thought aloud. "God how many?" he said as the first officers reached the lab.

Soon the lab was crawling with specialists. Paramedics cleaned and checked Andy who got the all clear. "You were lucky Guv,looks like old Bob saved your life", said Perkins

"Yes poor bastard took the full whack." Andy paused for a moment, then squaring his shoulders he said "Right you two back to the office, we need a plan, you going to be alright Denise?"

"Yes Guv just a bit queasy, can't seem to get used to it."

"Least some of his head's still there, says Perkins observing. 'Same as the others Guv?" he asked

"No, like I said, office, now!"

Once inside the office Andy said. "Right shut the door; this is not to leave these four walls, got it?"

Perkins and Denise nodded. "What we got Guv?" Denise leaned forward hungry for information.

"Not absolutely sure, Bob was prodding around in that tooth I had pulled and it blew up, we will have to wait for forensics to be cast iron. My theory is that the surgery where I had my tooth done, you know Denise where you dropped me off?"

"Yes Guv, go on". "Yes that surgery, the dentist there is called Steven; I am convinced that he put something in my tooth, some sort of explosive. My guess is that he has put explosives in other patient's teeth then blew them up with some sort of remote, what do you think? far fetched?

Perkins's piped up

"No Guv that certainly would explain it, I mean they didn't know till—boom".

"Exactly" Agreed the Guv.

"Motives?", Asks Denise.

"Some were wealthy some were not, so could be blackmail for money, revenge." Andy said
"Could be sexual" suggests Perkins; some of the women were drop dead, Err I mean really nice"

"Or he could just be a fruit cake?" Denise said.

They spent a few hours developing a plan of action then went home for the night.

Bright and early the following day Andy and his two sidekicks waited patiently as the surgery got into full swing.

"Right anyone in there we arrest, we want to get everyone, you got that?"

"Yes Guv"

"There's only one way out, so don't let anyone past"

"Yes Guv"

"I'm going to head straight for Steven's surgery"

"Yes Guv"

"Right, let's go!"

"Yes Guv".

They go in the entrance and up the stairs; Perkins guards the stairs, while speaking to Pauline the receptionist, flashing his I.D he tells her she's under arrest and to keep quiet. Denise has gone to the waiting room, which was empty. The Guv bursts into Steven's room where he has a patient on the chair. "Stay where you are your under arrest Steven" Andy shouted

"Oh I say, what the devil is going on?" said the posh speaking elderly man from the chair.

"Take it easy sir this man's under arrest for murder". For a second the Guv had taken his eyes off Steven, who taking his chance tried to make a dash for freedom. Andy rugby tackled him to the ground, and roughly handcuffing him read Steven his rights. Meanwhile Anthony watched with horror as the drama unfolded on the monitors.

Clutching a remote in his hand he taps in 007, with a finger hovering over the detonation button he is waiting for enough space between The Detective and Steven. Denise entered the room. "Denise, go get Perkins"

"Yes Guv."

"Perky the Guv wants you"

"Watch the stairs then" he tells Denise.

"Right"

Perkins entered the room. "Take him and don't take your eyes off him"

"Sure thing Guv", replied Perkins marching Steven out of the room.

Anthony seized his chance and pressed the button, nothing, "What the fuck?" he said pressing the button again, watching the Guv on the monitor he repeatedly pressed the button on the remote punctuating each attempt with "Fuck!" 'Sir, I must ask you . . . '. 'Sorry you'll have to speak up I'm a bit mutton Jeff', said the old boy. The Guv stepped a little closer and leaned towards the man. "Did the dentist do any major work to your teeth?" Just as the old man was about to reply . . . .

BOOMMM

His whole head exploded covering the place in blood, brains, and bone. Andy had taken a fair amount of the blast and was knocked to the ground.

Denise ran to the door un-prepared for what she was about to see. One look and her breakfast began to stage reappearance. Meanwhile Perkins had handcuffed his prisoner to the radiator pipe; reassured that Steven was going no-where he went to see what had happened. Denise brushed by him holding her hand over her mouth, vomit oozing between her fingers as she desperately raced to the toilets. Perkins peered in, even having seen all the other victims he felt a little queasy.

"Guv, Guv!" he shouted bending down over Andy's motionless body. Andy was badly injured but he was still alive.

"Hang in there Guv I'll get some help"

"Officer down!" he shouted into his walkie-talkie, Ambulance, back up, NOW!

Soon the place was crawling. Andy was taken away on a stretcher with a very green Denise in tow.

Anthony stood motionless, fear clutching his stomach as he watched the monitors. Should he stay put hoping not to be discovered, or make a break for it down the stairs and into the garden? After the surgery was cleared of people, the forensic team scoured the surgery top to bottom. Anthony held his breath when they opened the drug cabinet, and then expelled a sighed with relief when they moved on.

Once all was clear on the monitors he started packing the remotes and other important bits and pieces he may need. The whole lot fitted into two large carrier bags that he put at the top of the stairs.

Back in the secret room he left several of the devices, all tuned to the same frequency on his work bench and went quietly down the stairs and out into the back garden shoving whatever personal stuff he could fit into the top of the carrier bags. Making sure the coast was clear he noticed a copper guarding the front entrance and pulled back into the alley. Peering round he watched the policeman walking around, back and forth, back and forth. Once he had established a pattern of the man's patrol and when the policeman's back was to him Anthony slipped away, threw the bags on the back seat of his car. Further down, he stopped the car again. He could just see the roof of the surgery. For a moment he sat motionless then sighing slightly he hit the button. The building erupted into a cloud of fire and debris burying the copper. Anthony drove off looking back a thin smile on his face. He set his mind to the fact that he would have to look for lodgings now that his place of abode had been blown to smithereens. He thought about going home to his mother, but he did not want to draw any attention to her if the police went digging, and the same thing applied to Cathy, he loved her, and they were very close now, he did not want anything to jeopardise that. He thought about Cathy for a moment, how he had almost a double life, the life that he led with her, the sex that just got better, but even more than that the normality, meeting her colleagues going on days out, just normal things, that he had had no experience of before in his life. No he could not risk that, could not risk her finding out what his other life entailed. It was a nuisance, but he would cope and he had better lie low for now. At the police station Steven denied everything, they hadn't much proof, just more dead bodies with heads missing. Andy Sims was on the critical list and was also the main witness. After a quick run through with Perkins and Lawson, Superintendent Nyland decided they would take their chances with the CPA and charged Steven with eight counts of murder.

Banged up, Steven had a cell all to himself.

"Anthony can you hear me?" Both Steven and Anthony had fitted themselves with the most up to date version of their transmitter devices with no code word, so that they would be able to communicate at any time.

"Anthony?" Steven said a little louder.

"Yes mate, where are you?" he answered

"In a cell, they've charged me, I'm in court tomorrow." "Blimey that's quick!" said Anthony. "Well we are the thorn in their side that has been festering for months, they are slavering over me like hungry dogs, didn't expect anything else. Plus that twat Sims is in hospital now, was that your work Ant?"

"No, couldn't detonate him mate. In the end I offed old Culverhouse the guy you had in the chair, and Sims caught the brunt of it."
'Where are you?' asked Steven.

"In a crummy bed-sit, the surgery's gone; I had to blow it up"

"We can build another one when you get me out, go to another City eh?"

"Ye London, all those wealthy people", said Anthony a stream of wealthy businessmen in smart suits flashing through his mind."

"How are you going to get me out?" enquired Steven.

"Not sure but I'll be there tomorrow, you probably won't see me, but I'll be there"

"Okay I can hear someone coming, see you tomorrow"

An attorney was appointed for Steven. A dumb looking blonde, long hair, glasses, very plump, she was wearing a two piece that looked a size too small, the buttons and stitching were just about holding their own. "Hello I'm Angela Reese, I'll be representing you Steven", she said holding out her hand, which he accepted. The policeman accompanying her put a handcuff round Stevens's outstretched hand clipping it shut. Steven was startled
"We are just taking you to an interview room Steven" she said in a tone that was meant to be reassuring.

"Okay no sweat", he replied.

He couldn't of cared less what she had to say, or where they were taking him. Steven was a hundred percent sure Anthony was going to get him out anyway. He agreed to a plea of guilty.

With the blonde bimbo happy with her work he was escorted back to his cell.

"Hungry?" the copper said, "we got chicken or chicken".

"Guess it'll be chicken then" Steven replied not really giving a fuck.

The hatch was opened and the meal was placed on the shelf.

"Actually, poke it, I'm not hungry, you probably spat on it anyway," he said.

"Fuck you then, I'll eat it", said the copper taking it back.

Steven could hear the sarcastic bastard. "Mmmm lovely, Oh yes this is fucking handsome, Fucking melts in your mouth' the policeman taunted him from the corridor outside the cells till the meal was finished, and then all went quiet.

"Anthony?"

"Yes mate?"
"You're going to get me out, right?" said Steven anxiously.

"Yes mate, of course", Said Anthony.' get yourself a good nights kip'

"Yeah right, I might as well sleep on the floor, this bed's rock hard" moaned Steven.
"Mine too and it stinks, bed-sits, they're always the pits"

The pair talked into the early hours and confident that he would soon be free Steven signed off and drifted into a fitful sleep.

"Wakey, wakey sleeping beauty" an overweight copper stood over him, he smelt faintly of carbolic soap and stale cigarettes.

Steven was startled and nearly jumped out of his skin.

"What the fuck?" then realisation, as he remembered where he was.

"Breakfast?" said the policeman.

"Poke it", Said Steven.

"I just knew you were going to say that, jolly good, more for me. You got one hour then you're out of here".

"Where am I going?"

"To court, numb nuts!"
"Oh yeah" Steven said nonchalantly.

In court Steven sat expressionless, between two Detectives. Angela Reece was sitting to his left.

As the judge entered, the whole court rose and Steven was man handled to his feet. A large podgy man entered the court, clad in a black cloak and wig. Steven thought he looked vaguely familiar. Looking up at the visitor's gallery he glimpsed Anthony briefly, or rather his retreating back as he left the courtroom in a hurry.

"Where the fuck is he going?" Steven whispered to himself.

An hour passed as the machinations of the court ground slowly on, the charges were laid and bail was refused. The Judge asked Steven to stand.

"How does the defendant, Mr. Steven Smith plead?'

Angela Reece stood up 'Guilty to all charges my lord'

"Right court will adjourn for one hour," The judge said heaving his overweight body out of his chair.

The prosecution lawyer, Angela Reece and the judge sat in the Judges chambers half-heartedly discussing Steven fate.

"There's no fun in it if the bastards plead guilty" the prosecution lawyer grumbled glancing accusingly at Angela.

After tea and biscuits the three returned to court. Shortly after the legal teams had taken their seats, Steven saw, with relief, Anthony slip back into the court.

The judge eased his bulk back into this chair and said "Steven Smith, stand"

Steven did with a slight smile on his face.

"Steven Smith, you have entered a guilty plea, so I see no point in bringing your case to trial, I therefore charge you with eight counts of murder, you will go to prison for life, with a minimum tariff of no less than twenty five years. Do you have anything to say?"

Steven shrugged his shoulders and smiled slightly as though the judge had just let him off a speeding fine.

"Take him down," The judge said, mopping his waxy forehead with a handkerchief, it always made him uneasy when the buggers were so cool.

"He's innocent mate" Anthony's voice soft and precise appeared like an unexpected thought in the judge's brain. Like Steven he had recognised the portly man passing judgement and had dashed back to his grubby bed-sit room to fetch one of the remotes.

"What's that?" The judge looked up short-sightedly

"You got the wrong bloke, you fat fuck" Anthony said quietly, trying to wind the old fart up.

"You what?" the Judge spluttered, mopping at his face furiously with his handkerchief, "of all the impudent, I shall hold you in contempt of court sir, officers bring him to the bench!" A couple of police officers that were standing at the door to the courtroom looked confused, they could hear nothing, see no one.

"What's wrong with the judge is he all right". "What's the matter with him?" "Is he ill? He looks ill!" Angela said flustered, the judge was holding his head, looking around wildly for something or someone.

"It was me; your worst nightmare, let him go, or else you're going to die." Anthony's voice again.

"What? No! What's going on? Bring him down!" said the Judge his face darkening suffused with blood, he was agitated and sweating profusely. It looked like he might spontaneously combust at any time.

"Are you all right my lord?" the court usher asked solicitously.

"No there's someone talking can't you hear them?"

"No my lord, do you want to adjourn? It's plain your not feeling well!" The court usher said anxiously.

"Let him go NOW" the voice rang out in the Judge's head again.

"Stop it! Who's saying that?" The Judge was whimpering now, clapping his hands over his ears. He rocked back and forward muttering to himself, as though he was talking to someone. Around the courtroom officers and public, legal teams and ushers looked at each other. The judge was obviously having some sort of breakdown and they had no idea what to do.

"What's wrong is he going mad?" Angela whimpered as she and the opposing council stood transfixed.

"The noise, stop the noise!" The judge screamed falling out of his chair and landing with a loud thud on the floor of his courtroom.

BOOOMMMM

Blood, brains, and millions of little pieces of human tissue rained down on the courtroom, Angela Reese began to scream as she realised what she was looking at, and what was decorating her jacket, at the same time pandemonium erupted everywhere. The two officers flanking Steven jumped down from the defendant box their radios out summoning help. In the confusion, Steven vaulted down over the defendants box to the floor slippery with the judges grey matter and ran to the door. At the same time Anthony ran down the stairs from the visitors' gallery and together they slipped away unnoticed.

CHAPTER 13

"Thanks mate' said a relieved Steven sitting in the passenger seat of Anthony's car.

"That's okay Steve, lucky I remembered that fat fucker!"

"Yes I had a feeling, but wasn't sure, with his wig on' explained Steven. "But hey, what a fucking show we put on there, it was spectacular, and did you see all their faces?"

'Yes they didn't know what the fuck had hit them." Anthony said, "but we got a problem, that Detective's implant didn't detonate, he must have had it taken out by someone."

"No! How come it didn't blow up?"

'I don't know, maybe it did blown up, after all if he did have it taken out by someone then it might well have done, and if it only happened in the last day or so we would not have heard about it, may not have heard about it anyway depending on where and by whom it was removed. Anyway all is not lost, I think he's dead anyway, I detonated the old fucker in the chair, they were really close together, I think I got them both."

Steven looked at his friend, and thought that somehow Anthony had a developed a new maturity to go with his new look. There was something else too, a sort of downbeat note to Anthony's voice, as though he somehow regretted what had happened.

Although Steven had no clue, it was true that the time that Anthony was spending with Cathy had had a very calming effect on him. At the same time it had brought out in him a mature and more measured assessment of the world, a less hate filled view of things. His father was dead, and his mother was now coping very well, had even managed to graduate from her wheelchair to sticks now and had struck up a friendship with a man at the rehab group she attended. He was a nice man, Anthony had made sure of that. He was very protective of his mother still, and had flown around there when she had invited him to lunch with her new 'friend' Alan. Anthony had been prepared to hate the man on sight, but found that he couldn't. Alan was a big gentle bear of a man, an undertaker who had broken his back in a motorcycle accident. Like Anthony's mother Alan was on sticks and the two of them joked about nearly tripping each other up as they got used to walking. Anthony had not seen his mother looks so happy for a long time. She had lost weight, had her hair done and was wearing a really pretty dress, rather than the baggy trackies that she usually wore. She had a sparkle in her eye that made her look a lot younger than she was and Anthony began to relax as he saw how gentle and loving Alan was, anytime Anthony's mother would put down her fork Alan's hand would dart out to cover hers on the dinner table. In response she would give a little giggle and when Anthony left after lunch, they hardly seemed to notice. He had smiled to himself as he got into the car outside, heading for Cathy's; it was funny that both he and his mother were in love at the same time. He wondered if he and Cathy looked as soppy to observers as his mother and Alan did.

In fact Cathy and Anthony made a striking couple. Cathy, thanks to the efforts of the TV's make up department had developed a new, more sophisticated style. And Anthony was making the most of his makeover, he loved the way that heads would turn when they walked by although they did not go out that much, Anthony was always afraid for bumping into Steven. He supposed that at some point Steven would stop mentioning Cathy every few weeks but it seemed that just when Anthony thought Steven might be moving on he would make some remark about Cathy, about how she didn't know what she was missing, was a stuck up frigid bitch, or worse. Anthony had to bite his tongue hard and hope that Steven would meet someone else and would get over the massive blow to his ego that Cathy's rejection had obviously been. But Steven, it seemed who had a penchant for the rough side of sex, had taken up with an S&M group and took his pleasures mostly via his wallet.

"Don't want any stupid bint getting too close hey Ant?" he would say "Plenty of time for wall to wall pussy when we get out of this dump of a country and take ourselves off somewhere warm. I fancy Brazil myself, whadya think? Those Brazilian women are smoking hot, there was one in a group that I went to last weekend, she had a pussy like a vice, I swear she had teeth up there!"

Anthony had laughed, but in truth he and Cathy enjoyed gentle and tender lovemaking. They would make love for hours; he would stare into her eyes and tease her body to heights of ecstasy watching her expression change as she became more aroused. He would play with her willing body for hours, bringing her to orgasm after orgasm watching the expressions on her face the brightness in her eyes, the swelling of her nipples, her breasts, the soft folds around her vagina. When she begged him to stop he would gently enter her and just when she thought her over stimulated nerves could stand no more she would find herself exploding in a final orgasm along with Anthony. They were deeply in love. Early in their relationship Anthony had worried that she might be tempted by some of the slick types that worked at the TV station but one touch of his hands on her and she was back with him, under his spell, completely open to him and in love with him. Anthony could not have been happier with his relationship, he even fantasised about settling down, having children together. But none of that was possible while he and Steven were on the course they were on and he knew it. And now it had got a whole lot worse. He had thought of abandoning Steven to his fate but he couldn't do it and he knew that the trail would lead back to him anyway, after all Brian knew he worked there, for one. No the only way out of this mess was to attack it head on. Now as they sat deep in their own thoughts Steven said to him.

'What we going to do now mate?'

"I don't know." Anthony said

"We will have to start again somewhere else, and we'll need more money, the lab, the surgery all gone, just the remotes and a few bits and bobs left. "Have we got enough to get us some money? "Steven asked

"Yes," replied Anthony as he opened the door to the grubby little bed-sit.

"Hey cheer up mate, anyone would think you didn't want the money or to start again. You know we're going to have to disappear? Well mostly me, no one knows you, Anthony."

Anthony thought about Cathy, someone knew him, knew him very well, the thought of leaving her made his blood run cold. His mind went back to the night before, when, wrapped in each others arms they had watched the night sky from behind the balcony doors of her flat, they had made love and then sat snuggled up in a blanket together watching the stars, and the occasional blinking light of an aircraft.

"Anthony, I've been thinking."

"Sounds serious." Anthony had said kissing her upturned face.

"Well it is really, but I don't know if you might think I'm a bit, well, previous?"

"Go on, you're frightening me now." Cathy threw her arms around his neck "Silly, nothing to be afraid of, I just wondered if it would be easier if you, well moved in?" she smiled at him shyly.

Anthony's heart skipped a beat. He could think of nothing he would like to do more but he had to be careful.

He hesitated a moment too long and he felt her shoulders stiffen.
"Well if you don't want to!"

"No, of course I want to, it's just I do have mum to think of."

"Yes and that's another thing when are you going to introduce us?"

"I've told you Cathy, she's not well, can't see anyone, but I promise I will stay here as often as I can." Anthony hated lying to her but as it turned out it was just as well that no one, especially his mother knew that they were an item. It had bugged him at first when Cathy had asked him to keep the relationship a secret because she thought she would get on faster at work if everyone thought she was single. Now he thanked God for her insistence on secrecy.

"You can stay here for a bit till we sort money and that." suggested Anthony

"Thanks mate, you weren't wrong about the smell, frowsty." Steven sniffed the stale air.

"Yes nobody had stayed here for a while I bet, you'll be safe as houses here," Anthony said reassuringly.

"Can't be for long though, couple of weeks tops."

"You're right mate, about disappearing, I'm happy that my mum can look after herself now, I'll break it to her gently although she is pretty taken up with her new man, I doubt she'll even notice, and anyway I can visit, as you so rightly said, no one knows who I am. How you going to tell your mum Steve?"

"I'll have to write" he replied, 'I've got to, they're going to know soon enough what we've done, best I tell them myself." Anthony thought Steven looked less confident now.

Across town in the hospital Denise and Perkins stood outside Andy's room waiting to be allowed in. The ICU was always a frightening place, the beeping of the machines that kept patients who were clinging to life by a thread alive were bewildering and incomprehensible. Finally a nurse dressed in scrubs and wearing a mask appeared and asked them to put on gowns and masks before she led them into Andy's room.

"He looks bad," said Denise looking at her boss, his entire body seemed to be black and blue and grotesquely swollen, he was just a blob with no definition.

"He's a big old tough bastard he'll pull through!" said Perkins looking at all the tubes and wires trailing from the Guv's body. He swallowed hard. "Don't you make a liar out of me you fucker!" he said with forced jollity. Denise put her hand over his. She knew he didn't mean to be disrespectful; it was just his way of coping.

"I'm sure it looks worse than it is' she said a lump in her throat. "If he was able to, what would he be doing now?" she said

"Hmm, perhaps staking out Steven's home in case he turned up there?" Suggested Perkins

"You're not just a pretty face are you Perkins? Come on then let's go, we're no use here."

A while later they were parked outside Steven's house.

"Right you get your head down Perky I'll wake you in a hour then I'll have a kip."

Denise watched Perkins as he slept. She had a huge crush on him and thought he looked sweet his long dark eyelashes resting on his cheeks. The hour up Denise was getting drowsy and gave Perkins a nudge.

"My turn."

"Oh okay" he said wiping the sleep from his eyes.

"An hour?" Denise said reclining her seat.

'Will do Denise, nighty night'

Denise slept almost immediately, chuffing like a little steam train. Irritated by the noise Perkins reached over and twisted her nose. She shifted in her seat. Perkins's could barely believe his eyes, Denise's legs fell apart under her skirt that had hitched up and a button had come undone on her blouse. Dare he look for fear of being caught? What the hell he thought.

"Bingo! Red my favourite!" he whispered admiring the silky red triangle between Denise's legs, he was hypnotised, he tried to force his gaze away but his eyes kept being drawn back to the same spot. Is it me he thought or are her legs opening wider? Now he could spot a few pubic hairs peeping out the side of her red panties. Perkins's drew his hands up to his crutch to hold the erection he had developed. Fuck! I hope she doesn't wake up now he whispered looking at her eyes. Again his eyes were drawn downward, on the way he noticed the gap in her blouse, a white low cut bra, normally enough to hold things in place, but because of the way she was lying one of her pink nosed puppies had slipped out, the tight little nipple standing to attention. Perkins almost creamed his pants there and then. He was just debating whether he could get away with a wank, when suddenly Denise woke up.

"Fuck what's going on?"

"You tell me, you got your tits out, and you're spread eagled all over the place, think you just had sex in your sleep." Perkins voice was tight with lust.

"Sex what's that, haven't had any in months?" she said straightening herself.

"Me neither, and now I've got a raging hard on thanks to you, I was just thinking of doing some boys stuff."

"I can help you with that Perky." she said admiring his bulge, the very sight of it was turning her on. Thoughts drifted through her mind of the last time that she had been with a man, but it was a very distant memory.

"Really?" he said.

"Well have you had a better offer lately?" she asked feeling really horny.

"No, can't say I have." Perkins's voice was thick with desire.

"Well then," she said loosening the belt to his trousers.

Fearing she would change her mind he quickly helped her to gain access to his throbbing cock.
She slowly stroked it and whispered 'how about the real thing Perky?' into his ear.

"Yes, but quick I think I'm going to blow!"

Denise removed her silk red panties and brushed them across Perkins's face. He groaned as the musky smell filled his nostrils.

"Push the seat right back!" she said urgently

Perkins did as he was told and his excitement rose as she straddled him and lowered herself on to his cock.

"Oh yes Denise it's been a long time!" he breathed

"For you and me both!" she said bouncing up and down enthusiastically her breasts jiggling in his face, the nipples hard little bullets against his lips.

"I'm coming, I'm coming!" moaned Perkins.

"Go on then" she said as she felt his cock harden inside her. Perkins's orgasmed, months of stored up semen emptied into her and he deflated with a moan.

"Oh Denise, that was, well indescribable, brilliant, fantastic!"

"Okay don't over do it, let's go try it somewhere different next time, perhaps in a bed? And for now, I think you have some unfinished business" She moved back to her seat spreading her legs wide and guiding his hand to her engorged clitoris. Her orgasm, when it came, was as powerful as his and Perkins felt the start of a new erection.

"Definitely bed next time!" she gasped as they adjusted their clothing

"Goes without saying Denise, so there will be a next time?"

"Perhaps, like I said you had any better offers?" she smiled an impish grin.

"Nope, still can't believe my luck". He says smiling back. Denise was not his normal type but he was tired of the stick thin brittle blonde one-night stands he met in nightclubs, and even the last of them had been some time ago. Denise was soft and womanly and as sexy as hell! They settled down to watch the house their hands lightly entwined and the smell of sex pervading the interior of the car.

But Steven had no intention of going to his house. Up early the next morning Steven spotted a postman at the door of the building that housed the grimy bedsit "Excuse me mate?"

"Yes?" replied the postman.

"Here's a fiver, you know to cover the postage, could you deliver this letter for me?"

'Sure thing' said the man santching the fiver from Steven's hand.

"Cheers"

Some time later the letter dropped on to the mat, Mary picked it up.

"I know that writing it's Steven's, that odd, why would he be writing and look there's no stamp!"

"Well I guess you'll find out if you open it!" Brian said putting on his coat ready to walk to work.

Mary opened the envelope and began to read out loud.

> Dear Mum
>
> I have done things terrible things, don't blame yourself, if you want to blame anyone, blame the drunken bastard that made me this way. It was him that filled me with so much hate. It started off as a sort of revenge for the years of torture, but then it became a thirst for more.
>
> I have killed people Mother, many times and I can't stop, I won't ask for forgiveness, because how could you forgive

something like that? From this day forward as far as you're concerned I'm dead, you will never see me again.

Just know that I will be fine and that I will always love you and wish that your life is happy. I am sorry for the pain I know I will have caused you.

Steven

Steven's mother fell to the floor in a dead faint her brain unable or unwilling to take in what she had read.

Brian brought her round with a wet cloth and a gentle slap on her cheek.

"Well what a kick in the bollocks" said Brian his face as white as chalk as he helped her to the sofa "I'm fucking stunned!" he continued as they sat in shock. He glanced at Mary she was just sitting there motionless. Brian went and made a cup of tea, placed it on the coffee table, then sat with his arm around Mary offering comfort. They sat there for an hour their tea going cold beside them. There was a knock at the door, Brian knew who it would be. He was greeted by two tired looking detectives.

"Hello sir Detective Perkins and this is Detective Lawson, may we come in?"

"Yes please do" said Brian inviting them through. Mary remained motionless on the settee here eyes briefly flicking towards the detectives as they came in before settling on a point in the middle distance. Brian handed them the letter.

Perkins read the letter. "We will have to take this letter as evidence." He said and Brian nodded. Brian looked at Mary anxiously, there was something strange about her, almost like a detachment from the situation. Denise had noticed it too.

"Have you asked the doctor to come around?" she asked Brian

"No."

"I think you should, she has had a bad shock, it would be a good idea to have the doctor give her the once over."
Brian nodded.

"You haven't heard from Steven, other than this letter?" Perkins asked

Brian shook his head "No, we only got the letter an hour ago, delivered by hand apparently, it had no stamp on. Anyway, our post had already been delivered. Do you think he has run off, left the town?"

Perkins nodded. "I am sure he has, or gone to ground somewhere, we are looking for him, mob handed at the moment and it's just a matter of time till we catch him" Perkins said, and Brian felt Mary's shoulders tense slightly.

"Yes Detectives I hope you do", said Brian. "How did he do it? The deaths, I mean murders, how did he do it?"

"Well, he was a dentist, you know that."

"Of course, I trained him"

The two detectives exchanged glances.

"It looks as though he implanted explosives into the teeth of patients he treated somehow, then detonated them at a later date

Brian's mouth fell open. "He what?" he felt a wave of nausea wash over him

"Yes, sir, I am afraid so, you will remember the cases of victims blown up over the past few months?" Brian nodded silently. "We think he was behind them. I will come back with details of what we are sure of were his earlier victims and see if you can shed any light on why he would do this, why he would pick them."

"Him and Anthony?"

Perkins sat forward "Who's Anthony?"

"He's a friend of Steven's been friends since school, he worked with him at the surgery making and fitting dentures." Brian's voice shook slightly as he tried to take it all in.

"Address?"

"I'm not sure of the number or even if he still lives at home, but it is on Garton Avenue, I gave Steven a lift round there once, before he could drive."

"What is his surname?" Brian shrugged.

"Grace, and it's number 15." Mary's voice, soft and clear made them all jump.

"Thank you, I think you should really think about that doctor" Denise said. "Right we're finished here for now, and thank you both we'll be in touch and if he should contact you ..."

"We'll be in touch, don't you worry." Brian said "I'll show you out."

Brian closed the door behind the officers and returned to the lounge.
They sat in silence for the rest of the day, bedtime came and still Mary hadn't spoken another word.

Brian coaxed her into bed where she closed her eyes without speaking.

The next morning Brian awoke to an empty bed. He ran downstairs fearing the worst, and found Mary at the sink

"Good morning Brian love, fancy a fry up?" She said cheerfully

"Er yes, Mary are you okay love?"

"Yes why shouldn't I be?"

"Steven?" Brian said softly.

"Steven? Steven who?"

"You know, love, Steven your son'

"Goodness Brian what kind of cheese did you eat before bed? You're not making sense I haven't got a son, I couldn't have children, I told you that, don't you remember?"

"Uh, Oh yes." Brian sat down at the table, his mind whirring. He was going to have to call the doctor.

"Right then, breakfast, don't you think you might get dressed first love?" Mary gave him a sweet smile.

While he got dressed he tried to make sense of Mary's change of heart, he decided although it would be hard, he would try never to mention Steven's name again. And later when the doctor, a tall Asian man called, Brian told him "This is her way of dealing with it, I think. She really believes he does not exist!"

The doctor looked at him doubtfully.

"Really! In her mind he's dead, or never existed!" said Brian more convincingly

The doctor made reassuring noises and left some tranquillisers for Mary to take. He told Brian not to worry and to call again if he was concerned.

At Garton Avenue, Denise and Perkins had arrived and Anthony's mother and Alan were undergoing the same questioning.

"When did you last see you son Mrs Grace?"

"Oh about three months ago, just before he went abroad." Rose said.

"He went overseas?" Denise asked

"Yes, said that he had got tired of the dental business and wanted to travel, you know how these young people are!"

Alan looked at her sharply, why was she lying?

The truth was that Rose Grace was used to the police, she had become a seasoned liar in the years that her husband had supplemented his drinking habit with crime and she would do anything she had to, to protect her son. Although they had not said yet what it was that Anthony was supposed to have done, whatever it was, she was taking no chances.

"I see, but he did work with Steven Smith before he left the country?"

"Yes briefly but he said it wasn't for him, and he left!" Rose shrugged her shoulders looking as cheerful as she could. "Probably sunning himself in Thailand or some other exotic spot, lucky thing, eh? We could do with some of that sun couldn't we?" Denise smiled briefly.

"When did you last hear from him?"

"A couple of days ago."

"A postcard?" Perkins said hopefully

"No, a phone call, not one for writing postcards our Ant eh Alan?" Alan stared at her blankly and Denise and Perkins noticed the look.

"Did you speak to him when he called?" Perkins asked the big man.

"Um n—no." Alan stuttered. He's either is very shy and nervous our there is something fishy here Perkins thought to himself. Rose was thrusting her mobile in his face.

"See here, under calls received, that one, it says International." Rose said. The call had actually been from a mobile phone company trying to sell her a new package. As Denise and Perkins studied the phone she shot Alan a look, a look that said, screw up and you'll be sorry.

Alan escaped to the kitchen to make tea and gather his thoughts. As he did so he saw a familiar figure walking up the back path. It was Anthony! Alan hobbled to the back door opening it as quietly as he could and meeting Anthony half way down the path. Holding his fingers to his lips he took Anthony's arm and bundled him into the shed. Anthony was surprised, and noticed that Alan seemed to have graduated to using one stick now. Whispering Alan told him that the police were inside and watched as all the colour drained from Anthony's face.

"You better make yourself scarce, Anthony, your mother has said that you are travelling abroad and for the time being I think they believe her. What the hell is this all about?"

"Long story" Anthony said, pulling his collar up around his face, "I better go, you'll know soon enough and when you do Alan, tell mum that I never meant it, I'm really sorry, and thanks mate, take care of her!" As he disappeared down the road Anthony wondered what Alan would think when he found out the details, would he shop him? He would have to lie low, and it was a blow. They had thought that only Steven was in the frame but then of course his mother and Brian would have told the police about him, damn the whole thing was such a mess. Still if they had been convinced that he was travelling abroad, he had a bit of breathing space. Steven on the other hand was a wanted man; he could not go out at all and was getting more than a little restless in the stinking cramped bed-sit.

"Mate I've got to get out of this hell hole" moaned Steven "it's doing me head in, we said two weeks, I've been here a month already" he continued

"Sorry mate it's taking longer than I thought to find a place, there's nothing about" explained Anthony. In truth Anthony had spent a lot of the time he was supposed to be flat hunting, around at Cathy's. Luckily she did not expect him to take her out much, she did the weather in the evening at the TV station it was usually quite late before she got out and she was happy enough to spend the nights with Anthony in the flat that looked down over the river. Anthony loved getting away from the bedsit and was spending longer and longer away, a fact that was not lost on Steven.

Anthony was now even more determined to find a way to break free of Steven. All he did was talk about the rebuilding or the surgery somewhere else and the thought made Anthony feel sick. Yet he could not abandon his old friend, he just wanted to get away, somewhere where no one would find him. But that would mean leaving Cathy, and that he could not do.

As he watched Steven slumped on the bed, picking his nose he mustered his courage.

"Mate I've been thinking, we can't really set up here now, it would be only a matter of time before they found you. After all they know what we've done here, or at least I'm pretty sure they do, and if it started happening somewhere else in the country it wouldn't take them that long to put two and two together. I think, as well that it is going to be too risky for us to change accommodation now. This seems to be well under the radar, I think we should play it safe and stay here until we go. Then I thought we could go to America, what do you think?" Anthony held his breath

"I'm so fucked off I'd go to Timbuktu" groaned Steven. "I suppose you're right, better stick with this place till we get off, not that you're here much anyway, you got a bird on the go?" Steven shot Anthony a suspicious look. His friend looked totally out of place in this dump, somehow he managed to stay well groomed, and Steven noticed that for the little time that Anthony spent in the bedsit, he rarely sat down on the filthy two-seater or the bed. He must have a bird somewhere.

"Well? You got a bit of skirt?"

"Oh yeah, of course!" Anthony tried to sound sarcastic, "No like you said, I'm not on anyone's radar, I've been staying at mom's she's been having a bit of bother with her new man." He lied

"Really, does he need any dental work doing?" Steven chuckled.

Anthony forced a smile. Then changing the subject said "America it is then!" Anthony had to fight hard to hide his relief. This would buy him time.

"Oh yeah, I've checked and we'll have to change our transmitters they won't work out there on the frequency I have them set to. Here you do mine," Anthony handed Steven the device, and half an hour later it was in place.
"Right my turn I'll guide you through it."

"I've done it before!" insists Anthony

"Just be careful mate," said Steven

Just over the half hour and Steven's new device was fitted.

"Test run?" Steven said.

"Can't mate, we are on USA frequency now, the next time you hear my dulcets in your bo+nce we'll be Stateside!"

"Can't wait" Steven said.

"Right mate I'll be off start setting things up, I reckon if I go out there first, get everything ready for you so that you can come straight out there and get on with it. Maybe if you keep working on that beard and tash and grow your hair by the time I get a false passport for you and somewhere for us to work and live, we should be rockin' and rollin'!"

Steven looked doubtful. "I suppose mate, but I'm going to feel very vulnerable here on me own, how long will it take you out there do you think?"

"Hey you know I'll be as quick as I can, can't wait to get started again, the dream team, that's what we are!" Anthony high-fived Steven. "What do you want at the shops?"

'Bring back some beers I'm running out and some movies if you get a chance; I'm getting bored to death here. Do you know some people actually enjoy living like this; they must have a screw loose.

Anthony looked towards Steven, filthy, unshaven the smell of his body odour overpowering the usual aroma of the bedsit.

"Sure thing mate won't be long!"

Outside the door Anthony breathed a deep lungful of fresh air.

"Ah that's better!" he said to himself. Suddenly the door flew open behind him.

"Who you talking to mate?"

'Fuck you scared the shit out of me, I was talking to myself!' Anthony said

'Oh right' said Steven panning the area "See you in a bit then."

'Yes see you later' replied Anthony. Still shaken he hurried down the stairs and into the street. Once in the car he sat, his hands on the wheel, trying to work out in his head what he would do next. One thing motivated him. He was going to be with Cathy whatever happened, and if that meant abandoning his friend, well he was ready to do that. Steven was close to the edge now, the way he had come to the door of the flat just now, for instance, he looked like a mad man, he never washed and his eyes had a sort of crazed look in them. Anthony knew that Steven could be dangerous and it was going to be a matter of dealing with him before he lost it completely and did something that would bring the whole pack of cards crashing down on both of them. But just how long would that be?

CHAPTER 14

Anthony was in the little convenience store two streets away before he realised he had dropped his mobile in the bedsit. He felt a cold wave of fear wash over him and dropping his shopping in its basket on the floor in the middle of the shop, he bolted for the door. He rushed to the car, fumbling for his car keys as he went, praying under his breath that he would find the phone on the seat, maybe it had slipped out of his pocket . . . . It wasn't there.

Anthony jammed his fingers down the side of the driver's seat ripping the back of his hand on a jagged bit of metal. As blood dripped from his hand, he fumbled for an old pack of tissues Cathy had left in the car and wrapped his hand in it, securing it with duct tape. "Fuck fuck!" He continued to look, pushing the seat forward on its runners—nothing.

Back at the bedsit, Steven was slumped on the filthy bed, having a wank, an edition of Nuts in his hand. He was just building up a head of steam when a tinny bleep interrupted him. Ignoring it he continued staring at the plastically enhanced breasts of the cover girl and then aiming shot spunk all over her glossy face. As semen dribbled down her face and over her boobs then onto the sheets, he tucked himself back into his trackie bottoms and chuckled. He looked around for the mobile that had nearly put him off his stroke. It was Ant's and it was going off again now. He reached over for it where it had obviously fallen out of his mate's pocket by the chair and flicked it on.

"Where r u sxy?" The message read. It was signed Cathy. For a moment Steven stopped breathing. Cathy? Surely not his Cathy?. He flicked the message section open, there were a couple of messages he had sent to Anthony but most were from Cathy,

"c u l8r sxy" and "Can't w8 to c u sxy" "Cum soon, I'm missing u!" "Feeling sxy, how soon can u gt here?"

Steven felt sick. He flicked open the camera section and looked at photos that Anthony had taken. They were of Cathy. Cathy and Anthony in her flat, Anthony lying in bed, the sheets only just covering his groin, and a couple of them in the park, in the summer. One stabbed Steven right through the heart. It had obviously been taken on a crumpled bed, just after Cathy had come, her eyes were half shut, her face suffused with blood and there was just a glimpse of an erect nipple in the bottom corner of the screen at the tip of a breast blushed with the orgasm she had just had.

"The bastard, the total fucking bastard!" Steven muttered his hand shaking. He shut the phone. His mind was working overtime. Should he tell Anthony what he had discovered? No he would keep it to himself for now. Knowledge was power. At the moment Anthony had the upper hand, could abandon him in a moment, he would have to keep it to himself, think about what to do. He put the phone back on the threadbare carpet by the chair, where he had found it.

By the time that Anthony got back to the bedsit, praying that Steven had not found his mobile, Steven was in bed with the sheets pulled up over his head. He did not dare look at Anthony. Instead as Anthony came through the door he murmured.

"Just knocked one out, mate, having a nap, you got the stuff?" Anthony's glance took in the discarded magazine, Steven's semen congealing on it. He looked away.

"No, lost my wallet, I must have dropped out by the chair when I sat down—Oh here it is!" The relief in Anthony's voice was palpable. Got it now mate, I'll be back in a tick. I'll leave the door on the latch then I can put the stuff in without waking you. Sweet dreams!"

Outside Anthony leant against the stained wall of the stair well, a cold sweat evaporating on his skin. That had been close.

Steven did not move when Anthony came back with the shopping, but under the covers his eyes were open and burning with a hatred that he had not felt for a long time, not since Lucy, not since that day in the park.

As he drove to Cathy's Anthony thought about what a narrow escape he had had. It was possible that in their present situation Steven might have forgotten about Cathy, possible but not likely. There was something about Cathy that seemed to really wind Steven up, probably because she had effectively rejected him since he was a kid, and now that she was on the box every night, he had his nose rubbed in it on a daily basis. If he knew that Anthony, good old goofy Anthony, had snatched her from under his nose . . . It did not bear thinking about. There would be no reasoning with him, even although Steven had never gone out with her, but Anthony knew that that would make no difference if the chips were down. Steven, in his psychotic way had decided that she was his and nothing would be likely to deter him from that point of view.

In the bedsit Steven sat in his own filth, thinking. Could he trust Anthony to get them out of this predicament? Could he hell! If the spineless fucker couldn't even admit he had stolen his girl, how the hell was he going to rely on him to save his life? For all he knew he might be at the cop shop now spilling his guts. What remained of sanity in Steven's brain reassured him that Anthony could not do that without shopping himself. For now he was safe, but for how long and what was he going to do to punish Anthony, and Cathy? He could not let him get away with this, after all he hadn't let Barton get away with what he had done, and why should Anthony?

In the police station Denise and Joe Perkins were trying hard not to let their colleagues know that they were an item, but had just blown their cover when, as Denise stood beside Perkins desk going over some evidence, Perkins had been caught with his hand up her skirt caressing the warm smooth inside of her thigh.

"Aye aye! Bit of sexual harassment going on here then!" Jones one of the junior officers on the case came up behind them.

Joe removed his hand immediately but it was too late and the pair endured a day of teasing and ribbing. Denise found she didn't care. She had admired Joe Perkins from afar for a very long time and was delighted that he seemed not to mind that they had 'gone public'. She had always thought that he was a bit of a jock, always down the gym and always out on the town, she had even seen him a couple of times with girls who looked like models, she could barely believe her luck. She had put herself on an immediate diet and made an appointment to have a Brazilian and have her eyebrows shaped.

For his part Perkins felt pretty happy that he was with Denise, she was not his usual type, that was true, but in a return fixture at his flat she had proved to be a wildcat in bed and had given him the best blowjob he had ever had. Thinking about it made his cock twitch dangerously in his trousers and he picked up the statement from Rose Grace to distract himself.

"What do you think Denise, is she lying?"

"Dunno, I think so, but then the story is not so far fetched. Maybe we should get her mobile phone find out if that call really did originate in the Far East?"

"Yeah good thinking, not just a pretty face are you?"

Denise blushed.

"Come on then, let's go!" Joe slapped her lightly on the behind and Denise blushed again.

On the way over to Garton Road they sat in comfortable silence. Joe loved the noise her silk stockings made as she crossed her legs and as he imagined their silky tops on her thighs he felt his cock twitching again. He had always vowed that he would not go out with a woman on the force, but this had just sort of happened, and for now he was very pleased it had. Denise smiled at him. "What are you thinking about?" she said.

"Nothing I should be thinking about at work!" he replied and leaned over to squeeze the top of her leg. "I thought after we had been in to see Mrs. Grace we could go by the hospital, see the guv. What d'you think?"

Joe felt his erection deflate. He hated hospitals and he hated seeing Andy like that, a bit too close to home. There but for the grace of God and all that.

"Yeah, OK, you heard how he's doing?"

"Just that he is holding his own. I think he's going to have to have a lot of plastic surgery, he has first degree burns to his face."

Joe shuddered.

Rose Grace greeted the detectives like long lost friends and Denise was immediately suspicious, it was a well known ploy, to act as though you were delighted to see the police, and therefore could have nothing to hide. Denise thought that Mrs. Rose probably had an awful lot to hide.

"Come in come in, it's cold out there, I'm sure you could do with a hot drink, tea? Coffee? Hot chocolate? Oh and I've got some freshly baked cake, keep you going!"

"No thanks Mrs. Grace." Joe observed the woman hobbling around her kitchen like a demented scarecrow, her hair untidy and her eyes wild. She definitely had not been completely honest with them. He exchanged glances with Denise.

"Oh well, if you're sure?" Rose looked disconcerted "come and sit down then." Denise and Joe sat beside each other on a two seater settee as Rose lowered herself into a fire side arm chair.

"Has there been some news? Only I was saying to Alan yesterday, oh you remember Alan he's my partner, he was here last time, he's an undertaker you know and he's at a funeral today, only I was saying to him we hadn't heard from you although I did have another call from Anthony yesterday and I told him what had happened. He was shocked, so shocked!" Rose paused for breath "Anyway he said he might be home soon, he was really quite shocked you know!"

"You said" Joe glanced at Denise again.

"Yes, well, he was!" Rose said.

"Can I see your phone please Mrs. Grace" Denise leaned forward with her hand outstretched.

"That's the thing love, I can't find it. Going out of my mind I am, it's the only way that my Anthony can get in touch, I had it yesterday, I had a call from him, did I say?" Rose looked even wilder now and Denise crossed to her and put her hand on the woman's shoulder.

"Now just calm down Rose, think carefully, where did you have it last?"

"I was out in the garden, the signal is a bit dodgy sometimes indoors and I had gone out to talk to Anthony. When we finished talking I could hear the doorbell going. I need both hands for the sticks so I put the phone down on the bench and came in. When I got back outside again, it had gone."

Denise looked over at Joe, he had one eyebrow raised, he was obviously not buying it.

"Ok, is it contract or pay as you go?"

"Pay as you go, why?" There was a watchfulness in Rose's eyes now

"Well if it had been contract you could have got another phone with the same number, I'm not sure if you can with pay as you go. Who are you with?

"What do you mean? I don't really know anything about that, Anthony used to do all that for me, put money on and all, I don't know anything about it all!"

And methinks thou doest protest too much Denise thought.

They discussed Rose Grace on the way to the hospital. "She is obviously lying!" Joe said

"Yes, but then she would wouldn't she to protect her son. D'you think he is still in the country or has he gone abroad to avoid being caught?"

"My guess is he is still here. We need to get a good photo of him and circulate it. But I don't want to alert her that we are looking for him, at least not for a few days, so how do we get one?"

"There was one in the house it looked like a professional one done in a studio, he looks like a handsome young fella!" Denise said

"Right on the phone then and see if any studios have done work for a Mr. Anthony Grace."

"Fine, as soon as we finish here" Denise said drawing up at the hospital.

Joe steeled himself for the visit to Andy. He was still in ICU on a special bed for burn victims. He was in a lot of pain, on Morphine but even that did not seem to be helping all that much as his eyes were dull with pain and occasionally a low moan would escape his mangled lips. But he acknowledged them, the tubes that were keeping him breathing did not allow him to speak but he lifted his hand off the sheet in a feeble wave as they came in.

Joe stood behind Denise, he could not bear it, Andy looked like he was in hell, he looked as though he had been chewed up and spat out. It turned Joe's stomach and he felt in awe of Denise as she sat beside the bed her hand resting lightly over her bosses, bringing him up to date with how the investigation was going. As she spoke Joe saw a flicker of the old Andy in his tortured eyes as he took in the details and acknowledged what Denise said with the smallest nod of his head.

"So we're going back now to hit the Internet, get those photographic studios phoned, it seems strange that he would have a photo taken like that, more of a girl thing, I would have thought, but then it was for his old mum, I suppose!"

In fact Anthony had had the photos taken for his mum when he had finished having all his 'work' done. Rose Grace had always thought that her boy was a handsome lad, even although he patently was not, but she was delighted with his new film star good looks and he had had the photos taken for her birthday. Cathy had one in her flat as well.

Andy looked at her and his battered face moved very slightly into something that looked like it would be a smile. A single tear ran down his face from the corner of his left eye and Denise stood up quickly, feeling tears welling up in her own eyes.

"Right then we'll be off and get this thing put to bed! You can rely on us sir!" her voice wobbled with emotion and Joe led her from the room.

Their search turned out to be a short one. There were only three photographic studios in town and the second one that they called had done the studio shots for Anthony. Half an hour later they were distributing the shots amongst the task force.

Several days later when street surveillance had failed to spot any sign of Anthony, the photo that was destined to be used on the local news arrived in the TV studios at the same time as Cathy did for her early evening weather slot. She even carried it up to the newsroom in its police force envelope. Handing it over to Simon on the news desk she said.

What is it this time?

"Some weirdo who has been blowing people's noggins off their shoulders for some reason," Simon said opening the envelope that had one side made of cardboard to keep the photo flat.

"Go on then let's have a peek?" Cathy said as he took the photo out. She saw the name first. The police photographer had embossed it on the photo almost like a mug shot, ANTHONY GRACE. Her eyes flickered up the photo and in a surreal moment she recognised it as the one she had beside her bed in the flat, so that even when he was not there, Anthony would always be looking over her. Cathy put her hands to her mouth.

The face smiling back at her in a neat dark blue jumper, white shirt collar tips at the neck was the face that not an hour earlier had hovered above hers as they made love, those eyes had looked deeply into hers to share her pleasure and that mouth had caressed every part of her body. Cathy staggered slightly and held onto the side of the desk.

"Hey what's wrong with you? I know he's a good looking bloke, but steady on!" Simon said.

Cathy sat down, her mind working overtime. She could not believe what she was seeing there had to be some mistake, she could see Simon looking at her speculatively and she stood up forcing a laugh.

"Not as good looking as you though, eh Si? No I didn't have any lunch I feel a bit dizzy. There's usually something in the green room I'll have a look there don't want my tummy rumbling during the forecast, do we?." Simon smiled at her.
Back at the bed sit Steven was engrossed an old movie. It was a Hitchcock film about a woman who was in prison and was persuading the short-sighted janitor to help her escape. As the story unfolded he smiled to himself. He was about to change the channel when he stopped for a moment as the woman explained to the janitor how she wanted him to get her out of there. It was a great idea, genius and truly horrifying, this was one he had to file in his mental filing cabinet for later. He had been thinking of what he was going to do about Anthony and Cathy and a plan was formulating in his head now. Absently he flicked through the channels till he came to the early evening news. He wanted to see Cathy, see if she looked different somehow. As he clicked onto the channel the screen was suddenly full of Anthony's face.

"Just before we go to the weather, just a reminder that Police are urgently trying to trace this man, Mr. Anthony Grace, a dental technician thought to be connected to Mr. Steven

Smith the dentist who recently escaped from court where he was being prosecuted for multiple murders."

Steven sat up straight, his mouth open. "Shit!" he said under his breath. The door opened and the face on the screen was suddenly the face in the doorway. Looking at Stevens face Anthony crossed quickly to stand beside the bed. As they stared at the screen the newsreaders voice continued.

"Police are advising that anyone with any information should come forward immediately. This man is considered to be very dangerous and should on no account be approached directly. Anyone who has any information should contact detective sergeant Joe Perkins or detective constable Denise Lawson at Kenly Police Station.
The colour drained from Anthony's face and he sat down hard on the bed. His first thought was Cathy and the effect that this bombshell would have on her. His fear was confirmed, as the forecast started and she appeared on the screen, stricken, in front of the weather map. She stumbled through the bulletin dropping her pointer twice. She looked as white as a sheet despite her make up and her voice had a strange strangled tone as though she was fighting back tears. Steven watched his friend carefully as Cathy finished her slot. His face said it all. As Steven could not trust himself to speak,he made no comment. He was trying desperately to fathom out how this changed things, how the balance of power had shifted, what the possibilities were.

"Well old buddy" he clapped Anthony on the back, "Looks like we're going to be bunk mates again! Sorry if that pisses on your fireworks with your bit of skirt and all that, but we can't risk you wandering around being clocked!" Steven tried but did not succeed in keeping the venom out of his voice. Luckily for him Anthony was too stunned to notice.

"Yes," he muttered, "Lie low." He sounded almost robotic and Steven felt a surge of pleasure that he was suffering.

"Look I think I've altered in appearance enough now that no-one would recognise me if I went out, so I'll go and buy a camp bed, a couple of sleeping bags, all that sort of shit and some food." Getting off the bed Steven looked at himself in the mirror. He had certainly changed, even he hardly recognised himself, he had put on weight, about a stone and a half he guessed and lived permanently in the stained pair of trackies and a loose filthy tee shirt that Anthony had got for him when they had first gone to ground. Steven had a full straggling beard that had bits of food stuck in it and his hair was on his shoulders now. He doubted even his mother would recognise him. As he thought of his mother, a lump came to his throat. He could imagine the turmoil she would be in, she didn't deserve it, but there was nothing he could do about it now. Maybe once they had got away, started again, he could send her money, make sure that she never wanted for anything, but he had to come to the terms that he would probably never see her again. He looked over at Anthony.

"Did you hear me mate, I'm going to go out, buy some gear?"

Anthony nodded wordlessly. He was in deep shock.

Stepping out of the bedsit for the first time in weeks Steven blinked in the bright sunlight. His legs felt weak and wobbly as he walked up the road to the small shopping centre. He had hidden his car and dare not use it, it was sure to be on the most wanted list. By the time he had reached the shops two streets away, he felt a bit better. As he walked past a café he thought it would be great to have a decent meal for a change. He had just settled himself at a seat by the window when the waitress came over and said.

"Look, I'm sorry you can't sit in here." Her nose was wrinkled up and she had her hand half over it "If you like I've got some filled rolls from yesterday, you can take them—just . . . please leave!" Steven looked at her in astonishment for a moment then he realised what the problem was. He had not had a wash in weeks, he was stinking!

He walked back to the bed sit, the rolls the waitress had given him in a paper bag. As he climbed the stairs to the first floor he heard Anthony on the phone.

"Cathy I'm so sorry, I didn't think. I hoped . . . I never meant to . . ." Anthony started crying and Steven, waiting silently outside the door curled his lip, fucking baby, crying to his slut of a girlfriend, what a wanker!

"I can't Cathy, I can't see you, I can't risk it. Look we plan to go abroad, I will have to go ahead and then send for you, let you know where we are. In the mean time just don't say anything to anyone. I don't want you involved in this, do you hear me?" There was silence for a moment.

"I love you too, with all my heart!" Anthony's voice broke and Steven heard him flick his phone closed.

Steven scuffed his feet on the floor outside the door before letting himself in.

"I'm going to have to have a shower mate" he said to Anthony," there are clouds of flies following me up the road!" he laughed at his own joke.

Half an hour later and with the clothes he had worn in court straining at the seams Steven was in the small shopping centre again. It felt great to be outside again and he did not mind at all that he would have to make several trips back to the bedsit with what he had to buy. First he struggled back with a camp bed and two sleeping bags. Next he bought two tracksuits for each of them and socks and underpants. With those delivered safely back to the bedsit he started the food shopping, piling the trolley high with beer and bread and bacon, milk, margarine, ketchup cereal and biscuits.

As Steven came and went from the bedsit, Anthony appeared not to have moved. Steven pretended not to notice and busied himself cleaning up the tiny room, throwing out the filthy bedding and going back to the shops for some new pillows and pillowcases. His new-found freedom had given him a new lease of life and he was delighted to be out in the fresh air again.

"Cheer up mate, it might never happen!" he slapped Anthony on the back as he threw open the grimy window of the bedsit to let some fresh air in.

"It already has, it already fucking has" Anthony said.

On the other side of town Rose Grace was in shock. Her eyes kept darting to the photo of Anthony that she had on the Welsh dresser as if to check it was still there. She even took it out of its frame to see if Anthony's name was on the photo, out of sight under the edge of the frame. It wasn't, of course.

Alan hovered in the back-ground, not sure what to do. He was stunned by the news that his girlfriend's son, a boy he always found charming, even a bit effeminate, could be possible of such horror. He thought that there must be some sort of mistake. He was deeply in love with Rose and although she had hinted at a past that had been less than ideal with Anthony's father, he knew how close mother and son were and he could not believe that any child of Rose's would grow up to be such a monster. No, he had decided that Anthony was somehow an innocent victim in all of this, although if the truth was told, Rose Grace herself was not so sure.

Cathy had taken some sick days and for the rest of the week sat almost as motionless as Anthony, in her flat. She could not believe it, although when she thought back to Steven and how creepy and weird he had been she was not surprised that he had led Anthony into trouble. It made no difference to how she felt about her Anthony, none whatsoever, in fact like Alan she had convinced herself that it could not be anything to do with Anthony, it had to be Steven.

Anthony, when his brain finally emerged from its shocked state fell into a deep depression. Now the tables were turned and he was the prisoner, Steven was free to roam and he was deeply afraid that Steven might do something stupid, he was more or less mad, Anthony had concluded although he did seem a little better since he had been free to come and go from the bedsit. Now it was he, Anthony who was suffering from cabin fever, barely able to see through the grimy glass of the bedsit window, and within four walls that seemed to be closing in on him by degrees, he barely had the energy to get off the camp bed, and stared for hours at a suspicious brown stain on the peeling wallpaper beside his head.

Steven was thinking, day and night, about how he could get his revenge on Anthony and that low life bitch. That night as they sat eating chow mien from tin cartons that Steven had brought up from the Chinese on the corner Steven said.

"You know I always thought you and Cathy would make a nice pair" Anthony nearly choked on his food.

"You what?" he spluttered.

"Yeah, I mean I know I had my chance with her, but really she's not my type, whereas you and her, well that would be pretty good, I could see that, especially as she has smartened herself up a bit for the telly.

Anthony sat with his fork half way to his mouth, he could hardly believe his ears, all this time he had thought that Steven would go mental if he found out. It was a huge relief, he could confide in him now, maybe get him to send some flowers round for Cathy.

"Actually mate . . ." Anthony started.

Steven did a pretty credible job of looking surprised as Anthony told him the story of him and Cathy. When he had finished, he held his breath for Steven's reaction.

"Why you sly old dog! Why didn't you tell me mate?"

"Well I thought that you might, well be jealous?" Anthony said tentatively

"Fuck off! Got bigger fish to fry me! Sly old prick you are though, how long did you say this has been going on?"

"A long time now mate, it's really great, we're very close!"

Steven felt the pulse in his temple throb with the effort of keeping the smile on his face from slipping.

"Great, Ant, really mate, fill your boots! I'm pleased for you!" Anthony sighed with relief.

"I'm so pleased you know about Cathy and me Steve mate, it's going make things a lot easier.

Yes, it is, Steven thought to himself, it certainly is.

Neither of them woke early the next morning. Anthony had had a good nights sleep, the weight of keeping Cathy a secret was off his shoulders, he thought now that he might have misjudged Steven, well he obviously had, Steven didn't seem to mind about him and Cathy at all. Now that he's getting out and about more Steven had started going around to the waste ground behind the bedsit for a bit of dogging at night. It was a pretty notorious site for it and from the window of the filthy shared bathroom at the back of the building Steven would wait for cars to arrive then nip downstairs and out the back. His lurid descriptions of what went on cheered Anthony up a bit, but it also made him think with an almost painful longing of the tender love making sessions he had shared with Cathy.

It was a couple of days after Anthony had told Steven about Cathy that he asked Steven to get a top up for his phone. It was the only contact that they had now. Cathy wanted to come and see him but he could not bear for her to see him in this hell hole.

"Oh sure mate, we can't have you out of touch with old Cathy now can we?" Steven said through gritted teeth. Anthony looked up sharply, he had clocked the tone. What was this? He immediately felt wary. Steven, seeing his expression and realising his façade had slipped said.

"Ouch! Just bit the inside of my cheek mate," Steven made a big play of putting his fingers in his mouth to feel the sore spot.

"Fuck, that hurt!" Steven shut his moth and sat down opposite Anthony, composing his face into a reassuring expression. "As I was saying, since you can't get out to see her we have to make sure the phone is fully charged eh mate, maybe you can go for a bit of that phone sex, perhaps you'll let me listen in!" This time he smiled disarmingly at Anthony.

"Fuck off you pervert!" Anthony smiled, and relaxed.

"You know what Steven?"

"What?"

"D'you think that you could arrange for some flowers to be sent to Cathy when you're out? There's a florist next to the phone shop.

Steven could barely believe his luck.

Fighting to keep his voice even he said.

"Yes, mate, sure thing, what's her address?"

"Here, I'll write it down" Anthony said.

Steven took the paper and smiled.

"Sure you don't mind?" Anthony asked.

"Not at all, I'll sort her out for you, mate, leave it to me!"

CHAPTER 15

When Steven left the bedsit, Cathy's address in his hand, he went straight to the café around the corner. He sat there for hours, ordering one coffee after another while he thought. His every instinct was to run straight round there and sort the bitch out. But he knew that that would not be the right way to go. He had to think this out, make sure that he got the best advantage out of the situation. Maybe he could get her to trust him as well, then once he had them both under his spell he could . . . ? Could what? He wasn't sure yet. Thoughts and possibilities crowded into his head, in an unintelligible jumble. He put his head in his hands, closing his eyes to try to clear his mind.

When he opened his eyes again, a man was sitting opposite him. Steven felt fear clutch his spine in an icy grip. The man spoke softly.

"It's Steven isn't it?" Steven started to rise from his chair, but the man clasped his hand over Steven's pinning it to the table. He had a steely grip, an immense strength in his arms. Vaguely Steven noticed a stick leaning against the table.

"I'm not going to hurt you, you can trust me, I'm Alan, Anthony's mum's boyfriend."

Steven blinked; his overloaded brain could hardly take it in. He sat silently in front of this big bear of a man.

"Do you know where Anthony is?"

"Why? How did you know who I was?" Steven said warily

"Well your photo's on the box enough, yours and Anthony's and although you have changed a lot, I'm an undertaker, I'm used to people looking, well, shall we say different from their publicity shots?"

Steven's mind flashed back to the Alfred Hitchcock story he had seen on the TV. He pulled his chair up closer to the table and leaned forward.

"I might have something that I need you to do."

Now Alan looked wary

"To help Anthony," Steven continued quickly.

"Oh? You know where he is then?"

"Of course I do, we're in this together after all! Anthony is the best friend I ever had, almost like a brother." Steven looked down at his hands, hoping that the catch in his voice would be interpreted by Alan as emotion and not the naked hatred he felt for Anthony. It seemed to work as Alan relaxed and patted Steven's hand. But Alan was even surer that this shifty man with the dark cold eyes was responsible for leading Anthony astray and he was more determined than ever to do anything he could to get Anthony out of his clutches and back with him and his mother. They would have to run away, start again somewhere else, but it could be managed. He still had a tidy amount from the motorbike accident pay out. One thing was for sure he could not bear to see Rose suffer as she was suffering now, knowing nothing about where her son was, how he was, even if he was alive or dead. Now it was just a matter of getting Anthony away from Steven. He could see that he would have to tread carefully; Steven was as wary and as wily as a fox and his eyes seemed to penetrate Alan whenever he looked at him, making his skin crawl. There was something deeply disturbing about Steven. Those eyes, when they met his, looked wild, almost feral. Thankfully, during their conversation Steven mostly took pains not to make eye contact, but he was summing Alan up. The fact that he had to haul his huge bulk around on sticks explained the strength in his arms. He had a kind looking face, soft as a bag of tits in all probability, should be easy enough to get him to toe the line. Dangle poor little Anthony, as a carrot and he would be able to get him to do anything by the look of it. Steven knew that he would have to convince Alan that he was close to Anthony that he wanted him to be safe as much as Alan and Rose Grace did. He tried to squeeze a tear out and succeeded by thinking about his mother and how miserable she must be.

"I'm worried about Anthony." Steven sniffed loudly, "I don't know if he can take much more, we are going to have to get him out of the bedsit soon, he's losing it."

Alan looked at the overweight spotty man opposite him, his greasy lank hair straggling over his shoulders. It was true he didn't bear much resemblance to the photo the police were using. But there was something about him that rang every alarm bell that Alan had. He had been a Hell's Angel for many years and he knew a bull-shitter when he saw one, but for now Steven, however onerous a prospect he was, it's the only link he had to Anthony.

Mary Smith whom Steven had just managed to squeeze a tear out for couldn't have been happier. As she dusted the lounge she hummed to herself. Brian was upstairs clearing out the lodger's room. Odd that how the young fellow had just disappeared. And the stuff he had in there! She had not noticed him bringing it all in; she would have said something if she did, clutter from years back, and his school photos for heaven's sake! Whatever next! Still Brian had hired a skip and had made a dozen trips downstairs already. She had offered to help but when they came across a stash of very unsavoury magazines he had told her to go down and let him do the rest.

She had not argued. She thought herself very lucky that Brain did not like 'that sort of thing'. Their lovemaking was a pretty pedestrian affair. She did have flash backs to the rough brutal sex that she had endured with her previous husband. It had taken Brian a long time to coax her into the intimate side of things and now he very much 'proceeded with caution' She wondered if he would like things a bit rougher, a bit well, sexier, but he wasn't complaining and although she never had an orgasm, she enjoyed the closeness of their love making. "Let sleeping dogs lie" she said to herself as Brian passed the door on his way to the skip with another load.

"Let sleeping dogs lie? What's that about love?" he said.

Mary smiled, embarrassed, she felt as though he was reading her mind. "Nothing love just thinking, you know day dreaming!" Brian looked at her sharply. She was blushing. He shook his head. He would never understand women.

As he tipped the latest load of rubbish from under Steven's bed into the skip, a small diary caught his eye. There was a huge amount of stuff here even although the police had already been through it and taken anything they thought might be of use to them.

He picked it out from the piles of Nuts magazines and other porn mags that had their pages stuck together and almost made Brain gag. Still he pulled out the little book and began to read.

There were lists of names and dates and next to each one the word BOOM written in capitals and sometimes with so much force that the pen had broken through the page to leave marks on the page underneath. The name Barton caught Brian's eye, he knew that name, and it was one of the early entries and had been the monster who had attacked Steven and poor Lucy in the park. Alongside his name was the name of the woman, Sharon Bright, that Brian remembered had been blown up with him and next to her name Steven had drawn a little smiley face with a down-turned mouth. Brian felt the hair on the back of his neck stand up, he could not imagine the horror of that scene, he had had nightmares about it since the police had come round and told him what Steven had done, Steven who he had taught and nurtured, in a surgery that Brian had found for him and that had now taken on a museum like quality, what was left of it after the explosion. The press had had a field day, it was true it was a gruesome story, and for the first time in many years the dental profession were attracting headlines in every newspaper in the land on a daily basis.

"Afraid of the Dentist? You should be!"

"Open wide, this won't hurt a bit!"

"How to get that killer smile in one easy step!

The headlines screamed and proceeded to outline in gory detail how unsuspecting dental patients had had their teeth implanted with explosives and then by remote control had their devices detonated and their heads blown off.

Brian realised that what he had in his hand would be dynamite for the police. He knew from his contact with Detective Sergeant Perkins that the explosion at Steven's surgery had destroyed a lot of useful information, like what the devices were made of and how they were made, and detonated. This book that effectively listed the victims was going to be of great use to the police. Brian had to visit them at the police station mostly. Mary was still in complete denial and a doctor and psychiatrist had backed this up. The police were satisfied with the medical findings and opinions and were apparently convinced that Brian was genuine. God knows he was down at the station enough, trying to get information. He somehow felt guilty, responsible for the way that Steven had turned his training to such deadly effect.

As he arrived at the station Denise looked up from her desk.

"Ay up, here he comes again, I'm beginning to think that his missus isn't the only one with mental issues!" she said.

Perkins shot her a glance.

"Steady Eddie," he said a slight edge to his voice. "He's about all we've got at the moment, let's not blow it shall we?"

Denise looked chastened. It was sometimes difficult for her to remember that Joe Perkins, who had just been temporarily promoted to Detective Inspector, was her superior. It was especially hard when her jaw was still aching from her oral exploits on him the evening before and her vagina was still throbbing from accommodating Joe's impressive girth.

"Hi Brian, come on in, Detective Lawson, will you get Brian a cup of coffee, white with two isn't it?"

"Yes thanks." Brian took the seat in front of Joe's desk while Denise, her face flushed with indignation went for the coffee.

"I found this." Brian put the little book on the desk. Joe picked it up and flicked through it.

"Where did you find it?"

"I was clearing out Steven's room and it was amongst some of his magazines."

Joe had seen a selection of Steven's magazines, most stuck together with semen and all the hardest core porn that it was possible to have.

As Denise came back into the office Joe looked up"

"Who was in charge of the search at Smith's house?"

"I was." She said putting coffee cups down in front of Joe and Brian.

"Right, well you missed this." Joe held up the little book and Denise saw that a muscle in his cheek was twitching. He was obviously very annoyed or showing off in front of Brian. She wasn't having that.

"I wasn't the only officer in the house, where did you find it?" she asked Brian

"Amongst Steven's magazines." Denise shuddered as she remembered the sticky sordid mess under his bed.

"I didn't search those, sir" she said placing a sarcastic emphasis on the 'sir.'

Joe looked down at the book on his desk.

"Right, well, whatever, thank you Brian for this, it clearly is a very crucial piece of evidence, any news about Mary?" he tried to ignore the door slamming as Denise left the office. He had been warned more than once during his career about having relationships at work, and this was obviously what ignoring that warning led to.

"Not really," Brain replied, she still has it fixed in her mind that Steven was a lodger and apart from the disruption of the clearing of the room she is as happy as Larry. She even looked through his photos, with her and his dad in and didn't show any flicker of recognition, even of herself! It really is amazing what the mind can do, if it doesn't want to deal with things."

Joe nodded. He could see Denise through the glass wall of his office standing by the water fountain. He could tell by the set of her shoulders that she was very angry. He sighed. Brian in front of him seemed unsure whether to go or stay but Joe was not ready to face a pissed off Denise just yet, so he kept him talking.

"Hasn't Mary recognised any of Steven's belongings?"

"No, not a flicker, same goes for the photos of him around the house, she just thinks that the lodger put them around the place."

"The mind is a very complex thing." Joe said

Brian nodded. "Well if there isn't anything else?" he stood up.

"No, that's it really, just a big thank you for bringing this in, I wish I could say we had news for you, but so far nothing at all, not even a sign of Anthony Grace, although we have had every officer on the look out."

Brian hesitated, his hand on the door handle.

"Actually there was something, it's silly I know but I might as well tell you, see what you think."

"Sit down Brian, sit down, "Joe looked out at Denise who had started to make her way back to the office when Brian got up but was now staring daggers at him from the middle of the general office.

"Well it's probably a coincidence but on the night that Anthony's picture was shown for the first time on the TV, the girl who does the weather, a pretty little thing always looks relaxed and cheerful, well, she went to pieces. She stuttered, stammered and dropped her pointer thing. It was as though she had had a terrible shock, and it was just odd that it was immediately after the announcement about Anthony. It was Mary who noticed it. I was looking at Mary to see if there was any flicker of recognition once Steven's name was mentioned and she put her hand to her mouth, you know, the way people do when they are shocked. I thought for a minute that it had come back to her that she had remembered that Steven was her son but she was pointing at the girl doing the weather. She looked really upset, really she did, and Mary said it must be because she knew Anthony, in fact she said she thought she remembered her. I didn't really think much of it at the time but she hasn't been on the box since then, its probably just a coincidence, I feel a bit foolish even mentioning it, probably just Mary being Mary, you know . . ." Brian tailed off embarrassed, but Joe was listening intently.

"No Brian, not foolish, I think you might just have given us the breakthrough we need, now I'm going to ask you to leave us while we get on to this."

Before Brian could even leave the room Joe had grabbed his coat and was beckoning a still fuming Denise from the water fountain.

"Had a lead, the weather, girl you know that one on the local news with the big boo . . . ." He stopped as Denise shot him a murderous look. He was going to have to re think this whole relationship thing he decided, she was getting pretty heavy and it was in danger of affecting their work. For now though she was running behind him to the car. Once inside he didn't give her a chance to speak relaying what Brian had told him.

"Well I suppose that the girl, Cathy something isn't it? She, Smith and Grace are about the same age, maybe they went to school together." Denise said.

They drew up at the studios and made their way in past the security checks. A spotty girl who looked about 13 met them, saying that she was a producer. Joe whispered to Denise as they walked up the corridor after her

"They say you're getting older when the police look young, but maybe we measure our ageing by how young TV producers look!" His weak attempt at humour was rewarded by a frosty smile from Denise, but at least it was a smile.

An equally young looking man showed them into a small office where several monitors were on showing the programme being broadcast as well as programming from other channels.

Pushing his glasses nervously up his nose the young man asked them what it was they wanted. And Joe told them.

Diving into a filing cabinet he emerged with a file that had Cathy Barrett written in neat letters on the corner.

"Yes here is her address" he said, starting to write it down on a jotter pad.

"She has been off sick for a while, I do hope that she is not in trouble?" he said although his expression said that he would love to know what trouble she was in.

"Thanks for that, Mr.?"

"Crispin Hartley-Jeffries, you can call me Crispi, everyone does."

Joe suppressed a smile

"Ok then thanks, er Crispi, and please don't give her a ring to say we have been, we need to maintain the element of surprise on this one a bit, I'm sure I can rely on you?"

Crispi nodded earnestly

"Deffo, you can rely on me!"

Outside even Denise could not maintain her frown.

"Good God no bloody wonder local TV is so piss poor!" she laughed.

"Oh now then, I am sure Crispi has an excellent degree in Media Studies or something similar. D'you think he will phone her?" Joe smiled back glad that the ice was broken.

"Nah, too nervous, frightened of his own shadow that one! I bet he has a library book out over time the way he looked so worried when we came in!"

When they arrived at River Towers Joe and Denise had to knock for a good quarter of an hour before Cathy opened the door. Other doors along the corridor opened a chink as they shouted louder that they were from the police and eventually Cathy opened the door.

The flat was in darkness and for a moment Joe thought perhaps Anthony might be there. But as he surveyed the wreckage of the sofa, boxes of tissues and a half eaten pizza that was growing mould, he recognised the signs of a woman mourning her love life. He had grown up with four sisters and would know that stricken haunted look a mile off.

Denise walked briskly over to the window and drew the curtains back. Cathy blinked in the unaccustomed light. She looked even more dejected now, her hair had obviously not been washed in days and her clothes looked as though they needed a good wash. On second glance Joe realised she was wearing pyjamas and a dressing gown, she looked very vulnerable, young and vulnerable. He felt quite sorry for her. Despite the fact that she could do with a bath and hair wash there was no mistaking that she was a lovely looking girl, and he could see the swell of one of her ample breasts where her dressing gown was open slightly. Following his gaze Denise said harshly

"We are here to ask you about Anthony Grace." Denise looked at the girl ready to clock her reaction. There was none, or maybe that was just a slight twitch of her cupid bow lips? Bloody cow she thought, even looking like she had been dragged through a bush backwards she was still gorgeous. And Joe had obviously clocked that. She knew it was inappropriate to think about it now but she was getting a bit worried about him. It seemed that apart from blowjobs and bunk-ups she was not really on his radar.

"Well?" Denise asked impatiently and Joe shot her a warning glance.

"Come on now love" he said putting his arm around Cathy, we know all about you and Anthony, we just need to know if you know where he is?" After a moments silence, from somewhere Cathy gathered her senses.

"You know what about me and Anthony? I went to school with him that's all, him and that weirdo Steven." Denise shot him a hateful look but Joe kept his arm around the girl. Her shoulders felt bony under the thin material of her dressing gown and he thought he had copped a glimpse of a chestnut coloured nipple when Cathy shifted to accommodate his arm. He was going nowhere.

"Come on Cathy, don't play the innocent with us, we know all about it, we've been to the TV station!" Denise spat.

This did elicit a reaction from Cathy and she looked from Denise to Joe in concern.

"I should have called them, I've been off sick for a while I bet they're mad?"

"They didn't seem to be." Joe said reassuringly, "Just concerned about you, we all are Cathy." Denise gave a snort and Joe flashed her another warning look.

Cathy, despite her befuddled state was picking up on the animosity between the two detectives. She leaned her head on Joe's shoulder resting her hand lightly on his leg with a sigh and watched with pleasure as Denise's round face contorted with rage.

"Did they really seem OK?" she looked up through her long lashes at Joe and he felt his cock twitch in his trousers. He could hardly be in a worse place. He was between a rock and a rapidly developing hard place and Denise was taking it all in.

"Right," Denise said taking Cathy by the arm and yanking her off the settee.

"Let's have a look around shall we?"

Shooting a venomous look at the bulge in his trousers, Denise marched Cathy into the bedroom of the flat.

In comparison to the lounge it looked quite neat. Cathy had obviously been sleeping on the settee, the bed had only a bottom sheet on it, the pillow and duvet having been taken into the lounge. As Denise looked around with a practiced eye she saw Cathy glance at a bedside table. There was nothing on it, but as Denise took a closer look she saw that dust had formed a layer over the top of the table except for a neat thin strip near the front and a smaller strip about 4 inches behind that.

Perfect fit for a photo that has been recently removed, she thought.

"Where's the photo gone?" she asked Cathy and was pleased to see the girl flinch, bingo! Having got rid of his erection Joe had come into the bedroom and both women looked in his direction.

"Well where is it?" Denise said.

In an Oscar winning performance Cathy swooned into Joe's arms, her robe falling open and her full breast with its pointed dark brown nipple all but fell into his hand.

"For fucks' sake!" Denise shouted, pulling the girl's gown closed, snatching her out of Joe's arms and throwing her on the bed.

"For fucks sake Joe," she repeated "Can you get a grip? And not this stupid cows tit, just get a fucking grip!" Denise was half crying now her frustration obvious and her misery growing as she felt whatever she and Joe had had slipping away.

On the bed Cathy kept her eyes closed.

"Denise, listen to me, you are out of control, calm down, in fact go down and wait in the car for me."

"Oh yes, you'd like that wouldn't you? I'll go and then you can fuck this nasty little bitch. She's just about your level Joe, I don't know what I ever saw in you! Your dick is so much in control of you that you don't even know when you're being played, God I fee sorry for you!"

Now it was Joe's turn to manhandle Denise out of the room. He shut the door to the bedroom and hissed at her.

"You are completely out of control Denise, stop it now or I will have to put you on report."

"On report?" Denise squeaked "On report for what? Giving you blow jobs all night and then being treated like a sack of shit by you all day? Oh yes the super would be really interested to hear about that I'm sure!"

Joe was silent for a moment, cursing that night on surveillance. Why the hell had he done it? He had been so proud of the fact that he had never dipped his wick on his own door-step. He had poured scorn often enough on those who had, laughed even when their relationships fell apart. Now he was the fool and in a living hell. He said softly.

"Denise in case you have forgotten this is a very important case, I can't have it compromised by your behaviour. I'm going to have to take you off the case, it's obvious you can't handle it." Denise looked at him for a moment then slapped him as hard as she could across the face then turning her back on him she stomped out of the flat leaving him to it.

In the bedroom, Cathy lay with her eyes open listening to the argument in the next room. Then jumping off the bed she quickly wiped the sleeve of her dressing gown over the bedside table, removing the tell tale signs that Anthony's photo that was now stuffed into her knicker drawer, had once been there. Her mind was reeling with the events of the last half hour, it was obvious that the man detective was as horny as hell for her and she wondered if there was some way she could use that to her advantage. He was pretty hot looking, and if it would help Anthony, she began to get that familiar warmth in her groin and she realised that she had been missing the regular sex her body had come to expect.

By the time that Joe came back into the bedroom, rubbing his cheek that bore the bright red imprint of Denise's hand, Cathy had arranged herself on the bed with her gown slightly open to reveal her right breast, her nipple engorged and erect.

As Joe groaned, Cathy sat up, her gown now fully open showing both breasts.

"What happened?" she said groggily.

"You passed out, look I better go now, we may come back to you later." Cathy glanced at his trousers. It Looked like he was a big boy.

"Can you help me to the shower please officer? I'm afraid I might pass out again and I need to wash. Cathy made a half-hearted attempt to pull her gown together and flashed her wide eyes at him again.

"Haven't you got someone you could call? A girlfriend?" Joe said. His erection was hurting him now.

"No, but don't worry, if you'd rather not, she got off the bed, and immediately staggered. Joe caught her just before she fell.
"Ok I'll help you to the bathroom," he said
The bathroom was a surprise. Where there had once been a functional bath there was now a large walk in shower.

Cathy caught his glance and smiled. "I had the bath taken out and a shower put in, it's lovely, big enough for two."

"Yes, I see, well I'll leave you to it." Joe was desperate to get out now.

"Ok thanks officer, Ohhh" Cathy tottered again this time falling heavily against the wall. Joe was beside her again.

"You need to see a doctor." He said.

"No, I don't I just haven't been eating, as soon as I have had a shower I'll cook something, promise." She flashed him a weak smile.

"Right, well I'm going to wait outside while you shower, make sure you don't fall again."

"Thanks." Cathy began to undress and Joe beat a hasty retreat.

He was just wondering if he had enough time to knock one out when she called him.

"Officer, help, it's happened again!" Joe ran into the bathroom. Cathy was leaning against the back of the shower, water cascading over her and running in rivulets off her distended nipples and thick bush. Her legs were slightly apart and Joe groaned in defeat. Without another word he stripped his clothes off and joined Cathy in the shower.

Cathy's eyes widened as she saw the size of his cock, and she threw her arms around him in the warm water. She smelled lovely, of a rose soap she had been using and as his lips met hers, Joe tasted toothpaste. The minx, she had planned this! Still he was not complaining as she turned her back to him and let him explore her breasts while she leaned back on to him feeling his prick hard and insistent against her bottom. Joe had thought that her breasts had been surgically enhanced but as he cupped them in his hands running his thumbs over her large nipples, he realised they were all natural, firm and soft and utterly delicious. He turned her round and leaned down to run his tongue around one nipple then the other. Cathy groaned and leaned her head back into the stream of water. It was the sexiest thing that Joe had ever seen and he felt in danger of doing what he hadn't done since he was a teenager, shooting his load in an embarrassing premature ejaculation. Cathy's small hands were reaching for him now but he was afraid that it might be all over before it began. He pulled away. She opened her eyes questioningly.

"On the edge babe!" he smiled and she smiled back, pleased that she was having that effect on him. She had not realised how frustrated she was, all thoughts of Anthony were forgotten as Joe ran his fingers down over her stomach and burrowed into the thick hair of her pussy. He inserted a couple of fingers into her warm slippery depth and then withdrawing them found her clitoris. Gently he ran his finger around the edge, knowing better than to touch the sensitive centre and she opened her mouth to cry out in pleasure. With his arm around he continued the pressure until an orgasm rocked her and she half collapsed against him. He could wait no longer. Leaning down he picked her up by the waist and she wound her legs around him. In one practiced movement he was inside her, his long hot length making her blink in surprise. With her legs crossed at the ankle behind his back she let him rock into her, with rough powerful force watching him battle with himself, slow down when he thought his orgasm was near, his teeth clenched and eyes closed, and then start again, all the time holding her in his strong arms. This was animal sex compared to the gentle sex she had with Anthony and she thought she liked it. When they were back together again she would try to get him to be a bit more brutal, she knew that he adored her, but he made love to her like she was going to break. All of a sudden her thoughts were interrupted by an orgasm building, slowly at first and then, gaining momentum and rushing forward to collide with Joes'. Gasping for breath they sank to the floor of the shower, sitting, their legs entwined as the water cascaded down on them, strings of semen mingled with the water snaking down the drain.

It was five minutes before either of them spoke. Then Cathy began to wash him gently, taking a sponge to his cock and his hairy chest, kissing him where she washed. Then he did the same for her, washing her hair and watching the soapy bubbles dance down her body.

Downstairs Denise was waiting for Joe in the car. Joe thought she had gone but she hadn't and as she sat and time went by she became angrier and angrier, her hatred for Cathy and for Joe burning through her like acid.

When Joe eventually emerged from the building and saw her, she saw him hesitate, the look of shock and guilt on his face told her all she needed to know. She was not surprised when he got into the car smelling like an explosion at a perfume counter, nor did she make any remark. She was biding her time.

CHAPTER 16

The drive back to the station was an uncomfortable one for Joe. He kept touching his hair, which he was aware was still wet from the shower and he did not have to work very hard to interpret the look on Denise's face or the wrinkling of her nose as he exuded Channel no. 5 shower gel. She took every corner as though on a race track then screeching to a halt outside the station, she undone her belt and opened the car door snatching the keys out of the ignition at the last minute, leaving Joe to apply the hand brake.

Inside the building, by the time that Joe got into his office there was no sign of her. For a moment he thought she might have gone to the Super, a woman scorned and all that, but then as he glanced down into the car park he saw her stalking out onto the street. He sat down at his desk with his head in his hands. He had got himself into a right mess. He was under no illusion that Denise knew exactly what had happened in Cathy's flat, she knew as surely as if he had drawn her a diagram. And the fact that she had been rejected in such a manner could mean nothing but misery for him, he was sure of that. But there was the other side of things, the fact that he had slept with someone who was being investigated. His job could be on the line for that. He felt an awful sick feeling in the pit of his stomach, what was she going to do? Where was she now? Why was he so stupid?

Anthony was waiting for Cathy to reply to his text. He had to junk his old phone and get a new one and hers was the only number he could remember, so consequently she was the only person he ever spoke to, apart from Steven. While she was in the shower with Joe, Anthony had been calling her. Getting no reply he texted her three times, getting more and more worried. He knew she had not been into work, and that she was depressed, her voice was flat and dispassionate for the most part when they did speak. Had she done something stupid? He felt a wave of rage and helplessness wash over him. He almost felt like just walking out on the street and going straight around there, but Steven had told him that the police were patrolling regularly so it would not be long before they picked him up, and then there would be no chance of seeing Cathy at all. He felt tears well up in his eyes, tears of frustration and misery. Just then his phone rang.

"Anthony? It's me," Cathy sounded a little breathless, somehow animated, much better than she had sounded for a while.

"God Cath, I was going out of my mind, where the hell have you been?"

"The police came round, I had to hide the phone and put it on silent, they were here for ages."

"Did they know about us, or were they just guessing?"

"Guessing I think, I denied knowing you apart from being an ex classmate."

"And they bought it?"

"Think so, Oh Anthony what's going to happen to us? I miss you so much!"

"I know Cathy; I just want us to be together. The police must have some sort of an idea, Steven says they are around here all the time, prowling up and down the streets, he even saw one car that had been parked up all night. If it wasn't for that I would be over there, you know I would."

"I know but now that they have suspicions about me, that wouldn't even be safe." Cathy started to cry softly. She felt very guilty about the delicious session she had shared with Joe, she really did love Anthony it was just that her body was very fickle. For a while they sat silently then Anthony sighed deeply.

"God Cathy I need to make love to you."

"I know Ant, I know" she said softly. She was still in his towelling robe from the shower.

"I just had a shower, it was great, all that lovely hot water trickling down my body.

Anthony drew his breath in sharply, feeling his cock stir in his tracksuit bottoms.

"I got the soap and rubbed it all over me," Cathy continued in honeyed tones.

"Where did you rub it?" he croaked.

"Well first over my breasts, over the top and underneath and over the nipples. They got very hard when I rubbed them." She whispered and Anthony slid his hand down the front of this trackies to hold his cock which was now hard as a rock.

"Then what did you do?" he asked, his voice tense.

"Then I rubbed it down over my belly to the hair on my pussy and lathered it all up and that felt very good."

"Did it?" Anthony said starting to wank himself off now.

"Yes, then when I looked down, my pussy lips had opened and I could see my little clit poking out, all red and swollen." Cathy said, her breathing getting faster now as she began to rub herself, her legs spread wide.

"Then what?"

"Well it looked so lonely, my poor little clit, it missed your tongue so much I thought I should give it a bit of a treat so I got the soap and rubbed it right over it, and then round and round and then up and down, then when I was close to coming I stopped and stuck my fingers up my pussy, imagining it was your lovely cock."

Anthony groaned

"And then I rubbed it a little bit more like that and oh Oh OH!"

Anthony saw stars as his orgasm wracked him, making him drop the phone for a moment. He snatched it back up again and sighed as he heard the familiar sounds of Cathy's orgasm.

"God Cathy, I feel better for that" he said when he could speak.

"Me too Ant, I do love you."

"I love you too, I better go I'm just about out of credit, goodnight love, sweet dreams" He flicked the phone shut and settled down to dream of Cathy and her soft sexy body.

Outside the door of the bed-sit, Steven had been stood there a while with his ear to the door, smirking.

"Sad little wanker," he muttered. "What a fucking loser, resorting to phone sex!" As he put the key in the door Steven thought to himself. Don't' worry Cathy love, won't be long before you know what a real man feels like!

The next morning Steven slipped out without disturbing Anthony. He met Alan in the same café and Alan thought again what an onerous man Steven was. He was shifty, spotty, bloated and he smelled. But he was the only link he had to

Anthony, the only chance of getting him back. He had said nothing to Rose yet about his meetings with Steven; he didn't want her to know what was going on, not until she needed to.

"Last time we met you said that you might want me to do something to help Anthony?" Alan asked.

"Yes, it's an idea to get him out of the bedsit, he hates it there and the police are getting closer. I saw a patrol car parked up all night at the end of the street and they are up and down all day and night." Steven lied.

"Can I see him?"

Steven shook his head.

"Too dangerous, the amount of time that the police have been camped out round here they know everyone who comes and goes, we don't want them getting suspicious."

"Have they spoken to you?" Alan asked, and Steven hesitated for a moment. To say no would be to give the lie to what he had just said about the fact that the police were keeping a close surveillance of the area and the people who lived in it.

"Yes they have, but as you said, I look so different now they really didn't suspect a thing, just put me down as another low life living in grotsville!" Steven laughed and Alan tried to smile.

"So what did you have in mind, how can I help to get him out?"

"You said you're an undertaker right?"

Alan nodded.

"Fucking weird man, but hey each to their own!" Steven smiled a cold mechanical facial movement that did not reach his eyes.

"I was watching an Alfred Hitchcock film, there was a spoilt rich woman who was sent to prison for murder. In prison she befriends the handy man who amongst his other jobs has the task of putting any prisoner who died into their coffins ready for burial in the prison's graveyard. The old handyman is nearly blind and needs to have and operation to stop him losing his sight or some shit. He asks her to read a letter from the county benefit office who he has applied to for a grant to allow him to have the op. In fact the letter says that the grant has been approved but she tells him that it isn't, and promises to pay for him to have the eye surgery if he helps her escape."

Steven stopped looking at Alan for a sign that he was taking it all in.

Alan was feeling that the situation was taking on a surreal quality he could not imagine what this deranged man wanted from him, but he nodded and Steven continued.

"Anyway she hatches an escape plan, and that plan was that she would climb into the coffin with the next prisoner stiff and be buried alive. Then later, under cover of darkness the handyman would come and dig her up, genius eh?"

"Er, yes I suppose in that situation . . ." Alan tailed off, he knew now what he was going to be asked to do and his skin was crawling.

"There's no other way man!" Steven leaned over the table and put his hand over Alan's. Alan glanced down at the bitten dirty fingernails and had to resist the urge to snatch his hand away.

"Surely, if we got him out at night?"

"I fucking told you man" Steven hissed "The fucking police are just about moved in, it's not going to be long before they search the building, they're working their way down the street, but hey if you're not interested in helping Anthony, well I did my best!" Steven shot Alan a look that bordered on madness and slid his chair back. The screech that the metal legs made against the hard floor of the café made everyone look up.

"Wait!" Alan said and Steven stood over him one eyebrow raised, a vein in his temple pumping alarmingly.

This young man was very close to the edge, Alan realised.

"Please sit down, I'm sorry you just took me by surprise, it's really quite a brilliant idea!" Alan hoped he sounded convincing. Steven hesitated for a moment his mad eyes assessing Alan, seeming to bore into him. Alan forced himself not to drop his gaze. Eventually Steven sat down again, rocking forward in his seat.

"OK, don't fucking waste my time, are you in? Can I tell Anthony that you are going to help?"

Alan nodded. "But Steven you can't just bury people, willy nilly, there are procedures, a chain of events, that leads to a grave being dug."

"I know, I've thought of that." Stevens's eyes glittered again now as he warmed to his subject.

"How long before a funeral is a grave dug?"

"Usually the day before, but maybe a couple of days before if the funeral is to be on a Monday morning.
"Right that's what I thought!" Steven said triumphantly. "Then the next time you have to bury someone on a Monday, you come and collect Ant over the weekend put him in the grave, cover him over just enough to provide a

false bottom of the grave for the punter," Alan winced at the term "and then after the funeral we dig them both up and re-bury the real stiff!" Alan winced again.

"But surely, if we can get him out of the bed-sit to my funeral parlour then we don't need to bury him, we can simply let him out of the coffin at the funeral home?" Alan said.

"No!" Steven shouted, and everyone looked round again. "We do it my way or not at all. Besides which don't you think the filth are watching you? You're golden bollocks's step dad for Christ's sake?

Alan didn't think that the police were watching him, the front of his funeral parlour was a large glass window and the desk at which he sat was right behind it. He could see the street all day long and he could not remember the last time he had seen a police car. Still it was possible that they were using unmarked vehicles. And it was true that the police had seemed decidedly unconvinced by Roses' story that Anthony was overseas. He sighed.

"Better be safe than sorry, I suppose," he muttered.

"Good, so I'll leave it up to you to let me know when the timing is right?"

"Can't I at least phone Anthony? His mother is quite desperate you know."
"Sorry, no, we changed his phone when he came to the bedsit, threw the other one away, they can trace phone signals as well you now, probably got all your phones tapped. He doesn't need the phone really, but all that will change soon eh?" Steven said winking conspiratorially.

"What happened to the woman?" Alan asked.

"What woman?"

"The one in the Hitchcock film?"

"Oh her, yes it was way cool!" Steven said "The next time that she heard the bell ringing to signify that there had been a death she crept along to the place where the coffin was kept and got into it. It was dark and she was really grossed out but she shut her eyes, got in and lay down on the stiff. After a while she felt the lid being screwed on and the coffin being taken down to the graveyard. She heard the earth being shovelled in but she didn't care, she was laughing, really happy to know that she would soon be dug up and would be free." Steven looked at Alan a dangerous light in his eye. "Anyway time went by and nothing happened. She was starting to worry now, not a lot at first, but then more time had slipped by and she did start to panic. She had a little lighter in her pocket and took it out. She sort of craned her neck round in the coffin, trying to see who was beneath her. When she shone the light on the face she started screaming and screaming, and that's how the film ended."

"Well who was it?"

"It was the old handy man, the janitor!" Steven laughed delightedly and Alan felt his stomach turn over, he had rarely met anyone as repugnant as Steven, evil seemed to ooze out of him.

Back at the bed-sit, Anthony pounced on Steven as soon as he came in.

"Have you sent the flowers to Cathy yet?"

"No when I was going into the florist yesterday the police were in there nosing about, so I thought better of it. The fucking pigs are all over the bloody place, they were even in the café this morning." Steven sat down on his bed.

"Really, could you hear what they were saying?"

"Yes, they were showing your photo, have you seen this man, you know the sort of shit."

"What did they say?"

Well one of them seemed to remember you but she couldn't be sure." Steven was enjoying the effect that his lies were having on Anthony.

"The police have been round to Cathy's." Anthony said quietly

"What?" Steven jumped up from the bed.

"They went around yesterday, asking her about me, they had somehow found out that we were seeing each other."

"What do you mean, *somehow found out*?" Steven repeated Anthony's words in a whiny tone.

"Well we kept it a secret really; no-one really knew that we were going out."

"Oh, so I wasn't the only one then?"

"No." Anthony mumbled looking at his hands "Cathy thought that it would be better for her career chances at the TV station if she was seen as a single girl."

Steven threw his head back and laughed a hard unpleasant sound that owed nothing to mirth.

"Cathy thought that it would be better for her chances of whoring around, more like it! God she never fucking changes!" he said shaking his head in disbelief.

"And you bought that pile of crap did you? Jesus Ant, you're more of a wanker than I thought you were!" Steven laughed again.

Anthony felt the hairs on the back of his neck prickle and his hands close into fists. He wanted to flatten Steven, but he had to restrain himself, he was completely at Steven mercy, and did not dare upset him. He was closer to the edge than ever these days it wouldn't take much to push him over.

"Well you could be right, but we have been pretty tight, I think I would have known if she was seeing anyone else." Anthony said in a measured tone

Steven looked at Anthony annoyed that his attempts to goad him had apparently failed. Well he thought to himself, she would be seeing a lot more of Mr. Steven Smith soon, a lot more! He felt his cock twitch in his pants. He was looking forward to seeing Cathy again.

"I could take the flowers round myself, and then there won't be any trail?" Steven said.

"Would you?" Anthony felt very nervous of this idea, but, he reasoned with himself, he had already given Steven Cathy's address and he would have been round there by now, if he wanted to or if he had any ulterior motive. His head was pounding with the stress of speaking to Steven and trying to guess what was going on.

"And don't worry I won't give her one while I'm round there." Steven said making suggestive movements with his pelvis. Despite himself Anthony's eyes were drawn to Steven's thrusting groin, was that the beginning of an erection he could see?

"I'm well over her, in fact it's taking all my time to see to that Romanian waitress in the café, taken a real shine to me she has, lives over the shop too, so it's handy for a quick bunk up!

Steven was proud at how easy it was for him to lie. "In fact I think I'll be staying there tonight, give you the chance to have a bit more of that phone sex you and Cathy enjoy so much!" Anthony looked at him sharply.
"You heard?"

"Well just your side of it mate, "Oh oh Cathy I'm coming!" he mimicked and Anthony flushed with embarrassment and annoyance.

"Yeah well there's fuck all else I can do at the moment," he said.

"Well all that might change soon, Ant." Steven sat down on the camp bed beside Anthony and Anthony had to force himself not to turn away from the stench that emanated from Steven. It was a mixture of BO and stale clothes, and other smells that Anthony did not want to guess at.

"I've got a plan."

"What is it?" Anthony asked and Steven began to tell him about the film he had seen and his meeting with Alan.

"Woah! No way! I am not going to be put in a coffin, no fucking way!" Anthony said.

Steven shrugged, "Up to you mate. I thought you wanted out of here, but if you're happy enough to stay, no probs! See ya!" With that Steven heaved his bulk off the camp bed and crossed to the door slamming it loudly behind him.

Anthony stared after him, speechless. Every fibre of his body wanted to go after him and to talk to him about the madcap plan, to ask what Alan had said, if there was any news about his mother. But he couldn't. In a rage he punched the wall that gave way easily spraying the room with ancient dust from the rotting plasterboard. He paced the floor of the bed-sit swearing under his breath, tears of rage and frustration streaming down his cheeks. He wanted to speak to Cathy but he was out of credit and Steven had forgotten to buy him a card when he went out in the morning. Now, God knows when he would be back! Anthony swiped the tears from his face. He felt like screaming. But, he reminded himself, there was a lot at stake. Maybe he should consider Stevens's hair brained plan, because presumably he would only have to be in the coffin until it got to Alan's funeral parlour? Anthony was not claustrophobic, but the thought of being confined in a coffin made him breathe faster and cold sweat stood out on his forehead.

"Fuck!" he shouted as loud as he could and saw a couple walking out on the street in front of the bed-sit turned their faces up towards the window. The shock of seeing their eyes straining to focus on him through the grimy window brought him back to his senses and he sat down on the bed. He thought about the explosive that Steven was innocently carrying around with him. Believing it to be a USA standard transmitter. In the side of his rucksack he had the detonator. Every fibre of his being wanted to get it and blow the fucker off the street, he didn't even care who else he took with him, he hated being under his control, he wanted to be rid of him and his sick plans. He did not trust him, yet he had to. And he had given him Cathy's address, and that was niggling at him all the time now. He thought perhaps the fact that he had told Steven that the police had been round might put him off. It would be very difficult to know whether the police were in the flat or not, especially if they came in an unmarked car.

In her flat Cathy had just finished tidying up when the doorbell rang. She had been feeling better since her romp with Joe and phone sex with Anthony and she was pleased with how nice the flat looked now. She even thought that she might go back to work. They had been ringing and making veiled threats about long term sick being difficult for them and how Sophie the TV Station's sports reporter's niece was standing in and making a pretty good job of it. Cathy herself was not so sure. Sophie had mispronounced anti cyclone last evening and pointed at Cumbria instead of the West midlands in her report. She hummed to herself as she went to answer the door. It was likely to be the post-man, she had sent for some new shoes on line and she was expecting them any day.

But when she opened the door her face fell and her eyes darted down the corridor.

"Sorry, Cathy, I'm on my own, you quite wore Detective Sergeant Perkins out, you naughty girl!" Without asking for an invitation Denise pushed past Cathy and into the lounge. Too late Cathy realised that she had replaced Anthony's photo on the bedside cabinet. Denise strode through to the bedroom and scooped it up.

"Thought so!" she said dropping it triumphantly into an evidence bag.

"Look, constable, er." Cathy said\

"Lawson, detective constable Lawson."

"Yes, right, look I'm sorry that you were annoyed that Joe, I mean Detective Sergeant Perkins was flirting with me . . . ."

"Annoyed? Why should I be annoyed, I fucking hate the bloke, he's just a prick on legs, literally, whores it around anywhere with anyone who will open their legs for him. Luckily I only have to work with him, although that's hard enough!"

"Oh I thought you and him . . . ." Cathy said.

Denise threw her head back and laughed, "Please give me a bit more credit than that! But hey don't feel bad, you're not the first one he's done it to, and if you want to put in a complaint about him, well it would be added to the pile, it's really about time he got what was coming to him! Was it worth it? I've heard from others that he's pretty much the stud."

Cathy thought back to the shower, the delicious hard thrusts as Joe pushed into her driving her to intense orgasm as she clung to him, her arms around his muscled shoulders.

"Nothing special" she muttered, feeling really cheap now.

"Right shall we sit down and you can tell me about the real man in your life?" Denise said. She was pleased to have got the confession out of Cathy that she had slept with Joe and she was sure as hell going to make her write out a complaint, she was going to take Joe down every way she could, and for a start she was going to be the one to crack the case, she was convinced that Cathy knew where Anthony was, and now that she had got her on side it wasn't going to take much to crack her.

"It must be very difficult for you Cathy" Denise put her hand on Cathy's as she held the photo in the clear evidence bag up. Anthony's face smiled out at them.

"You must think I'm awful, with Anthony in so much trouble then sleeping with your officer."

"No of course not" Denise said soothingly "You've been under a lot of pressure, anyone can see that."

Cathy began to cry. "There, there" Denise said, recognising with distaste the smell of her soap, the same smell that Joe had reeked of.

The doorbell interrupted them.

"It's probably the post man" Cathy sniffed, "I'm waiting for some shoes."

Denise found she was feeling slightly better. But Joe was still going to have to suffer for this. She was just imagining her interview with the Superintendent, when Cathy burst back into the room.

Denise looked up in surprise and saw Cathy, half lifted off the floor, just her toes scraping the carpet being carried in to the living room. Around her waist was a man's arm, his other arm around her neck where he held a knife to her throat. Cathy's eyes were bulging in terror and although her mouth was open she seemed incapable of sound. Cathy's captor was apparently as surprised to see Denise as she was to see him and he loosened his grip on Cathy for a moment. It was enough for the terrified girl to break free and run into her bedroom, slamming the door behind, coughing and half screaming.

Steven pounced on Denise before she could get off the settee, pinning her face down on cushions that smelt vaguely of old farts and baby oil. She struggled but he was strong and she felt the tip of the blade pierce her neck, little flames of pain spreading from where it had broken the skin.

"So who have we here then?" Steven hissed "Another one of Cathy's little whoring friends?"

From the bedroom he could hear Cathy crying

"Detective Lawson, are you still there?" she whimpered through the closed door, and Denise shut her eyes bracing herself for the thrust of the knife that would surely follow now that this man knew she was a police officer.

"Oh a pig are you? Thought so with a lard arse like that!" Steven slapped her bottom and then lifted her skirt, shoving her knickers half down and started to fondle her buttocks. Denise felt a cold heavy weight in her stomach, this man, whoever he was, obviously had no intention of her getting out of this alive. She called on her training, stay calm and to try to reason with the assailant. But Cathy wailing in the bedroom distracted Steven. Someone would hear her if he didn't shut up.

"Come out here Cathy, now! Or I'm going to stick my knife right down this pig's throat. It's up to you, do you want her to live or die?" he jabbed the knife at Denise's throat again and she let out an involuntary cry of pain.

The door opened and Cathy came nervously through it. Now that she could see Steven's face clearly, she recognised him immediately and terror clutched at her spine.

"Steven, what do you want?" her teeth had started chattering now and her voice wavered. She was as white as a sheet and Denise thought she might faint.

"Oh shut up Cathy you big baby, and get over here! I'm here to give you at treat and there's plenty to go round so that the detective here won't be left out, but before that, you come over here and tie this pig up."

"What with?" Cathy's voice quavered.

"Christ how thick are you Cathy?, a belt, whatever!" Steven was getting annoyed now. Cathy brought a belt and held it out to Steven her eyes drawn to Denise's bare backside.

"You do it you stupid bitch!" he snapped and Cathy did the best she could. Satisfied that Denise was secured after a fashion Steven took the knife from her throat and tightened the belt around her wrists. He stood her up and half pushed half dragged her to the bedroom. Then lying her down on the bed with one movement he pulled off her tights and pants and skirt, leaving her exposed, tying one leg to each of the metal bedposts of Cathy's bed. Cathy stared in horror, she could see traces of talc on Denise's bush and along the insides of her plump thighs that were a bit red, maybe because they rubbed together when she walked. A very thin line of hair ran up over her rounded belly to her belly button and Steven spotting it at the same time as Cathy ran his knife up it leaving a little trail of pin prick beads of blood. Denise flinched but said nothing. Using the knife, Steven cut through her shirt and bra and her large breasts tumbled out, their nipples stiffening as they left the warmth of her bra.

"Now you—strip!" he ordered Cathy and as she stood paralysed Denise said.

"Do it." Cathy stepped out of her clothes and stood naked in front of Steven and Denise. Steven recalled to mind his sexual exploits with the two prostitutes and how when they touched and played with each other really turned him on. An opportunity not to be missed he thought as he said.

"Now, on the bed, get one of her tits and suck it!". Cathy looked at Denise and she nodded. Tentatively she took a nipple in her mouth. It felt strange, but not unpleasant, and she sucked like a baby.

"Go on put your back into it, finger the other nipple!" Steven said. He was struggling out of his tracksuit bottoms now a huge purple erection springing free and releasing a foul smell of unwashed body and stale urine.

"That's good, he said perching on the side of the bed, working his hand up and down his huge shaft.

"Remember him?" he said to Cathy, "he's missed you, now lick her out, go on, I've spread her legs for you, he pushed Denise's pussy lips apart roughly, "get in there!" he grabbed Cathy by the hair and forced her head between Denise's legs. Cathy sobbed into Denise's bush as Steven ground her face into the warm folds of Denise's vulva. Then grabbing Cathy's upturned rump Steven shoved his cock into her hard as he could and Cathy screamed into Denise's warm flesh. For a moment or two he rode her then he came with a loud shout, collapsing on the bed beside the women with eyes closed in ecstasy. Denise signalled to Cathy with a nod, and despite her terror

Cathy too had been waiting for an opportunity and grabbed the knife from where Steven had dropped it on the bed. It was a huge sharp and deadly looking thing, she cut through one of the belts that tied Denise's legs like butter. Her hands shaking Cathy cut the second belt and was just about to cut Denise's hands free when Steven opened his eyes. She dropped the knife on the bed and Denise held her legs in position. As long as he did not look at her ankles, they would be OK.

"Right then Piggy, your turn, let's hear you squeal now but you're going to have to give me blow job to get me back up again, you'll like it, I promise, I bet you've never seen such a big boy?" Denise tried not to gag as the foul odour of Stevens's unwashed genitals hit her. He positioned himself bedside her head and started to shove his half erect cock into her mouth.

Using all her strength Denise spun and kicked a leg out catching Steven full on the jaw. He went down like a sack of potatoes, and a terrified Cathy cut Denise's wrists free. "Get my bag!" She ordered wiping the rancid taste from her mouth. Cathy pulled on a dressing gown and threw Denise Anthony's towelling robe. Denise rubbed her ankles and picked up Steven's knife. He would be out for a bit she thought looking down at his prone body.

Cathy returned with the bag from the lounge and handed it to Denise who hurriedly took out her police radio. She was about to put the call in when in a single movement Steven jumped up from the floor snatched the knife and drove it into her back. The same knife driven into Cathy's throat changed her screams to a gurgle as she sank to the floor in a rapidly growing pool of her own and Denise's blood.

CHAPTER 17

It was only the fact that the neighbours in River Towers were always so interested in what was going on, that prevented their being two deaths in Cathy's flat. As Steven blundered out into the corridor, grabbing Cathy's phone off the hall table, he almost bowled over a man in scruffy slippers and a string vest who was saying over his shoulder.

"Don't worry love, I'll get the bitch to shut up, Christ she's like and alley cat that one!" As Steven collided with him, the man was spun one hundred and eighty degrees his last word coming out as "wuhuhn" as Steven ran past him making for the stairs, a trail of bloody footprints on the worn lino followed Steven and like him disappeared down the stairs of the communal corridor.

"Fucking watch out mate!" the man said his voice tailing off as he as saw the bloody footprints leading away from him. He looked fearfully at the open door of Cathy's flat. From the flat's interior he could hear a terrible gurgling noise, and he had to force himself to look inside.

On the floor a woman was lying with a growing crimson rose spreading from the middle of her back. Her legs were twitching wildly and it reminded the man of the time he had seen a cat hit on a motorway, it had been flung into the air, it's back broken, making grotesque twitching movements. Close to the woman was another, her throat gaping, blood pouring down her dressing gown. The gurgling noises were coming form her.

Scrabbling for the phone the man called the police and ambulance and all the while the woman whose throat had been cut stared at him with terrified eyes. He recognised her, she was his neighbour the weather girl, and her hands were clutching at her gaping throat. She was on her knees beside the settee.

"Linda! LINDA!" he shrieked at the top of his voice, and a few moments later his wife appeared at the door.

"Oh my good God!" she said holding her hands up to her mouth.

"What do we do?" he said his voice shaking.

"I don't know, have you called an ambulance Bill?"

"Of course I called a fucking ambulance, what are we supposed to do till it gets here?"

Sirens arriving at the towers cut off any answer she might have had.

The woman on the floor had stopped twitching now and Bill wondered if that meant she was dead. His neighbour, the weather girl was getting paler by the minute as her blood trickled down her gown onto the carpet. In her eyes was the most naked animal fear that Bill had ever seen, but still they followed his every move. His blood ran cold as she managed to communicate a terror to him that seemed to reach out and try to envelope him, just before her eyes finally flickered shut.

And then suddenly the flat was full of ambulance crew and Bill and Linda found themselves, shell shocked, out in the hall. The police were behind the ambulance crew and two of them pushed into the flat leaving the other two officers with Bill and Linda. A tall man in plain clothes but with a police high visibility jacket on took them back into their flat.

His face was white, almost as white as the face of the girl next door whose lifeblood had seeped out of her before his very eyes, Bill thought.

"What did you see?" The officer asked.

"And you are?" Bill said.

"Sorry, Detective Inspector Joe Perkins" Joe stood up and took his badge out.

"Right, we are Bill and Linda. Bill patted Linda's knee, she was crying quietly now, and her hands were shaking so much that he had to light her fag for her.

"This bloke ran out of the flat, that's his footprints on the lino, the blood." Bill pointed in the direction of the landing.

"Yep, we saw that, thanks, did you get a good look at him?"

"No he ran into me as he was leaving the flat and I sort of spun round." Bill said, "But he needs stringing up for what he's done to those women in there, it was horrible." Bill shuddered.

Joe had noticed Denise's car in the car park at the foot of the flats as he came in, and his stomach had turned over.

"Were the women conscious when you went into the flat, did they say anything?"

"You'll be fucking lucky, one of them had her throat cut and the other was stabbed in the back."

"I see, so were they dead?"

"No I don't think so, well one of them was just kneeling there, gurgling, you know clutching her throat where she had been stabbed, that's our neighbour, you know the weather girl off the box?" Bill shuddered as he thought of the girl the hungry terror in her eyes.

Joe nodded, he could barely bring himself to speak.

"And the other one?"

"Well she was twitching her legs when I went in but then that stopped, mind you the weather girl keeled over too in the end, just went out like a light, I expect they're both gone now."

Joe got up abruptly and went to the door. The paramedics were taking a stretcher out. The face of the victim was covered.

"Both dead?" Joe said to the policeman on the door.
"No, this one is but the other went off in the ambulance straight away."

"What were the injuries of the one who died?"

"Not sure gov."

Joe went back to Bill and Linda and half listened as they told him about Cathy's lifestyle, their damning judgement of her loud love making hinting at but not saying that she had been asking for it. Almost robotically Joe went over everything they had heard.

Finally, he could not put it off any longer and he made his way along the landing where forensics had cordoned off the area that bore Steven's footprints.

Inside Cathy's flat the sweet cloying smell of blood greeted him. One of the crime scene investigators showed him a clear evidence bag with a handbag in it.

"Looks like one of ours Joe, a Denise Lawson?"

"Yes she was working with me on the Kenly case."

"Oh right, I didn't know the name."

"No she was seconded in quite recently, was it her who died?"

"No sure, neither of them were dressed, well they were in towelling robes, and it looks as though the bedroom has seen some action . . ."

Joe was trying to piece together what could have happened in the flat. Either Anthony or Steven Smith had come round to see Cathy and surprised Denise there. Since the constable had said there had been action in the bedroom Joe thought it was probably Anthony, maybe he and Cathy had been having a session when Denise turned up, he probably wouldn't be able to stay away too long either if he was sleeping with Cathy, Joe thought, she was a tigress!

Steven was bundling the knife into a discarded newspaper that had been fluttering down the road. He looked down, his dark blue tracksuit was covered in blood and there were splashes like fallen red tear drops on his trainers. Because his tracksuit was dark unless you looked closely you probably wouldn't notice the bloodstains, but the trainers, he would have to clean them off somehow. He had reached the park now and made for the public toilets. He waited until the place was empty then heaved one foot then the other into the sink and let the tap run over them. As he left the toilets he could feel the cold water squelching around in his trainers as he walked, but at least he had removed the bloodstains. Sitting down on a bench, he suddenly felt very tired. He took Cathy's phone out of his pocket, no messages from Anthony. Steven remembered that he had not bought him the phone card he had asked for and made a note to do that when he went up to the charity shop for some more clothes.

In the distance he could hear more sirens. Fear gripped him as he wondered if Cathy and the pig were alive or dead. Like some deranged teenager he dragged his tired body up and made his way back into town. He bought another tracksuit, trainers and a phone card and changed in the alley behind the co-op shoving the stained tracksuit and his soaking trainers, down deep inside a big waste container outside the shop. He suddenly felt very vulnerable and walked as briskly as his increased weight would allow him, back to the bed-sit. He hesitated before he opened the door. As soon as he did open it Anthony leapt off the bed.

"Have you got the phone card?" he said and Steven said

"Yeah sorry mate, forgot it before, here it is."

"Is that a new track suit you're wearing?" Anthony said sharply

"Yeah, mate look sit down I need to speak to you, and it's not good news." Steven turned the TV off, he couldn't afford for Steven to hear what had happened.

"I went round to see Cathy, to give the flowers you know, that's why I bought the new trackie, couldn't turn up there looking like a sack of shit."

Anthony was on full alert now, and eyed Steven warily.

"Anyway mate, it's not good news, she was with another bloke, some skinny stuck up wanker from the TV station. She told me to tell you that she doesn't want you to ring her."

"You're lying!" Anthony fumbled with his phone to load his credit and rang her number. In his pocket Steven closed his hand around Cathy's phone. He had turned it off and he had to suppress a smile as Anthony waited for her to answer.

When Anthony finally put the phone down Steven said

"Sorry mate, it's a bastard."

"What did she say exactly?" Anthony had tears in his eyes.

Steven shrugged. "Not much really, the guy was in the bedroom and she was in her robe, hair all messed up you know like they'd been at it."

Anthony winced.

"She only let me get as far as the hall. She said she couldn't really take it with you on the run and everything, had to think about her career and all that shit."

Anthony looked up doubt clouding his face. It was true that she had been very keen on progressing her career, not letting people know that they were an item, for instance. Anthony felt sick. He couldn't believe what Steven was saying, but she wasn't answering her phone. He sent a text. Nothing.

"Look mate," Steven said, "remember the little plan that I had for you to get out of here?"

"Yes." Anthony said flatly, he really could not care what happened to him now. If Cathy was not going to be waiting for him, then he didn't really care about anything.

"I think we need to do it sooner rather than later, mate, you can't move for fucking cops on the high street and now that you and Cathy have um broken up" Steven tried to look regretful, "it's going to be a whole lot less complicated. We still have plenty of money and we can get out to South America no trouble. "I reckon you're pretty much unrecognisable, now with your hair longer and darker, I didn't know you dyed it mate! You're going the same way as me sitting on your arse all day" Steven pointed to Anthony's swollen belly. "I'm organising false passports, they should be ready soon. But first we've got to get you out of here. Let's just hope that Alan comes up with a stiff needing burying soon!"

Hearing Alan's name and making the connection with his mother pushed Anthony over the edge and he started to cry, long low sobs, into his pillow.

Steven curled his lip, he hated weakness but nevertheless he went over and patted Anthony's shoulder.

"Come on mate, Cathy was always a bit on the adventurous side, there are plenty of really beautiful girls in Brazil, they'll knock your eyes out!"

At the hospital Joe sat quietly in the waiting area of A&E, He could go up and ask for what he wanted, the woman who had been admitted, her details how she was etc. but for now he didn't want to know. He thought about Denise, if it was her who had died then he would be safe, unless Cathy survived and wanted to complain about him. But he doubted that, she would be too pleased to be alive. He felt wretched for wishing Denise dead, Denise who had warmed his bed and given him the best blow job he had ever had, Denise who was keen as mustard and destined for a great future in the force, had he really stooped so low that he would wish her dead to save his sorry backside? Joe knew that however much he tried to dodge the question, he did. He had ambitions too and he didn't want anything to stand in his way. And after all, it was not as though he had attacked her himself.

Eventually and very wearily he hauled himself off the chipped plastic seat and approached the desk. He flashed his badge and the receptionist began to stab at the buttons on her computer.

"Still no ID on either the deceased or the injured person, could you ID either, officer?

"Both, probably" Joe said.

"Oh right!" she smiled brightly at him. "I'll let the doctor know, the injured woman is still here in A&E, waiting for theatre."

Joe returned to his seat to wait.

A doctor who looked about as tired as Joe felt came and sat beside him on the seat.

Joe showed him his badge.

"Well officer, the woman we are looking after here is very badly injured. She is very confused, and has been trying to speak, but nothing yet, perhaps you can come through and see if you know her, that would be a help" The young doctor ran his fingers through his dishevelled hair and Joe followed him through A&E. He held his breath as the doctor pulled back the curtain to one of the cubicles and as the young medic stepped out of the way the woman on the bed swivelled her eyes to him.

"Hi Joe" she croaked.

Joe swallowed hard.

"Hi, Denise." He said.

In his funeral parlour Alan put the phone down on its hook. It was an old fashioned Bakelite one that he had on his desk because it was more in keeping with the traditional sober surrounding of the interior of the parlour.

He had had the call he was waiting for. Alice Smedleys' family had been in touch to say that they had arranged her burial for Monday morning. The old lady was already in the back of the funeral parlour and Alan wandered back there now, resting his hand on the walnut casket with the plaque on it that read:

Alice Smedley

3rd April 1924 to 8th November 2010

R.I.P.

The Smedleys wanted her buried on the 15th, Monday morning at St. Gabriel's. Alan swallowed hard. He had a bad feeling about this, a very bad feeling, but then he reasoned, anything to do with Steven left a bad taste in his mouth, quite literally some times as the stink of him seemed to pervade the air and actually find its way to Alan's taste buds.

He retuned to his desk and texted Steven. Steven answered his text almost immediately. He was in the café, and wanted Alan to meet him there as soon as he could. Steven had left the bedsit telling Anthony that he was going to replace the TV set that he had accidentally on purpose pushed off the rickety chair it stood on. Steven could not afford for Anthony to see the news, but he knew that Anthony was close to having a break down so when he received Alan's text he had said "Yes!" so loudly that some of the café customers had turned to look at him again. He was becoming a bit of a curiosity at the café and he had to try to remember to keep it down, not to draw attention to himself. His leg jerked up and down as he waited impatiently for Alan to arrive. Across the street was the high streets Curry's and he watched as one of the big screens in the window showed a picture of first Cathy and then Denise. He felt the colour drain from his face as the women's faces stared out at him. Then suddenly they were gone and in their place Anthony's photo and then a police contact number. Steven laughed out loud. He didn't need to hear the commentary to know what was being said. Again the clientele of the café looked at him. his leg jerked up and down harder now and he kept his eyes trained on the door.

When Alan arrived he was agitated and almost before he had sat down he asked Steven. "What the hell is this on the news? They are saying Anthony attacked those two women, murdered one of them, his mother is beside herself!"

"Bloody typical of the filth!" Steven said "They're so fucking lazy if they've got someone in the frame for something they just pin anything else that happens on them!" he shook his head in mock disbelief. "Hell we both know he couldn't have done it! One of the women died, did they say which one? "Why do you ask, do you know them?"

"No, why should I know the stupid bitches?"

"Well why would Anthony be suspected?"

"No idea, but obviously golden bollocks didn't do it!"

Yes but *I* don't know that you didn't. Alan thought to himself. He felt sick, thinking that he might be sitting in front of a man who murdered a woman and attacked another horribly not that long ago.

"Anyway, you texted me, someone snuffed it?" Steven said eagerly.

"Yes, and old lady has died, she is to be buried at St. Gabriel's next Monday morning.

"Brilliant, nice one love!" Steven said. "So when is the grave being dug?" Steven asked eagerly.

"I've checked with the church, and it will be ready by tomorrow lunch time.

"OK then you come round and get him tomorrow night and we get him in there, then dig him up again after the old dear's been planted on Monday."

Alan tightened his jaw. He knew that it would be the wrong thing to do to antagonise this unstable young man further but he seemed to have no respect for anyone or anything.

"Right, got it." Alan said flatly. He thought about the talk he had had with Rose that morning. He had asked her about Steven, about what he had been like when he and Anthony had been at school together.

"Oh he was a nice lad, he was always ever so polite when he came round here, always asked after my health and always had a chat with me. I know that it must be him behind all this malarkey but it really is hard to believe, he was always such a smart good looking young lad."

Not any more, Alan had thought to himself, Steven was stinking and spotty, lardy and callous. He wished he could talk to Rose about his meetings with Steven but he knew that it would be unfair of him to burden her with this especially now that this latest thing about Anthony having attacked a police woman and raped and killed another had come up. Rose had wept for hours when the police came around to tell them what was going to be on the evening news.

Alan couldn't believe it either, he was convinced that if it had been anyone it had been Steven. He wanted very much to go to the police and tell them where they could find the revolting man but he did not dare while he had Anthony under his control God knows what he would do to him if he suspected Alan might shop him to the police. It had crossed his mind that he might be able to get some clue as to what Steven was likely to do from his mother and Stepfather and he went around to their house.

Brian answered the door and recognising Alan from the television where he had put out an early appeal for Anthony to give himself up, he quickly steered him around the corner of the house. There he explained to him about Mary's total amnesia where Steven was concerned and arranged to meet him in the pub on the corner of the road 10 minutes later.

"Who was that love?" Mary had asked when Brian came back in.

"One of my old dentist friends, a few of them are down at the pub and asked if I wanted to join them."

"Oh that's nice, are you going to?"

"Thought I might." Brian said.

Ten minutes later the two men sat opposite each other in a quiet corner of the pub.

"Have you heard from Anthony?" Brian asked.

"No but I think that's because he doesn't want to drag his mother into all this, didn't want her to have to lie to the police."

Brian nodded. "Yes Steven sent his mother a note saying that he would not be in touch for the same reason, I suppose that's something."

The two men sat in silence for a moment. Alan wanted with all his being to unburden himself to Steven's stepfather, to tell him what Steven was having him do, but he did not dare to. Several times during the time that they sat together he opened his mouth to speak and then shut it again. He liked Brian and he thought Brian liked him. They were both in an intolerable position, virtual stepfathers of two of the most wanted men in the country, but unlike Alan's opinion of Anthony, Brain seemed to have no affection at all for his stepson.

"I hate what this has done to Mary." Brain said and Alan nodded agreement.

"I think she must know deep down that he is a baddun and because of guilt or denial or whatever she has just blotted him out, as though he never existed!"

Alan thought that he would love to blot out the smelly obnoxious man that was Brian's protégé. It was hard for him to imagine that Steven was once a dentist, a respected member of the community, smart and clean in a white dentist's tunic and talented too if Brian was to be believed.

As the men parted outside the pub, they shook hands and Alan said.

"What's the post code here?"

"Why?" Brain said

"Just so that I can drop you a note if I need to, if I find anything out." Brian nodded and handed Alan a card.

"It's all on there, the address, phone, email, postcode, the lot!"

"Thanks." Alan said and they went their separate ways,

Steven had forced himself to stay in with Anthony all day. Alan would be coming round to get him later, in a coffin. Steven chuckled to himself. Anthony was jumpy and snappy, and very angry that Steven had not replaced the TV.

"Look mate, you're out of here tonight, what was the point?" he said.

"I'm fucking going out of my mind here!

"I know that, it won't be long now." Steven said. He had had a text from Alan saying that he would be around as soon as it got dark. Anthony looked and felt terrible. The more he thought about being shut in a coffin the more he felt sick. And what if he was sick and swallowed it and choked? Would there be enough air? He tried to comfort himself. Alan would make sure that he was OK and it wouldn't be for long, just till they go to the funeral parlour.

As night fell a hearse slid silently to a halt outside the bedsit. The coffin slid silently out of the back and onto a small trolley. Alan had brought his youngest and most inexperienced trainee with him and when they got to the bottom of the stairs, Alan hobbled up and knocked on the door. Steven answered. Behind him Alan could see Anthony, as white as a sheet his eyes dark and haunted. His heart went out to the boy.

"You're going to help get the coffin up the stairs" Alan waved his stick.

"Right" Steven put the hood of his hoodie up and went downstairs. The young lad standing by the coffin on its trolley looked at him quizzically and Steven turned his back to him as they lifted the coffin up to the flat.
"Now fuck off!" Steven hissed and the boy bolted down stairs.

Inside the flat Alan smiled at Anthony

"How are you son?"

"Been better" Anthony said, he could not take his eyes off the coffin.

"Won't be for long." Alan said

"Will I be able to breathe?

"Yes of course, I've made extra holes underneath the plaque."

"You won't screw the top on will you?"

"No of course . . . ."

"Hold up there Alan we are going to have to screw the lid on, I don't want any accidents." Steven said

"Fuck off Steven, I'm not being nailed into a coffin you can just FUCK OFF!" Anthony's voice was panicky now. Steven looked at him his cold dark eyes seeming to bore through him.

"Right, well it's off then, thanks for coming Alan but it looks like our Ant is happy with the way things are!"

"Now just hold on lads." Alan said. "Look Ant it won't be for long, honestly it's not going to make any difference if it's fixed on."

Anthony hesitated. Alan was pleading with him, his eyes trying to send him a message. Without another word he got into the coffin and lay down, sweat standing out on his upper lip and his brow.

Once the coffin lid was fixed on Alan warned Anthony again that one of his trainees would be helping Steven down the stairs with the coffin.

"Don't move or make a sound, all right?"

Steven sat in the back of the hearse on the way back to the funeral parlour, his hood up, obscuring his face. Once they were there Alan dismissed his assistant once he had helped Steven put the coffin on the stand in the relatives room.

"I'm very sorry for your loss" the boy mumbled to Steven and bolted.

Standing on either side of the coffin, Steven and Alan's eyes met. What Alan saw in Stevens dark mad eyes terrified him and in the instant that his terror froze him to the spot, Steven jumped over the coffin and plunged a knife into his chest. Alan thought almost dispassionately that it was amazing that a man of Steven's bulk could pull off such a feat, but then they said madness gave you the strength of 10 men. Alan had half raised his stick to defend himself and the knife gashed his arm as it made it's way to its target. The serrated edge of the knife sliced the left ventricle of his heart in half stopping it before he even hit the floor. Steven jumped back so that the blood would not splash onto him. He watched with satisfaction as blood spread in a pool around Alan. He was getting quite fond of this hands on killing lark! He looked down, not a speck of blood on him, hey he was getting better at this!"

From the coffin he could hear Anthony's muffled voice, asking what was going on.

He did not bother to reply. Steven screwed the plaque a little tighter over the air holes, he didn't want to cut off the oxygen supply completely, he wanted to think that Anthony would suffer a slow lingering death! Next he manhandled the coffin back onto the little trolley it had been brought in on and wheeled it out to the street again where the hearse still stood. Heaving it into the back he shut the big hatch back of the vehicle. He could hear Anthony banging on the inside of the coffin now, and he smiled to himself. He went back into the funeral parlour and opened the top drawer of Alan's big desk. A cash box inside held a couple of cheques and some cash and he put them in his pocket, throwing the cash box across the room, pulling out more of the drawers of the desk and throwing stuff around the room. With a bit of luck the cops would think it had been a druggy looking for cash.

He had noticed Alan had put the keys for the hearse on a hook in the back room and he retrieved them before shutting the door of the funeral parlour behind him.

When he got to St. Gabriel's he left the hearse in darkness and scouted around the graveyard. He was in luck, the grave was next to the wide drive way. He drove the hearse up till he arrived opposite the pile of newly dug earth. Opening the hatch back of the hearse he heaved the coffin out and slid it across the grass to the edge of the grave. The soil that had been shovelled out was piled up to one side of the grave and he positioned the coffin now at one end of the deep hole. He had bought a torch on an elastic headband, the type that postmen used in the winter to see what they were doing, and he shone it down now on the blank plaque on the front of the coffin. He could feel the sturdy coffin vibrating slightly where Anthony was kicking and banging on the inside. Sitting down and leaning over the plaque Steven said "I wouldn't be doing that if I were you Ant old mate, once you get under there won't be that much oxygen to play with, but then on the other side do you want to use it up quicker, or die slowly, ah well it's your call I suppose. Oh I forgot to tell you, Cathy died, sad it was, although she did enjoy her last hours, I could see from her eyes that she had never had anyone so big, I think she wished she had given it up to me earlier, she really enjoyed it anyway, so I doubt even if she hadn't died and you hadn't been 6 foot under she would have had much time for you, I know that you had the skill, but believe me Ant it's the size they really want, you should have heard her scream, God she was insatiable." Steven looked up at the clear cold sky

"Shame it's had to end this way really, we had a good thing going and I'm really going to miss having you to spend the money with me—not!" Steven laughed into the night, a sound colder than the frosty air itself.

Inside the coffin Anthony through fear had lost control of his bowels, diarrhoea and urine ran freely from his body. Now lying in a pool of his own waste his breath came in short gasps, the foul smell seeming to invade his nostrils and his mouth and make him want to gag. His heart was racing and pure terror gripped him making sweat stand out on his brow. The heat in the coffin was unbearable and the stench sickening. He could not even move his hand to his face to cover his nose and mouth and tears ran down his face and into his ears. And all the while Steven's voice spoke softly to him from outside the coffin, outside in the cold clear night air. He knew now that Cathy was dead and he assumed Alan was too. He cursed himself for being led into Steven's trap and he wanted to scream at the naked grief of losing Cathy. But he was helpless, hopeless and he knew he was going to die.

A fear like none that he had never felt before took hold of the far reaches of his mind and for a few blissful seconds he passed out. When he came to, the coffin was on the move, he was being tipped head first into what he could only imagine was a grave. He screamed as his faeces and urine sloshed up his back to his head as the coffin slid into the grave. Eventually after some manipulation from Steven if came to rest level, but Anthony was now covered in shit, he could taste it, feel it on his hands and down his neck.

His brain seemed to be shutting down and he reached out with the same desperation as a starving man would for a crumb of bread. He felt a strange sensation in his head a strange numbness, God was he having a stroke? The absurdity of what he was worrying about struck him. So what if he was having a stroke or a heart attack or a fucking bout of piles? He was going to die, what did it matter? And as Steven shovelled earth in on the coffin the sound of Anthony laughing drifted up through the holes under the plaque. Steven stopped momentarily the hairs rising on the back of his neck, quickly he continued shovel after shovel until the laughter befitting a church yard was deadened.

CHAPTER 18

On Monday morning Brian was rushing out, late for his first appointment when the postman came through the garden gate.

"Here you are then mate!" He said smiling at Brian.

"Thanks" Brain took the post and hesitated. Should he go back and open the door to put the post in, or put it through the letterbox. There were several bulky magazines, He really didn't have time, and Mary had already left. He ran for his car and threw the bundle on the passenger seat. His new surgery was further away from home now and the traffic through town was always a bitch at this time of day.

At the funeral parlour, the young lad who had helped Alan with the coffin on Saturday night was first there, that morning. As he stood stamping his feet to keep warm in the doorway, he glanced inside and let out a high-pitched scream that sounded for all the world like a little girl's shrill shriek. Inside, through the door that led to the back room he could make out half of his employer lying in a pool of blood that had gone black over the weekend. Taking out his mobile phone, with hands shaking the young lad eventually managed to put in a garbled call to the police.

In the hospital Joe was at Denise's bedside. When he had seen her on Saturday he offered to ring any relatives she had, her shoulders dropped as she told him the sad truth that she had no relatives. The news unsettled Joe making him feel that he owed it to her to stay for a bit. He did not want to admit to himself that he was trying to get her onside, win some brownie points in the hope that she would not blow his career out of the water. She slept a lot of the time but she had been able to tell him that her attacker was not Anthony. She was not sure if it was Steven, there was a slight resemblance but Denise told Joe she was not sure. Then Joe had been asked to wait out in the corridor while yet another doctor, one Joe had not seen before, came in to examine Denise.

As the doctor came out of the room he came over to Joe.

"Good news Mr. Lawson, your wife has not lost the baby!"

Joe stood staring at him his face draining of colour. The doctor looked confused. He looked down at his chart and then up at Joe.

"You are Mr. Lawson aren't you?"

Joe could not speak. Instead he took out his badge.

"Oh dear, I'm sorry officer, I didn't think, with you not being in uniform . . ."

"Plain clothes." Joe croaked.

"Well I really am very sorry, Oh dear, this is terrible, patient confidentiality and all that!" the doctor looked very agitated and Joe pulled himself together.

"Oh it's all right doctor, I know about Denise's er, pregnancy I just had convinced myself she had lost the baby, that is why I looked so shocked"

The doctor relaxed visibly.

"Oh good, Oh well that's a relief, yes indeed, well goodbye!" he said taking off down the corridor leaving Joe staring at the closed door of Denise's room. His mind was racing. The baby was probably his, hell who was he kidding, it was definitely his, Denise had been so besotted with him that the torch she was carrying could have lit up a small town. He thought it could have been her almost suffocating attention that had shoved him into the shower with Cathy, in fact he knew it was. And so now what was he going to do. Had she known before this happened that she was pregnant? Squaring his shoulders he went back into the room.

Denise was crying and for a moment his heart went out to her. As well as everything else the doctor's had said it was unlikely that Denise would ever walk again.

"I'm pregnant!" she blurted out. "I didn't know it, apparently it's very early but the doctor says that the baby is OK." She started crying in earnest now and Joe crossed to the bed and patted her shoulder awkwardly.

"Am I? . . ."

"Of course you're the fucking father!" she turned her face blotchy from crying to him and he wondered, not for the first time, what he had ever seen in her.

"Don't worry though, I don't expect you to hang around, I mean you were off like a rat up a drain pipe as soon as that little tart gave you the come on."

Joe winced. Denise had a dangerous look in her eye and he feared again for his future. The word was that his acting DI status was about to be substantiated and he couldn't let anything jeopardise that. He could just imagine the scene, the Super sitting beside Denise's bed as he was now listening to the tearful account of her seduction while on duty, his infidelity with a witness and the fact that he had impregnated her.

"Hey hey!" he said sitting on the edge of the bed "That was a blip, I'm sorry I really am but what we have was special, I don't know why I risked it, it's been destroying me ever since!" Joe thought back to an edition of Jeremy Kyle he had seen recently.

"I think I knew that I was falling hard, it was a last attempt to resist the inevitable, I was just scared, scared and weak!"

Denise looked at him doubtfully from blood shot eyes but she didn't say anything.

"Please say you'll give me another chance?" Joe tried to look as contrite as he could

"I've been to hell and back, "said Denise

"Oh my God I can't believe it I'm going to be a Dad, that's fantastic!" Joe said and even to him his voice sounded strangled. But it seemed to convince Denise and her blotchy face broke into a grin.

"You really mean it?" she said.

Joe took her hand.

"I've been a fool, but for the time that I didn't know whether it was you or Cathy that had died, I didn't know what I was going to do." Joe hung his head and Denise reached out her hand and lovingly placed it to the side of Joe's face. "It's alright darling, I'm going to be with you forever!" she whispered and Joe's stomach turned over. His phone was vibrating in his pocket.

He reached for it and answered it. He listened for a few moments.

"Right I'll be there in ten." he said, planting a hurried kiss on Denise's forehead.

"What is it darling?" Joe cringed at Denise's use of the endearment.

"Someone offed Anthony's step father and stole a coffin!" he said

"What?" Denise said, her eyes showed how much she wanted to be by his side

"I'll be back as soon as I can!" Joe said quickly exiting the room.

At the funeral parlour Joe took in the scene and the snivelling boy in the corner of the office.

"Hello" Joe flashed his badge. "Don't be scared" he continued reassuring the boy

"What happened when you got her this morning?"

The boy told his story to Joe haltingly and also told him about the man from whom they had picked up the coffin on Saturday night.

"Where was the bed sit?" Joe asked sharply

"Warren street, number 16a—a right dump" the boy said.

"Anyone round there?" Joe asked the uniformed officer guarding the funeral parlour door.

"Yes two uniforms and a DC."

"Which one?"

"Jim Roberts."

"Oh? He's back from sick leave then?"

"Yeah and keener than mustard to get this bastard. I think he suspects he had something to do with Matheson as well. Seems like really bad things happen to people involved with this case, look at DC Lawson!"

"Yes thanks constable, that's all for now." Joe returned to Alan's apprentice. But the lad didn't really know much, hadn't even got a very good description of the guy from the bed sit but he did mention a filthy grey hoody and Denise had mentioned that too.

It had to be Steven.

Back at the bed sit Jim Roberts was surveying the filthy squalor that Anthony and Steven had been living in. Steven had cleared nearly everything out of the bedsit. Now forensics busied themselves going over what remained, the bedding and sleeping bags they had left behind would yield rich pickings by the look of them. The place stank and whoever had cleared it out hadn't been very careful, there was loads left behind. Jim set his jaw. These bastards needed catching and now that he was better he was going to do everything he could to help. Joe Perkins was no Sammy Matheson, hell he wasn't even an Andy Sims, poor bastard. Jim had been to see Andy in the rehabilitation unit in the next town. It was sad to see, Andy had been so desperate for any snippet of information it had brought a lump to Jim's throat. Still al though Joe Perkins was very much third best, Jim was determined to give everything he had to the investigation.

Now as he surveyed the bedsit he was looking for anything that might give him a clue as to where these two bastards might have gone next. Apparently Anthony had been involved with the weather girl that lived in River Towers, when forensics had gone round after she was killed and Lawson attacked, they had found a photo of Anthony already in an evidence bag. But why had Lawson gone round there by herself. From what he had heard in the gossip at the station, Lawson and Joe Perkins were a bit of an item, and procedure was that they should be interviewing suspects together. From what Jim had read in the notes so far, they had both been round to interview Cathy so why had Denise gone back on her own? He would have to talk to Joe and see if he knew why.

One of Alan's friends and fellow funeral directors, Bill Johns had taken over the Smedley funeral for him while his wife sat with Rose who was deeply in shock. Every now and again she would sob violently and then stop just as suddenly. The doctor was on the way to administer a sedative but for Rose it was as though her world had ended. First Anthony and now this, she couldn't take it in and when the doctor arrived and gave her an injection she slipped into sleep gratefully.

As the Smedley funeral arrived at the graveside, Bill Johns, Alan's colleague looked at the messy grave surround. "Bloody lightweights" he muttered under his breath, leaving the grave in such a state, and it didn't look like they had dug a very deep grave either. He glanced at the mourners, he hoped none of them would notice that the grave seemed to be a good couple of feet shallower than it should have been, but they were so shaken by the days events that they were all more or less in a state of shock. Bill was beside himself, he could not imagine who would want to kill Alan, he was a big bear of a man but as gentle as a kitten with a heart of gold. Bill pondered over Alan's life since his bike accident, thinking how rough times had been for him, but then the last time Bill had seen Alan socially he had looked the best he'd seen him in a long time and was obviously really happy with Rose. It was a crying shame, and Bill supposed that it had something to do with Rose's lad Anthony, bad business that. Still the coffin was in the ground now and the first mourner had sprinkled some earth that Bill had offered to him in the time honoured fashion on it. As the mourners dispersed and went back to their cars parked beside the church the gravediggers, two of them slouched over to begin filling the grave in. Bill pointed two fingers towards his eyes and then at them and they flicked him the V's. He would speak to them later, lazy bastards.

In his surgery Brian had just shown out one of his patients. The consultation had been a struggle, try as she might, the young woman could not sit still in the chair and every time he put his fingers and instruments in her mouth she would try to clamp her jaw shut and her hands would fly up to try to drag his arm away. He had eventually carried out his examination and identified that she needed a filling, but it was a marginal case and he decided not to mention it this visit, maybe next time she would need something less and he could give her a sedative to do the work, she was going to need it. His next patient was a denture fitting and he had left the three front teeth on their hooks in the car where he had picked them up at the end of last week from the dental technician he used. He ran downstairs, retrieved the dentures and picked up his post. He was due to have a coffee after this one he could go through it all then.

The denture fitted perfectly and the rugby player was pleased with them. With 15 minutes before his next appointment Brian sat down to pen his post and have a welcome coffee. He had been so late this morning he had not had anything yet. As he leafed through the magazines and junk mail a small handwritten envelope caught his eye. In the corner opposite the stamp URGENT was written in red and underlined. He tore the envelope open and started to read. Suddenly he sat up and spat his coffee out, it sprayed in a graceful arc across his little office and his hands started shaking as he reached for his mobile. He rang the number on the letter and a voice answered.

"Can I speak to Alan, the undertaker please?"

"Whose calling?" the voice did not sound very friendly

"Brian Henderson"

"What do you want?" the voice asked and Brian thought again that it was not exactly a comforting image for a funeral parlour.

"I want to speak to Alan."

"He's not available, goodbye"

"Wait!" Brian shouted "Is he dead?" There was silence for a moment then the voice said.

"Why would you ask that?"

"Because I have a letter from him, posted on Saturday morning, saying that I had to find out if he was dead today." Brian realised how bizarre what he was saying was, but he had got the attention of the person on the other end of the line.

"Yes Mr. Henderson, he is dead, this is Police constable Sharp." Brian felt faint. If he was dead then according to his letter Anthony was . . . ."

The last of the Smedley's relatives were still in the church yard when three police vans screamed in through the graveyard gates and officers clutching shovels leapt out and sprinted over to the recently filled in grave. The relatives of the deceased watched in horror as the officers aided by the gravediggers swiftly emptied the grave of earth and dumped a coffin unceremoniously on the side of the hole in the ground. A few minutes later to their utter horror, another coffin was pulled out of the grave and the policemen were prising the top off it.

As the top sprung off the policemen stumbled back the stench almost knocking them off their feet.

"Jesus Christ!" one of the officers said holding his hand over his mouth and gagging.

Inside the coffin Anthony lay still his eyes closed.

"Is he dead?"

"Fuck me the smell alone would have done that!" Anyone in suits?" he shouted.

Some forensic officers in their traditional white hooded suits with masks on hurried themselves to graveside. By the time they had finished getting Anthony out of his coffin onto the grass they were covered in excrement. As if responding to their touch Anthony opened his eyes then blinked in the unaccustomed light of the winter sun.

"Is there an ambulance coming?"

"Yep, on its way" One of the forensic team looked into Anthony's eyes. What he saw there was barely human, an expression that was feral, completely insane.

The ambulance arrived and two medics were soon kneeling on the grass in front of Anthony. Now that his arms were free of the confines of the coffin Anthony was trying to reach up to the pocket inside his thin jacket that was covered in urine and faeces. His nails and the tips of his fingers were a pulped mess where he had clawed at the inside of the coffin.

"What's your name sir?" one of the ambulance crew asked him and his eyes swivelled to her. He opened his mouth to reveal a mangled tongue that he had bitten repeatedly and muttered something unintelligible.

"Ok let's get him to the hospital."

Anthony tried to get up but they rolled him onto a stretcher and took him to the waiting ambulance.

As the officers watched the ambulance pull away Jim Roberts said.

"Fucking hell, poor bugger, whatever he's done that was pretty horrible!" They stood in silence for a while trying to imagine the feeling of being buried alive, thinking that you were never going to be discovered, that you were going to die slowly of suffocation.

"That was Anthony Grace then?" one of the officers said and Jim nodded.

"Apparently his step father met up with Steven Smith's step father and I suppose the undertaker fella, Alan must have had an idea of what might be going to happen. He sent a letter to Brian Henderson, Steven Smith's stepfather asking him to check that nothing had happened to him and saying what he had done—taken Anthony out of the bed sit to the funeral parlour with a view to burying him.

"Why the fuck would he want to do something like that?" a young uniformed police officer asked.

"Steven Smith" Jim said through clenched teeth. "You thought the Moors murderers, the Yorkshire Ripper and Fred West were sick bastards, well Steven Smith makes the lot of them look like pussycats!

The young constable swallowed hard, he knew he would not be sleeping well that night. The sight of the man covered in his own shit, his eyes mad and desperate at the same time. That was the sort of sight that would haunt a man.

Joe Perkins came straight back to the hospital from the funeral home to see Anthony. As he looked at him in his cubicle, he thought it was interesting that he had been his competition with Cathy, he wondered absently which of them she had found better.

Apart from the state he was in and the mad look in his eyes Anthony was obviously a handsome lad, hardly the type that Joe would suspect would do the horrific things that he knew he and Steven Smith had done. By the look of him though, they wouldn't be getting very far with Anthony. Joe wondered if he knew where Smith was. He doubted it; if Smith was happy to plant his friend in the graveyard he probably wasn't in the frame of mind to be sharing secrets with him.

On the other side of town, Steven chuckled to himself. Sitting in the same doorway as the old tramp he had bumped into all those months ago he wondered if anyone who passed by even realised he was a different man. He had been surprised at the amount of money that people were willing to throw into the old cap he had found in a dumpster. He didn't need the money but it pleased him anyway to see them looking at him expectantly when they threw down a few coppers expecting him to be really grateful. He would hold their eyes for a mo then hiss "Fuck off!" Most of them reeled away as though he had slapped them and he thought it was funny. None tried to take their money back.

He was trying to think what to do next. He felt for the money belt around his waist that bulged with cash. But it would not take them long to piece together what had happened, even they weren't quite that stupid and of course now that he knew Miss Piggy had survived his attack she would be oinking his name all over the place. He wondered if Anthony was dead yet. He laughed as he thought of him screaming and squirming in the coffin. Serve him right for fucking his girl; still he had had the last dip of the wick! He could go for another change of look and try to evade attention that way. Yes that is what he would do. Standing up from the doorway he let the old cap with the money he had collected fall on the pavement and strode off.

In the town hospital, as the nurses started to undress Anthony in A&E he became more agitated, trying to get hold of his jacket. The inside pocket sagged slightly with something and a nurse reached her gloved hand in gingerly and took out what looked like a remote for an electric gate. As she held it up Anthony tried to grab it and Joe stepped forward.

"I'll take that thanks." He held out an evidence bag and the nurse dropped it in.

Anthony gurgled and thrashed on the bed and Joe frowned. Given what he knew these lads had been up to, this could be one of the devices they used to blow up their victims. Everything in him wanted to press the button in the centre of the small device, but he dare not, until he knew what would happen if he did. The doctor stepped forward to administer a sedative and Anthony slumped down on the bed.

Several floors above the Super was visiting Denise. He sat beside her bed and his presence instantly dominated the room. He was a tall man and in his uniform he looked impressive.

"Well, then Denise, this is a sad day for us, one of our finest cut down in the line of duty." Denise smiled at him and he thought for someone who had been told that they may never walk again and was almost certainly not going to be able to work as a police woman again, she looked remarkably cheerful.

"Brave girl." He said patting her arm.

"Thanks Sir, well I have had some good news today as well. I haven't lost the baby I'm carrying."

The Super's eyebrows shot up.

"Yes acting DI Perkins and I are expecting a baby, we're delighted!" she said.

"I. I didn't know, er congratulations!" he said. He had not seen that one coming. He knew Joe Perkins MO and it did not usually include nest making with plain Jane's like DC Lawson. Still that might take the flack off a bit if Perkins was going to be setting up home with this particular injured bird. He would have to try and push the selection board forward and make sure that Perkins got the substantive post. Effectively losing three officers in a short period of time was beginning to raise eyebrows higher up the food chain.

At a barbershop deep in the now mostly boarded up precinct area of town Steven admired his new hair cut and thought that it looked very city boy fucker. His next call was a shop that sold men's suits. It was closing as many of the shops were in this area of town and there were good discounts off many of the suits there. The assistant gave him a very old fashioned look as he took in his stained track suit, now at odds with his smart new haircut and cut throat razor shave.

Steven tried on a couple of suits. The difference they made was amazing. Even his own mother wouldn't know him now. He bought a couple of shirts and a small leather holdall some new underwear and a beautiful dark blue long wool coat. By the time he left the shop he looked every bit the professional. Steven headed straight for the centre of town to the upmarket hotel that was opposite the police station. He could hardly stop smiling as he checked in paying cash in advance for a weeks stay. The room he had requested overlooked the police station and through the glass walled building he could see the little pigs scurrying around inside. He quickly stripped off his new clothes and hit the shower. It felt good, after so long to have a nice shower and afterwards as he wrapped the hotels soft towelling robe around himself he looked at himself in the mirror. He was still a bit tubby and with his hair dyed he really would have been hard pressed to recognise himself! Also he had heard someone say once that if you looked as though you were meant to be somewhere or doing something, no one would question you, and if anyone had the balls to pull that off he did, and he intended to do just that!

He flicked the TV on. Images of the graveyard filled the screen and Steven grabbed the remote raising the volume

" . . . . .this morning. The police say that a man was buried alive in a grave. A letter left by the undertaker, himself found murdered, alerted a member of the public to the fact that someone had been buried alive. The funeral had already taken place before the police got to the graveyard and they had to dig out the grave remove the coffin and dig deeper to uncover another coffin in which the man had been buried. He is now recovering in the hospital."

Steven felt himself go cold. "Fuck" he shouted. That bastard Alan, he obviously had been cleverer than Steven gave him credit for. Steven stared out at the police station, watching people come and go, some in uniform some not. He was going to have to get out of town, there was soon going to be nowhere to hide, Anthony would make sure of that. He had more or less admitted to him that he had killed Cathy and he knew that Anthony would come after him for that at least. And no doubt the filth would offer him all sorts to spill his guts on what he knew. And Anthony would take whatever it was they offered him, Steven knew that. He cursed himself that he had not already started looking into getting a false passport; looking as he did now he would stand out like a sore thumb in the parts of town he would need to go to get one. He sat down hard on the bed. Then he thought back to when he had checked in at the Castle Hotel. He had been in a line of men who looked, give or take an inch in height or shade in hair colour, almost identical to himself, corporate drones buzzing around the hive of the privileged, from the liveried doorman to the plushly carpeted lift, it all shouted wealth. Well, not shouted maybe, that would be unseemly, but an idea was germinating in Steven's brain. A couple of the men he had seen in the queue to check in had bags that had airline labels on their handles, and they would have their passports on them wouldn't they. Steven dressed quickly and went downstairs. Picking up a newspaper from a complimentary stand he sat down in an armchair close to the check in desk.

He did not have to wait long. A man roughly the same height and with an almost identical haircut greeted the check in clerk.

"Well hello Mr. Connor"

"Good afternoon" the man said in a thick Irish brogue.

"And how was the flight over?"

"Oh you know, a flight is a flight, the airport in Dublin is getting busier all the time."

The clerk laughed politely and said.

"Room 114 as usual, have a nice stay!"

Steven let the man turn away from the desk before he got up and followed him to the lift. In his hand he had his room card key sticking out of the passport from the Irish Republic. Bingo! Steven thought and smiled at the man as they made the journey to the fourth floor together. The man smiled back. His face was a little thinner than Steven's but they did not look that dissimilar and if Steven made a joke with the airline check in dolly in a thick Irish accent . . . ." Steven felt his blood begin to pump faster; he could do it he knew he could!

In the hospital Joe decided to visit Denise before he took the evidence bags with Anthony's clothes and the remote device back to the station. He locked them in the boot of his car and took the lift up several floors to Denise's private room. He tapped lightly on the door and gingerly opened it slightly then shut it again as he recognised the broad back of the super sitting at her bedside. But it was too late, and the super opened the door and ushered him in.

"Great news Perkins I hear that you're going to be a father, congratulations, I think you make a splendid couple!" Joe swallowed hard and composed his face to what he hoped was an elated expression.

"Yes sir, it was quite a surprise, and I am so grateful that Denise was not killed and that the baby is OK . . ." he tailed off and cleared his throat as though choking back the tears. In actually fact he was choking back absolute horror. He had been neatly manoeuvred into a corner now and he felt his blood run cold.

In the hotel, Steven followed the Irish man along to his room, he would have the element of surprise on his side, he would strike while he was closing the door. Steven felt for the knife with its big serrated blade in his pocket, one of the linen handkerchiefs from the gent's outfitters wrapped around it. Pulling a mobile from his pocket he pretended to examine it as the man put his card key into the door of the room. As he entered inside, Steven heard the man say.

"Oh good you're here already!" Steven stopped, frozen to the spot as a voice he recognised said;

"Yes, I'm here, nice to see you again!"

CHAPTER 19

As the door to the Irish man's room closed behind him, Steven stood rooted to the spot in the corridor. A niggling feeling that he had seen this man before was distracting him and now he could not hear what the Irish man was saying, just the murmur of voices as his brain tried to take in what he had heard. It was not so much what he had heard as the tone of voice of both the Irish man and —Brian! Yes there was no doubt in his mind that the other man in the room had been Brian! What the fuck was he doing there? And what was with the soppy tone of voice? It was the same tone exactly as Brian used to greet Steven's mother when she came home. "Oh my God!" Steven said out loud, "He's a fucking shirt lifter!" He went back to his room. He felt, as though his life was unravelling, he felt exposed, vulnerable and he needed to take stock. He opened the mini bar. As he looked at the array of bottles inside the small fridge an image of Anthony's father flashed into his brain, along with the words he had said to Anthony what seemed like light years ago "I'm never drinking." He wondered if a psychiatrist could trace his and Anthony's behaviour back to the treatment meted out to them by their fathers. Who was he kidding? A first term psychiatry student could make the connection. The temptation to have a drink was overwhelming. His head felt as though it was going to explode as he tried to make sense of what had just happened. For a moment or two more he hesitated and then took four scotch miniatures and poured them into the glass provided. Then, without adding either ice or water, Steven knocked the burning liquid back in one swallow. He spluttered slightly at the unaccustomed strength of the dark brown fluid but before long warmth seemed to spread up from his stomach to his brain, taking the sharp edges off his anxiety and confusion. He realised that he was very tired and getting undressed wrapped himself in the soft bathrobe kept warm by its own heater in the bathroom, he curled up in the foetal position between the soft clean sheets of the bed—and slept. While Steven slept, Anthony's mother Rose had arrived in the hospital to see her son. The boy who stared vacantly at her, grinning like an imbecile was far removed from the boy that she knew. She cradled him in her arms with tears running down her cheeks she noticed his bloodied fingertips.

"Oh Anthony, what's happened to you?" she wept and Anthony giggled inanely. The Consultant Psychiatrist looking after him tried to explain the situation to Rose. "Post-traumatic stress disorder, which Anthony is suffering from, is simply a special variation of mental conflict. Not everyone who uses defence mechanisms to help them cope with horrible situations suffers from Post-traumatic stress disorder. But you have to realise that what has happened to your son has been the most horrendous of experiences and one that he did not expect to survive."

Rose nodded sadly, closing her eyes briefly against the pain, she could not bear to think of what her boy had been through.

"Fundamentally," the doctor continued, "Post-traumatic stress disorder is not a tangible thing, like a virus or a brain tumour. It is simply a label therapists use to describe specific psychological symptoms. Those who either support social structures that perpetuate the causes of trauma or are simply embarrassed to confront the causes of trauma have often dismissed trauma victims as exaggerators but in Anthony's case we would not expect any of that sort of accusation. Rose glanced towards the door of her son's room where a policeman stood on guard. She knew what Anthony would be facing when he was well enough, could she really blame him for retreating into his own world. The doctor followed Rose's gaze and smiled at her gently. "As it is currently defined, Post-traumatic stress disorder can be described as a psychological disorder that results from a traumatic experience that overwhelms a person's normal defence mechanisms as it has done with your son. The shock of this experience is so great that his defence mechanisms have become disorganized and disconnected from reality, either temporarily or for a prolonged and indefinite period of time."

"How long will that be in Anthony's case?" Rose said,

"We have no way of knowing at the moment" the doctor replied, "But quite often people do recover spontaneously. Over the coming days and weeks we be looking for the symptoms of hyper arousal in Anthony when we would expect to see high levels of emotion, alternating with periods of a pronounced numbing of his emotions. This alternating reflects a form of mental conflict. Through constriction he will seek to avoid thoughts and memories related to this trauma. By means of intrusion, the subconscious draws attention to some aspect of the traumatic experience, resulting in a period of hyper arousal. As he swings through this approach-avoidance cycle, you might observe that Anthony is constantly alternating between feeling emotionally numb and feeling emotionally overtaxed. It is very likely that the emotionally overtaxing periods will be triggered by thoughts or events that symbolically force him to relive aspects of this traumatic event."

Rose looked hopeful.

"So he won't stay like this then?" she looked at her son

"No we have every hope that, given time, he will progress to the stage that I have mentioned to you now. Then we can work with him to deal with what has happened to him.

"Will you be allowed to?"

"How do you mean?" The doctor said kindly.Rose looked again at the policeman,

"Will they let you?"

"Oh the police? I am aware of what Anthony is wanted for Mrs. Grace but that will take a back seat for the moment until we can get him well again. After all it is in the police's best interest to have him, shall we say compos mentis so that he can help with their enquiries."

Rose looked at the psychiatrist gratefully. She didn't know how she was going to cope with all this, with losing Alan and now with poor Anthony, but she knew that she was going to have to, somehow! Sitting beside Denise's bed Joe wished that his phone would ring. It seemed inconceivable to him that with all that was going on he was not needed somewhere. Denise was still sleeping a lot and in the times that she was awake she would just stare at him with that adoring look on her face. Joe was getting a headache with the strain of keeping up the pretence. In fact the more he tried to talk himself into life with Denise the more appalled he became by the prospect. He tried to concentrate on that first time in the car together and the great sessions that they had had in the early days.

But he knew now that they had been the product of two healthy sexual beings going through dry spells, the' any port in a storm' scenario. It had been fun but it should never have happened, it was too difficult when you worked together. And now it looked like what should, at best, never have taken place and at worst should have been written off as a bit of temporary fun was turning into the template for the rest of his life. But there was nothing he could do about it now. He had been greeted as a hero at the station, his colleagues patting him on the back congratulating him on the baby, commiserating about Denise,—if there was *anything* they could do? Joe felt like shouting "Yes, get me out of here, put the clock back 3 months!"

The Super had been especially nice to him hinting that the board, when it came up would be a shoe-in for Joe. Joe was not stupid; he knew that the Super could mitigate the PR damage done in recent months considerably by keeping Denise happy and ensuring that 'her man' got on! Joe was also not so deluded that he thought it would be easy for him to achieve the promotion in the normal way. He was OK as a detective but there were others who would wipe the floor with him at the board. Knowing that he was using Denise again in this way did not feel good to him, but on the other hand, if he was going to have to provide for her and a baby, well he needed all the advantage he could get. Roberts was the next phone call that he took.

"Hello, Joe" Joe noticed the junior officer did not call him Guv or sir, but he let it go.

"Hi, Jim, you feeling better?"

"Yep, just had the path reports back on the stuff from the bed sit. Definitely Smith and Grace.

"What about the device that I sent to the lab?"

"Yep, that's definitely a detonator, they can't disable it, it has a trip device, and if we try it will blow. they've got it in a safe."

"Good" Joe looked over at the bed.

"Right, bye then Joe" Roberts said.

Denise was stirring. As she opened her eyes and looked at him sleepily Joe said "Right Roberts I'll be straight over there," to a dead line, then flipped his phone shut and got up from his chair.

"Oh do you have to go?" Denise said.

"'Afraid so, I think we are getting quite close now."

"Really?"

"Thinks so, I'll come back and give you a full update later." Joe kissed his fingers and planted them on Denise's forehead.

"Bye darling!" she said smiling at him.

When Steven woke up the niggling feeling he had had about the Irish man had transformed itself into a realisation of who he was. He was a rep from Dublin from where Brian had bought most of the surgery's dental supplies. Steven had only seen him once or twice but remembered now that he had even teased Brian about how excited he seemed to be getting over buying amalgam! Brian and the Irishman had shut themselves away in his small office for what seemed like hours. Steven tried to remember if Brian had gone out on the evenings around the reps visit but he couldn't. He had often wondered in a sort of yuck way about his mother and Brian, his mother seemed pretty much a cold fish to him, another legacy from his lovely father, and maybe that was what Brian liked about her, he could live a respectable life as part of the establishment with her and then see his bit on the side when he was in town. Steven laughed out loud and shook his head. "Whatever, different strokes for different fucking folks!" He said to the empty room.

In his office Joe looked at the findings from the lab. Nothing very startling there. He was just about to go down the pub for a drink when the Super came in and closed the door.

"Joe, there's something we need to talk about." He said shutting the door behind him. "Sir?" Joe said.

"It's about the girl, Cathy Barrett"
"Oh yes, I've been meaning to ask about her parents, how are they, they're not local are they?"
"No not anymore, they went to France when Cathy left home to rent out a gites in a very remote part of France, as far as I

know. I believe it is a sort of get away from it all, a place with no TV, phone signal or even electricity. "

"I suppose they're back now then, do you want me to speak to them?"

"No, they're not, thing is they don't know what happened to Cathy."

"You mean you haven't been able to get in touch with them?"

"No, I mean Cathy is not dead." In the silence that followed Joe could hear the voices of officers in the main room on the phone.

"Sorry sir, I thought you said . . ."

"I did, look Perkins, we let the word go out locally that she was dead because we thought if Smith knew she wasn't he would come after her, and we couldn't take that risk or the risk that another of our officers might get hurt protecting her."

Joe stared at his senior officer open mouthed. "But have her parents not heard from people, seen the news?"

"So far we haven't heard anything from them, as I said they are very remote, but we will be telling them that she is not dead, in fact she is doing well in a London hospital."
"I see." Joe said. "But when the truth gets out, the press . . . ."
The Super nodded and lowered his head into his hands. "Sometimes we have to take extraordinary measures; I have cleared it with the Home Secretary."

Joe looked startled.

"Look Joe this is becoming as high a profile case as the Yorkshire Ripper, I don't think you realise how much National attention is focused on us."

"No, I suppose I've taken my eye off the ball a bit." Joe said and the Super's expression softened. "Yes, yes, quite understandable, with Officer Lawson, er . . . Denise and all. "Anyway Perkins, the reason I am telling you this now is so that you are completely in the picture. When the attacks at River Towers occurred I was contacted immediately and in conjunction with forensics and the ambulance service, we flew Cathy to London."

Joe was speechless. He thought about Cathy about the time in the shower together and all of a sudden she seemed like a beacon showing him a way out of the mire that he had gotten into. Her uncomplicated enjoyment of the sex they shared, had made it all the sweeter to him and his dreams were populated with images of her soapy body her nipples jutting out from the foam and her wide eyes hungry for him. He had begun to think of that abandoned afternoon as the end of his carefree existence, and the thought of Denise in her hospital bed smelling of illness and medicine plunged his soul into depression. He liked Denise, he did, and he admired her determination, but he did not and would not ever love her. And even if he had had any idea that he could keep up the charade for a while and then leave her, now there was a baby in the equation and with the fuss that everyone was making about it all, he could see no way that he could be seen to be leaving Denise disabled and with a child. He knew that the Super was pulling strings for him and that the unspoken part of the deal was that Joe kept Denise happy.In his room Steven was considering what to do next. The possibility of seeing Brian again was tempting him, he wondered if he was still in the Irish man's room. He dressed quickly and was soon standing outside the door of the Irish man's room. In his pocket his hand tightened around the handle of the knife. He pressed his ear to the door and could hear the murmur of voices. Good Brian had not left. He raised his right hand and rapped his knuckles on the door. "Just a minute!" the Irish man called out and Steven gripped the knife harder. The Irish man came to the door wrapped in the same hotel bathrobe that was supplied in Steven's room. His hair was messed up and he smiled pleasantly at Steven a hint of recognition in his eyes, mixed with a slight bewilderment as he looked for and did not identify a hotel uniform. But before he could speak Steven had, in one fluid movement pulled the knife from his pocket and buried it up too its hilt in the Irish man's neck. The soft blue eyes widened as blood poured from his mouth and Steven shoved him into a chair as he swept into the room. He looked around. The room was bigger than his, the bed, obviously recently used, but there was no sign of Brian. Steven listened at the bathroom door. He could hear humming, that was Brian alright, he always hummed in the shower, a tuneless rendition of nothing that Steven had ever been able to identify. Steven flattened himself against the wall beside the bathroom and waited. Eventually the door opened and Brian emerged a towel around his neck and a semi erect penis.

"Look what came up when I was in the shower Liam, I was hoping you were going to join . . . ." Brian's voice tailed off as he took in the sight of Liam slumped in the chair by the door, the front of his bathrobe crimson with his blood.

"Hello Brian" Steven said grabbing the older man's cock and spinning him around with it before abruptly letting go. Brian tumbled onto the bed.

"Well well, who would have thought you were a fudge packer, tut tut, whatever would mother say?" Steven smiled. Brian was staring at him, his eyes bulging in their sockets as he scrabbled for a sheet to cover himself with. His mouth was moving but he seemed unable to speak.

Steven took the knife he had used to stab Liam in the throat out of his pocket and wiped it slowly across the bed sheet. It left congealing stains of the Irish man's blood behind it and Brian stared at it as though hypnotised. A little strangled whimper came from between his white lips and he drew his legs up to his chest, pulling the blankets and sheets of the bed around him. Now that he was almost up at the head of the bed his dead lover was in his eye line and his eyes took in the gaping wound in the Irish man's throat and the darkening blood stains down his robe. He knew that Liam was dead and that he should be keeping his eyes on Steven, who was now apparently completely mad, had a look in his eye that made Brian's blood run cold. With an effort Brian turned his attention back to Steven.

"Steven, come on son, you've made a mistake but we can put this right, don't you worry." Brian surprised himself at how calm he sounded all of a sudden. His voice also took Steven by surprise and for a moment the penetrating stare of pure evil wavered and Brian thought he saw something of the old Steven. Encouraged he said.

"Look Steven It's true I was seeing Liam but I didn't want to, he threatened to tell everyone if I stopped seeing him, I'm so grateful you killed him, thank God you did, now I can get back to my life and help you get away from here."

Steven's hand that had been wiping the blade back and forth across the sheets hesitated and then stopped. Brian thought he saw Steven's grip loosen around the knife's handle.

"Bull shit!" Steven said

"What?" "You're full of bullshit!"

Brian felt his heart beat speed up, the madness was back in Steven's eyes and he had adjusted his grip on the knife handle so that it was upright in his fist the blade down like a dagger. Brian felt terror playing his spine like a harp. He had to keep his cool. "I'm not full of bullshit; I am genuinely pleased to be rid of him." Brian said a silent prayer for forgiveness, "and you know how much I care about you, I've promised your mother I would do anything at all to help you get away."

There it was again, the glimmer of uncertainty in Steven's eyes, a look almost of vulnerability. Brian realised that it was the mention of his mother, Mary.

"Yes I promised her, pass me my trousers and I'll ring her for you, she'll be so pleased to know we are together." Brian held out his hand his palm open towards the trousers that he had hung over the back of a chair. Steven followed his gaze to the trousers and he reached out for them. As he lifted them towards Brian's outstretched hand he looked at his stepfather. He was making little beckoning movements with his fingers, his head nodding slightly as the trousers got closer. Then when they were almost within his grasp Steven released his grasp and the trousers fell to the floor, just short of the bed, the keys in the pocket jangling as they landed. Part of Steven wanted more than anything else to speak to his mother but he had vowed that she should not be involved and that was before Cathy, before the cop, before Anthony, before arse bandit Liam. No he would never be able to speak to her again and without that nothing else really mattered that much. He would get away, use Liam's passport and start again and all this, and his mother, would be forgotten.

Brian was prattling on about his mother, saying her name every other word as though that was some sort of magic key to stopping Steven cutting his throat. Now Brian was saying how his mother had sent him out every day to look for Steven.

"I don't believe you, you fucking shit shovelling liar!" Steven hissed and in one movement was beside Brian on the bed, pressing the serrated edge of the knife to his throat.

Brian's hair was still damp from the shower and smelt of the same vague citrus smell as Steven's had when he had washed earlier. Brian had stopped his prattling now. Steven needed time to think. He should be able to make use of Brian if he could figure out how.

In the hospital Rose Grace was listening as the doctor told her what medications Anthony was on. Suddenly from the bed a cracked hoarse voice said. "Mum?" The doctor and Rose were on either side of the bed in an instant and Rose noticed that Anthony's eyes were focused on her, the vacant imbecilic stare replaced by fear.

"It's alright son." She said, cradling his head

"What's going on mum?" he said The doctor nodded at her and she said gently "You're in hospital son, you had a little um accident, but you're alright now, you're safe."

"Where's my jacket?" "Hush now; what do you want that for? Just relax, get better!"

"Must have it mum, please!" Anthony croaked.

Rose looked at the doctor

"Anthony, your clothing has been taken away, it was dirty." The doctor said to him and Anthony looked up at him.

"In the pocket, I need it!" he clutched at the doctors sleeve urgently

"Well now, you just wait, we'll get everything you need in due course, just rest now,"

Anthony started to sit up, kicking his bedding back and trying to swing his legs over the side of his bed. Rose watched transfixed as the doctor swiftly prepared a syringe and expertly applied a tranquilliser to Anthony's arm. As her son sank back onto the bed Rose asked the doctor.

"Is this the hyper-arousal that you talked about?"

"Yes and it is important that we make sure that your son is kept on an even keel."

Rose nodded, part of her wanted to celebrate the fact that her son seemed to have returned to his right mind, but even as he was doing that she could see the activity increasing at the door, before long the police would be taking advantage of Anthony's new ability to communicate. There were already three of them where there had only been one. Rose recognised the tall man in plain clothes, he had come to the house with the lady policewoman, the same one that had been so badly injured in Anthony's girlfriends flat. As she caught his eye he beckoned her with a long finger. Rose glanced down at Anthony, who was sleeping peacefully now.

Joe smiled at her as she joined him outside the room. "Thanks Mrs. Grace, let's go somewhere a bit private shall we?"

Rose followed Joe down the corridor to small room that she guessed doctors used to break bad news to relatives.

"How is Anthony?" The tall young man said, and Grace eyed him warily. She knew that it had been his girlfriend that had been attacked in the flat and although Anthony had not done it, he was hardly an innocent in all this. Still, he looked genuine enough.

"Well he seems to have come to his senses, talking sensibly, at least."

"Oh, what has he been saying?" Joe leaned forward and Grace felt as though he was closing in on her. He seemed to realise that and sat back in his chair again.

"Nothing really, asking for his jacket, obviously still not quite himself but it's a start?" Grace looked at Joe hopefully.

"Indeed it is!" Joe smiled. "Did he say why he wanted his jacket?"

"Not really, he just kept asking for it."

"Well that's great Mrs. Grace." Joe concluded the interview. He was getting nowhere with his mother and Joe was desperate to get in to see Anthony but he doubted his doctor would let him.

In the hotel room Steven was trying to think. He would be able to use the passport recently made redundant by Liam but what he had to work out was whether Brian would be of any use to him alive. He thought about his mother, she loved Brian whatever kind of a pervert he was, did Steven really want to deprive her of a man who provided for her and kept her safe and happy? Someone who would look after her once he had gone to South America? Steven looked around the room. Liam's big heavy sample case was sitting by the bed.

"Stand up!" Steven said and Brian obeyed wrapping the bed sheets around him. "Stand in front of the window" Steven said. Brian whimpered. He closed his eyes tight waiting for Steven's hand to come over his shoulder and the cold blade of the knife to plunge into the soft flesh of his throat. He thought his legs were going to give way and opened his eyes to look out at the grey winter sky. Was this the last sight he was going to see? A reflection of movement in the glass of the tall sash window caught his eye and he tried to make out what it was. As he did so the edge of Liam's sample bag hit him squarely on the back of the head knocking him out immediately. There was a loud crack and Steven said

"Whoops" He was not sure what that had been but it didn't sound too good! He felt Brian's pulse; it was there, weak, but there. He should be out long enough for Steven to get down stairs and pack and get out of the hotel. He would look in on him before he went.

He looked around and found the key card for the room and took it with him along with Liam's passport that was on his nightstand.

Downstairs he packed quickly and casting a last look around the room to make sure he had left nothing behind went back upstairs. As he let himself in he heard a moan from beside the window where Brian was lying in a tangle of bed sheets. Steven stood over Brian's prone body for a few moments. A few more moans escaped his lips but his eyes remained tightly shut and he showed no sign of coming round. Steven considered hitting him again but then thought better of it, something had given way after the last blow, he had probably fractured his step father's skull, if he hit him again he might kill him. As Steven gathered up the cash and credit cards from Liam and Brian's wallets he felt a little thrill of excitement. For the first time in months he would be leaving this shit hole of a town and by tomorrow, all being well, he would be starting a new life in South America. Pity that Cathy had died, he could have taken her with him, she would have loved a life in the sun.

As an afterthought he got the ropes that were used to tie back the heavy curtains of the room and tied Brian's feet then his hands behind his back. Then taking the cord from the dressing gown that hung in the bathroom he put it around Brain's mouth tying it as a gag. Brain started to breath raggedly through his nose, but his chest was moving rhythmically up and down and Steven was satisfied he would not suffocate. Taking the 'do not disturb' sign he hung it on the handle on the outside of the door and pulling the collar of his coat around his face went downstairs, paid his bill and slipped away down the street. At the corner of the street he stood for a moment looking back at the police station, it seemed particularly busy this evening, or was that his imagination. He smiled as he thought of the scene he had left behind in the hotel, right opposite the cop shop. Hell Brian had probably been looking into one of the offices in the police station when Steven had smashed the case down on his head. Still smiling, Steven hailed a cab.

"Where to mate?" the cabbie said without turning round.

"Heathrow please." "Right, traffic's a bitch tonight, what time is your flight?"

"Oh I'm on standby, not really expecting to get one but we've got to try eh?"

"Oh yes, you got that right mate, we all got to try!" the cabbie laughed. Steven was aware that this cabbie might be questioned about him in the days to come so he told him that he was on the waiting list for a flight to Cape Town. That should put the filth off track for a while. Once he was in Brazil he would be safe as houses, him and Ronnie Biggs!

CHAPTER 20

Joe Perkins stood at the end of Anthony's bed and the two men eyed each other warily. Now that he had been allowed in to speak to Anthony to ask him about the detonator in his jacket pocket, Anthony was denying all knowledge of both the device and of asking for it. His mother fussed around him but said nothing as her son continually denied having or asking for the detonator although her eyes kept flashing in Joe's direction. She knew that he was lying but he was her boy, she was not going to take Joe's side over Anthony's

Back at the station Joe spoke to the Super.

"I know that Anthony can tell us about the detonator, I want permission to take it into the hospital to actually show it to him. That should get a reaction!"

The Super pursed his lips. "Let me think about it. It's a very high risk strategy; we don't know what it is for or how it is activated. If anything was to go wrong, we could be looking at half the hospital going up in smoke."

"I'm pretty sure that there is no risk to the hospital, it will be targeting an individual like all the others."

"Yes but we don't know that for sure Joe!" The Super looked annoyed. "Leave it with me I'll talk to our explosive boys and see what they say."

At the hotel Jim Roberts was standing over the corpse of Liam the once crimson stain on the white bathrobe now a malignant black. He put a call into Joe.

"Hi Joe, we just got called over to the Hotel, we've got a stiff here and another almost a gonner."

"Any obvious connection to Smith?"

"Pretty much so, the guy that was whacked over the head is his step dad."

"And the stiff?"

"Liam O'Rourke, dental supplies salesman from Dublin."

"Over on business?"

"Bit more than that I would say, the two of them look like they were having a bit of bum fun before someone interrupted them. O'Rourke's passport has gone and so have the credit cards from both wallets.

"Right get on to all the airports and ferry ports."

"I have done" Jim said and Joe detected a slight edge to the junior officers voice.

"Good I'm going to be tied up at the hospital for now, with Grace, but I'll be with you later."

"Right." Jim cut the line and Joe looked down at his phone, annoyed. It was irritating that Jim was obviously not taking him seriously as a superior officer but he had bigger fish to fry. Just before he had left the Super's office the senior man had taken a call from the hospital in London where Cathy was being treated. She was up to questioning now and the Super had asked Joe to go and see her. Joe's stomach had lurched at the thought of seeing Cathy again. He was to be driven into the hospital in an unmarked fast police car and driven straight back again afterwards.

"I know you won't want to be away from detective Lawson, er. Denise for very long." The Super had smiled gently and Joe realised that he had not even given Denise a second thought.

"No of course not, but I think it is important that I conduct the interview." Joe said and the Super nodded approvingly.

Sitting in the back of the car that sped him up the motorway to the capital Joe thought about his life. He was trying hard to keep his feelings for Cathy in perspective; he knew that it was only because of the situation with Denise that he was seeing Cathy in such a positive light. He tried to rationalise that she was really just a little prick tease, who, despite supposedly being beside herself with worry over her murderer boyfriend was quite happy to lure Joe into her shower. His cock twitched in his pants as he remembered their lovemaking, the first time that he had felt any kind of sensation in his groin for a long time. The thought that any erection he had from now on would have to be the property of Denise had worked on him like a bucket of cold water.

Joe was taken in through the Hospital laundry area at the back of the building, the steam from the huge generators hung like a blanket of fog in the winter air. The service lift whisked him to the fifth floor where he was ushered into a private room. The name on the door read Vanessa White. There was no obvious police presence although Joe's trained eye spotted two plain clothes detectives sitting reading newspapers on some plastic chairs in the corridor. The slight bulge in their suit jackets attesting to the fact that they were armed, as he was himself.

Inside the room as the door opened, Cathy looked towards it, her eyes even wider now in a face that had lost all its plumpness. For a moment she looked puzzled and then recognition hit her and she smiled a weak mechanical movement of her face muscles that did not reach her eyes.

"Hi Cathy" Joe said softly. He felt a lump in his throat; she looked so frail, so frightened and vulnerable.

"Hi Joe" Cathy's voice sounded hoarse and Joe took in the bandaging around her neck and the tubes draining the wound.

"How are you feeling?"

"Better." Cathy smiled again but the smile did not replace the terror that had been etched into her face.

"Are you up to talking to me?"

"Think so" Cathy said.

Joe went through the questioning as quickly as he could. He did not want to cuase her more pain by making her recall that awful day, but it had to be done. She was brave and told him what he wanted to know. As she spoke he recorded the interview on a portable recorder. He put his hand over hers on the sheets and was alarmed to feel how thin and bony her hand felt. He wanted to gather her up in his arms and hold her tight, promise her that he would protect her. But he could do none of that and his heart felt as though it was going to break. As she described how Steven had raped her, her hand curled around his thumb like a child's and he had to fight back the tears.

When the interview was over, they both sat for a moment in silence and Joe wiped away a single tear from Cathy's cheek.

"I'm so sorry, so sorry." He whispered and she smiled at him.

"Not your fault."

"No, but you should never have had to . . . ."

"How is Denise?" Cathy asked and Joe almost jumped.

"Oh, she's coming along." He said.

"And Anthony?"

Joe looked up sharply. There was a hopeful look in Cathy's eye a yearning, a real desire to know something about her lover. Joe had not considered the fact that she might still love Anthony, so invested was he in what they had shared together.

"He's in hospital." He answered shortly. Cathy's eyes widened with a real fear.

Joe thought quickly. He could not tell her what had happened to Anthony, it would be too much for her to deal with in her current fragile state.

"Oh don't worry, he's fine, just a little accident, he's helping us with our enquiries." Joe said more harshly than he intended to. He took his hand away from Cathy's a cold feeling in his stomach. It was obvious from her reaction that she still loved the slime ball. She didn't seem to notice that he had taken his hand away and bombarded him with questions about Anthony. Joe felt sick; he had been an utter fool, no better than a schoolboy with a crush. The cloud of depression that hung over him thickened. Suddenly and he felt the need to get out of there.

The radio in the cab gave out Steven's name on the news bulletin just as they approached the airport.

> *"Police are watching all airports and ports after another murder is believed to have been committed by Steven Smith known as the Dental Detonator, in which a passport of Irish national Liam O'Rourke was taken. Members of the*

*public are warned not to approach Smith, but if they have
any suspicions to contact the police immediately."*

Steven looked in the rear view mirror of the cab expecting
the cabbie to be looking back at him suspiciously. He wasn't,
instead he was prattling on about a prang he had had and how
difficult it had been to get a matching wing for his car.

The terminal was in sight now and as they drew up, Steven
jumped out of the cab and paid the driver as quickly as he could.
Then he waited for another cab to draw up and discharge its
passengers, a harassed family of four, clambered out shivering
onto the pavement outside the terminal already optimistically
wearing shorts and Hawaiian shirts. Steven asked the cabbie
to take him to a hotel, The Regency midway between Kently
and the airport.

"What you doing over here mate? This isn't arrivals!" the
cabbie asked. Steven wanted to tell him to mind his own
fucking business but instead he smiled and said.

"Yes been a bit of a day, I flew in this morning and the wife's
just flying out so we've had a key handing over ceremony here.
And to cap it all one of my business associate is at the Regency
hotel and I have to go there first and meet him for lunch!"

"Cor blimey mate, life in the fast lane eh?"

Steven laughed. He was very conscious that he had to be as
normal as he could be. He was annoyed that his plans had
been thwarted for now, it looked as though he was going to
have to get another passport, he was beginning to feel that the
net was closing in on him, but he knew that any false or hasty
move could be the end for him. He was going to have to wait
it out.

As Joe travelled back up the motorway to Kently he felt the
dark depression tighten its grip on him a bit more. It was
bleaker than the one that he had been under before he knew

that Cathy was still alive. Knowing that she was had boosted him, given him hope. Now that hope was dashed, there was nothing ahead of him expect living a lie with a woman that he did not love and a child he did not want, forced into domesticity like some pathetic animal, caged and thrown a piece of meat each day, left to pace up and down for the rest of its miserable life. Ahead of him he could see a life of snatched pleasure where he could get it, prostitutes, anyone, he knew himself, pushed far enough he wouldn't be fussy, and he would be pushed. He closed his eyes and swallowed the bitter bile that was rising in his throat.

When he arrived back at the station he put the tapes in for transcription and went up to see the Super. As he entered the office his eyes were drawn immediately to the large evidence bag on the desk, inside it the detonator that had been concealed in Anthony's jacket pocket.

"How did it go?" The Super asked tilting back in his plush leather chair.

"Fine, she gave a good statement, I've dropped it in at the pool for transcription." Joe could not take his eyes off the detonator.

"Good, well I see you've noticed that I got you the detonator as you asked, I'm not at all sure about this, I'm putting my neck on the line for you Joe, but we need something to push us over the line with Anthony Grace. You have to keep it in this padded reinforced explosives case at all times alright and two armed guards are going with you to the hospital"

Joe nodded as the Super held up the black case. The Super made a phone call and Joe was soon on his way to the hospital with two Incredible Hulk look-alikes dwarfing him, the one holding the brief case with the detonator in, had it handcuffed to his wrist.

In the hospital he felt almost like a criminal himself being marched to Anthony's heavily guarded room by the men.

Entering the room Joe nodded to Rose Grace who was at her son's bedside as usual. Joe thought that Anthony looked a good deal better than he had, the haunted, edge of madness glint in his eye had been replaced by a more resigned watchfulness. Joe had briefed the guards on the way in as to what he wanted them to do, and without a word the three men moved further into the room, the guard with the case, put it on the bed opened it and removing the detonator held it in front of Anthony just out of his reach. Joe had deliberately hung back so that he could gauge Anthony's reaction. At first Anthony's face registered confusion, as he took in the two goons with Joe behind, but when the guard opened the case and took out the detonator his face changed and he moved to grab for it. Joe tried to interpret the look. It was almost as though Anthony had been waiting for this moment, his eyes fixed on the detonator, a real purpose in them. The guard swung the detonator away before Anthony could get near it and put it back in the case. Then moving to the back of the room he and the other guard stood their legs apart, their arms folded in front of them, their right hands holding their left wrists. Joe stepped forward.

"That the detonator you want is it Anthony?"

Anthony slumped back on his pillows. He realised he had given himself away.

"It's not a detonator."

"Oh? That's not what our explosives team says?"

"All-right, it is a detonator, but it's not armed."

"Again, not what our explosives team says" Joe said.

"Who has the dental implant that this detonator will explode Anthony?"

Anthony shrugged.

"I can't remember, there were so many."

"You see, I just don't believe you Anthony, I think you know very well who it is."

"Well I don't."

Joe thought for a moment. This was not getting them anywhere. He looked at the goons and Rose Grace.

"Can you give us a moment please?" The guards looked doubtful and Rose looked fearful but they left.

Joe drew up a plastic chair next to Anthony's bed.

"I went to see someone this morning that I think that you would like to speak to, even see."
"Oh?" Anthony's eyes looked dull and uninterested.

"Cathy, I went to see Cathy." Anthony sat up bolt upright in his bed, his eyes alive and wary at the same time.

"Fucking liar, she's dead!"

"She's not dead, and she was asking about you."

"But" Anthony said . . . I saw it on the news . . . I don't understand."

"We kept it quiet in case Smith came after her. Better he thought she was dead, better for her and for us, he seems to have taken quite a toll on us one way or another." Joe said.

"She was asking about me?"

"Yes, very concerned. She's in hospital in London and she is doing very well, it won't be long now till she's out. If you want to speak to her I can arrange that and I can even arrange for her to visit you when she's better, but I want the information on that detonator."

Anthony hesitated.

"Prove it, how do I know you're telling the truth?"

Joe got out his phone and called the London hospital.

"Vanessa White please, room 206."

"Detective Inspector Perkins"
A moment later Cathy's voice answered

"Hello?"

"Hello Cathy, it's Joe Perkins here how are you feeling now?" Joe turned on the loudspeaker on his phone and held it up to Anthony.

"Not so bad, better since you told me the news that Anthony is doing OK, thanks."

Anthony grabbed for the phone but Joe put it back to his ear.

"That's great Cathy, we'll talk soon." And he flipped the phone shut.

Tears were streaming down Anthony's face.

"You bastard!" he said but he was smiling broadly, the woman he loved was alive! For now, that was all that mattered.

In his hotel room Steven was watching the news. The new photo-fit of him as complied by the fucking busybodies in the Town Hotel, was pretty good, he was going to have to change his appearance again. Taking out his razor he lathered his head and shaved it. He changed out of the suit he had been wearing and into some of the smart casual clothes purchased from the gent's outfitters. He looked like a country boy Rupert trying to look hard, a bit 'twat about town' but nothing that would raise attention and quite a lot dissimilar to the photo fit. Steven felt a lot more confident and decided to go down and have something to eat in the hotel café, check out his new look.

Although a couple of people looked up when Steven entered the little lobby café no-one paid any particular attention and he sat down, giving a pretty Romanian girl an order for an all day breakfast and coffee. He looked around at his fellow guests. It was not going to be so easy to find a passport here. The Regency was too far from the airport to serve as a hotel for travellers. Most of the people there seemed to be business people, probably staying for a night or two. He frowned. Once he had finished his food he was going to have to get a paper and sit in the lobby to see who was coming and going. Steven felt weary. The fact that he had had to turn back from the airport at the last minute had rattled him. He knew that if he was going to get out of the country it was going to have to be soon. There was no way that he could spend the rest of his life in prison. The thought of it made him feel sick and a deep dread. No he had to get away. Sighing heavily he got up from his table and took up position in the lobby. The newspaper that he picked up had his face on the front of it and he smiled to himself as he sat behind it watching the unsuspecting public come and go.

In the hospital Joe had taken a break from talking to Anthony to go and see Denise. He wanted to let the young man think over what he had said, to appreciate the carrot that was Cathy that Joe was dangling in front of him. He was pretty sure that Anthony was going to go for it and give Joe what he wanted. The goons who had accompanied him were not too happy with the set up as even although Joe had given them back the detonator, he had not allowed them to leave the hospital yet.

In Denise's room she was sitting up, and looked better than she had for a while.

"Hi Denise." Joe said, pulling up one of the hospital plastic chairs.

"Where have you been?" Denise crossed her arms across her chest, here eyes suspicious.

"Working, murder case to solve and all that." Joe tried a smile and Denise gave a sort of half hearted smile back.

"It's not easy being here on my own, wondering what you're doing all the time. Oh yes and the Super told me about your 'work' today, that you went up to London to see 'poor Cathy' she dropped her voice to a mock sympathetic whine, did you manage to get a quick one in while you were there?"

He looked down at his hands, a nerve twitching in his temple was the only sign of his irritation.

"I took Cathy Barrett's statement, she's is in a hospital bed, a bit like you, hooked up to all sorts."

Denise's expression softened for a moment. She was not a spiteful girl by nature, but she felt so vulnerable, so helpless in her hospital bed.

"Sorry." She murmured and Joe took her hand.

"Silly!" he said. "Don't you know that all I'm doing I'm doing for our future, with the baby and everything I am determined to get that promotion."

Denise smiled at him warmly. He looked at her, she did have lovely eyes and she was a pretty girl. But Joe felt sick to his stomach, he was like a kid trying to console himself that that second place trophy he had won was almost as good as a first, and failing miserably. The now familiar hopeless dark depression that had been hanging round him for a while now threatened to derail him for a moment and he got up to leave.

"Got to get back down to Grace. I think I've got him on the ropes, I wish you were there with me, we'd nail him!"

Denise smiled at him adoringly and he left hastily as the bile of his hopelessness again soured his throat.

Half an hour later, sitting beside Anthony's bed, Joe finally heard the words that he wanted to hear.

"The explosive that the detonator will activate is implanted in Steven Smith's tooth." Anthony murmured.

Joe leant forward.

"You're not lying to me are you Grace?"

"No, can I speak to Cathy now?"

"Not yet." Joe was thinking.

"Are there any other detonators, anywhere?"

"A couple back at home I suppose, I had a little cubby-hole under a loose floor board in my room with a couple of spares in, I don't think I removed them."

"Right Anthony I am going to get your mother in, you tell her where to find them and get one back here to me. She is to say nothing to anyone, understand?"

Anthony nodded.

"But what for? There are no more live ones." Joe did not reply "Then can I speak to Cathy?"

"Yes, of course, hell I'll arrange for you to see her!" Joe lied and Anthony's face lit up.

An hour later, the goons had just been in to ask how much longer they would be. Joe was getting anxious. The Super had already phoned, nervous about the detonator and Joe had bought himself a little more time, but if Rose Grace did not get back soon . . ."

And then suddenly she was there, and handing over an identical little device.

Joe went outside the room, the device carefully hidden in his pocket.

"Listen guys, he said to the goons outside with the briefcase.

"I'm nearly there, but I need the device, for a moment or two. The men got up and started towards the door.

"No, on my own, he clams up when you guys are in there, look cuff him if you like, but let me have just two minutes; I think I'm almost there."

The goons looked unsure, but eventually after cuffing a terrified Anthony they handed over the evidence bag and went to wait outside.

Opening the bag, Joe quickly replaced the detonator with the one that Rose Grace had brought from home.

For good measure he shouted a bit before he returned the bag to the goons winking at a confused Anthony.

"What are you going to do with it?" Anthony said.

"I'm going to get even with that little shit, I'm going to find him and blow his fucking head off his shoulders!" Joe said and Anthony smiled weakly.

"Not a word!" Joe said "or no Cathy." Anthony swallowed hard and nodded.

Outside the room where Rose and the goons were waiting Joe shook his head sadly.

"No good I'm afraid, he's not talking, I think you might as well get this back to the station, lads, thanks anyway."

The goons nodded and lumbered off down the corridor. Joe returned to Anthony's room he was not finished with him yet.

"Can we tell where he is from this device? Is it a tracking device of any sort?"

"Well I had experimented with a crude kind of tracking, but you'll have to give it to me for me to see if it is still working.

"No funny business, keep that safety catch on or no Cathy!" Joe warned.

Anthony took the little device. On the side was a small button, he turned it on and Joe jumped.

"It's OK, the safety is still on, look." Anthony said.

A little light started to flash on the side of the device, Joe judged it to be at approximately seven second intervals.

"That means he is still in range, but only just." Anthony said, feeling a cold fist around his spine. It is pretty crude, like I said, sort of like a metal detector, the closer he is the nearer together the light emissions.

Joe looked at Anthony. It was hard to imagine that he could be a cold blooded murderer. Joe had no doubt that it was Smith who had been the instigator and the driving force behind their reign of terror but Anthony had played his part. He wondered how long Cathy would wait for him.

As he got into his car Joe placed the little detonator on the dash board. From now on it was going to be him against Smith. Before this day was over, he was going to get his man. He drove West first and within a few minutes the little light was extinguished. North yielded the same and South although a bit longer also ended in the cessation of the flashing light. Turning the car East, Joe gripped the steering wheel. He almost imagined that he could feel the evil of the man reaching out to him like a dead man's grasping rotting fingers from the East. The light began to flash strongly now at four then three second intervals. Joe drove slowly responding to any little variation until he had the light flashing strongly. He was driving towards the airport, but Smith could not have made it there as it was too far away for the signal to be so strong.

Joe carried on driving blindly and began thinking about Denise. The depression that had settled over him had lifted a bit as he tracked Smith, but at the very thought of her and the life that he would be expected to lead the dark cloud seemed to settle around him again seeping into his pores and threatening to choke him. The thought that his career rested on his being with Denise and 'doing right by her' made the situation seem even more hopeless and he had to drag his thoughts away from her to concentrate on the little light flashing away on the detonator.

Meanwhile Steven was getting more frustrated. He had seen no-one check in yet who was likely to have a passport. A large group of BT employees were staying in the hotel for a conference, which did not help and it seemed that they had most of the rooms apart from his own. Time and time again he had heard the reception staff tell callers that the hotel was full. A seed of panic had started to germinate in his stomach now. What if he couldn't find a passport, what was he going to do? He could almost feel the police closing in on him now. He knew it would not be long. He had just got up to change his newspaper when he saw a car cruise by in front of the hotel, something about it reminded him of the cars that Kently police used for their plain clothes filth. He shook his head. He was getting paranoid, he needed to sleep. Putting the paper back in the stand and smoothing out the creases over his tabloid image face, Steven smiled to himself and made for the lift.

Outside Joe was passing the hotel for the third time. The light was more or less solid now. He looked at the hotel. It was anonymous enough, just the sort of place that you would choose to hide out in, the sort of place where people came and went and no-one bothered to ask questions or even notice. Parking the car Joe went inside.

Flashing his badge he asked for the manager. Joe asked to see the register, anyone who had recently checked in. Apart from the BT group there were only two others who had checked in that morning. An elderly couple from Glasgow and a man who had paid for his room in cash. Joe felt a chill travel up his spine. That was Smith, he knew it. He asked for the manager to identify Steven's room. It looked out over the front of the hotel. Over the next half an hour the manager and one of his deputies quietly emptied the building assembling the guests and staff and the conference room of BT employees in the back car park, while in his room, Steven slept.

Joe knew he should call for backup. But this was his baby. He was going to see it through himself.

When the building was empty Joe sat by himself in the lobby. He took out the detonator and looked at it. Then with the safety off and the pass-key for Steven's room in his hand, he travelled up in the lift to the third floor.

The door to Steven's room opened with an almost inaudible click. Joe had turned the lights in the corridor off so that they would not alert Steven. Now as the dim light shone in to the room on Steven's sleeping face, Joe took in the features of the most wanted and most evil man in the UK. He looked barely more than boy. Joe closed the door softly behind him. There was some light in the room from where Steven had not pulled the curtains properly. Suddenly Steven's eyes flew open and in one fluid movement he was out of bed.

Joe pulled the curtains and took out the gun that he had been issued, pointing it at Steven.

"Hello Smith." He said quietly

"What the fuck?"

"Sorry chum the game is up" Joe sat down on a chair underneath the TV. Steven stood still, his eyes darting back and forth, assessing the situation.

"Why did you do it?"

"Do what?"

"Kill all those people, it's not normal you now."

"Oh no? Well if only someone had said something!" Steven said his voice heavy with sarcasm.

"Anthony has been very helpful, I must say." Joe said and Steven's face changed.

"And Cathy's doing very well, they are so happy together, it's lovely to see!" Joe lied, watching for a reaction.

"You fucking liar, the news said she died, and so she should have the slag!"

Joe tutted. "I don't know they just never seem to get it right on the news do they?"

Steven looked like he might fly at him, so Joe took out the detonator.

"Recognise this?" Steven took a step back.

"Yes Anthony gave it to me, remember when he said you both had to have new transmitters fitted for the States?" Stevens face contorted.

"Well seems you pissed your mate off, see this little button, press that and it's bye bye Stevie boy!"

Steven said nothing for a moment. Then he sat down opposite Joe and said.

"That pig woman that I stuck in the back that was your bit of stuff wasn't it?"

Joe stiffened.

"Gotta say mate, thought you could do a bit better than that, bit of a porker and that bush, well I'm glad it was Cathy face down in there not me, a bit on the rough side, still nice thing for you to think of when you're giving her one, my critique of her twat eh?"

Joe's jaw tightened. The thought of Denise and him spending their life together tugged at him hard now, the depression tightening its grip, clouding his brain. He sighed, he felt weary, it was nearly over now.

He held the detonator out to Steven.

"Come on then mate, take it!" Steven looked at him for a moment then lunged towards him.

Joe pressed the button as Steven landed on him.

It took six months for forensic pathology to sort out and assign all the human tissue left from the explosion. In that six months, Anthony went to jail for life, Cathy took up with a doctor and Joe's baby son, Joe was born. Denise got close to Jim Roberts and they married 2 years later.

As for Steven Smith, he became the thing of nightmares, a definition of pure evil and the screaming, bowel twisting horror that haunts us all in the small dark hours of the night.

THE END

About The Author

Chas Coakley was born in County Cork Ireland May 1957, and at the age of 6 months his parents moved to England and settled in a sleepy little village in Essex called Wakering. Both his parents worked the land and from the moment he could walk he worked with his mother potato, pea, strawberry, picking, and turkey plucking near Christmas. Siblings would soon start to arrive and young Chas would be on hand to change nappies and help raise his three brothers and one sister. Great adventures were had on the acres and acres of farm land that surrounded their tiny little two up two down farm house. The local farmers looked forward to bailing time as the Coakley clan would gather the bails to make castles, obstacle courses,tunnels, so all the bails were in one place, saved the farmers a fortune.

At the age of fifteen young Chas started work as an apprentice welder. Nowadays he is a contracts manager in the heating industry.

Married some thirty years with two children Colleen and Ryan. Chas still lives in Essex

Favourite pass times, walking his three dogs with wife Maria, Trying his hand at writing, and last but not least, a lifelong passion for boxing of which he competed to a high level, and is now an England boxing referee.